UNHOLY MURDER

Lynda La Plante was born in Liverpool. She trained for the stage at RADA and worked with the National Theatre and RSC before becoming a television actress. She then turned to writing and made her breakthrough with the phenomenally successful TV series *Widows*. She has written over thirty international novels, all of which have been bestsellers, and is the creator of the Anna Travis, Lorraine Page and *Trial and Retribution* series. Her original script for the much-acclaimed *Prime Suspect* won awards from BAFTA, Emmy, British Broadcasting and Royal Television Society, as well as the 1993 Edgar Allan Poe Award.

Lynda is one of only three screenwriters to have been made an honorary fellow of the British Film Institute and was awarded the BAFTA Dennis Potter Best Writer Award in 2000. In 2008, she was awarded a CBE in the Queen's Birthday Honours List for services to Literature, Drama and Charity.

✉Join the Lynda La Plante Readers' Club at
www.bit.ly/LyndaLaPlanteClub
www.lyndalaplante.com
◻Facebook @LyndaLaPlanteCBE
◻Twitter @LaPlanteLynda

Lynda La Plante

UNHOLY MURDER

ZAFFRE

First published in the UK in 2021 by
ZAFFRE
An imprint of Bonnier Books UK
4th Floor, Victoria House, Bloomsbury Square, London WC1B 4DA
Owned by Bonnier Books
Sveavägen 56, Stockholm, Sweden

A CIP catalogue record for this book is
available from the British Library.

Hardback ISBN: 978–1–78576–542–1
Trade paperback ISBN: 978–1–78576–543–8

Also available as an ebook and an audiobook

3 5 7 9 10 8 6 4

Typeset by IDSUK (Data Connection) Ltd
Printed and bound in Great Britain by Clays Ltd, Elcograf S.p.A.

Zaffre is an imprint of Bonnier Books UK
www.bonnierbooks.co.uk

Thank you for reading my books, you keep me writing

CHAPTER ONE

The yellow JCB digger was backhoeing a deep trench for the concrete foundations to be laid. As Barry, the driver, started to scoop up another load of rain-sodden soil he knew, from the tension on the digger arm, the bucket had struck something solid under the ground.

Opening the cab window, he shouted to his colleague who was sitting in a large open-top dumper truck waiting for the digger to empty its next load of soil.

'Oi, Dermot, I've hit something hard. See if you can make out what it is.'

Dermot did a thumbs up and slowly stepped down from the dumper truck.

'Get a move on, Dermot,' Barry shouted.

'Whatever it is, it's still under the soil. Give it a prod with the bucket so I can hear if it sounds like stone or metal.'

Barry raised then lowered the bucket. When it struck the unknown object, there was a clanging sound.

'I reckon it's something metal,' Dermot said.

As Barry pulled back on the bucket the sudden unbearable screech of metal scraping on metal made Dermot wince. He frantically waved his arms. 'Whoa, stop digging!'

Barry repositioned the bucket, so it was lower in the ground. This time he was able to pull the unknown object up so part of it was sticking out of the soil. It was still covered in dirt, so Barry jumped down from the cab into the trench and brushed away the topsoil with his hands. 'It's a bloody coffin!'

'We'd better let Lee know about it. This area could be the old convent graveyard,' Dermot said warily as he walked off.

Barry grabbed him by the arm. 'We've been digging the new foundations for two weeks now and we ain't uncovered no other coffins, so this can't be a proper graveyard, can it?'

'Better safe than sorry, Barry.'

'You'll be sorry if Lee calls the Old Bill and the site gets shut down. No work means no bloody wages. I say we dig a hole somewhere in the woodland over there and put the coffin in it. No one will be any the wiser.'

Dermot shook his head. 'You can't treat the dead like that. We have to tell Lee. He's in charge of the site.'

'Let's have a look inside first . . .'

'No way. That would be sacrilege,' a shaken Dermot exclaimed.

'If it's an empty coffin, there's no harm in moving it.'

'I told you, I ain't touching it.'

'You're frightened, aren't you?' Barry scoffed.

Dermot went to the builders' hut and returned a couple of minutes later with Lee, the site foreman.

Lee looked at the coffin and sighed. 'That's all we bloody well need.'

'I think we should move it or at least have a look inside,' Barry suggested.

'I don't know . . .' Lee said hesitantly.

'If you do, I'm having no part of it,' Dermot said firmly.

'All right, Dermot, calm down. You two wait here while I go speak with Mr Durham. And don't touch the coffin.' Lee headed towards the walled gardens of the old convent.

Dermot waited until Lee was out of sight before walking off.

'You going back to the hut?' Barry asked.

'No, I'm going to the phone box down the lane to call the police.'

'Tosser,' Barry muttered under his breath. He watched as Dermot got in his Vauxhall Astra and drove towards the lane. Barry nipped to his van and looked in a toolbox. 'You'll do the job nicely,' he smirked as he pulled out a crowbar.

CHAPTER TWO

Detective Sergeant Jane Tennison was sitting at her desk in the Bromley CID office, reading the night duty detective's report about the arrest of two young men trying to break into a house in Beckenham. As she got to the part where the two burglars were disturbed, she couldn't help but laugh out loud.

'What's so funny?' Detective Inspector Stanley asked Jane as he walked in.

Jane had known Stanley since she'd joined the force and had worked with him on a number of cases, but his Christian name was still a mystery to her and, like everyone else, she just called him Stanley – or 'guv', now that he was a DI. When she had first met him, he was a long-haired, scruffy-looking undercover officer, who not only looked like a tramp, but smelt like one as well. With promotion to DI, he had tidied up his appearance and now had short combed-back hair and dressed smartly in a dark blue two-piece suit, white shirt, and Flying Squad tie with its swooping eagle emblem. Present and former members of the elite 'Sweeney' proudly wore the tie which symbolised the way its officers would swoop swiftly on armed robbers.

Jane smiled. 'Morning, Stanley. This night duty report is funny. Two lads broke into a house at two in the morning and disturbed the owner, who just happened to be a police dog handler. His Alsatian, Rumpus, bit one of them in the arse and he needed twelve stitches. The other lad jumped up a tree in the back garden fearing he was next on the dog's menu.'

Stanley laughed. 'That'll teach the little shits.'

'They're still in the cells awaiting interview and their home addresses need to be searched. Me and DC Boon can deal with—'

Stanley shook his head. 'Don't worry, I'll sort them out. The duty sergeant just informed me a coffin has been dug up on a building site in Bickley and they don't know what to do. I need you to deal with that.'

Jane was puzzled. 'Since when was that kind of incident a CID matter?'

'It's on the grounds of an old convent, which means the land might be consecrated and have other bodies buried in it.'

'I still don't see how it's a CID matter,' she said, glumly looking out of the window at the torrential rain.

'Uniform are down to minimum strength today and well tucked up with a major RTA in Widmore Road. Besides, as you've only been here for four weeks it'll give you a chance to get out of the office and do some investigation – and take DC Boon with you,' he added, handing her a page from a police memo pad with the address on it.

'I was just asking why CID, not trying to get out of dealing with it,' Jane explained. 'I've heard the term consecrated ground, but what's the legal procedure?'

'I don't know. I've never dealt with an unearthed coffin before.'

'Then that makes two of us.'

'I suggest you go speak with the foreman and see if there's a body in the coffin for starters,' Stanley said.

'And if there is?'

'Then you'll need to inform the Bromley coroner, who'll advise you accordingly. And maybe speak with the local Catholic church authority as well. They should know if it's consecrated ground or not.'

Jane looked up as a dripping wet DC Boon sauntered into the office, removing the earphones from his Sony pocket radio.

'Bloody hell, it's wet out there' he remarked as he removed his rain-sodden coat and shook the water off it, some of which landed on Jane and the night duty CID report.

'Watch what you're doing, Boony!' she said, wiping the report with a tissue and unintentionally smudging it. 'And keep your coat on, we've got an incident to attend.'

'Anything exciting for a change?' he asked.

'We won't know till we get there, but it involves an unearthed coffin,' she replied, grabbing her raincoat from the coat stand.

'Grave diggers?' Boon asked hopefully.

'In a manner of speaking, yes,' Stanley smiled.

'Have I got time for a coffee and bacon sarnie?' Boon asked.

Stanley frowned. 'No. If you want breakfast have it in your own time before you come on duty. I don't like my detectives coming to work and going straight to the canteen for a bite to eat and a chat. It pisses off the uniformed officers who do three to four hours on the beat before they get their official refs break, so I expect you all to do the same. Refs at twelve or one for detectives on a nine-to-five shift in future and five or six on a two-to-ten shift.'

'Yes, guv, point taken,' an embarrassed Boon replied.

Jane was somewhat surprised by DI Stanley's remarks, especially as he'd never been a stickler for the rules as a detective sergeant when they worked together on the Flying Squad in North London. However, she was aware that he'd 'blotted his copybook' whilst awaiting promotion to DI, and he regarded his transfer to Bromley CID, on the quieter outskirts of the Met, as a punishment posting.

Stanley nipped into his office and returned with an umbrella, which he handed to DC Boon with a grin.

'You might need this. Keep me informed.'

Jane picked up the keys for the maroon Hillman Hunter CID car and tossed them over to Boon.

'You can drive.'

He tossed the keys back. 'Sorry, sarge, but I'm still suspended from driving 'job' motors after the POLAC I had last month.'

Jane frowned, remembering that he'd driven into the back of a privately owned Mercedes at a roundabout. 'Right. I'll drive, then.'

'So where exactly are we going?' Boon asked as they walked down the stairs.

'What used to be a convent in Bickley.' Jane then repeated what Stanley had told her.

Boon sighed. 'And there was me thinking it might be something exciting for a change. It's obvious why DI Stanley didn't fancy dealing with it.'

'I suspect the miserable weather might have had something to do with his decision to send us instead,' Jane said.

'And they say a good copper never gets wet,' Boon chuckled.

*　　*　　*

As Boon directed Jane to the site of the old convent the rain got heavier. There was a sudden flash of lightning in the distance. Boon looked at his watch and started counting the seconds. He got to five and there was a loud crack of thunder.

'Why are you counting?' Jane asked.

'I'm doing a flash, bang count.'

'A what?'

'You take the number of seconds between the lightning and thunder, divide by five and it tells you how far away the lightning is . . . which at present is roughly a mile.'

'A meteorologist as well as a detective,' Jane smiled.

'They say you should take cover if the time between the lightning flash and the rumble of thunder is thirty seconds or less.'

'Talking of cover, where's that umbrella Stanley gave you?'

'Shit, I left it in the locker room toilets when I went to the loo.'

'Why am I not surprised,' she sighed.

'Sorry, sarge, I've got a plastic bag in my coat pocket if you want to use it to cover your hair.'

Jane raised her eyebrows and shook her head in disbelief. 'Thanks but no thanks.'

She'd only known Boony a few weeks, but found him to be polite and cheerful, though somewhat scatty. He had been a detective for two years, was in his early twenties, tall, dark-haired and good-looking. He was always smartly dressed, and Stanley felt he had the makings of a good detective, but needed guidance, which from her first impressions Jane considered to be a fair assessment. He was also a good footballer and played for the Met's first team, to the annoyance of some of his CID colleagues because his duty shifts were often arranged to enable him to play and train.

'St Mary's Lane is next right. It's a dead-end,' Boon said, putting the small London *A-Z* street atlas back in the glove box.

Jane followed his instructions, passing two small cul-de-sacs on either side of the road, each with six large detached houses, some of which were mock Tudor in style.

'Those houses look new and expensive,' Boon remarked.

Jane nodded. 'Looks like a lot of this area was old land that's been built on recently.'

Just past the second cul-de-sac, on the left, was a small brick-built parish church with stained-glass windows and a large double wooden door. On the church wall next to the door was a six-foot concrete statue of Christ on the cross and underneath it a large green sign saying ST MARY'S CATHOLIC CHURCH, along with holy mass and confession times. Beyond the church there was a long hedgerow and woodland.

'I can't see any convent. Are you sure you've got the right road?' Jane asked.

'I'm just going by what's written on the duty sergeant's note – that *you* gave me,' he said cheekily. He pointed down the road. 'There's a high brick wall way down there on the left, maybe the building site is on the other side of it.'

'I'll drive on a bit,' Jane said. 'There may be an entrance further down. If not, then you can nip into the church and see if there's anyone about you can ask.'

A hundred metres down there was an open metal gate leading onto a gravel drive.

'That big house in front of us with a statue of what I assume is the Virgin Mary looks like a convent to me,' Jane said.

The impressive two-storey grey stone and brick building had a seven-bay front, comprising a shallow gabled entrance flanked by a bay either side, with a further gabled two-bay projection on both ends. The large bay on the right had a holy cross on top of it and a large, pointed arch, with a stained-glass window, making it look like a chapel. A high brick wall with wooden gates abutted either end of the building.

'I can't see any building site. Bloody Stanley's having a laugh and sent us out on a wild goose chase just to get wet,' Boon said.

'There are obviously people living or working in there and, judging by the expensive cars out front, I doubt it's nuns. If a coffin's been dug up, it might be somewhere else on the grounds,' Jane suggested.

Jane parked the car, then she and Boon ran through the rain to the front entrance, where two stone steps led up to the timber-panelled door, next to which was an intercom with thirteen buzzers.

'Looks like the convent might have been converted into flats,' Jane said as she pressed the visitor buzzer and waited for a reply.

'Can I help you?' a well-spoken, deep-voiced man asked as he approached them from behind.

He was tall, well-built, looked to be in his late fifties, with a rugged complexion and a dimpled chin. He had a large golf umbrella in one hand and wore an ankle-length green waxed coat. By his side was an unleashed golden retriever, which suddenly jumped up at Jane, depositing muddy paw marks on her raincoat.

The man grabbed the dog by the collar and pulled it back. 'Heel, Bella,' he said firmly. 'Sorry, she's young and I'm still training her,' he added, as he attached a lead to the dog's collar.

'I'm Detective Sergeant Tennison and this is Detective Constable Boon. We were wondering if there's any building work occurring on the grounds,' Jane said.

'Yes, out the back of this building down the far end of the gardens. The site access is off a lane over the back of here. Has something happened?'

'Nothing for you to be concerned about, sir,' Jane replied.

'They dug up a coffin,' Boon said casually, and Jane frowned.

'On the site?' the man asked, looking worried.

'We don't know the full details yet, sir,' Jane told him.

'Is this building still a convent?' Boon asked.

'No, all the Sisters of Mercy nuns have long gone now. The buildings have been converted into private apartments.'

'I like how they've kept the outside like an old building, especially the stained-glass window there,' Boon remarked, pointing.

The man nodded. 'It's a listed building, so the exterior remained as is, though obviously the stone and brickwork were cleaned up and some double glazing put in. The stained glass is original, and that part of the convent was the oratory.'

'What's an oratory?' Boon asked.

'It was the chapel used by the nuns.'

'I bet a flat in there costs an arm and a leg,' Boon said.

The man forced a smile. 'Yes, the apartments are expensive.'

'Thanks for your help, sir. Can you give us directions to the building site?' Jane asked.

'The temporary road leading up to it will be very muddy and you might well get stuck. It would be quicker to walk through our rear communal gardens. Please follow me.' He wiped his wellingtons on the outside doormat, then unlocked the front door.

Boon was about to step inside, when Jane whispered to him to wipe his feet on the mat. Inside there was another large doormat which the man also used, before picking up a neatly folded towel from the floor and wiping the dog down with it.

The hallway was large with a beige marble floor and a stunning Gothic-style dark oak L-shaped staircase. Halfway up the stairs to the upper floor was a pictorial stained-glass window, the centre-piece of which depicted the virgin Mary, Joseph and baby Jesus in the stable at Bethlehem.

'Excuse me for a moment while I put Bella inside.' The man went over to a large arched wooden door in the right-hand corner, opened it and went inside.

Jane took Boon to one side. 'You shouldn't have mentioned the coffin. The residents might start worrying about dead bodies in their back garden.'

'Sorry, sarge, but they're going to find out sooner or later, aren't they?'

Jane was about to reply when the man returned carrying a large umbrella. 'Sorry, I've only got the one, but it's better than nothing.'

'Thank you,' Jane said, taking it from him.

The man then led them to a rear entrance off the hallway where he opened the door. Outside was a vast garden with high walls and Gothic-style arches.

'Blimey, the back garden is massive,' Boon remarked.

'It's the same as it was when the nuns tended it, though we did have to do quite a bit of work to restore it to its original splendour. All the residents chip in and help maintain it. It's absolutely stunning in the summer,' he said proudly. 'Follow the gravel path towards the far end and go through an arch midway on your right into the herb garden. You'll see another arch on your far left which leads to the building site. I'll leave the back door open, but I'd be grateful if you could slip the latch back on and leave the umbrella outside my door when you leave.'

'It's like stepping back in time,' Jane remarked as they walked, the gravel crunching under their feet. 'The nuns who lived here must have led a very peaceful life.'

'Bit like working at Bromley nick, then,' Boon grinned. 'You've worked at some real busy stations, and the Flying Squad, so what made you want to come to Bromley?'

'I bought a house in Chislehurst a few months ago,' Jane said. 'Travelling uptown to Gerald Road nick by train was getting expensive.'

'That's the problem living south of the river,' Boon agreed. 'There's no tube trains for us to use our warrant cards on for free travel into Central London. Did you not fancy working somewhere like Lewisham? That's a busy South London nick.'

'Not really,' Jane said. 'I wanted a quieter posting so I can study for next year's inspectors' exam.'

Boon grinned. 'You'll get plenty of time to do that at Bromley.'

They followed the man's directions to a large expanse of land with a wood and small lake in the distance. To their right were six burnt-out buildings, one of which had a rusty old school bell precariously hanging from an arched recess in the wall above a fire-damaged door. Just beyond the burnt-out buildings they saw a dumper truck, two vans and a small car parked outside a Portakabin.

'That must be the builders' hut over there. Looks like there's a few people working here,' Boon said.

Approaching the Portakabin door they could hear a man talking in a raised voice. Jane closed the umbrella.

'It's a fucking joke stopping everything! This is all your fault, Dermot,' Barry shouted.

Lee remained calm. 'He did what he felt was right. Besides, it may only be a temporary setback.'

Barry was still angry. 'Why can't we dig the south-side founda-tions? That's well away from the bloody coffin.'

Boon was about to knock on the door when Jane stopped him, putting her finger to her mouth and leaning closer.

'Because the police told us to stop,' Dermot said defensively.

'Shut the fuck up, Dermot. Or I'll fill your big mouth with my fist,' Barry threatened.

Lee had had enough. 'Knock it off, Barry. I'm the site foreman, not you! Do as you're bloody well told, or you'll be joining the dole queue.'

Barry shook his head in disgust, 'I may as well piss off home then.'

'Maybe that's best for now,' Lee agreed.

Jane was about to knock on the Portakabin door when it was abruptly opened by Barry, who barged past Boon, nearly knocking him over.

'Sorry, mate, was I in your way?' Boon said sarcastically.

'Fuck off,' Barry muttered as he got into the red minivan. The wheels spun in the dirt as he accelerated away from the site.

Jane held up her warrant card and introduced herself and Boon.

'I'm Lee Holland, the site manager. Sorry about Barry. He's just worried about the site closing down and being out of work.'

Lee was in his late forties, bald, with a large beer belly and a double chin. He wore a black donkey jacket, white T-shirt, blue jeans, and Doc Martens workman's boots.

Compared with the cold weather outside, the Portakabin was stiflingly hot. There were two paraffin heaters, the interior windows were covered in condensation and there was also an overpowering musty odour, a mixture of dampness and sweat, which Dermot and Lee seemed oblivious to. The cabin had a couple of desks and some filing cabinets and pinned up on the wall were plans for the site. The floor was covered in muddy boot prints.

'Who found the coffin?' Jane asked.

'Barry hit something hard when he was using the digger,' Lee said. 'But Dermot here was also there. They cleared the surrounding soil away so you can see it better. I'll put the kettle on while he tells you about it.'

Dermot recounted how the coffin had been uncovered, not mentioning that Barry had wanted to open it.

'Did you find anything else which might indicate the area was a graveyard?' Jane asked.

Lee shook his head. 'No, not a thing. And we've dug out quite a large area so far. Would you like to see the coffin now or have a coffee first and see if the rain eases off?'

'May as well see it now,' Jane said, holding up the umbrella. 'This should help keep the worst of it off us.'

'It's pretty muddy out there. Have you got any wellies in your car?' Dermot asked.

'Unfortunately, no,' Jane replied.

'I've got some plastic shopping bags you can use as shoe covers,' Lee said, opening a desk drawer and taking some out.

'They might make it more slippery as they've no grip, but thanks anyway,' she replied, thinking she'd look ridiculous wearing the bags.

'I'll have some,' Boon grinned. 'These shoes were expensive!'

* * *

Dermot took them round the back of the Portakabin to the building site, which was bigger than Jane had expected. At about half the size of a football pitch, it was clear that quite a few flats or houses were going to be built on the land. Jane stepped carefully through the mud, whilst balancing herself with the umbrella, but her shoes quickly became covered in the brown sludge.

Standing at the edge of the footings trench, the large grey metal coffin was now clearly visible as the heavy rain had washed away the topsoil. It was over six feet long with an inlaid silver cross on top and fresh scratch marks caused by the digger bucket. It looked old, with patches of rust.

'Looks like it's been in the ground for a while,' Boon said.

'There's no name plate on it, though. It might be a nun, or a priest connected to the old convent,' Dermot suggested.

'Looks a bit big for a nun's coffin,' Boon said.

'Nuns, like us, come in all shapes and sizes. The fact is, we won't know who or what's inside until it's opened,' Jane said.

'Might save some time if we have a quick look inside now,' suggested Boon.

'Barry wanted to open it,' Dermot said. 'Then if it was empty, we wouldn't have had to call you lot. Being a Catholic I was a bit wary, so I said best to leave it and tell Lee.'

Jane could tell Dermot was nervous and gave him a reassuring smile. 'Don't worry, we won't open the coffin here. I'll arrange for it to be taken to the mortuary where we can do it in a more controlled and dignified manner.'

'How're we going to get it out?' Boon asked.

'I can dig under the coffin with a shovel and put some heavy-duty straps around it. If I attach them to the digger bucket and lift it out you can put it in a police van,' Dermot said, thinking they would remove the coffin in one go.

'The undertakers will come in their van to remove it to the mortuary,' Jane told him.

Dermot pointed to his right. 'We've made a temporary road using the rubble from the old buildings we knocked down. It's a bit bumpy and muddy in some bits, but they should be able to get their van up from the lane down the far end.'

Jane could see that the makeshift road was about a hundred metres long and a section of the woodland had been cut away to allow vehicles in from the lane.

She turned to Boon. 'I need you to go back to the car, radio the station and ask them to inform the Bromley coroner's officer about the coffin and request the attendance of the undertakers' van. Give them the location of the entrance and a heads-up about the muddy conditions. See if they can arrange the opening of the coffin for this afternoon.'

'Will do, sarge. Do you want a lab liaison sergeant to attend?'

Jane shook her head. 'It's not a crime scene. Besides, I don't think there's anything they can do to assist us here.'

As Boon turned to leave, the ground on the edge of the footings trench suddenly gave way and his feet started to slide out from under him. As he fell forward, he instinctively grabbed the nearest thing to stop his fall, which unfortunately for Jane happened to be her left arm. She let out a loud shriek as she lost her balance, dropped the umbrella, then toppled over and landed in the mud. Boon, however, managed to regain his balance and stay upright.

'For Christ's sake, Boon, what are you playing at!' Jane shouted.

'Sorry, sarge, it was an accident,' he said sheepishly as he put out his hand to help her up.

She flicked it away and got up. 'Look at the state of me. I'm covered in bloody mud.'

'I'll pay for your clothes to be dry cleaned,' he said, looking crestfallen.

'Too bloody right you will!' she barked as she shook her mud-covered hands in an effort to get some of it off. 'Do you have a sink and hot water in the Portakabin?' she asked Dermot.

'No, but there's a cold-water hose outside that's linked to the main supply up at the flats. We've got some loo roll in the cabin you can use as well.'

'That will have to do for now.'

'Can I have the brolly?' Boon asked, not wanting to get soaked as he returned to the car.

Jane headed back to the Portakabin without replying.

'I'll take that as a no,' Boon muttered to himself.

'Bloody hell, what happened to you, detective?' Lee asked.

'Her mate slipped and knocked her over. She nearly fell in the footings trench,' Dermot said as he handed Jane a toilet roll.

'You all right, officer?' Lee asked.

'Yes, thank you,' she replied, forcing a smile.

Jane did her best to wipe the mud off her coat using scrunched-up sheets of the toilet roll dipped in hot water from the kettle, but her efforts only seemed to make things worse.

'Is the land you are working on part of the old convent?' she asked Lee.

'Yes. We're building more flats,' he replied as he handed her a mug of coffee.

'Thanks. What was on the land before you started?'

'Nothing, apart from the fire-damaged outbuildings, which we've yet to demolish.'

'Do you know if the land you are building on was ever a graveyard or consecrated ground?'

'If it were, I doubt the developer would have got planning permission,' Lee said.

'Is he aware of this morning's discovery?'

'I tried ringing him at his office, but he was out at another site, so I left a message with his secretary.'

Jane removed her notebook and pen from her coat pocket. 'I'll need the developer's name and contact number, please.'

'It's Nicholas Durham. His office is in Bromley, next door to Biba's nightclub.' Lee handed Jane a piece of headed paper embossed with THOMAS DURHAM AND SON BUILDING DEVELOPERS, 27 WIDMORE ROAD, BROMLEY, TELEPHONE 014673281.

'I take it Nicholas is the "son",' Jane said.

Lee nodded. 'Tom Durham started the company, but he's sort of retired now, and Nick runs it.'

'Do the Durhams own the land or are they just doing the building work?'

'Tom Durham bought the old convent and land years ago and turned it into high-quality apartments. Now he's building some more.'

'Were you involved in the initial build as well?' Jane asked out of curiosity.

'No, I came on board after that, but I've been working for them a few years now.'

As Jane wrote some notes, Boon returned to the Portakabin. He told her he'd brought the CID car round and let her know the duty sergeant had spoken with the coroner's officer, PC Rogers.

'The undertakers' van should be on the site in about an hour, and the coffin can be opened at one.'

Jane looked at her watch. It was a quarter to eleven. 'Where's the mortuary?'

'Queen Mary's Hospital, just off the A20 between Chislehurst and Sidcup. Not far from your house, actually.'

'A hospital? Why aren't they using a local council mortuary?' Jane asked.

'Bromley and Bexley division regularly use the hospital mortuary for suspicious deaths and murder post-mortems. Two coroner's officers work there as well,' replied Boon.

Jane closed her notebook. 'Thanks for your time and help, gentlemen. As soon as we've opened the coffin, I'll notify you of the result. In the meantime, I think it would be best if you don't do any more work on the foundations.'

'Can we do other stuff?' Lee asked.

'As long as it doesn't involve any digging.' Jane headed towards the door and Boon followed her. She turned round and looked at him.

'I want you to remain here and supervise the removal of the coffin. I'll see you at the mortuary later.'

'How am I going to get there?'

'Get a lift in the mortuary van. I'm sure they can squeeze you in the back,' Jane said, knowing very well that three people could sit in the front of the van.

Boon frowned, as if he thought this was payback for landing Jane in the mud.

Jane gave him her brightest smile. 'For the sake of evidence continuity, I need you to stay with the coffin.' She handed him the umbrella. 'Don't forget to return this to its owner before you leave.'

CHAPTER THREE

As Jane drove up St Mary's Lane, towards the main road, she saw the small parish church they'd passed on the way to the building site and noticed the door was open. It occurred to her that if the coffin did have a body in it, she didn't have a clue what should be done concerning a reburial, and even if it was empty the coffin would probably be the property of the Catholic church. Deciding it might be worth chatting with the local priest, Jane stopped and parked the car. She took off her dirty raincoat and left it on the passenger seat before going into the church.

Glancing around, Jane couldn't see anyone, but noticed the cut-out cross on top of a confessional box had some light shining through it from a small electric bulb. The curtains on each side of the box were closed. Walking towards it, she heard the muffled sound of voices coming from inside. Not wanting to disturb anyone, or hear the actual confession, she moved out of hearing to wait at the back of the church. A couple of minutes later, a young woman carrying a small baby in her arms exited the box and hurried out of the church with her head down. It was obvious to Jane she was in a distressed state and had been crying. Jane felt an instinctive impulse to ask the woman if she was all right, but realising the circumstances and surroundings said nothing.

She walked over to the confessional box. 'Excuse me, Father, I wonder if I could have a word with you,' she asked through the closed curtain.

'Please, enter the confessional box and confess your sins to Almighty God, my child,' he said with a slight foreign accent.

Jane thought he might be Italian. She wasn't quite sure what to do and, fearing she might alarm the priest, didn't open the curtain he was behind. She stepped into the confessional booth, sat down, and held her warrant card up to the mesh.

'Sorry, Father, but I'm not here for confession. I'm Detective Sergeant Jane Tennison from Bromley CID. I'd like to speak with you about an incident I'm dealing with.'

'Have you found the lead that was stolen from the church roof?' he asked.

'Not personally, Father, and to be honest that's not what I need to speak with you about.'

He sighed. 'Pity. The police officer I reported the theft to thought the local gypsies might be responsible. I was hoping the lead would be recovered and save the church the cost of replacing it. How can I help you, Sergeant Tennison?'

'I don't wish to appear rude, but could we speak face to face outside the confessional box?'

He laughed. 'Of course.' Pulling back the curtain, he stepped out at the same time as Jane.

Jane had expected a small, elderly man and was surprised to see he was in his mid-thirties and about six feet tall. He was slim and handsome, with dark, swept-back hair, olive skin and almond-shaped brown eyes. He wore a neatly fitting black priest's suit, which accentuated his athletic build, a black shirt and white dog collar. A purple stole, with embroidered gold crosses and golden tassels on each end, hung from his neck.

He held out his hand.

'I'm Father Christopher Floridia, but everyone calls me Father Chris.'

Jane shook his hand. 'Is that an Italian accent?' she asked.

He laughed. 'No, I'm Maltese.'

'Oh, sorry,' Jane said.

'No apology needed. People often think I'm Italian when they hear me speak.'

Jane was relieved he wasn't offended, recalling her father once telling her the Italians, under Mussolini, had dropped a barrage of bombs on Malta in 1940. She told Father Floridia about the unearthing of the coffin at the old convent building site, and how it was being taken to the mortuary to be opened.

'I was wondering if you could help me with the correct procedure if there is a body inside the coffin, and who I need to inform within the Church.'

'I've never actually dealt with anything like that before,' he said thoughtfully. 'I'd imagine, as the coffin was found on the grounds of the old Catholic convent, there would need to be a reburial.'

'And who should I speak to about that?'

'Our South-East area bishop should be informed. He may want to inform the archbishop as well.'

'Can I have their names please?' Jane asked, getting out her notebook and pen.

'The bishop is Robert Meade and Andrew Malone is the archbishop of Southwark.'

'And how would I go about contacting them?'

'The diocesan head office is at Archbishop's House in St George's Road, Southwark. The archbishop is currently visiting the Vatican, helping to organise Pope John Paul II's forthcoming visit to the UK.'

'I never realised churches in Bromley would come under Southwark,' Jane remarked.

'The archdiocese covers a wide area of London, Kent and Surrey. There are 180 parishes in it.'

'Do you know much about the old convent?' Jane asked.

'Not really. I only became the parish priest here ten months ago. I was told the Sisters of Mercy nuns lived and worked at the convent from the mid-1800s until the mid-sixties, then a local man bought it and built a load of flats.'

'Why did the Church sell the convent?' Jane asked.

'One of my regular Sunday worshippers told me that during the early sixties the number of nuns slowly declined, and the convent became unmanageable for the few that remained. Eventually escalating running costs meant they had to move out.'

'Would the convent land have been consecrated when it was first built?'

'I'd have thought the church and any graveyard land would have been.'

'Sorry if this sounds like a silly question, but what exactly is consecrated ground according to the Catholic faith?'

'Catholic burials are steeped in tradition, with specific rules that date back thousands of years. Our doctrine requires human remains be buried in consecrated ground, or ground blessed by a bishop and deemed an appropriate final resting place by the Church.'

'We haven't found any indication that the coffin was in a communal cemetery,' Jane said.

'What sort of coffin was it?'

'No name plate, grey metal, with a large inlaid silver cross on top and about six to seven feet long.'

'A priest or bishop might be buried in that type of coffin. Nuns are usually buried in a wooden coffin, but that's just conjecture on my part.'

'Don't worry, Father, as a detective I'm often guilty of conjecture myself. Quite a bit of digging work has already been done by the developer and no other coffins or headstones have been found on the land . . . as yet.'

'If any nuns or priests were buried on the convent grounds then they'd probably have had a small wooden or metal cross in the ground to remember them by. Headstones are too expensive. It's also possible any nuns who died at the convent were reburied in another graveyard on consecrated ground.'

'Would it be local?'

'Possibly. St Luke's, Magpie Hall Lane, is the nearest cemetery.'

Jane made a note. 'There's one last thing. I wondered, if the coffin is empty, who should I restore it to?'

'If it's helpful, I can speak with Bishop Meade for you. I'm sure he'll know a lot more than me about the old convent and what should be done with the coffin and its contents.'

'I'd appreciate that. Is there a phone number I can contact you on to let you know if there is, or isn't, a body in the coffin?'

'I don't know it by memory yet, I'm afraid. The presbytery is next door; I'll go and get it for you.'

'Is it in the phone book?'

He nodded.

'Don't worry. I can look it up when I'm back in the office. It's been a pleasure meeting you, Father Chris, and thanks for all your help.'

'My pleasure.' He smiled. 'I look forward to hearing more about your mysterious coffin.'

CHAPTER FOUR

As it was half past eleven, and her house in Oakdene Avenue was nearby, Jane decided to nip home, have a wash, and change out of her muddy shoes and tights before going to Queen Mary's Hospital.

Jane had recently bought the two-bedroom property for £25,000. It was cheap because it needed a lot of work done on it, which, at present, she couldn't afford to do. However, she looked on modernising and decorating it as a long-term project. Above all, she was pleased to have a house of her own with a nice, if small, garden.

Arriving home, the first thing she did was phone DI Stanley.

'Where are you?' he asked.

Jane said she was at home, then recounted how Boon had knocked her over at the building site and being covered in mud she needed to change her clothes.

Stanley laughed. 'I wish I'd been there to see that.'

'Yeah, well, it wasn't funny for me. Boon's a walking disaster zone,' she replied before telling Stanley about the coffin being taken to the mortuary.

'If the coffin's empty, you've wasted 'job' money by calling out the undertakers and arranging a post-mortem. You could have opened it at the site to save time and money.'

'I didn't feel it was appropriate to look inside it on the site,' she countered. 'What do I do if there is a body in it?'

'Under the coroner's rules, a pathologist has to do a routine examination before it can be released for burial, and they won't do it for free!' he told her.

'I'm sorry, I didn't realise that would be the case.'

'What time are they opening the coffin?'

'One o'clock. I was going to go to Queen Mary's straight from here. Will you be attending the mortuary?'

'No, I won't. I've better things to do,' he said dismissively.

'I spoke with the local priest, Father Christopher Floridia. He's helping me regarding the correct religious procedure, and he said—'

'I'm not interested in what he has to say! Body or no body in that coffin, hand the bloody case over to the coroner's officer and he can deal with it,' Stanley barked before putting the phone down.

Jane was annoyed at how disrespectful Stanley had been – not just to her but also to Father Chris, who was only trying to help. She went to her bedroom to change her clothes and looking in her dressing-table mirror noticed a smear of mud on her face. She felt mortified realising it must have been there when she met Father Chris and he hadn't said anything so as not to embarrass her. She also knew Boon must have seen the mud and deliberately failed to mention it just because she'd told him to stay at the building site.

Having washed and changed, Jane made a cheese and tomato sandwich, which she ate with a packet of crisps and a mug of hot chocolate. Sitting at her breakfast bar, she looked up the phone number for St Mary's Church in the phone book and jotted it down in her notebook. She looked forward to meeting Father Chris again and wondered if she should call him and let him know that her DI wanted a coroner's officer to deal with the case and not her. She picked up the phone, started to dial, then put it down, deciding she would visit him at the church and tell him personally after the coffin was opened.

* * *

Arriving at Queen Mary's Hospital Jane went to the coroner's staff office, next to the mortuary. The cramped, rundown office had two desks facing each other and a chalkboard on the wall. On the board was a list of deceased people, cause and date of death and their fridge numbers. Jane noticed some blood-stained mortuary overalls on a coat stand and white mortuary boots next to it, which made the room smell like a mixture of death and disinfectant. A swarthy, chubby man in his late forties was sitting at a desk typing, whilst puffing on a cigarette that was hanging out of his mouth. His brown two-piece suit was badly creased and ill-fitting. A black tie hung loosely round his neck and the top button of his white shirt was undone.

Jane introduced herself and said she was dealing with the coffin discovered on the old convent grounds.

'I'm PC Roger Rogers, the coroner's officer,' he said with the cigarette still in his mouth. A lump of ash fell onto his desk. He brushed it off and onto the floor.

'My DI has asked that the case be handed over to a coroner's officer as it's not really a CID matter,' Jane said.

Rogers raised his eyes in disapproval. 'It's not for a DI to decide what happens next, it's up to the coroner after I've appraised him of the results of the coffin examination.'

'I've got the details of the local priest who's happy to speak with his bishop and assist regarding any reburial and restoration of the coffin to the church,' Jane told him.

'Having been a coroner's officer for many years, I am aware of the necessary procedures in cases like this,' he said tartly.

Jane decided to ignore his confrontational tone. 'Has the coffin arrived?' she asked.

He continued typing. 'It's in the mortuary examination room, as is your colleague DC Boon.'

What a pompous little man, Jane thought, turning to walk out the door.

'No need to rush,' he said. 'The pathologist is running late.'

'Is it Professor Martin?' Jane asked, having worked with him on previous murder investigations.

Rogers sighed. 'No, it's Dr Pullen.'

She picked up on his uneasiness. 'I've not met him before. Is there a problem?'

Rogers frowned. 'She's a woman, and about to be fully registered as London's first female forensic pathologist. Personally, I think it's a bit early to let her go solo.'

Jane could tell by his tone he was a chauvinist. 'Well, there's a first time for everything. If Dr Pullen was trained by the renowned Professor Martin, I've no doubt she will be as good at the job as her male counterparts,' she said.

'That remains to be seen, love,' he smirked.

Jane had had enough of Rogers' attitude. 'I'm not your "love", PC Rogers, I'm a sergeant and that makes me your superior officer ... and as such I prefer to be addressed as sergeant.'

'Yes, sarge,' Rogers said, with a mock salute and look of disdain, before going back to his typing.

At that moment a woman appeared in the doorway, breathing heavily and wiping a bead of sweat from her forehead with a tissue. 'Sorry I'm late, PC Rogers. I've just run all the way up the hill from Sidcup railway station.' She paused for breath. 'Bloody hell, I'm knackered ... and there was me thinking I was reasonably fit.' She turned to Jane. 'I'm Dr Samantha Pullen, but everyone calls me Sam or Sammy.' Pullen was in her late thirties, about five foot seven, thickset, with dark collar-length bob and a straight fringe. She had green eyes, a round face and wore red lipstick, which accentuated her rosy cheeks and broad smile.

Jane thought Pullen looked rather trendy in her burgundy raincoat and matching Baker Boy hat.

'Pleased to meet you. I'm Detective Sergeant Jane Tennison from Bromley CID. Congratulations on your forthcoming appointment as a Home Office forensic pathologist.'

'Thank you, Jane. I've a couple of weeks to go yet ... hopefully I won't screw up before then,' she added with a big smile.

Rogers stood up, took two stained mortuary gowns from the coat stand and handed one to Jane. 'Right, let's get this coffin open.'

'I'm fine without the gown, thank you,' Jane replied, putting the gown back and wiping her hand on the side of her skirt.

He shrugged. 'Please yourself.'

'I'll just nip to the mortuary technician's locker room to get changed, then we're good to go,' Pullen said.

Jane followed Rogers to the examination room where Boon was leaning on a work surface, reading a newspaper while eating a Mars Bar.

'Food is not supposed to be eaten in here, DC Boon,' Rogers barked, scowling at the resident mortuary technician, Jack, for allowing it to happen.

Jane thought this rather rich coming from someone who was wearing a dirty blood-stained gown that he kept in his office.

The coffin was on an adjustable examination table and Jane went and stood beside Boon. 'I've got a bone to pick with you, Boony.'

He looked alarmed. 'What have I done now?'

'It's what you didn't do.' She touched her face where the mud had been.

'Sorry, I thought you were going straight back to the station.'

'You're lucky I saw the funny side of it,' she said, half-smiling. 'But remember, revenge is a dish best served cold.'

*　*　*

'Right, let's get started,' Dr Pullen said as she entered the room, now wearing protective clothing and carrying a clipboard and pen. 'I just need everyone's names for the records, please.'

Boon's eyes lit up. 'Nice-looking for a mortuary technician,' he whispered to Jane.

'PC Rogers, Jack the mortuary technician and DS Tennison I already know.' Pullen looked at Boon. 'And you are . . .?'

Boon who was still admiring Pullen's figure didn't hear her question. Jane nudged him with her elbow. He stood straighter, and puffed out his chest.

'Detective Constable Simon Boon, Bromley CID. I accompanied the coffin from the building site to the mortuary. I am also assisting DS Tennison with this case and will perform the role of exhibits officer.'

'Good for you, Simon,' Pullen said with a wry smile.

'May I say how refreshing it is to meet a lady mortuary technician,' he said. 'You must have a strong stomach for this job.'

'I'm not a mortuary technician,' she said, still smiling.

Boon looked confused. 'Oh . . . are you a coroner's officer?'

'No. I'm Dr Samantha Pullen, a forensic pathologist.'

Boon flushed and mumbled an apology.

'I'm so sorry, doctor . . . I didn't realise . . . I was expecting a man . . . I mean Professor Martin.'

'I'll do my best to live up to your expectations, DC Boon,' she said, not smiling anymore.

Pullen put her clipboard down on a work surface then picked up a mortuary hammer and chisel. She looked at Boon with a steely expression. 'These should do.'

'Do for what?' he asked nervously.

'Opening the coffin.'

As Dr Pullen lowered the examination table, Boon whispered to Jane, 'Why didn't you tell me she was the pathologist?'

'Remember what I said about revenge,' Jane replied. 'And by the way, your chat-up lines are awful.'

'Was it that obvious?'

'Blindingly!'

'Right, let's unseal this coffin,' Pullen said.

'What's it sealed with?' Boon asked Pullen, but Rogers answered.

'Metal coffins are normally sealed with a rubber gasket that goes all the way around the edge of the lid. The sealing clasps then lock the lid in place.' He pointed to one. 'And the rubber gasket forms a tight seal that prevents air and moisture from getting in.'

'So, if there's a body in there it might be in good condition?' Boon asked.

'Not necessarily,' Pullen said. 'Sealing a casket won't prevent a body from decomposing, even if it's been embalmed.'

Pullen undid the clasps, then put the chisel in between the two halves and gave it a knock with the hammer. To her surprise, the chisel slid in easily. 'Looks like the rubber seal has degraded.' She pushed the handle of the chisel down, and the top of the coffin started to open. 'Although it may be heavier than it looks, I think this lid will come off fairly easily.' She looked at PC Rogers and Boon. 'Can you give us a hand to lift it off, please? The protective gloves are over there.'

Boon was worried about his clothes. 'Have you got a spare overall?'

Jane frowned. 'I'll help,' she said, putting on a pair of latex gloves.

They stood round the coffin, one at each end and two in the middle, waiting for Pullen's order.

'One, two, three . . . lift.'

Boon inched forward, eager to see what was inside as they put the lid on the mortuary floor.

'Jesus, that stinks of rancid cheese!' Boon exclaimed, putting his hand to his mouth and starting to retch.

'Don't be so squeamish, it's just a dead body,' Rogers scoffed.

'Dead bodies don't bother me, I just hate cheese!' Boon retched again.

'If you're going to be sick, do it in the sink,' barked a stern-faced Rogers.

Jane thought it strange the body didn't smell of decay and rotting flesh as she'd expected. The face looked gruesome, yet fascinating. The skin was shrivelled and cracked, with a chalky white, almost yellowish colour to it with flecks of grey. There were empty sockets where the eyes had once been, but the mouth was eerily wide open revealing an intact set of teeth. The cracked and shrivelled hands were clasped together. A rosary with a small wooden cross was wrapped around the right hand.

Parts of the clothing were disintegrating and discoloured, but it was clear the body was dressed in a black ankle-length gown and black lace-up shoes. A black veil covered the head and shoulders, with a stiff white wimple under it. The wimple was tight under the chin and hung in a semi-circle below the neck. Tied around the waist was a brown cord with tassels on each end. The interior of the coffin was lined with satin, which was now covered in mildew and a dirty grey colour.

'It looks like the body of a nun from the clothing,' Jane remarked.

Pullen nodded. 'I agree, though I will have to confirm it by further examination.'

Boon laughed. 'Imagine if . . .'

'Imagine what?' Jane asked.

'Imagine if it turned out to be a transvestite priest! That would raise a few eyebrows at the Vatican,' Boon grinned. 'Then again, maybe not.'

'I expected a corpse that would be badly decomposed, but in fact the face and hands look almost mummified,' Jane remarked.

Pullen was about to explain the phenomenon when a smug-looking PC Rogers interjected.

'It's due to adipocere on the body, which can occur in sealed coffins when no air can get in.'

Pullen picked up her clipboard and pen. 'That's a very astute observation, especially as it's a condition that's quite rare to observe.'

'I have an excellent memory, Dr Pullen,' Rogers replied pompously. 'I first observed adipocere a few years ago, in a case Professor Martin was dealing with.'

'What's adipocere?' Boon asked.

Pullen explained. 'Adipocere is Latin for fat wax . . . *adipo*, meaning fat, and *cire*, wax, though pathologists generally refer to it as grave or corpse wax. Although rare, you are more likely to find it on females and the obese, due to their higher fat content.' She looked at Jane. 'Adipocere looks similar to mummified flesh, but it's actually quite different and varies in colour from dirty white to light brown or grey. It's also what causes that rancid cheesy smell DC Boon dislikes so much.'

'What causes the adipocere to form?' Jane asked.

'Basically, after death, fat tissue in a corpse starts to break down. Bacterial enzymes from the intestine and the environment convert unsaturated liquid fats to saturated solid fats, which causes the development of a soft waxy, soap-like material on the body. Adipocere acts as a barrier against the usual process of decomposition and in turn preserves features of the body.'

'But the hands look dry and shrivelled, not waxy or soapy,' Boon observed.

'Recent adipocere tends to be white, yellow or reddish brown. The older it is, the greyer and more solid it will become . . . as on this body. We'll need to be careful when we remove it as dried adipocere can crumble and split.'

Jane was pleased Pullen described the condition of the body in layman's terms, unlike Professor Martin who, she knew from experience, loved to play to the gallery during a post-mortem and use obscure medical jargon.

Pullen crouched down and looked at the rim of the coffin. 'I think this coffin's been opened recently.'

'How can you tell?' Jane asked.

'There's fresh indentation marks on the rim, possibly from a jemmy, plus the sealing glue has been stretched and separated . . . which would also explain why we were able to remove the lid so easily. It looks as if someone has used a crowbar to prise it open.' Pullen pointed to the marks. 'The state of the body suggests this coffin was previously airtight, and yet there are some beads of water on the rim and inside.' She dabbed her finger in a droplet and showed it to Jane. 'It could be recent rainwater.'

Jane turned to Boon. 'Do you know anything about this?'

Boon looked offended. 'No, I don't! You said not to open it, so I didn't. I also know for a fact no one went near it after you left the building site.'

'Well, someone's opened it since it was dug up,' Pullen said.

'What about the undertakers?' Boon suggested. 'I nipped to the hospital canteen to get a drink and a Mars Bar when we got here.'

PC Rogers shook his head. 'No way. I watched them unload the coffin and leave, as did Jack, who then had a cup of tea with me.'

'Dermot the builder said his mate Barry wanted to open it, so it could have been him before we even got to the building site,' Boon recalled.

'Good point,' Jane said. 'It may also explain why Barry was in a hurry to leave when we got there.'

Pullen pointed to the nun's habit. 'There's some distinct marks here that look like the outline of a crucifix . . . and two faint lines that run up towards the neck, which could be from the chain.'

'Whoever opened the coffin might have taken it, especially if it was silver,' Boon suggested.

Jane frowned. 'I think we need to have a word with Barry.'

'He's not that bright if he thought we wouldn't notice the coffin had been opened,' Boon added.

As Pullen wrote her notes, Jane asked if adipocere could help to determine how long a person had been dead.

'To be honest, this is the first time I've actually seen it in the flesh, so to speak. From my pathology training, I know adipocere can take weeks if not years to form due to different factors such as temperature, embalming, burial conditions, and materials surrounding the corpse. It's even been found on bodies that have been dead for hundreds of years. When I do a closer examination of the corpse on the mortuary table, I might be able to give you an approximate idea of physical age, though it might be worth consulting an anthropologist for a more exact—'

Rogers was quick to interject. 'I don't think an anthropologist will be necessary, Dr Pullen.'

'Why not?' Jane asked.

'Now we know it's the body of a nun, I don't see a lot of point continuing.'

'Are you telling me to stop my examination, PC Rogers?' Pullen frowned.

'The coroner will want the body handed over to the Catholic church for reburial,' he said.

'You can read his mind, can you?' Jane retorted.

'I'll phone him and seek his opinion,' Rogers replied smugly, then left the room.

'He really is an objectionable little prick,' Pullen remarked.

'I couldn't agree more,' Jane added, surprised but also pleased with Sam's candour.

'Is that dried flower petals on the chest and forehead?' Boon asked, pointing to the body from across the room because of the smell.

'They look more like shreds of fabric,' Pullen replied, using tweezers to lift a piece off for closer examination. 'I'd say they are bits of satin . . .' She noticed something odd. 'Jane, could you pass me the magnifying glass from the table, please.'

Pullen held the magnifier over the piece of satin. 'There appears to be a tiny fragment of a fingernail embedded in it.' She put the satin and nail in a small container before delicately lifting the left hand of the body. 'Thankfully, the adipocere has preserved the hands and the fingernails are still attached,' she said, examining one of the hands with the magnifier.

Jane noticed a look of concern on Pullen's face. 'Is there something wrong?'

'The fingernail on the left index finger is broken . . . same on the third finger . . . and there appears to be a tiny bit of satin attached to a broken nail tip.' Pullen moved round the coffin to examine the right hand.

Jane was pretty sure she knew what Pullen was thinking. 'Boony, help me turn the coffin lid over,' she said, grabbing one end.

'What are you looking for?' he asked.

'I want to see the condition of the satin lining.'

'The right hand on the body has a broken fingernail and the others are worn down to the fingertips,' Dr Pullen informed them as they gently turned the lid over.

The mouldy white satin lining was torn and hanging loose at the head end. Jane gently brushed it to one side, revealing deep fingernail scratch marks on the interior metal.

'Oh my God, she was buried alive!' Jane exclaimed. 'Her mouth must be wide open because she died gasping for air.'

Pullen looked closely at the scratch marks and torn satin, then pointed to a strand. 'There's a bit of fingernail just there.' She used the tweezers to pick it up then looked at Jane. 'I'd like to treat this as a suspicious death and carry out a full post-mortem.'

Jane nodded. 'I agree, and I'm sure the coroner will concur when he hears what we've found.'

'I don't mean to sound silly, but could she have been buried alive by mistake?' Boon asked.

'It's possible but highly unlikely,' Pullen said. 'There was a case from my medical studies which has always stuck in my mind. In the early 1900s Essie Dunbar, who was thirty, suffered a severe epilepsy attack. It was so bad she passed out and everyone thought she was dead. Even her doctor couldn't detect a pulse. For religious reasons the funeral was arranged for the next day and the body was put in a burial coffin. Essie's sister, who lived out of town, arrived after the coffin had been covered in soil, and demanded the body be removed so she could see her sister one last time. When the coffin lid was opened, Essie sat up and smiled at everyone around her . . .no doubt frightening the crap out of them at the same time.'

'No way,' a disbelieving Boon grinned.

'Apparently it's true, and then she lived for another forty-seven years.'

'So, if our body was deliberately put in the coffin when she was alive, murder could be hard to prove,' Jane remarked.

'As strange as it may sound – and excuse the pun – but the hand of God might help us here,' Pullen replied.

'I didn't take you as the religious type, Sam,' Jane said.

Pullen laughed. 'I'm not. The last time I was in a church was at my sister's wedding, eight years ago. It's the adipocere that might help us. It sometimes preserves the soft tissue and internal organs, thus allowing a pathologist to identify internal injuries on the body. She may have been attacked, knocked unconscious and then sealed in the coffin, so I want to do some X-rays on the body and skull for any fractures before we remove it for a full examination.'

Jane looked at Boon. 'Go tell Rogers what we've found and make sure he tells the coroner and asks for a full post-mortem.'

'It will be my pleasure, sarge.'

'I think it may be advisable to have a lab liaison sergeant present and take photographs before the body is examined any further,' Pullen said, removing her latex gloves.

'I'll call the lab sergeant after I've deflated Rogers' ego,' Boon smiled.

'See if you can get DS Paul Lawrence to attend,' Jane said.

'Any particular reason?' Boon asked, clearly wondering if she had a soft spot for Lawrence.

'I've known him since I joined the Met and he's the best at what he does when it comes to forensics and murder. Something tells me this case isn't going to be straightforward, so his knowledge and experience may prove invaluable.'

'Looks like a dull day at Bromley just got exciting,' Boon remarked as he hurried out of the room.

'You're right about DS Lawrence being good at his job,' Pullen said. 'I've met him a few times whilst assisting Prof Martin, who also rates him highly. Paul is a very nice man.' She hesitated. 'Do you know if he's single?'

Jane wasn't sure what to say as Lawrence had confided in her he was gay and lived with his boyfriend. 'Paul's not married, but he's in a relationship with someone.'

'Is it serious?'

'As far as I know . . .'

Pullen sighed. 'That's a shame. I was thinking of asking him if he'd like to go for a drink sometime.'

* * *

A smug-looking PC Rogers was on the phone as Boon entered his office.

'I've some new info for you about the—'

Rogers put his hand over the mouthpiece. 'Can't you see I'm speaking to the coroner?' he growled, before resuming the conversation. 'Yes, sir. I'll write the death up as natural causes on my report and contact the Catholic archdiocesan office in Southwark so they can arrange a reburial of the nun.'

Rogers was about to put the phone down when Boon grabbed it from his hand.

'Sir, it's Detective Constable Boon from Bromley CID—'

Rogers reddened. 'What do you think you're doing!'

Boon ignored him. 'Dr Pullen has found evidence that suggests the nun was alive in the coffin, which means she might have suffocated to death. DI Tennison would like your permission to treat the death as suspicious and also asked if Dr Pullen could carry out a full forensic post-mortem examination.'

As Boon informed the coroner of Pullen's findings, Rogers' face turned pale and he slumped back in his chair. Boon handed the phone to Rogers, whispering, 'He wants a word with you . . . and he don't sound happy.'

As Jane walked in, a glum-looking Rogers was putting his raincoat on. 'I take it DC Boon has updated you?'

Rogers said nothing as he trudged out of the room and Jane looked to Boon for an explanation.

'Coroner said he wanted to see him pronto in his office.'

'I wouldn't want to be in his shoes, but he's only himself to blame. We OK for a full PM?'

'Yeah, and he's happy for Dr Pullen to do it as long as Prof Martin agrees. Shall I give him a call first then ask for a lab sergeant to attend?'

'Yes, please, and I'll update DI Stanley,' Jane said, lifting the phone receiver on another desk.

'Do you think he'll form a murder squad?' Boon asked.

Jane shrugged. 'Depends on the outcome of the full post-mortem and X-rays.'

'Surely the coroner will want further inquiries made to ascertain who she is and when she died,' Boon suggested.

'Yes, but that doesn't mean we'll be making them,' Jane said.

'Why not? We were assigned the investigation so surely we should continue it.'

'I agree, but more senior officers may not. If there's no other post-mortem evidence to justify a murder investigation the coroner may NFA the case, and return the body to the Church.'

'I hope it is a murder,' Boon said.

'Well, don't get your hopes up. Like I said, even if it is you may not be on the investigation.'

'I know I've not been a DC long, but this would be a good case for me to gain more experience,' Boon said, looking hopefully at Jane.

Jane remembered the excitement she had felt on her first murder investigation. 'If they do form a squad, and I'm on it, I'll recommend you be part of the team.'

His eyes lit up. 'Thanks, sarge.'

Jane then rang DI Stanley.

'We found the body of what appears to be a nun in the coffin . . .'

Stanley was quick to interrupt. 'Well, no surprise there then.' He sounded like he was in a bad temper. 'Hand the case over to the coroner's officer then get back here pronto. I need you to deal with an indecent assault allegation against a local councillor and take a statement from the victim.'

'I'm sorry, but I'm tied up here at the mortuary,' Jane told him. 'The coroner wants the death treated as suspicious and a full post-mortem done.'

'On what grounds?' Stanley retorted.

'The death may not have been from natural causes,' Jane said, then recounted her observations and Dr Pullen's comments.

'She was buried alive? Bloody hell, I wasn't expecting that. What about the body – any idea how long she's been dead or who she is?'

'No to both at present, but the Church might be able to help us. The full PM should tell us more about her age and when she died, and we might find something in the coffin to give us an indication of who she is.'

'So, you haven't started a full PM yet?'

'No, we're waiting for a lab sergeant to attend and Prof Martin's permission for Dr Pullen to do the PM.'

'I thought you said a pathologist was already there?'

'Yes, but . . . she's not quite fully qualified yet.'

'Then her initial conclusions could be wrong.'

Jane was getting irritated by Stanley's attitude. 'She explained her suspicions to me and pointed out visual evidence to back it up. I think she's right and the nun may have been murdered.'

'You're not a pathologist, Tennison . . . and Pullen is a rookie. Personally, I think it best if Prof Martin does the PM.'

She sighed. 'You're beginning to sound like PC Rogers.'

'Who's he?'

'The coroner's officer dealing with the case.'

'Oh, so he agrees with me?'

Jane waved her hand at Boon who was still on the phone. 'Have you spoken to Prof Martin yet about Dr Pullen doing the PM?' she whispered.

Boon nodded as he put the phone down. 'Yep, he's happy for Doc Pullen to do the PM and said to ring him if she needed his assistance or advice. DS Lawrence is already working on a murder in North London, so another lab sergeant will be allocated this case and be with us shortly.'

Jane smiled and did a thumbs-up. 'Prof Martin is happy for Dr Pullen to . . .'

'I heard what Boon said,' Stanley interrupted.

Jane smiled. 'Well, the Prof obviously has faith in her ability and judgement . . . unlike some people.'

'I'll be with you in half an hour. Don't start the PM without me,' he added and banged the phone down.

CHAPTER FIVE

While Boon went to the hospital canteen to get a sandwich, Jane looked in the *Yellow Pages* for Father Floridia's phone number and called to update him about the discovery of the body, but there was no answer. She was about to return to the mortuary examination room when Pullen walked in. Jane told her that the coroner wanted a full post-mortem and Professor Martin was happy for her to do it, and if she needed his assistance to call him.

'Thanks, Jane,' she replied nervously.

'You don't look pleased.'

'I know it sounds silly,' Pullen sighed, 'but I feel like a schoolkid about to do my first recorder solo on stage.'

Jane smiled. 'You'll be fine. Believe me, Prof Martin wouldn't let you go solo if he didn't think you were up to it. Plus the audience will be much smaller.' Jane added, 'Are you going to do the X-rays in the hospital radiography department?'

Pullen shook her head. 'For health reasons they won't let me, due to the state of the body. But it turns out they have a mobile X-ray machine on site and the radiographer is doing them as we speak. I had a quick look in the nether regions of the body and can definitely say it's a female. I also measured her height and she's only five foot two.'

Jane frowned. 'That's a small body for a big coffin.'

Pullen nodded. 'The coffin is just over seven feet long.'

'Father Floridia thought a nun would normally be buried in a wooden coffin,' Jane said.

'The plot thickens,' Pullen said, raising her eyebrows.

The more Jane engaged with Sam Pullen, the more she liked her down-to-earth attitude and affable personality. Jane told her about

PC Rogers' *faux pas* with the coroner and Sam said he had it coming and deserved no sympathy.

Jane was making a coffee for the two of them and had her back to the door when she noticed Pullen look towards it. Thinking it was Boon she put a teaspoon of instant coffee in another cup.

'Can I help you?' Pullen asked.

At the door was a handsome black man in his mid-thirties with short afro hair and a smooth complexion. Dressed casually in dark grey Farah slacks, a blue-and-white striped shirt and woollen jacket, his clothes accentuated his slim body and muscular frame.

'Believe it or not, I'm actually here to help you,' he smiled. He spoke with a London accent.

Jane thought the voice sounded familiar and, looking at the reflection in the window in front of her, instantly recognised her former colleague from her days on the Flying Squad. She felt a rush of affection on seeing him, yet at the same time a mixture of anxiety and guilt, wondering how he would react on meeting her again, nearly two and a half years since the day he had been shot and nearly killed by an armed robber.

'Hi, Lloyd,' Jane said.

His smile widened with a look of delight. 'Bloody hell, Treacle Tennison . . . long time no see.' He gave her a hug and kiss on the cheek.

Jane instantly felt more at ease. She'd got used to being called 'Treacle' and knew he only used it as a term of endearment.

'Treacle Tennison?' Pullen said, looking at Jane for an explanation.

'We used to work together at the Sweeney. "Treacle" was my nickname on the squad. It comes from the cockney slang: treacle tart – sweetheart.' She turned to the newcomer. 'It's good to see you, Lloyd. How are you?'

'I'm fine – and all the better for seeing your lovely face again.'

'I'm Dr Sam Pullen.' Pullen put her hand out and he shook it.

'Sorry, rude of me not to do the intros first. Pleased to meet you, doc. I'm Detective Sergeant Lloyd Johnson. I'm here to assist you with the body in the coffin.'

'Has the coroner sent you as a replacement for PC Rogers?' Pullen asked.

Lloyd laughed. 'No, I'm your laboratory liaison sergeant. Anything you need forensic-wise, I'm your man.'

'Oh, right, I didn't realise . . .'

'Don't worry, doc, it surprises everyone. Unfortunately, there were no white lab sergeants available, so you're stuck with me.'

Pullen looked embarrassed. 'I'm sorry I didn't mean to sound offensive.'

He grinned. 'You didn't . . . I was just joking. I'm actually very proud to be the first black lab sergeant, though I'm still on trial in the role under the excellent tutelage of Paul Lawrence.'

'Is he here with you?' Pullen asked hopefully.

'Not today. He's busy on another job and let me go solo on this one.'

Jane could see Pullen was disappointed, even though she was smiling.

'Well, I'm pleased to meet you. And so far we have two things in common. I'm the first female forensic pathologist and also on my first solo case.'

'Well, we'd better look after each other and make sure we don't mess up. I've heard a lot of good things about you from Paul Lawrence and believe me, he doesn't hand out compliments easily.'

Pullen blushed. 'I was fortunate to have Prof Martin as my mentor, as were you with DS Lawrence.'

Lloyd nodded. 'That's for sure.'

'I'm just making a coffee – would you like one?' Jane asked, holding up a cup.

'I wouldn't say no,' he said.

Pullen picked up two of the coffees. 'I'll take one through to the radiographer and see how he's getting on.'

'She seems a nice lady,' Lloyd said when Pullen had left the room.

'She is. Sam's got a good sense of humour – unlike some pathologists I could name. You still take milk and two sugars?'

'You've a good memory Jane. How have you been keeping?'

'Fine, thanks. I'm working at Bromley now and studying for the inspectors' exam.'

'You'll pass that with flying colours. I always said you'd go far in the job. Bit of a schlep from your flat in Marylebone to Bromley though, isn't it?'

'I'm living over this way now. Oakdene Avenue in Chislehurst.'

'The posh stockbroker belt, eh? So, found yourself a rich young man yet?' he grinned.

She laughed. 'There's nothing posh about my place. It's a little semi that desperately needs a shedload of work done on it . . . which I can't afford right now. And I've no time for romance with all the studying I'm trying to do.'

'You need to get out a bit more. Let the bees come to the honey pot. Whoever nabs you as a missus will be a very lucky man.'

'What about you? How you been since, you know . . .?'

Lloyd could see she was having difficulty asking the obvious.

'I got shot in the chest? I told you when you visited me in hospital that it wasn't your fault, Jane.'

'I should have visited you more. It's just that every time I saw you, I felt responsible for what happened,' she said, hardly able to look him in the face.

Lloyd sighed. 'I missed your visits, but I knew that was why you stopped coming.'

Jane felt close to tears. 'I nearly got you killed. If I'd just stayed in the OP that day, then it would never have happened.'

'Rubbish. Every time a Flying Squad officer does a pavement ambush, they know they risk being shot. If it wasn't that time, it could

have been the next. DCI Murphy knew you suspected he was bent . . .
all he needed was an excuse to get rid of you, and being there when I
was shot gave him what he needed. He twisted what happened to suit
his purpose, Jane. Thankfully, you and Operation Countryman got
him in the end and now he's behind bars where he belongs. His life is
now in danger every day and I have no sympathy for him.'

'Yeah, but I alienated a lot of people assisting Countryman's
investigation and setting up Murphy for a fall. To be honest,
studying for the exam wasn't the only reason I requested a move
to a quieter station. My name was mud in a lot of places. A colleague nicks a seasoned villain or solves a complex crime and
they instantly become a great detective. I help arrest and convict
a colleague who organised armed robberies and I'm a grass for
snitching on one of my own. Where's the sense in that?'

'You've got to move on for your own sanity, Jane. I know the
Flying Squad officers were glad to see Murphy go down and they
respected and admired you for having the balls to do it. Ignore
what the halfwits say and do what you do best – being a bloody
good detective. Anyone who disses you is only jealous of your abilities. I heard Stanley is the DI at Bromley now. Has he been giving
you a hard time about Murphy?'

'No, not at all. In fact, he's never mentioned it,' Jane said.

'Good. That's probably because he knows you did the right thing.
You think you get it rough? Try being in my skin, woman!' he said
in a thick Jamaican accent, making her smile.

Jane had never worked in uniform or in the CID alongside a
black officer until she met Lloyd on the Flying Squad. There
were no black officers at Bromley. She knew that despite efforts
to encourage black and other ethnic minority applicants to join
the police force, the response had been poor. Many in the Afro-
Caribbean community believed, with good reason, that if they
joined the police they would be subjected to racism within the force
as well as opposition and hostility from their own community.

Lloyd took a sip of his coffee and put his notebook and pen on the desk. 'I take it you're dealing with the body in the coffin?' She nodded. 'Right, give me a rundown on what's happened so far.'

Jane brought Lloyd up to speed with details of the case. As he closed his notebook, Boon walked into the room eating a sandwich and carrying a brown paper bag.

'Where have you been?' Jane asked him.

'Sorry, sarge, I got delayed giving a nurse some advice regarding home security.'

'More like chatting her up, knowing you, Boony,' Lloyd said as he turned round.

'Bloody hell, Teflon, how you doing, mate?'

'Not bad my friend . . . and you?'

'Good, thanks. I'm working a really interesting case with DS Tennison. It looks like it could be a murder.'

'I know, she just told me all about it.'

'DS Johnson is assisting us as the lab sergeant,' Jane told him. 'So how do you two know each other?'

Boon spoke with a mouthful of sandwich. 'Teflon was helping coach the Met football team until he got himself shot. Then his wound got infected, and he ended up with sepsis, which damaged his liver and kidneys . . .'

Seeing that Jane was shocked by this new information, Lloyd raised his hand. 'I'm sure Sergeant Tennison doesn't want to hear all the gory details, Boony.'

'We all thought you was a goner at the time, mate,' Boon continued, ignoring the hint. 'I even heard they called a priest in to give you the last rites.'

'That's rubbish. I'm fine now and hope to be back coaching again soon.'

The mortuary technician put his head round the door. 'The radiographer just finished developing the X-rays and Dr Pullen is ready to start the post-mortem.'

As they left the room, DS Johnson sidled up to Boon and tapped his arm. 'I'd prefer to be called Lloyd now, Boony. Teflon was a Flying Squad nickname, which doesn't really go with my new role as a lab sergeant.'

'No problem.' Boon nodded. 'Personally, I always thought Teflon sounded a bit racist.'

As they entered the mortuary room Pullen was examining an X-ray on an illuminated viewer.

'Found anything interesting, doc?' Boon asked as they gathered round the viewer.

'This is a close-up X-ray of our victim's upper throat region,' Pullen explained. 'If I get too technical, or you don't understand anything, let me know.' Using a mortuary scalpel, Pullen pointed to a small bone at the top of the throat on the X-ray. 'This little horseshoe-shaped bone here is called the hyoid bone. It helps support our tongue movement and swallowing. The dark line just here is a small fracture of the hyoid, which indicates trauma to the neck. Although a fracture like this can occur in road traffic accidents or as the result of a contact sports injury, it is most commonly associated with strangulation.'

'A manual strangulation?' Jane asked.

'Or a ligature may have been used.'

'There may be some fibres deposited on her neck and headdress from a ligature. I'll take some tapings. We might find something to help identify the type of ligature used,' Lloyd said.

Boon looked confused. 'If she was strangled to death and put in the coffin, then how did the scratch marks get on the inside of the lid?'

'Good question, DC Boon. However, you don't have to be strangled to death for the hyoid bone to fracture,' Pullen said.

'So, she could have been strangled to a point of unconsciousness, put in the coffin, then regained consciousness,' Jane suggested.

'And in a state of sheer panic scratched the lid before suffocating to death,' Boon added.

'That's what I thought at first . . . until I saw this.' Pullen replaced the X-ray with another one and again used the scalpel blade as a pointer. 'This is the top section of the spine, which is made up of small bones known as the vertebrae, which protect the spinal cord and nerve roots that run through them. We refer to the top vertebra, where it joins the skull, as C1, the next C2, then C3 and so on. Can you see the tiny shaded triangular shape in between the C3 and C4 vertebrae?'

'Is her spine broken?' Lloyd asked.

'Severed possibly, but I can't be certain until I dissect the neck and examine the spine,' Pullen said. She then held the scalpel blade just below the triangular shape on the X- ray and the similarity to the tip of the blade was obvious.

'She was stabbed with a scalpel!' Boon exclaimed.

'The X-ray images are smaller than the real thing, but yes, she may have been stabbed. The object in between the vertebrae could be the broken tip of a knife blade.'

'If her spinal cord was severed would it have caused paralysis?' Jane asked.

Pullen nodded. 'Yes. A cervical vertebrae injury in the C1 to C5 section is the most severe. In the worst cases all communication between the brain and bod, below the injury, would instantly be cut off, including the ability to breathe properly, which would lead to a terrifying death.'

Jane looked shocked at the thought. 'Her assailant must have strangled her, then put the body in the coffin thinking she was dead and secured the clasps . . . which would explain the scratch marks.'

Pullen agreed. 'If she was originally put in the coffin on her back then a rear entry wound that high up on the spine would suggest she sat up or was let out before being stabbed. It's also possible the killer heard her cries for help and opened the coffin to stab her.'

Boon let out a long sigh. 'That poor woman. What kind of person could do that to a nun?'

'Murderers come in all shapes and sizes, Boony,' Lloyd said as he took some photographs of the body in the coffin.

Boon looked at Jane. 'Do you think another nun or a priest might have done it?'

'Right now, who knows. Father Floridia said the Sisters of Mercy lived and worked at the convent from the mid-1800s until the 1960s. Let's say 1850 to 1969, which gives us a possible time span of . . .' Jane paused to work it out.

'A hundred and nineteen years,' Boon said instantly, looking pleased with himself.

'Whoever killed her could be long dead by now,' Lloyd remarked, as he placed some sticky-backed ruler paper on the coffin lid to photograph the scratch marks.

'Finding out who she is and when she was born should help narrow the time frame down,' Jane suggested.

'That's not going to be easy if she's been dead for a hundred years,' Lloyd said.

Pullen picked up her mortuary gown and latex gloves. 'Right, I think it's about time we got the body out of the coffin and onto the examination table. I'm going to need everyone to help move her. We'll have to be gentle as I don't want any bits of her crumbling or coming away in our hands.'

The mortuary technician picked up a roll of green disposable post-mortem aprons, tore some off and handed one to Boon, then pointed. 'There's some plastic arm sleeve covers in the box over there.'

Jane noticed Boon grimace. 'If you want to get involved in murder investigations, then you need to learn to cope with the unpleasant side of things.'

'Yes, sarge,' he replied glumly, putting on the plastic gown.

When everyone was appropriately dressed and ready to go, they gathered around the coffin which was on an adjustable table. Pullen lowered it to a suitable height and the mortuary technician put the portable examination table in front of it.

LYNDA LA PLANTE | 49

'The mortuary technician and I will take either side of the torso and arms,' she said. 'Jane and Lloyd take the legs and feet, and DC Boon hold the head. We will lift on my count of three, then once we're all steady and ready to go, shuffle forward and slowly put her down on the table in front.'

Everyone got into position. Boon was turning his head away as best he could to avoid the smell. They all lifted the body on Pullen's count and when everyone said they were ready she gave the order to shuffle forward.

'I distinctly told you *not* to start the post-mortem without me, Tennison!' Stanley bellowed as he stormed in the room.

'Keep moving, we're nearly there ...' Pullen said, trying to ignore him and concentrate on what she was doing.

Boon, startled by Stanley's entrance, froze on the spot. As the others kept shuffling along there was a grating sound followed by a pop as the nun's head, still in the veil and wimple, came away from her body. Jane, Pullen, and Lloyd glared at Boon.

Boon started to retch as he put the head on the mortuary table.

'Shit. Sorry, Sam, I forgot to tell you DI Stanley wanted to attend the PM,' Jane whispered.

After the nun's body was placed on the table, Sam winked at Jane before turning to Stanley. 'Ah, DI Stanley, a pleasure to meet you.' She took off one latex glove and shook his hand. 'I'm Dr Pullen, the forensic pathologist on this case. DS Tennison informed me you would be attending. I thought I'd get the body laid out on the table so I'd be ready to start when you got here. Perfect timing, wouldn't you say?'

'Sorry, I thought you'd started,' an embarrassed Stanley replied.

'Well, we can, now you're here,' Pullen said, putting her glove back on.

'Stanley, how are you?' Lloyd asked.

'Teflon, what you doing here?'

'I'm your lab liaison DS.'

'I heard your injuries had rendered you unfit for front line duties. Didn't expect to see you in this role, though,' Stanley said.

Lloyd smiled. 'I figured it would be less traumatic. After all, dead people can't shoot you.'

Stanley took Lloyd to one side saying, 'I'm a DI now. I don't mind you calling me Stanley when it's just the two of us, but when there's junior ranks present, I'd prefer guv or sir.'

'No problem,' Lloyd said. 'I like to be called Lloyd now and not Teflon, if you don't mind.'

Stanley laughed. 'Why? You've been known as Teflon for years.'

'Unlike you, I like my Christian name. However, if you want to call me Teflon, I shall call you Evelyn.'

Stanley frowned. 'I told you that in the strictest confidence. It's not my fault my parents liked Evelyn Waugh's novels.'

'You told me that when you were pissed, and I haven't told anyone . . . yet,' Lloyd grinned.

'All right, point taken,' Stanley replied.

Lloyd took some photographs of the body then examined the interior of the coffin for any further forensic evidence but found nothing. Dr Pullen examined the head, whilst Jane showed Stanley the X-rays and pointed out the injuries.

Stanley shook his head in disbelief. 'After the attempted strangulation, the poor woman must have been terrified when she woke up in the coffin.'

Jane sighed. 'As awful as it sounds, I'd like to think the stabbing killed her instantly. To be totally paralysed, unable to do anything as you watch your killer slowly close the coffin lid, is unimaginable.'

Stanley nodded. 'Whoever did this was clearly determined to kill her.'

'Will you be forming a murder squad?' Boon asked brightly.

'It's not up to me, Boony. DCS Barnes will decide if a squad should be formed and who will be on it.'

'When will you be speaking with him?' Boon asked.

'I already have. He wants to wait until the full post-mortem is completed and speak with the coroner before making a decision.'

'From the injuries detected on the X-rays it's pretty clear we're talking murder here,' Pullen remarked.

'If DCS Barnes does form a squad, I think me and DC Boon should be on it,' Jane said.

'I don't have a problem with that,' Stanley said. 'But Barnes might.'

'Have I done something to upset him?' Boon asked with a worried frown.

'Not to my knowledge.' Stanley took Jane to one side. 'Tony Barnes wasn't very complimentary when I mentioned your name.'

'I've never even met the man,' Jane responded. 'Hang on, is Barnes another DCI Murphy sympathiser.'

'No. He said he'd been told you weren't a good team player and liked to do things your own way, that's all.'

'You know that's not true. I've always shared any leads or information I get with my colleagues.'

'Be honest, Jane, sometimes you keep things to yourself.'

'Only until I get further evidence to corroborate my suspicions, which, as you know, is because my male counterparts often doubt my abilities.'

Lloyd, who was eavesdropping on the conversation, joined them. 'Barnes and Murphy used to work together on the Flying Squad, but it was a good few years before you were on it. Barnes was the DI then and Murphy a DS.'

'Thick as thieves, were they?' Jane asked pointedly, looking at Stanley.

'I think you're jumping to conclusions Jane,' Stanley said curtly.

'No, I'm not! Murphy knew I was good detective. He had me kicked off the Flying Squad because I was a threat to him. And now his pal Barnes wants to stop me investigating murders.'

'To be fair, Jane, I've never heard any mention of Barnes being corrupt,' Lloyd said.

'Nor me,' Stanley added. 'If he were, then Countryman would have been after him as well. As for Murphy, all the evidence at his trial indicated he became a bent copper when he was a DI – which was a few years after he worked with Tony Barnes.'

'Maybe Barnes lured Murphy into a world of corruption,' Jane said bluntly.

'You're becoming paranoid, Jane,' Stanley said firmly. 'Me and Lloyd worked with Murphy . . . does that make *us* corrupt?'

Jane could feel herself getting angrier. 'You know that's not what I meant.'

'Well, it's what you're inferring.'

Jane turned away. 'This is ridiculous . . . I need to get some fresh air.'

'You feeling sick as well?' Boon asked.

'Only with the way I'm being treated!'

Stanley sighed. 'If it makes you feel any better, I'll insist you continue to be involved in the investigation, whatever Barnes says.'

Jane let out a heavy sigh. 'It would have been nice if you'd done that when you first spoke to him.'

Dr Pullen could see that things were getting heated. She deliberately spoke loudly. 'If you'd all like to gather round, I can show you the neck injuries and retrieve the object stuck in the vertebrae.'

She instantly got everyone's attention. The head of the nun lay on a separate examination table. Her dark blonde hair was well preserved under the wimple. It was cut to just above the earlobes, untidy and not very straight.

'I had to cut through the nun's wimple so I could dissect the skin and muscle around the neck.' Pullen handed the wimple to Lloyd.

He laid it out on a large brown exhibits bag and proceeded to tape it for any fibres which might have come from the ligature.

Pullen used tweezers to pluck some of the hairs from the scalp, then put them in a plastic exhibits bag which she handed to Lloyd.

'To be tested by toxicology for any drugs, I take it?' Lloyd asked.

Pullen nodded. 'Just in case she was poisoned as well, I'll remove her stomach and contents for testing when I examine the internal organs.'

'Has my little mishap with her head caused any problems?' Boon asked tentatively.

'Thankfully, there's no further damage to the vertebrae,' Pullen told him. 'As I suspected, the spinal cord has been severed between the C3 and C4 sections and the hyoid bone is fractured.' She looked at the notes she'd made prior to dissecting the throat. 'The width of the entry wound in the neck is two and a half centimetres and the penetration depth five centimetres. However, the knife could have had a longer blade than the penetration depth. There were no signs of serration on the vertebrae which suggests the knife had a smooth blade.'

Pullen used the tweezers to lift out the small triangular-shaped object she'd seen on the X-ray. She placed it gently down on a piece of blue paper cloth. It was clearly the tip of a knife.

Pullen took some measurements. 'It's quite thin, two centimetres wide at the break point and narrowing to a curved tip.'

Lloyd took some close-up photographs as Pullen held the ruler next to it. 'She must have been stabbed with some force to severe the spine and break the knife tip off.'

Pullen nodded. 'Yes, it's rare. The tip was embedded between the vertebrae and probably broke off when the knife was removed at an acute angle.'

'Do you think two people could have been involved in her murder? Lifting the body and putting it in the coffin wouldn't be easy,' Boon suggested.

Pullen shrugged. 'It's possible. However, the victim is small and quite light, even though the body has mummified.'

'If the coffin was on the ground, a single person could lift the upper body in first then the lower half,' Jane suggested, and Pullen agreed.

'The initial strangulation may not have taken place near the coffin,' Lloyd suggested.

'Could another nun have done it?' Boon asked.

Pullen shrugged. 'Metaphorically speaking, God only knows. All I can say at present is she was strangled then stabbed, by a person or persons at present unknown.'

'This is all wild speculation at the moment, anyway,' Stanley said.

'Finding the knife with a broken tip would be good,' Boon said enthusiastically.

'If she was murdered in the 1800s, it will be long gone,' Stanley retorted.

'It might be buried somewhere in the old convent grounds. We could use one of those metal detector things to look for it,' Boon suggested.

'A mechanical fit between the knife blade and broken tip would prove it was the murder weapon,' Jane added, and Lloyd agreed.

Stanley shook his head, 'searching the old convent grounds would take weeks, if not months. Spending a fortune on a murder that could have happened in the last century might not be justifiable, especially if the killer and any witnesses are all dead.'

'So, we just forget about it . . . is that what you're saying?' Jane asked.

'Like I said, Jane, I don't make the decisions.'

'Well, the coroner may want a full investigation. As I see it, the priority has to be to find out who the poor woman is,' Jane said.

'I think the coroner is likely to agree with DCS Barnes's thoughts rather than yours,' Stanley replied.

'I'm not qualified in forensic odontology, but I can say her teeth are in reasonably good condition, which may help to give you her age range,' Pullen interjected. 'I can contact Dr Martin.

He's the top forensic odontologist in London and lectures at King's College.'

'Have they got an anthropology department?' Jane asked.

'Yes, they have,' Pullen replied, 'and they also have a senior lecturer there, Richard Eaves. He's an expert in anatomical art and doing some ground-breaking work on facial reconstruction.'

'What's facial reconstruction?' Boon asked.

'Basically, he layers the skull of a body with modelling clay to create a three-dimensional facial likeness of the deceased person. It may lead to someone recognising the reconstructed face of the nun and help you identify her.'

Stanley raised his hand. 'Slow down, the lot of you. Before we start calling every forensic expert in the phone book, let Dr Pullen finish the PM, then I'll speak with Barnes.'

Pullen continued the post-mortem, dissected the body, and examined the internal organs, which had remained intact and become leathery due to the adipocere. The stomach contents had dried up, but there were some remnants of digested food which Pullen put in a glass container.

Pullen finished the post-mortem in nearly three hours. 'Her liver, heart and other internal organs were preserved by the adipocere. They are all in good condition which makes me think she was a healthy young woman . . . possibly aged between twenty and thirty, but don't quote me on that. Cause of death is the stab wound to the back which severed the spinal cord. I'll type up my report and send it to Jane in the next couple of days.'

'Thanks, Sam. You've given us some interesting details to work on. You also did an excellent job on your first solo PM,' Jane said.

'What about me?' Lloyd asked, looking forlorn.

Jane laughed. 'You as well, Lloyd.'

'You've a long way to go to beat Paul Lawrence's track record,' Stanley joked.

Pullen removed her gown and gloves. 'Please let me know if you decide to call in an anthropologist or odontologist. I'd like to be present when they examine the body. Anyone fancy a drink at The Sydney Arms? It's just up the road.'

'I've got time for a pint before heading back to the lab,' Lloyd said.

'Sorry, I'll have to decline as I need to get back to the station,' Stanley said.

'Can we join them for a drink?' Boon asked Jane.

'Sorry, Boony. We need to write up our reports of the day's events.'

'Just a quick one, sarge . . .' Boon said.

'Do as you're told, Boon,' Stanley said firmly. He turned to Jane. 'I want to go over everything that's happened before I speak with DCS Barnes. I'll see you in my office when we get back to the station.'

Jane waited for Stanley to drive out of the mortuary car park before having a private word with Lloyd, who was putting his forensic case and exhibits in the boot of his car.

'Can you do me a favour?'

'What is it?' he asked cautiously.

'Would you contact the odontologist and Richard Eaves, the facial guy at King's College anthropology department? I'd like to know their availability over the next couple of days.'

Lloyd sighed. 'I'm not sure that's a good idea. You heard what Stanley said about doing things your own way. Let him speak to Barnes before calling them.'

'It's already clear Barnes won't be interested in my opinion, but he can't argue with the experts. That nun was murdered, and whoever did it needs to be held accountable.'

'If she was murdered in the mid-1800s, the case would be over 150 years old. There'll be no one alive to arrest or convict.'

'That's my point. We won't know how long she's been dead, or how old she is, until we get further expert opinion. For all we know, it could have happened in the fifties or sixties, before the convent was sold for development. There may be a grieving family out there, still alive, wondering what happened to their daughter.'

'Then they might have reported her missing. The convent records might help as well,' Lloyd suggested.

'I know. I was going to do the relevant checks when I get back to the station. Will you contact the other experts?'

'I don't like being used, Jane,' Lloyd said as he shut the boot of his car.

'I'm not trying to use you, Lloyd. All I want to know is if they would be available and willing to examine the nun's body. I'll take full responsibility if you get in any trouble.'

Lloyd shook his head. 'I don't want to risk my job as a lab sergeant . . . not when I've just started. If I got sent back to division, you know I can't do front line duties with my problems. I'd be stuck behind a desk pushing paper.'

'I'm sorry, I shouldn't have said anything. I'll make contact with King's College myself,' Jane said.

'For your own sake, why not just wait and see what Barnes says? If he authorises a full investigation, calling in the experts won't be an issue.'

'You're right. I shouldn't be so impatient,' she said, fully intending to make the call whatever Barnes said.

'No, you shouldn't.' He got a card out of his pocket with his office number on it and wrote his home number on the back. 'If you fancy going out for a drink one evening give me a ring. Be good to catch up properly.'

She took the card. 'Yes, I'd like that . . . maybe at the weekend if I'm not on a murder squad.'

He gave her a big wink. 'They couldn't solve it without you, Jane.'

CHAPTER SIX

Jane found it hard to concentrate on the road as she drove back to the station, nearly going through a red light had it not been for Boon warning her to stop. The thought of how the victim suffered an agonising death, paralysed and unable to breathe, made her feel nauseous. She wondered what could make someone so determined to kill a nun and whether it was a spur-of-the-moment incident or planned. There was no way of knowing where it had taken place, but somewhere within the old convent grounds seemed most likely.

Boon was looking out of the window, as if in a daydream, when he suddenly sat up and clicked his fingers. 'I've just had a thought about Barry the builder opening the coffin, and there being a cross on the body that's missing. Perhaps he nicked it. And what if the knife that was used to kill the nun was still in the coffin, too.'

'It wasn't,' Jane said. 'Lloyd searched the coffin.'

'I know,' Boon said. 'But Barry might have nicked the knife as well.'

'That's good thinking, Boony,' Jane replied in a positive tone, though she thought it unlikely.

He looked pleased. 'Thanks, sarge. It would be a right result if Barry did have it. Teflon – sorry, Lloyd – might get some finger-prints off it.'

'When we get back, I'll start the report. It's a long shot, but I'd like you to phone missing persons and make an enquiry on what we know so far,' Jane told him.

'Which isn't very much. What about asking the Church if they have any records of missing nuns?'

'I'll ask Stanley if it's OK to speak with Father Floridia about that. You stick to the mispers for now.'

'I doubt mispers will go back to the 1800s,' he sighed.

Jane knew identifying a female missing person as a possible victim would put pressure on DCS Barnes to fully investigate the nun's murder – even more so if any of her family were still alive. 'We know she was a nun, her height and hair colour. Confine your initial search to the 1960s for blonde-haired women, aged between sixteen and thirty . . . then we can go back to the 1950s if we need to.'

Boon made some notes in his pocketbook. 'She might have been from out of town. Missing Persons Bureau only covers the Met. Should I send a telex out to the surrounding county forces to search their misper records?'

Jane worried that sending a telex to other forces might get back to Barnes or Stanley. 'It's best to start in London, then widen the search if we have to.'

'We could end up with hundreds of possible hits . . .'

'Agreed, but one of them might lead us to who she is. Investigating murder is never easy, Boony. It can take a lot of time and hard work to solve a complex case like this, even more so when the victim is unknown.'

'You really like this side of the job, don't you?' he said.

'Yes. As macabre as it may sound, the thrill of the chase excites me. Solving a murder and getting a conviction is very satisfying for everyone involved, even the dead person's family to some extent.'

'They say it gives them closure.'

'Maybe a bit, but you can never forget the death of a loved one,' Jane said, thinking of her parents and the grief they went through at the loss of their only son, four years old when he drowned.

*　*　*

It was just after five when they got back to the office. While Boon phoned Missing Persons, Jane went to Stanley's office. He was on the phone, and from what she could hear of the conversation she guessed he was speaking to DCS Barnes. Stanley pointed to the chair. Jane placed it in front of his desk and sat down.

'Yes, sir. I'll pass your thoughts on to Tennison and make sure it's ready first thing in the morning.' Stanley put the phone down.

'Make sure what's ready?' Jane asked suspiciously.

'He wants to see your report before he makes a decision.'

'What for? You know as much about the case as I do.'

Stanley shrugged. 'He was busy. I didn't get the chance to give him all the details.'

'What were his thoughts on the details you *were* able to give him?' Jane asked, feeling Stanley was being evasive.

'He sounded positive. Like I said, he'll make a decision after he's read your report in the morning . . . so I suggest you get on with it.'

'The coroner asked for a full forensic PM. Dr Pullen's findings prove the nun was murdered. What more does Barnes want?'

'For fuck's sake, Jane, why do you always think everyone's got it in for you? You've never met Tony Barnes and know nothing about him, yet you already assume he's the devil in disguise. He has a reputation for being a stickler for the rules. He likes to know the ins and outs of a duck's arse before making a decision.' Stanley opened his desk drawer, pulled out a thick blue folder and pushed it across his desk.

'What do you want me to do with that?' she asked, assuming it was another case file.

'It's a copy of every bloody report I've had to do for him in the nine months I've been here. He got screwed over once when he was given duff information by another officer, who then denied what he'd said when the job went tits-up. Barnes ended up getting a reprimand. He quickly learnt the lesson that signed reports can't be denied.'

'Sorry, I didn't realise . . .'

'Please, Jane, for my and everyone else's sake, just do the bloody report. Barnes will be in his Orpington office at ten.'

'He wants me to take it to him?' Jane asked.

Stanley sighed. 'No, put it in a stamped envelope. I'll post it to him on my way home.'

'There's no need to be facetious. I'm just surprised he'd want to meet me.'

'I've no doubt you will do a decent report, but there's bound to be a few questions he'll want to ask.'

'I asked Boony to run our victim's description through the Missing Persons Bureau,' she said hesitantly.

'I don't mind that under the circumstances.'

'Am I OK to do some overtime to finish the report?'

'Of course, Boony as well. You've both worked hard today in pretty shitty conditions.' He wagged his index finger at her. 'And no further investigation until Barnes gives you the go-ahead, understood?'

She realised it was pointless asking if she could speak to Father Floridia. She stood to attention and saluted. 'Yes, sir.' Then as she walked towards the door, she suddenly spun on her heel. 'I just remembered something I forgot to mention earlier.'

'God help me. What now?'

Jane told him about the jemmy marks on the rim of the coffin and why she and Boon suspected Barry the builder had opened it and stolen a crucifix from around the dead nun's neck.

'He must be a sick bastard to steal from a dead nun! Get a couple of the late-turn detectives to nick him and search his home address ASAP.'

'I haven't got a home address for him. He was leaving the site as we arrived. Me and Boony were going to nick him tomorrow morning.'

'You're meeting Barnes. Get Boony to do it with a couple of the lads and some backup. If Barry resists arrest, they've my authority to give the scumbag a good right-hander.'

Jane felt a bit miffed at not being able to take part in Barry's arrest, but knew her meeting with DCS Barnes was more impor- tant, especially if she could persuade him to form a murder squad. She nodded and went back to the CID office.

'How did it go with mispers?' she asked Boon, who was sitting at his desk doing some paperwork.

'Do you know they get about 25,000 misper reports a year. Nearly fifty per cent of them are under eighteen, with thirty per cent in the eighteen to thirty age range, of which females make up—'

'Anyone matching our nun's description?' Jane interrupted, wanting him to get to the point.

'The officer I spoke with said it will take a few days to trawl through the sixties females aged eighteen to thirty. He'd never heard of a nun being reported missing and he's been working there for fifteen years.'

'That's an interesting point,' Jane remarked.

'What is?'

'That he's never heard of a nun being reported missing. If a nun did suddenly disappear from a convent it should have been reported, and would then in turn attract press attention.'

'So, there might have been a previous investigation into her disappearance, years ago?'

'It's possible, if there were any suspicious circumstances, so we might get lucky with mispers.'

'Not if it happened in the late 1800s or early 1900s. We can only go as far back as 1929 when the Missing Persons Bureau started. Plus, she may not even be from the convent,' Boon replied.

'Whatever the case we need to do all the necessary checks to try and find out who she is. When you were at the building site, did the manager mention what time they started work?'

Boon shook his head. 'Not to me personally. Dermot asked if he should come in tomorrow and the manager said yes as there was a big brick and breeze block delivery. I think he suggested they start at seven thirty. Obviously Barry wasn't there, so it's unlikely he'll turn up if he thinks the site is still shut down.'

'The manager must have his home address, though.' Jane worked out some timings in her head. 'Right, I'll meet you in the bottom lane by the site at seven. Get a couple of uniformed officers to come with you. Hopefully Barry doesn't live far away. We should be able to search his premises in an hour or so.'

'Why the rush?' Boon asked.

'I've got to be at DCS Barnes's office in Orpington with my report by ten.'

'I can deal with Barry if you want,' he offered.

'I know you could, but I'd like to be there and hear what he has to say for himself. You can make the arrest.'

'Thanks, sarge. If Barry admits nicking the crucifix, you'll have plenty of time to spare.'

'Somehow, I don't see him putting his hands up and saying, "Fair cop, guv."'

'Do you want any help with the report?'

'No, thanks. You've done a good job today. Get off home and have an early night.'

'Thanks, sarge. Sorry about the incident with the nun's head.'

'Don't worry about it. I'm sure she didn't take offence.'

Jane sat at her desk, put a piece of paper in the typewriter and opened her notebook. She noticed Father Floridia's name and phone number and remembered she had promised to call and update him about the coffin. She leaned back in her chair and sighed. Jane realised she knew very little about St Mary's Convent, or the practices of the Catholic Church, and Father Chris's knowledge could prove invaluable in trying to identify the nun. She went to Stanley's office.

'Sorry to bother you, guv. There's quite a bit of distraction in the office and it's hard to concentrate. Is it OK if I type up my report at home?'

'I don't care where you do it as long as it's done by ten in the morning.'

'Thanks. I'll see you in the morning after my meeting with Barnes.'

'You'll be fine. Whatever happens, he knows he can't brush a nun's murder under the carpet. It's just a question of manpower and the cost of investigating something which may never be solvable.'

'I know,' Jane said. 'I shouldn't have reacted like I did at the mortuary or here earlier.'

'It's all right. I get why you're upset over the way you've been treated in the past. There's many an officer who would have handed in their warrant card by now.'

She gave him a wry smile. 'It's crossed my mind a few times.'

'That's the thing I most admire about you, Jane. You're a fighter, not a quitter.'

'It's good to know you're on my side.'

'I always have been, Jane. I remember the first time I met you in the back of an observation van in the early seventies.'

She laughed. 'So do I! You told me to keep watch and then went to sleep.'

He grinned. 'Happy days. For what it's worth, my advice is not to bottle things up and let them eat away at you. Listen to other people's viewpoints, then speak your mind calmly and objectively.'

Jane knew he was right, though it seemed odd coming from Stanley. This wasn't the scatterbrained man she'd worked with when he was a DC and DS. Promotion to DI seemed to have somehow made him a lot more thoughtful.

CHAPTER SEVEN

There was a slight drizzle of rain falling as Jane knocked on the door of the old Victorian presbytery, tucked round the back of St Mary's Church. The paint on the timber sash window ledges was peeling away and in need of repair, as was the slate roof which was missing a few tiles and covered in moss.

As she waited, Jane knew she should have asked Stanley's permission to tell Father Chris about the murdered nun, and he probably would have told her to wait and see what Barnes had to say. But as she'd told Father Chris she would update him after the coffin was opened, Jane felt it only right that she did it personally.

Thirty seconds passed and there was no answer. Jane wondered if he was out and knocked again a little louder. She was about to leave when the door opened a bit and Father Chris stuck his head round. Jane could see his hair was dripping wet.

He seemed surprised to see her. 'Detective Tennison. Please excuse the state of me . . . I was just having a shower.'

'No need to apologise, Father. I should have phoned ahead to let you know I was coming.'

'Is it about the coffin?'

'Yes, but I can call back tomorrow.'

'No, please come in. Give me a minute to get dressed and I'll be right with you. The living room is first on the left,' he said.

The door creaked open, allowing Jane to see Father Chris holding a thigh-length towel round his slim waist. He had broad shoulders with muscular arms and his calf muscles flexed as he briskly climbed the stairs two at a time. When he got to the top, he started to remove the towel and Jane smiled to herself as she glimpsed the cheeks of his backside.

The small living room was tidy, but sparsely furnished, with two shabby grey armchairs, a side cabinet, and an old oak writing desk with matching chair by the window. The green-painted plaster walls had numerous cracks and the carpet was threadbare in some places. The smoke from the log fire gave off a nice woody smell, reminding Jane of her family home when she was a child. She was surprised that the only religious objects in the room were a wooden crucifix above the fireplace and a large bible on the writing desk.

She also noticed there was no television. A transistor radio was on the side cabinet, alongside some framed photographs, which Jane presumed were of Father Chris's parents. She noticed a picture of him suspended in mid-air, in a hitch kick position, about to land in a long-jump pit. He looked to be in his early twenties, and she could see a large, terraced stadium in the background, filled with spectators.

'Would you like a coffee or tea?' he asked as he entered the room wearing a grey tracksuit and flip-flops.

'I'm fine, thanks. I see from the photograph you were a long jumper.'

'That was actually the last competition I jumped in.'

'Where was it?'

'Meadowbank Stadium, 1970. I represented Malta.'

The place and year rang a bell with Jane. 'You were in the Edinburgh Commonwealth Games?'

'Yes, but I didn't win a medal. In fact, I was second to last.'

'It's still a fantastic achievement to have represented your country in such a prestigious event. Your family must have been very proud of you,' Jane said.

'My parents were there. The whole thing was an experience I'll never forget.'

'How old were you then?'

'Twenty-one. I became a priest shortly after, so that was the end of my long-jumping career.'

'You obviously still keep yourself fit,' she said, recalling the sight of his semi-naked body.

'I try to run three or four times a week or go to the Walnuts Leisure Centre.'

'Where's that?' she asked.

'Just near Orpington police station. There's a 33-metre swimming pool and gym.'

'I've only recently moved to Chislehurst and haven't been to Orpington yet. I'll have to check it out sometime as I like to try and keep fit.'

He removed the fireguard and put some more logs on the fire. 'Let me take your coat.'

Jane removed her coat and handed it to him.

'Please, take a seat,' he said, then hung her coat in the hallway. He sat down in the other armchair. 'What was the outcome with the coffin?'

'There was a female body inside dressed in nun's clothing.'

'That's sad. Do you know her name?'

'At the moment we have no idea who she is or when she died. Does the diocese keep records of all the nuns who lived and worked at the convent?'

'I'm not certain, but I would think so. I had to give them my details and next of kin should anything happen to me. I suspect the convent would have kept their own records as well. They would have been passed on to the diocesan archives when the convent closed.'

'Where are the archives kept?'

'Archbishop's House in Southwark. I'm sure the diocese will arrange for her to be reburied in a cemetery.'

'I was wondering if you'd informed the bishop about the coffin?'

'No. I was waiting to hear back from you first. I'll call him now.' He walked towards the phone on the writing desk.

'This may sound odd,' Jane said, 'but I'd be grateful if you didn't just now.'

He turned back to her with a puzzled look. 'Why?'

Jane realised she'd dug a bit of a hole for herself. 'I shouldn't really be here discussing the investigation. My senior officers won't be very pleased with me if they find out.'

He frowned. 'And I'm afraid Bishop Meade will be angry with me if he finds out I didn't tell him.'

'I'm sure I'll be able to tell you tomorrow. Look, I'd better go . . .'

'This is putting me in an awkward position as well,' he said. 'Is there more to the nun's death than you're telling me?'

'I'm sorry, but I can't say at the moment,' Jane said.

'Trust works both ways, detective,' he said with a meaningful look.

Jane sighed, but felt she had no other option than to trust him. 'The post-mortem revealed she was murdered.'

'Murdered? Bloody hell! How was she killed?' he asked, clearly stunned. 'I'm sorry, I apologise for swearing.'

'Tragically, she must have suffered a slow, agonising death,' Jane said before telling him about the examination of the coffin and the post-mortem findings.

Using his right hand, Father Chris traced the sign of the cross.

'*In nomine Patris et Filii, et Spiritus Sancti.* Amen.' He held his hands together, eyes closed in silent prayer for a few seconds before looking up at Jane with a sorrowful expression. 'It saddens me when I hear what human beings are capable of doing to each other.'

Jane was moved by his words. 'If whoever killed her is still alive, I'm determined to find them.'

'I hope you do.'

'We also think a builder on the site forced open the coffin and stole a crucifix from the nun's neck. The outline of a cross and chain was on her clothing.'

He shook his head in disgust. 'That's sickening. But you do realise a crucifix and a cross are not necessarily the same thing.'

'Really?'

'A crucifix is a cross with Jesus depicted or engraved on it. A cross is just a plain cross, though a nun's cross often has the Sacred Heart of Jesus engraved on it.'

'Is it the same as a normal heart shape?'

'Pretty much. The symbol represents Jesus' love for all humanity. It can be depicted in different ways. The most common is a heart with a circle of thorns, which represents the crown of thorns placed on Jesus' head. There may also be a cross on top of the heart, which represents the crucifixion.'

Jane nodded. 'That's useful to know when we search the builder's premises.'

'I spoke with my housekeeper after you left this morning,' Father Chris said. 'I didn't mention the unearthed coffin but asked her about the convent. She said it was an orphanage with about twenty or thirty children living there. Apparently, there was a fire and the convent closed, but she couldn't remember exactly when.'

'The building site manager mentioned there was a school which burned down before the convent closed. I've got a meeting tomorrow morning with my detective chief superintendent. I don't know what course of action he will take – or if I'll still be involved in the investigation. He may even contact the bishop himself. So I'd be grateful if you could keep this conversation between the two of us.'

'Of course. The last thing I want to do is get you into trouble. I appreciate your honesty, and I'm still happy to help in any way I can.'

Jane gave him a relieved smile. 'I could do with your help to identify the nun.'

He nodded. 'Will you call me after you've spoken with your chief superintendent?'

'Yes. I'll only tell him about your offer of assistance. I'm sure he'll appreciate it as well.'

'Thank you for confiding in me. Is there anything you need from me just now?'

'There's a million questions I'd like to ask you about nuns and the Catholic Church, but they can wait until tomorrow.' She looked at her watch. It was half past seven. 'I'd best get off home. I've a lengthy report to type up.'

'Have you had supper yet?' he asked.

His question surprised her. 'I was going to get a takeaway on the way home, actually.'

'I've some *soppa tal-armla* simmering on the stove. It should be just about ready and there's plenty for two.'

She was in two minds. Staying a little longer would give her the opportunity to discuss the case a bit more, but it would also mean a late night typing her report. She didn't want to appear rude by declining his offer, although she didn't have a clue what he was cooking.

'I don't want to put you to any bother,' she said in the end.

'It's no bother at all. I've a small table in the kitchen where we can eat. Please, after you,' he said, ushering her through the living-room door before him.

The small kitchen was antiquated, with Thirties-style green cupboards, a stone floor and an old gas stove, which reminded Jane of the one her grandmother had. A Raleigh drop-handle racing bike was resting upside down against the kitchen table, with one wheel on the floor next to it.

'Excuse the bike. I got a puncture this afternoon. I need to repair it so I can get out and about tomorrow.' He opened the back door and put the bike and wheel outside.

'You don't have a car?'

'My vows of poverty mean I can't have one. The bike keeps me fit; though I must admit I dislike riding in the rain.'

A pot was simmering on the stove, giving off a mouth-watering aroma which instantly made Jane feel hungry.

'It smells delicious. What did you say it was called?'

'*Soppa tal-armla*. It's a popular Maltese winter soup made with vegetables, potatoes and tomatoes. I just need to add some cubes of goat's cheese for a few minutes, then it's ready to eat.'

'Does *tal-armla* mean vegetables in Maltese?'

He started stirring the soup with a large wooden spoon. 'The literal translation is "of the widow", thus it's commonly known as widow's soup. The name originates from the medieval practice of gifting penniless, widowed women with vegetables and other available produce, which they would use to make filling soups.'

'I can't wait to try it, Father.'

'Please call me Chris,' he smiled.

'Well, seeing as we are both technically off duty, you must call me Jane.'

He placed two wicker table mats, side plates, cutlery, and napkins neatly down on the small table, then pulled out a chair. 'Please, take a seat.' He gently slid it back in as Jane sat down, then unfolded a napkin and handed it to her.

'Would you like a glass of red wine with your soup? It's a Chianti,' he said, holding up the bottle.

'Only if you're having one.'

Chris poured two glasses and handed one to Jane. 'Cheers,' she said, raising her glass.

He smiled. 'Cheers. Here's to a successful outcome to your investigation.'

'Let's hope so,' Jane replied, taking a sip of wine.

'I made some Maltese sourdough bread earlier. Would you like some with your soup?'

She nodded. 'You obviously like cooking.'

'I used to help my mother in the kitchen when I was young. I find cooking relaxing, though it's generally just meals for myself. Having company is a pleasant change.'

He cut four slices of bread on a wooden chopping board which he then placed on the table. He ladled some soup into two bowls, sprinkled some chopped parsley on top, then put the bowls on the wicker mats before sitting down.

'It can be served with a poached egg on top, but I used my last two for breakfast, I'm afraid.'

'It looks delicious as it is,' Jane said, picking up her spoon. She noticed Chris had bowed his head, with his palms pressed together. On impulse, she followed suit.

'Bless us, O Lord, and these, thy gifts, which we are about to receive from thy bounty. Through Christ, our Lord. Amen.' He made the sign of the cross. 'Help yourself to some bread, Jane. I like to dunk it in the soup,' he said, picking up a spoon and fork.

Although the soup looked appetising, she noticed it had cauliflower florets in it, a vegetable she had never liked. Using her fork to cut a small bit off she scooped it up in her spoon with some of the soup. Her opinion of cauliflower was instantly transformed as the flavour enveloped her taste buds. Next, she tried a bit of the cheese, which literally melted in her mouth. She dipped her bread in the soup, took a bite, and raised her wine glass.

'My compliments, Chef Chris. I can honestly say I've never tasted a soup like this. It's absolutely delicious.'

Chris raised his glass with a smile. 'I'm glad you like it.'

'Without a name for our victim, finding out what happened to all the nuns living at the convent over a hundred years is going to be a massive task. My intention is to work backwards in ten-year periods from the day the convent closed.'

'Some of the nuns will still be alive,' he pointed out. 'They may be working in other convents or parishes.'

'They shouldn't be hard to trace, then.'

'There is one problem you may encounter, though.'

She raised her eyebrows. 'Which is . . .?'

'In some convents, nuns change their names to reflect the change that has happened in their lives. Sometimes they can suggest a new name, but it's often up to the Mother Superior to decide on it.'

Jane sighed. 'That could make things a lot more complicated.'

'It might be worth trying to locate the last Mother Superior. The diocese should know where she is.'

Jane nodded, swallowing a mouthful of soup. 'What about the orphan children who lived in the convent? Will there be a record of them?'

'I'd imagine so, and Bromley Council may have a record as well. Would you like some more wine?' he asked, lifting the bottle.

She picked up her glass. 'Just a drop, thank you.'

He topped up both their glasses and offered Jane another slice of bread.

'It's just a thought,' she said, 'but is there a specific religious shop where nuns and priests get their clothing?'

'There is for us. I'm not sure about nuns. Why do you ask?'

'I didn't check the habit at the mortuary. A maker's label might help identify a period when it was made and narrow the timeline of our victim's death. I'll get our forensic guy to take a look.'

'That's clever thinking.'

'Not really. It's something I picked up from an experienced colleague on a previous case. I should have thought to do it at the mortuary.'

He admired her modesty. 'It must be hard to concentrate after such a gruesome discovery.'

'You kind of get used to it, but I'd be lying if I said it's never upsetting – not so much at the time, as you've a lot to think about, but later, when you are off duty. Dealing with grieving families is hard, but you have to be strong for their sake. It must be the same for you.'

He nodded. 'Yes, it is, especially when it's children or babies who have died. I was wondering . . . would it be possible for me to visit the deceased nun in the mortuary and say a prayer for her?'

'Certainly. Under the circumstances that would seem to be very appropriate. Are you free tomorrow afternoon?'

'Yes. After one would be best.'

'I'll pick you up at around quarter past one,' she said, knowing he didn't have a car.

'There's no need to put yourself out. If you give me the address, I'll cycle there.'

'It's no bother. I can let you know how my meeting went on the way to the mortuary.'

Jane savoured her last spoonful of soup and put the spoon in the bowl. 'That was pure heaven.'

'I doubt the angels make it as good as my mother did,' he joked, and Jane laughed. 'Would you like some more?'

'I'm full, thanks,' she said, patting her stomach.

'Would you like some more wine . . . or a coffee?'

Jane said a coffee with milk would be fine. Chris filled a kettle, put it on the hob and spooned some instant coffee into a cup.

'Would you like to try some *kwarezimal* with your coffee?' he asked, picking up a round cake tin from the work surface and removing the lid. He put the tin on the table.

'Did you make these as well?' Jane asked, admiring the inch-thick, oval-shaped, chocolate-coloured biscuits.

'Yes. Basically, they're made with orange water, cocoa, ground almonds and spices, then coated with honey and almond slivers. They're best straight out of the oven, but I can warm some up for you.'

'No need. They look delicious.' She picked one up and took a bite.

'These are to die for as well. What are they called again?'

'*Kwarezimal.* It's a traditional Maltese Lenten food, which derives its name from the Latin word *Quaresima*, meaning the forty days of Lent. During Lent, adult Catholics abstain from eating meat and often had these instead. They're quite fattening, but I love them . . . naughty but nice,' he said, picking one up and biting into it.

The kettle started whistling. Chris made Jane a coffee, emptied what was left of the wine into his glass and offered her another *kwarezimal*.

'If I eat any more, I'll burst. But I'd love to know the recipe for the widow's soup.'

He opened a drawer and removed a worn leather-bound note-book with an elastic band around it. 'My mother kept all her recipes in this book. Cooking Maltese food reminds me of my parents and my old life in Malta.' He removed the elastic band and handed the book to Jane.

She noticed some old burn marks on the back, which made it look as if it had been dropped on a stove at some point. 'Do your parents still live in Malta?'

'Sadly, they're both dead now.'

She realised they must have died quite young if Chris was in his early thirties. 'I'm sorry,' she said, wondering if he had any brothers or sisters but didn't want to ask.

'I miss them, but they are still with me in spirit . . . and never more so than when I'm cooking something from my mother's recipe book.' He smiled. 'What about your family?'

'My parents live in London, and so does my sister.'

'Is she also in the police?'

Jane laughed. 'No, she's a hairdresser. She's married with two young children.'

'Does she do your hair?'

'Yes. I'm due to see her for a trim next week, though it may depend on how this case works out.'

'She's obviously very good. I'll swap her details for the soup recipe.'

Jane laughed. 'Deal . . . though I better check with her first as she doesn't usually cut men's hair – apart from my father's and her husband's.' She opened the recipe book. It hadn't crossed her mind that all the recipes would be written in Maltese. 'I think I'll need you to translate again,' she said, handing him the book.

Chris read out the ingredients and the method for making the soup and Jane wrote it down in the back of her notebook. He asked if she'd like the recipe for the *kwarezimal* biscuits as well.

She smiled. 'I think they may be beyond my cooking abilities.'

Chris closed the recipe book, put the rubber band around it, then gently kissed it and made the sign of the cross.

Jane looked at her watch. 'I really must be going, or I'll never get my report done by tomorrow morning. Would you like a hand with the washing up?'

He stood up. 'No, it's fine. My housekeeper will do them in the morning. She actually gets annoyed if I do the dishes – or cleaning of any sort.'

Jane laughed. 'Thanks for a lovely meal.'

'My pleasure. Thanks for the company.'

'Hopefully, I'll see you tomorrow.'

'I hope your meeting goes well. It would be a great shame if someone as determined as you wasn't allowed to continue the investigation.'

In the hallway, Chris helped Jane on with her coat and opened the front door – then he asked her to hold on for a second and nipped back to the kitchen, returning with the biscuit tin.

'Please, take these.'

'Are you sure?'

He nodded. 'I can easily make some more.'

'Thank you. Goodnight, Chris.'

'Goodnight, Jane,' he replied, closing the door.

Chris went to the living room, turned on the radio and sat in the armchair to listen to the evening news. After a couple of minutes, he got up, turned off the radio, then picked up the phone and dialled a number.

It was quickly answered. 'Bishop Meade speaking, how can I help you?'

'Good evening, Bishop. It's Father Floridia. I've just rung to tell you a coffin was uncovered today in the grounds of the old St Mary's Convent . . .'

CHAPTER EIGHT

Driving home, Jane felt nervous about her conversation with Father Chris. She knew it could land her in trouble, and she only had herself to blame if it did. She hoped he'd meant it when he said 'trust works both ways'. It was that remark that had persuaded her to confide in him. Her only two previous encounters with a priest were at a friend's wedding and the funeral of a murder victim she had attended in her official capacity. In both instances the priests had been in their sixties and rather dour. Father Chris seemed proof that not all priests were the same, with his warmth and humour.

It was obvious he still grieved the loss of his parents. She wondered if he'd left the Mediterranean island of Malta to become a priest because of their deaths.

Arriving home, she parked her Mini Cooper on the small driveway. As she got out of the car, Jane noticed a man in his late sixties walking past with a small Jack Russell terrier, which cocked its leg on her front wall pillar and peed on it. The owner looked embarrassed and was gently tugging the dog's lead.

'Naughty boy, Spud. I'm so sorry. I'll get a pitcher of water . . .'

'No need,' Jane said. 'I can do it.'

'No, I insist. I won't be two seconds,' he said, hurrying to the house next door.

Jane removed her briefcase from the passenger seat, opened her front door and flicked the hallway light on. It lit up briefly, popped and went out.

'For God's sake, not again,' she said to herself.

'Everything all right, love?' the neighbour asked, pouring some water on the pillar.

'There's a fault with the hallway light. It works fine for a bit and then the bulb blows.'

'I can have a look at it if you like. Have you got a ladder?'

'Sorry, I haven't. Don't worry, it's pretty late and I'm sure you've better things to do.' She switched on the living-room light which lit up a section of the hallway. 'That will do me until the morning.'

'It's not nice entering a dark hallway. We don't want you tripping over anything on your way upstairs,' he said, noticing the storage boxes in the hallway Jane had yet to unpack. 'I'll just nip and get my ladder and tool kit.'

Jane really wanted to get on with her report but didn't want to offend him. It wasn't long before he returned with an old wooden ladder and a metal toolbox, from which he removed a torch.

'Can you switch the main fuse off for me, please?' he asked as he unfolded the ladder.

'Certainly,' she said, assuming it was somewhere in the hallway coat cupboard next to the kitchen door.

'I think you'll find it in the small floor cupboard next to the front door,' he told her, turning the torch on.

'Sorry, I haven't had a chance to get to know where everything is yet.' She opened the cupboard while he shone the torch on the fuse box.

'I'm Gerry, by the way. I live next door with my wife Vi, that's short for Violet. Would you hold this for me while I remove the bulb and light shade?' He handed her the torch.

'Pleased to meet you. I'm Jane.'

'Welcome to Oakdene Avenue, Jane. How are you settling in?' He removed the light bulb and handed it to her.

'Fine, thanks. Still got a lot of unpacking to do, though. Sorry I haven't popped round to introduce myself yet.'

'I expect a young woman like you is very busy with her work. Are you in the police?' he asked, as he removed the lightshade.

'What makes you ask that?' Jane asked.

'I saw you at lunchtime in the Hillman Hunter when I was walking Spud. My grandson told me if you ever see a deep red Hunter behind you, it's wise to slow down as it's probably a plainclothes police car.'

'Can't argue with that.' Jane smiled, as everyone in the CID knew the Hillmans stuck out like a sore thumb.

'Do you work locally?'

'Yes. I'm a detective sergeant at Bromley.'

'Not far to travel for work, then.'

'Thankfully, no.'

He unscrewed the drop cap and asked Jane for the torch so he could examine the wires inside.

'As I suspected, the bulb's blowing because there's a loose connection in the cap, which is causing an arc to jump across the contact rather than flowing through it.'

'Is it a big job to repair it?' Jane asked, wondering how much it might cost.

'No. I just need to reconnect the live wire.' He got a small screwdriver from the toolbox and secured the wire. 'Do you have a spare bulb?'

She held up the blown bulb. 'This was the last one I had.'

'I came prepared.' He smiled, removing a spare bulb from his toolbox and fitting it in the cap. He switched the main fuse on and tested the hallway light, which lit up instantly. 'There you go . . . nice and bright now.'

'Thank you so much. Are you an electrician?'

'No. I'm a retired cab driver. But I've learned a lot about electrics and plumbing doing up my house over the years. Sorry to say this, but your fuse box and wiring is very old. I'd say it was fitted when the house was built in the mid-Thirties.'

'Is it dangerous? The last thing I want is for the house to catch fire.'

'You'd be best to get a qualified electrician to look at it. Edith, who lived here before you, was in her eighties and didn't bother to update anything after her husband died twenty years ago.'

Jane nodded. 'The estate agent did mention an elderly lady lived here for nearly forty years.' Jane knew the house had been offered at a well-below-market price due to its antiquated state. It would have been sensible to get a full survey done, but she couldn't afford it.

'Poor Edith got dementia before she died.'

'In a care home?' Jane asked.

'No, she had a heart attack in the living room. I had a key for the place and used to check on her a couple of times a day. Walked in to find her slumped in the armchair and cold as ice. Mind you, she made it to eighty-two, so it wasn't a bad innings.'

'Funnily enough, the estate agent never mentioned that,' Jane said, unhappy at the thought that someone had died in the house.

'I bet you see a lot of dead bodies as a detective,' he said cheerily.

'Quite a few. It's all part of the job.'

'Rather you than me, dear. Right, I'd best be off and let you get some shut-eye. You must pop round for a drink and meet Vi,' he said, before picking up the ladder and toolbox.

Jane opened the front door. 'That would be nice, thank you.'

'Any time you like . . . our door is always open.'

'Goodnight, Gerry.' As she closed the door, she wondered if she should have offered him some money for fixing the light, but thought he'd probably have refused. She decided to buy Gerry a nice bottle of wine and drop it off the following day.

She looked at her watch and sighed. It was nearly nine and she still hadn't started her report.

Having washed and changed into her pyjamas, Jane went to the kitchen and poured herself a glass of wine. 'God, this kitchen is old and tatty,' she said to herself, looking at the dripping sink tap and skew-whiff cabinet doors. She needed something to cheer herself up and got one of Father Chris's *kwarezimal* biscuits from the tin. Taking a bite, it reminded her how delicious the meal he cooked had been. It had certainly changed her mind about soup being a

boring starter. She'd love to be more adventurous in her own cooking and couldn't remember the last time she'd entertained someone at home, other than her parents. She'd only cooked meals for
herself in her new home and wondered if she should invite someone over for a meal.

Jane set down her glass of wine and got her typewriter out of
the cupboard, then sat down at the living-room table, opened her
notebook, and started typing her report. Although she was a fast
typist, Jane took her time, making sure her report was well written
and contained all the relevant facts to assist DCS Barnes in making
his decision about the next step in the investigation.

It was nearly two in the morning before she finished, feeling
exhausted. She put the report in a folder and went straight to bed.
Setting the alarm for six, she regretted not letting Boon deal with
the arrest of Barry the builder, as it would have allowed her a couple more hours in bed before the meeting with Barnes. It wasn't
long before she was in a deep sleep.

*   *   *

When the alarm sounded, Jane felt nauseous and struggled to get
out of bed. After a tepid shower, she put on a smart two-piece grey
suit, a dark blue blouse with a bow at the neck and grey court shoes.
Pushed for time, Jane had a quick breakfast of tea and toast then
grabbed her briefcase, hurried out of the door and drove to the old
convent building site.

Boon was already waiting in an unmarked car with two plainclothes crime squad officers when Jane arrived. He got out of the
Hillman Hunter and went to speak with her.

'Morning, sarge. You are looking very smart this morning. Anyone would think you've got an important meeting,' he grinned.

'I didn't finish my report until two, so I'm not in the mood for
any jokes. How many radios have you got?'

'One in the car and a portable as well.'

'Tell the two lads with you to park up the road out of sight. Bring one of the radios and jump in with me.'

'I thought you wanted backup?'

'I do, but the Hillman sticks out as a police car. If Barry sees it, he might turn round and drive off. I can park my car round the back of the workmen's hut, then if Barry tries to leg it we can radio the others to block him off.'

'But he might not even turn up for work.'

'I know, but we need to speak to the site manager first to find out whether he has or not.'

'OK, I'll be back in a second.' He rushed back to the Hillman to speak to his colleagues and quickly returned. Once in Jane's car, he made a call on the radio.

'Papa Romeo from DC Boon ... this is a test call ... are you receiving ... over.'

'Yes, signal loud and clear ... control over.'

'Received.' He turned to Jane: 'The late-shift detective left a note for you in the office message book. Dr Pullen rang yesterday evening and asked you to call her this morning.'

'Did she leave a number?'

'Yes, I jotted it down for you.' Boon started to rummage in his trouser and jacket pockets. 'I could have sworn I ...'

Jane shook her head, 'You've lost it, haven't you?'

'I'm sure it's here somewhere ...'

'Don't bother. I'll call the office later for it.'

Approaching the site, Jane noticed the lights were on in the Portakabin and the white Transit van was outside.

'Looks like the foreman might be here already,' Boon remarked, as Jane parked next to the Transit.

'It could be Dermot,' Jane suggested.

'Nah, he drove off in an Astra yesterday,' Boon told her. 'Isn't that the man who lives in the old chapel?'

Jane looked towards the garden wall that led to the site. 'Where, I can't see him?'

Boon pointed. 'Over there . . . he just came out of the builders' hut with his dog.'

Jane saw he looked angry about something. But his expression instantly turned to a smile when he saw them getting out of the car.

'Good morning, officers. How are you both today?'

'Good morning. Everything all right? Jane asked.

'I was just asking the site foreman what was happening about the coffin, as some of the residents are a bit concerned. He wasn't very helpful. Are you able to tell me what's going on?'

'It's still under investigation,' Jane told him.

'I see,' he said with a frown. He turned and walked off towards the walled gardens.

Boon was about to knock on the Portakabin door but, to his surprise Jane just opened it and walked straight in. She saw Lee sitting at a desk, with his elbows on it, rubbing his forehead with his fingers.

'Morning, Mr Holland,' Jane said.

Startled, he jumped up from his chair. 'Christ, I nearly had a heart attack!'

'Sorry, I should have knocked first.'

'What can I do for you?'

'We're here for a couple of reasons. The first is to let you know we found the body of a nun in the coffin.'

'Does that mean the whole site will have to shut down?' he sighed.

'I've yet to speak with someone senior in the Church to determine if the ground is consecrated or was ever used as a graveyard, but—'

'So you are shutting us down?'

'No, just suspending any digging work for now.'

He frowned. 'But nothing else can be done until all the foundations are dug out.'

Jane could see he was distraught. 'I'm sorry, but I'm just conveying what my senior officers told me. I'm sure things will be back to normal soon.'

'Have you told Nick Durham about the nun?' Lee asked.

'Unfortunately, I didn't get a chance to speak to him yesterday. Did you?'

'Yeah. I spoke to him on the phone. I told him the coffin had been taken to the mortuary, gave him your details and said you'd be in touch. Naturally, he wasn't happy about the situation.'

'That's understandable, but we have a job to do. I will speak to him personally, hopefully later today.'

'What's the other reason you're here?'

'We need to speak to Barry. Is he coming to work this morning?'

'I don't know. Dermot was going to tell him to be here for half seven as we've got a brick delivery coming in at eight.'

'Do you have a home address for him? Just in case he doesn't turn up. And what's his surname?'

'His surname is May.' Lee went to a filing cabinet, removed a file with Barry's details and handed it to Jane. She jotted down his address in her notebook and showed it to Boon.

'Do you know where it is?'

'Yes. Crundale Tower is on the Ramsden Estate in St Mary Cray. It's mostly council flats and maisonettes. What's Barry done?' Lee asked.

'Did he say anything to you yesterday about wanting to open the coffin?' Jane asked.

'Not at first. Dermot told me about the coffin, and I went out to look at it. Barry was worried about the site being shut down. He said if the coffin was empty there'd be nothing to worry about and we could just get rid of it. I specifically told him not to touch it.'

Jane looked out the window and realised the original position of the coffin couldn't be seen from the Portakabin. 'Was Barry with you from the time you called us to the time we got here?'

'No. I went to call Nick Durham. Barry was sulking in the hut when I got back. He opened the bloody coffin, didn't he?'

'It appears that someone did,' Boon said.

'Well, I can assure you it wasn't me or Dermot,' Lee replied. 'Is it even a crime to open a coffin?'

'No, but it is to steal something from it,' Jane told him. 'We believe a silver cross may have been taken from the body.'

Lee was visibly shocked. 'I know Barry can be an idiot at times but stealing from a dead nun is beyond belief. If it's true, he's never working here again . . . or any other site if I can help it.'

Boon heard the sound of a vehicle approaching and looked out of the window. 'This looks like Dermot.'

Jane took him to one side. 'Go and have a word, just to make sure his recollection of events is the same as Lee's.' She turned to Lee. 'Is it all right if we wait here for a bit and see if Barry turns up?'

'Sure, would you like a tea or coffee?'

'A coffee, please. Just as a matter of interest, who was the elderly man who was with you earlier?'

'He doesn't work here, but he lives in one of the old convent flats.'

'I know. But having spoken with him again this morning, I realised I don't know his name.'

'To be honest, I don't either. I think he's one of those nosey types who likes to know what's going on.'

'He seemed a bit angry when I saw him earlier,' Jane said.

'Probably because I told him to mind his own business when he walked in here asking about the coffin.'

'Yes. Unfortunately, my colleague let slip why we were here yesterday.'

'Milk, no sugar, wasn't it?' Lee asked.

'Yes. Does Barry have access to a crowbar?'

'The workmen have their own toolkits. He keeps his in his van.'

* * *

Boon was satisfied that Dermot's account of events corroborated Lee's version, and was about to go back to the Portakabin when they heard the sound of a vehicle. Boon turned to see a red minivan driving towards them.

'Here comes the thieving bastard now,' Dermot said.

The van suddenly stopped, then started to reverse back down the driveway.

'Are you not going to chase after him?' Dermot asked, surprised at Boon's calmness.

Boon removed the radio from his pocket. 'Papa Romeo five receiving, over.'

'Yeah, go ahead,' his colleague in the Hillman Hunter replied.

'Block the red minivan that's attempting to leave the building site.'

'Received, Boony, we already got eyeballs on him.'

Boon ran to the Portakabin to tell Jane.

Barry saw the Hillman approaching in his rear-view mirror and hit the brakes hard, stalling the engine. Pulling up behind him, the two crime squad officers jumped out of the police car. Barry locked the door and tried to start the engine. One of the officers tapped the driver's side window with his truncheon.

'Get out of the car or I'll break the bloody window!'

'All right, all right!' Barry shouted.

He flung the door open, hitting one of the officers and knocking him off balance. The other officer dragged Barry out of the car, forced him face down on the muddy ground and handcuffed him. Both officers then lifted him up by his arms and escorted him up the dirt path to where Jane and Boon were waiting.

'Barry May, I'm DC Boon. I'm arresting you on suspicion of theft. You do not have to say anything unless you wish to do so, but what you say may be given in evidence.'

'I want to make a complaint about these two assaulting me!' Barry growled.

'You were resisting arrest and they restrained you,' Jane said calmly.

'Did you open the coffin and take a cross from the nun's body?' Boon asked.

'What! No way. Dermot said he wanted to open the coffin, so you best fuck off and ask him.'

'You really are a piece of shit,' Boon said, shaking his head. He put Barry in the back of the Hillman and then got in next to him.

'Where you taking me?' Barry asked.

'To search your premises.'

Barry grunted. 'Where's your fucking warrant, then?'

'We don't need one as we've arrested you on reasonable suspicion of theft,' Boon told him.

Jane found a toolbox in the back of the minivan and removed a small crowbar. She knew Lloyd could do some tests to see if it matched the indentations on the coffin. She then followed the Hillman to Crundale Tower in her car.

'Is your wife or any other family at home?' Boon asked Barry.

'My wife will have gone to work by now.'

'Any kids?'

'Yeah, two girls. Katie drops them off at her mother's and she takes them to school.'

'My colleagues and I are going to search your premises from top to bottom.'

'How many times do I have to tell you, I didn't open that coffin or steal any bleeding cross, so you won't find nothing.'

Boon shrugged. 'Have it your way.'

Arriving at Crundale Tower, Boon got out and went over to speak to Jane.

'I think he might have got rid of the cross . . . maybe pawned it or sold it to someone. If we don't find it, we'll have to release him.'

'We might find a pawn ticket – or even the missing knife,' Jane said hopefully.

'I haven't mentioned the knife to Barry. I thought if we find a crucifix, he might roll over and tell us what else he took from the coffin. The search could take an hour or two; me and the crime squad lads can do it if you want to head off to your meeting.'

She looked at her watch, it was a quarter past eight. 'I've still got a plenty of time. I'll stay for an hour then drive to Orpington.'

Boon used Barry's key to gain entry to the flat. Jane told the crime squad officers to search the bedrooms and made Barry sit in an armchair in the living room.

Jane looked around the room. 'We'll start in here, then do the kitchen. Make sure you look inside the cushions, as well as down the sides of the—'

'I know how to do a proper search, sarge,' Boon interrupted.

The high-pitched sound of a woman's screams suddenly filled the flat.

'Stay with Barry,' Jane told Boon and hurried to the main bedroom.

A buxom, dark-haired woman in her late twenties was sitting up in bed tightly clutching a white bed sheet under her chin. She looked terrified, her eyes wide open and her body shaking.

'Please don't hurt me?' she pleaded, close to tears.

'It's all right, love, no one's going to hurt you ... we're police officers not burglars,' the crime squad officer informed her, holding up his warrant card. 'Are you Barry May's missus?'

She still looked worried. 'Yes, has something happened to him?'

Jane stepped between the officers and the woman. 'There's no need to be alarmed, Mrs May. Your husband is fine and here with us.' Jane waved to Boon to bring Barry to the bedroom.

'What's going on, Barry?' his wife asked, seeing the handcuffs.

'These idiots think I nicked some jewellery and want to search the house for it. I've told them they're wasting their time,' he said.

'No work today?' Jane asked Mrs May.

'I swapped shifts with a friend.'

'Are the children in their bedroom?'

'No, they're with my mother. I dropped them off earlier and came back to bed for a bit of peace and quiet.'

'I'd like you to get dressed, please, then we can search your bedroom,' Jane told her.

'What, with them in here?' she asked, nodding towards the male officers. 'I ain't got no clothes on.'

Jane told her colleagues to go to the living room with Barry and start the search. She then closed the door.

'Sorry, Mrs May, but I need you to stay in here while I search your bedroom . . . it's normal procedure.'

'This is ridiculous,' she sighed. 'Can you hand me the dressing gown on the back of the door.'

Jane lifted it off the hook and threw it on the bed. Katie didn't move.

'Do you mind turning around while I put it on?'

Jane sighed as she turned. 'Please, Mrs May, just get a move on so I can search the room.'

'You can turn around now,' she said a few moments later.

Jane noticed Mrs May was holding the dressing-gown collar tightly around her neck.

'Do you have a jewellery box?' Jane asked. She noticed Mrs May's hand tremble slightly as she pointed to the dressing table.

'It's in the top right drawer.'

Jane removed the jewellery box and looked inside. There were some cheap rings, bangles, and a chain with a K pendant. Jane held it up. 'Is this yours?'

'Yes. K for Katie.'

'And this is all your jewellery?'

She nodded and pulled the dressing-gown collar up.

'Are you wearing a necklace of any sort just now.'

'No,' she replied nervously.

'I'd like you open your dressing-gown collar, please,' Jane said.

'Do I have to?' Katie started to cry.

'I understand you're trying to protect your husband . . . but please don't put me in a position where I have to arrest you on suspicion of handling stolen goods and forcibly search you.'

Katie let out a sob. 'I swear I didn't know it was stolen. He said he found it on the building site.' She removed the chain from her neck and handed it to Jane.

Hanging from it was a silver cross measuring about two and a half by one and a half inches with a Sacred Heart engraved on it, along with a small cross and circle of thorns.

Jane removed a small exhibits bag from her pocket and placed the cross and chain in it. 'Thank you for being honest with me,' she said.

'Please don't tell Barry what I told you,' Katie said, looking desperate.

Jane sensed fear in her voice and now the dressing gown was loose below the neck, she noticed two large bruises above Katie's left breast. 'Did Barry do that to you?' she asked, pointing to them.

Katie closed the dressing gown. 'It was an accident . . . he didn't mean to.'

Jane wasn't convinced. 'Have you got any other bruises?'

'No,' she replied nervously.

'Can you show me your arms, please.'

Katie started shaking as she pulled the dressing gown tighter around her body.

'I'm on your side, Katie. I can help you . . . but I need to know if you have any other injuries.'

Tears began to trickle down Katie's face as she slowly opened the dressing gown, let it fall open and stood with her hands covering her crotch.

Jane gasped as she saw the extent of bruising on Katie's arms, legs and stomach. They were clearly the result of punches, grab marks and kicks to her legs, deliberately inflicted in areas where

Barry thought other people wouldn't see them. Katie pulled the dressing gown around her.

'This is wrong, Katie, so wrong. You can't let him treat you like a punch bag. If you make a formal allegation of assault against him, he will be charged. I'll ask the court for him to be remanded in custody pending trial . . .'

'I can't . . . it would only make things worse.'

'What about the children? Has he ever hurt them?'

'He'd never do that. Barry's loves his children.'

'Believe me, as they get older, he will treat them in the same way. You also need to know we believe he forced a coffin open and stole the cross and chain from the body of a dead nun.'

Katie looked horrified and her legs started to buckle. Jane managed to grab her and sit her on the bed before she fell over. The tears rolled down her cheeks.

'How could he do that then give it to me?'

'I don't know. I'll tell him I saw the cross when you got out of bed; that way, he won't know about our conversation and take it out on you.'

'Thank you . . . but he'll still be angry with me.'

'Have you thought about leaving him?'

Katie choked back a sob. 'Is there anywhere you can go?'

'My parents live down the road,' she managed to say. 'I'm sure they'll take us in until I can find somewhere else.'

'Will you be safe there?'

'I don't know for sure, but it's the only place I have to go.'

'Barry will be taken to the station for interview. It will give you time to pack some belongings for yourself and the children.'

'How long can you hold him?' Katie asked, pulling a small suitcase out from under the bed.

'Depends on whether or not he admits to stealing the cross, but at least eight to twelve hours. That should give you plenty of time to get out of here. If you want to press charges about the assaults . . .'

'Let me think about it.'

Jane didn't want to force her. She got a pen from her pocket and picked up a piece of scrap paper from the dressing table. 'I'll give you my details. Ring me and let me know you're OK. If you change your mind and want to press charges, I will personally arrest him and deal with the case.'

'Thank you.'

'You know where I am if you need me. There's one other thing. Did Barry say if he found anything else yesterday?' Jane asked, thinking about the missing knife.

'No. He only mentioned the cross.'

Barry was sitting back in the armchair yawning as he watched Boon and the crime squad officers search the living room.

'We haven't found anything, sarge,' Boon said as Jane walked in.

'I said you wankers were wasting your time,' Barry sneered.

Jane removed the cross from her pocket and briefly held it out for Barry to see.

'As luck would have it, I just found this around your wife's neck.' She put it back in her pocket.

Barry shrugged. 'So what, lots of women wear a cross . . . not just nuns.'

'I asked her where she got it. The strange thing is, she didn't want to tell me. Did you give it to her?'

'It ain't a crime to give your missus a present.'

'I'll take that as a yes,' Jane said.

'Take it how you like, love.'

'You opened the nun's coffin yesterday and stole the cross, didn't you?' Boon said.

'I already told you, Dermot wanted to open the coffin. You should nick him and search his fucking gaff. I wanna speak to my missus!' Barry demanded, getting up from the armchair.

Jane pushed him hard in the chest so he fell back into the armchair, then pointed a finger at him. 'The only place you are going is to the station for interview. Take him down to the car,' she told the crime squad officers.

She waited until they were alone in the flat, then told Boon about Katie and her bruises.

'He's a real low life.'

'Barry mustn't know what his wife told me. Do everything slowly with him so she has plenty of time to pack some bags and get out.' She took the exhibits bag with the cross in it from her pocket. 'Take this to the SOCO. Get him to photograph it and print some enlargements for me.' Boon held it up and looked at it, and was about to put it in his pocket when Jane stopped him.

'Hang on a sec . . . there's something on the back of the cross.' Boon handed it to her. 'Stupidly, I didn't think to look on the other side when his wife handed it to me.'

She looked closely. Engraved on the back was 20.02.58 and the initials MB.

'Those numbers must relate to a significant date. It could be when she became a nun. This is an important find, Boony. It could help to identify the body and narrow the time frame of the murder.' She was looking forward to showing it to Father Chris and asking his opinion on the significance of the engraving.

CHAPTER NINE

Jane arrived at Orpington police station at a quarter past nine, with time to spare before her meeting with DCS Barnes, so she decided to have a poached egg on toast with a cup of tea in the canteen. After ordering her food, she sat at an empty table and opened her briefcase to have a quick read through her report. Her heart immediately sank. 'No, no, no,' she said to herself on finding the file was not in the case. She instantly knew that in her rush to get to the old convent, she'd left the report on the dining-room table.

'Excuse me,' she said to the uniformed officer on the table next to her. 'How long does it take to get to Chislehurst High Street from here?' Her house was a two-minute drive from there.

'About fifteen, twenty minutes tops.'

'What's the quickest way?'

The officer gave her the most direct route which, to her relief, was pretty straightforward.

'Thanks,' she replied, hurrying to the canteen door.

'You forgot your briefcase, love,' the uniformed officer shouted.

'Shit,' she muttered, then turned, grabbed the case and ran as fast as she could to her car.

Thankfully, the traffic wasn't heavy, and she made it home in seventeen minutes. She dashed inside and grabbed her report.

'Good morning, Jane, you off to work?' Gerry was walking his dog.

'Yes,' she replied, opening the car door, and throwing the report on the passenger seat.

'Everything OK with the light socket?'

'It's working fine now, thanks.'

'Any problems, you know where I am.'

'Sorry, Gerry, but I have to go as I'm running late for an important meeting.'

'You got far to go?'

'Orpington,' she replied, wishing he'd stop asking questions.

'You know what they say . . . more haste, less speed.'

Jane looked at her watch, it was a quarter to ten. Angry with herself, and knowing she'd be late for the meeting, she banged her hand on the steering wheel. She didn't drive fast and the return journey took her twenty minutes. She parked her car, ran to the station and up the stairs to DCS Barnes's office.

Jane knocked on Barnes's door whilst dabbing the sweat from her forehead with a tissue. She knew her hair must be a mess from all the running around, but there was no time to do anything about it.

'Come in,' Barnes said in a gruff voice. 'I take it you must be DS Tennison.' He looked over the top of his half-moon glasses as he put a folder in a filing-cabinet drawer, then used his foot to close it.

Barnes was a short, thin man in his early fifties, with combed-back grey hair. He looked quite dapper, dressed in a brown two-piece suit, light blue shirt, navy blue tie and brown shoes.

'I'm really sorry I'm late, sir, but I was—'

He held his hand up to stop. 'In my book, if I give up my time, you should be respectful by arriving on time.'

'Sorry, sir. I was on an early morning search which took longer than expected. I got here as fast as I could,' Jane said, feeling foolish.

'That's obvious from the state of you.'

Jane dabbed her forehead again and Barnes told her to take a seat. She was surprised at how soft, yet strong his voice was.

'Was the search connected to the nun's murder?'

'Yes, sir. We suspected one of the builders had forced the coffin open and stolen a silver cross. He's denying it, but we found the cross at his flat.'

'Good. I like positive results.'

'I also told the site manger to stop all digging work while I made further inquiries regarding the body.'

'Is he aware the nun was murdered?'

'No, and neither is Barry May, the builder who stole the cross.'

'Good, those sorts of people have big mouths, so keep it that way for now. Have you done a report for me?'

She handed him the folder.

'I think I'll have a coffee while I read it.'

Jane stood up, intending to go to the canteen. 'I'll get it. Milk and sugar?'

He pulled a sour face. 'I never drink the dishwater they serve in the canteen.' He pointed to a cabinet in the corner of the room, on which was an electric kettle, a cafetière and a china teapot.

'The ground coffee is in the cabinet. If you want tea there's lapsang souchong. I don't take milk or sugar. If you want anything different, the canteen is on the next floor.'

Jane flicked the kettle on and put some coffee in the cafetière. She watched Barnes out of the corner of her eye as he slowly read the report, occasionally turning back a page to check something. She decided to have a tea and put some tea leaves in the pot.

She put the coffee on his desk, and he nodded a thank you. She took a sip of the tea, which was surprisingly refreshing after all the running around she'd been doing. A few minutes later, Barnes put the report down on the desk and removed his glasses. He opened his desk drawer and removed a packet of Sobranie Black Russian cigarettes and a gold Dupont lighter. Opening the pack, he offered one to Jane, who politely declined. He removed one of the long black cigarettes by its gold filter, which was decorated with a double-headed eagle, lit it and inhaled deeply before slowly blowing out the smoke. He folded his reading glasses and put them in the breast pocket of his jacket.

'Your report is very informative and well written, Tennison. Is there anything you'd like to add?'

She told him about the cross, detailing the engraving and possible significance of the date and initials on it.

'If the cross is the victim's, it would be reasonable to assume she was murdered sometime after February 1958,' Barnes surmised.

'That's what I was thinking,' Jane said. 'I've been told the convent was sold to the developer in 1965, so we are only looking at a possible seven-year time span.'

'I agree, but you must also consider the cross may have been put on the nun to fool anyone who found her.'

'You think the cross could belong to whoever killed her?'

He took a puff of the cigarette. 'It's not beyond the realm of possibility someone religious, such as a priest, killed her. Once you eliminate the impossible, whatever remains, no matter how improbable, must be the truth.'

Jane knew the quote was from Sherlock Holmes, and wondered if Barnes was trying to impress her.

'I was told the diocese keep records of all the nuns in their district, so it shouldn't be difficult to identify individuals with the initials MR,' Jane said.

'Who gave you the information about the diocesan records?' he asked.

'Father Christopher Floridia. He's the priest at St Mary's, which is just down the road from the old convent.'

'I didn't see his name mentioned in your report.'

Jane hesitated. 'I didn't think it relevant to the investigation, though he was very helpful and informative regarding—'

Barnes folded his arms and tilted his head. 'Did you tell him the nun was murdered?'

Jane suspected that if she said yes, she'd be taken off the investigation.

'No, sir,' she said quickly. She then explained that she'd sought his advice prior to the post-mortem. 'I wanted to know what the religious rules were regarding consecrated ground and who I should inform if there was, or wasn't, a body in the coffin. He did ask me to let him know the outcome, so out of courtesy I phoned him after the PM—'

He leaned forward to interrupt. 'And what did you tell him?'

Jane took a deep breath. 'Only that we'd discovered a mummified body in the coffin dressed in a nun's habit. He offered to introduce me to the bishop and help identify her.'

Barnes straightened in his chair. 'At present I don't want Father Floridia, the bishop, or anyone connected to the Church knowing this is a murder investigation.'

Jane was taken aback. 'Surely, sir, the priority is identifying our victim and ascertaining if she was a nun at the old convent. Father Floridia's assistance would be very useful.'

'I don't trust priests or the hierarchy of the Catholic Church to be truthful when dealing with something that reflects badly on them. They'll make empty promises to keep you at bay,' he said bluntly.

'Will it not reflect badly on us if we don't tell them?' she countered.

'I've made my decision, and I expect you to obey it,' he said, stubbing out his cigarette.

'Yes, sir,' Jane replied. She wanted to ask why Barnes didn't trust the Church, but thought it best not to. 'Does that mean you want me to continue with the investigation?'

'Yes, for now.'

'Thank you, sir. Will the murder squad be based at Bromley or here?'

'I'm not forming a full murder squad just yet. I want everything played low-key for now and no press involvement. If whoever killed her is still alive, the last thing we want to do is give them a heads-up and the opportunity to disappear. Do your best to identify the nun over the next three days, then I'll review my decision on Monday.'

Jane was confused. 'How do I do that without speaking to anyone connected to the Church?'

'I never said you couldn't talk to them. You've already got one foot in the door with this Father Floridia. Tell him the post-mortem is still ongoing.'

'I don't think I'd feel right lying to him.'

'You don't have to lie. Your report said further expert opinion is needed to determine the nun's age and how long she's been dead. That's quite true, and it's also true we need to identify her as soon as possible. I'd call it a means to an end. However, if you're not happy about it, I can always find someone who is . . .' He paused to let her answer.

'I take your point, sir. Of course, I'll do as you ask. DC Boon's also been assisting me . . .'

Barnes frowned. 'DI Stanley said he's not very experienced.'

'But he's keen and eager to learn,' Jane said. 'He's liaising with the Missing Persons Bureau and was with me at the building site and post-mortem, so he's up to speed with the investigation.'

'All right, but if he screws up it's on you.'

'What about the building site? Can they start work again?' she asked.

'Not yet. To be honest I'm not that concerned about whether or not the land is consecrated. The priority is identifying the nun and finding out who murdered her. That said, it can be used to our advantage as a cover to get information out of the diocese and identify the nun. Once you've done that, I'll review the situation regarding the building site.'

'Should I report back to you directly?'

'I'm in meetings at Scotland Yard for the rest of the day and away at a family wedding over the weekend. DI Stanley will super-vise you in my absence. Are you rostered to work this weekend?'

'No, sir, but I'm more than happy to do so without overtime, and re-roster my rest days.'

He nodded. 'You can claim overtime if your inquiries justify it. Same goes for DC Boon if you need him. We can have another meeting in DI Stanley's office on Monday morning at ten. Is there anything else for now?'

'I was wondering if it would be worth getting an anthropologist to do a facial reconstruction. It's a fairly new thing which involves—'

'I'm fully aware of what it is, Tennison. Circulating a facial reconstruction this early in the investigation could lead to a lot of erroneous identifications and cause more problems than it's worth. I'm happy for a forensic odontologist to examine the victim's teeth to give an estimate of her age at death. If you do identify the victim and recover any dental records, the odontologist can then compare the two; that way, you'll have a confirmed ID.'

Jane already knew, from a previous investigation, what a forensic odontologist could do and thought she'd raised it in her report. 'Thank you for letting me continue the investigation. I won't let you down,' she said.

'That remains to be seen. From what I've heard, you had quite a chequered history during your eight years' service in the Met. My advice to you is, be a team player and don't go behind people's backs. It only causes friction and distrust.'

Jane thought he was criticising her part in the downfall of DCI Bill Murphy. 'DCI Murphy was a corrupt officer, and a jury found him guilty,' she said. 'If I had to do the same again, I would.'

'And I commend you for that. I knew Murphy when he was a DS. Like you, I served with him on the Flying Squad. Back then he was an honest, devoted detective who quickly rose to the rank of DCI. Unfortunately, he got himself in financial difficulties and was going through a divorce when he started taking bribes. Then, as you know, he progressed to organising armed robberies.'

'It's no excuse for what he did. His actions endangered the lives of other officers. It's lucky no one got killed.'

'I agree with you.'

'I wish more people on the force did,' Jane said.

'That's your problem, Tennison. You think the world is against you. Because of that you sometimes fly solo, which in turn annoys your colleagues and turns them against you. Contrary to what you may think, I've heard many a good word said about you. If you want to make inspector, you need to learn how to communicate better with both your superiors and subordinates. Teamwork is based on trust and respect.'

She nodded, knowing he was giving her sound advice.

He looked at his watch. 'I've got to head off to the Yard in a minute. Photocopy your report and leave the original on my desk. And remember, tread carefully with Father Floridia and anyone else you speak to at the diocesan offices. Don't take their word as gospel,' he smiled.

She couldn't help asking before she left his office: 'I don't wish to appear nosy, sir, but have you had a bad experience with the Catholic Church. I mean, in an official way?'

Barnes nodded, removed another cigarette from the pack and lit it. 'It was over twenty years ago now. I was a young DS in North London, investigating a case where a twelve-year-old boy called Stephen Phillips had gone missing from a children's orphanage run by a priest and nuns. I instigated a search of the nearby woods and found him hanging from a tree.' He took in a deep breath and let out a sigh. He rubbed his chin and shook his head as he recalled the memory. 'The poor boy had taken his own life.'

'That must have been a shocking thing to witness,' she said.

His voice trembled. 'Cutting Stephen down from the tree and holding his limp body in my arms still haunts me to this day. I didn't even know him . . . yet it was if I'd lost my own son.' He took a steadying breath before continuing.

'At first, I couldn't for the life of me understand why a mere child would want to commit suicide. It was during the post-mortem I discovered the answer. When we removed his clothing, there were black and blue welt marks over his lower back and buttocks. He'd been beaten so badly you could see the outline of the belt and buckle on his skin. The pathologist said some of the marks were old and some recent. I knew right away whoever was responsible for inflicting Stephen's injuries had to work at the convent.'

Jane felt sickened by the idea. 'Was it the priest or one of the nuns?'

'At first, I suspected it was just the priest in charge of the orphanage, but I later found out some of the nuns also beat the children. He was a pompous, self-righteous man who believed it was "God's will" that children who were unruly should be punished and the use of a belt was appropriate. He described Stephen as a "problem child" who needed to learn right from wrong,' Barnes said, his sadness turning to anger.

'What did the priest say when you told him Stephen had committed suicide?'

'He considered it to be a mortal sin. His exact words were, "We must say what we know is the truth – taking your own life is a sin against God who made us." The church even refused to hold a funeral mass for Stephen because he'd committed suicide.'

'I never realised the Catholic Church could be so strict.'

'Neither did I. The sad thing is, it took a child's suicide to open my eyes. An orphanage should be a safe place where children are loved by adults they can trust, not a place that fills them with fear of physical abuse.'

'Were they sexually abused as well?'

'I don't know for certain. But I believe the priest got a sadistic pleasure out of humiliating and inflicting bodily harm on the children under his care, some of whom were only six years old. It beggars belief that anyone of any faith could mistreat innocent children the way they did.'

Jane could see the sadness in Barnes's eyes, but thought it strange he never said the priest's name.

'What was the outcome?'

'The archbishop got involved. He informed my DCI the diocese would carry out a thorough investigation and I was told to await the outcome. A week passed and I'd heard nothing, so I went to the orphanage and said I wanted to interview some of the older children and have them examined by a police doctor. The priest refused to let me in the door.'

'On what grounds?'

'That the archbishop was still conducting his investigation and I would cause the children undue stress and disrupt their daily routine. The next thing I knew the divisional commander wanted to see me in his office. The archbishop had complained that my behaviour was overbearing and accused me of persecuting one of his priests. I was told to mark the case file up as a suicide by a mentally unstable child.'

Jane was staggered. 'That's awful. How could a commander condone serious assaults against young children?'

'The archbishop used the law to his advantage. Corporal punishment in schools and orphanages is justified by the common-law doctrine known as *in loco parentis*, whereby teachers are granted the same rights as parents to discipline and punish children in their care if they do not adhere to the rules.'

'But what about the welt marks from the belt on Stephen's buttocks? Surely that was physical evidence the priest had gone too far.'

'The archbishop said the priest and nuns had had justifiable grounds to chastise Stephen on a number of occasions as he was so unruly. The Met solicitors said without Stephen as a witness it was impossible to say who was actually responsible for inflicting the injuries, and therefore there wasn't enough evidence to charge anyone. The archbishop said the priest had been given some advice on his future behaviour and moved to another post.'

'Where did they send him?'

'I don't know. They wouldn't tell me. As far as I'm concerned the whole thing was a big cover-up by the Catholic Church to protect its reputation.'

'Did Stephen have any family?

'No, both his parents had died in a car crash when he was six. One minute he was alone in the world and the next he was in a living hell.'

'Where was he buried?'

'The coroner helped me arrange an Anglican burial for him. No one from the Catholic Church even bothered to attend. It was a really sad day, but the whole of the CID office attended, and uniform formed a white-gloved guard of honour outside the church. I visit his grave a few times a year and lay some fresh flowers in his memory.'

Jane was deeply moved by Barnes's shocking revelations. It was clear he would never forget Stephen Phillips, and was still deeply frustrated and angry at not being able to charge and convict the priest for the assaults he'd no doubt inflicted on numerous children. His distrust of the Catholic Church now made perfect sense. But she also worried that in the current investigation, it might cloud his judgement of decent, caring priests like Father Chris.

CHAPTER TEN

As she drove back to the station, Jane felt relieved her meeting with DCS Barnes had gone so well. He certainly hadn't come across as the kind of authoritarian stickler for the rules Stanley had described.

But although she was pleased that Barnes wanted her to continue the investigation, Jane was also worried she might come to regret not being honest about telling Father Chris the nun had been murdered. It had also put her in an awkward position with Father Chris, as he understandably didn't feel comfortable lying about a nun's death to Bishop Meade. She just hoped Barnes would quickly form a full murder squad once the dead nun had been identified, and this would allow her to tell the bishop the cause of death.

After parking her car in the station yard, Jane walked the short distance to the office of Thomas Durham and Son in Widmore Road. She pressed the intercom and explained she was the detective dealing with the unearthed coffin on the building site and had come to speak with Nick Durham.

'Hang on second, please . . . I'll see if Mr Durham is available,' said a female voice.

Jane was surprised and a bit annoyed not to be simply buzzed in. It was nearly a minute before she got a reply.

'Sorry for the delay, Ms Tennison. Please come in. Our offices are on the first floor.'

Entering the office Jane couldn't help but notice how modern and bright it was, compared to the drab, green-painted walls and worn brown carpet of the CID office. On one wall were numerous pictures of houses and flats, which presumably had been designed and built by the Durhams. On the opposite wall were two large-scale drawings of different modern-style houses, next to which was a separate glassed-in office, with a kidney-shaped glass desk and two small sofas. Jane could see the back of a tall man with collar-length blond hair. He was smartly dressed in a light blue suit and holding a phone to his ear whilst looking at a large building plan on the wall.

An attractive blonde-haired woman in her mid-twenties looked up from her typing as Jane walked in.

'Welcome to Thomas Durham and Son, Ms Tennison. I'm Judy, the office secretary. Mr Durham is on the phone. He'll be with you as soon as he's finished. Would you like a coffee or cup of tea?'

'A black coffee, no sugar, would be lovely thanks,' Jane replied, hoping it would perk her up after her lack of sleep.

'Please take a seat.' Judy pointed to a two-seater sofa. There was a small coffee table next to it with a pile of glossy house brochures.

Judy returned with Jane's coffee in a bone china cup. 'I'm sorry to keep you waiting. Mr Durham is on a very important business call.'

Jane wondered if it was about the coffin and the shutting down of his building site. She picked up a brochure for a five-bedroom house and flicked through it. Looking at the interior photographs, she was amazed how contemporary and bright the rooms were, especially the fitted kitchen with its modern appliances. It made her realise how old and rundown her house was. It struck her that Nick Durham might be able to recommend a good electrician to look at her fuse box and wiring. Her thoughts were interrupted when she heard a man's voice call out.

'Detective Tennison. I'm so sorry to keep you waiting. Please come through to my office.'

Jane looked up and instantly thought the man, in his mid-thirties, looked familiar. He was good-looking, with an engaging smile and slim physique. She picked up her coffee and followed him to his office, where he pointed to one of the sofas.

'I'm Nick Durham. Please take a seat.' He went and sat on the other sofa.

Even his voice sounded slightly familiar to Jane. 'Excuse me for asking, but have we met before?' she asked.

He put his hands up. 'Honestly, I've never been arrested in my life!'

She couldn't help smiling. 'Well, there's always a first time for everything.'

He raised his eyebrows. 'If a policewoman like you had arrested me, I'm sure I'd remember.'

'Clearly, I must be thinking of some other Casanova I met,' Jane said drily.

'I usually get mistaken for Robert Redford,' he said with a grin.

'Not Woody Allen?'

He laughed. 'Ouch, that hurt.'

Although Jane was enjoying their banter, she thought it best to get to the point of her visit.

'I'm sorry I didn't contact you yesterday. Things got busy at work and I didn't get a chance to call you before your office closed.'

'That's OK. Lee, my site manager, told me about the discovery of the coffin last night. He also rang this morning and said you'd found the body of a nun in it. Do you know who she was?'

'Not at present. Her body was mummified, so she probably died some years ago.'

'Lee also said you'd arrested Barry May for stealing a cross from the corpse,' he said with a frown.

'Yes, that's correct. We found a cross and chain at his flat, which we believe to have been taken from the nun's body after he forced open the coffin.'

'He'll never work for me again, that's for sure,' Nick said angrily. 'How does all this affect our building work at the convent?'

'My detective chief superintendent has said that you have to close the site for now.'

'Can we at least knock down the fire-damaged buildings?'

'He wants to know if the land is consecrated and identify the nun first, then he'll review the situation.'

'I doubt the outbuildings would be. I was told they were badly damaged by a fire while the nuns were still there. The structural damage meant we couldn't rebuild them. We were going to knock them down and make it into a parking area.'

'Like I said, the final decision is my boss's. As soon as he's made it I'll let you know.'

'Thanks. My dad's a stickler for doing things by the book. He made sure everything was in order before buying the convent and starting the renovation work.'

'I don't doubt that,' Jane said. 'But we still have to make the necessary checks. Do you know in what year your father purchased the buildings and land?'

His brow furrowed. 'I remember him showing me round. He was chuffed to bits, proudly telling me his vision of turning it into luxury flats. I'd just finished my A level exams at the time, so it must have been the summer of 1965.'

Jane wrote the date in her notebook. 'Why the long gap before the current redevelopment?'

'Financially my father needed to sell all the flats built in the first development to fund further development. Then he decided to buy land near St Mary's Church and build detached houses on it. When they were completed and sold, I persuaded him to use the money to build more flats on the convent grounds.'

Jane recalled passing some new houses on the way to the convent. 'Does your father know about the coffin?'

'Yes. I spoke with him last night. He said his solicitor liaised with the Church and Bromley planning department. They supposedly checked everything before he purchased the land and there was no indication that any bodies were buried there.'

'Unfortunately, I know nothing about religious or legal rules covering consecrated ground,' Jane admitted. 'I'm meeting the diocesan bishop this afternoon. Their archives office should have records concerning any burial sites on the land and the sale of the convent.'

'Would you like me to dig through our old company files for any paperwork relating to the original purchase?'

She nodded. 'That would be helpful.'

'Where do we stand as a building company if it is consecrated land?'

'It wouldn't be a matter for the police to investigate, unless there was any fraud involved in the original purchase,' Jane told him.

Nick looked offended. 'My father would never do anything dishonest. His reputation in the building trade is second to none.'

'I wasn't casting aspersions on your father. I was just stating how and why the police might be involved. A civil court would probably deal with any legal arguments about the purchase.'

'Sorry, I didn't mean to sound tetchy. My dad has got a dodgy heart, so I get a bit worried about him. He's supposed to be retired and enjoying life, but this coffin thing has got him all worked up. As a company we stand to lose thousands of pounds if the development is stopped, which won't do his stress levels any good.'

'I appreciate your concerns,' Jane said. 'It might be advisable to consult your solicitors as they will be able to give you far better advice than me.'

'I'll do that. It is what it is for now, I guess.'

'I'm sure the bishop will be able to tell me more about the convent land, and I'll call you later if I've any more information.'

'Thanks, I'd appreciate that.' He went to his desk and picked up a business card. 'I'll put my home number on this as well. Don't worry if it's late. I doubt I'll manage to get much sleep with this hanging over us.' He handed Jane the card.

She couldn't help noticing he wasn't wearing a wedding ring. 'Is there anything else you'd like to ask me?'

'Will you need to speak to my father?'

'Considering his heart condition, I wouldn't want to cause him any further stress. For now, it's probably best I contact you if I have any further questions. That way you can decide what you want to tell him.'

'Thanks for your understanding of our situation. Is there a number I can contact you on if I need to?'

'I work at Bromley in the CID office. I don't have a business card, but the station number is in the phone directory.' Jane stood up. 'It's been a pleasure meeting you.'

'Likewise,' he replied as they shook hands.

'There is something I'd like to ask you that's not police related, though,' she said. 'I was wondering . . .'

'Yes, I would love to have dinner with you this weekend,' he said with a straight face. 'What time suits you?'

She laughed, unsure if he was just trying to be funny or was genuinely asking her out.

'Actually, I was wondering if there was an electrician you could recommend.'

'Is it a big or small job?'

'I don't really know. I recently bought a house in Chislehurst and I think the fuse box and wiring need looking at.'

'The guy who does the wiring on our new builds might be able to look at it for you. It could be a week or two before he's free, though.'

'I'm in no rush.'

'Leave it with me. I'll have a word with him and get back to you.'

Jane thanked him and walked towards the door.

'You didn't answer my question about dinner.'

Now she knew he was being serious. She smiled over her shoulder but didn't reply.

She stopped at Judy's desk. 'Thanks for the coffee. I was wondering if you have any brochures for two-to-three-bedroom houses or flats Mr Durham has built.'

'Yes, we do.' She opened one of the filing cabinet doors behind her. 'Are you thinking of buying one of his properties?'

'No. I've just bought a small house which needs some modernisation, especially the kitchen. The one I looked at in your brochure earlier was incredible, but much bigger than mine.'

Judy selected various brochures and put them in a large envelope. 'You should ask Mr Durham's advice. He designs all the interiors for our properties. He even designed our office.'

'Really? I thought he was a building developer?'

'He's actually the company architect. He does all the plan drawings for the new builds and conversions but now he runs the business, people tend to think of him as a developer.' She handed Jane the envelope.

'Thanks for these. Where did he learn about interior design?'

'Self-taught. He's very creative and has a good eye for beautiful things.'

'He certainly has,' Jane replied with a knowing grin.

Walking back to the station, Jane felt flattered that Nick Durham had found her attractive and wanted to have dinner with her. Although he was handsome and seemed charming, she wondered if he was like some of the men she'd met in her life – a chancer who only wanted to get her into bed. Whatever his intentions, she knew she'd have to speak with him again and she had to admit she was looking forward to that.

Crossing the yard, Jane stopped by her car and put the brochures on the passenger seat, before going to the CID office.

'Is Boony about?' she asked a detective who was writing a report at his desk.

'He's in the charge room with DI Stanley interviewing that low life who stole the nun's cross.'

She remembered Boon telling her Sam Pullen had tried to contact her. She looked in the message book for Sam's number, then went and sat at her desk and dialled it.

'Hi, Sam, it's Jane Tennison. Sorry I didn't get back to you earlier. I've been out of the office since yesterday.'

'That's OK. I just wanted to let you know that I spoke with the anthropologist Richard Eaves. He's agreed to examine the nun's body and do a facial reconstruction.'

'I'm sorry, Sam, but DCS Barnes said no to using him. He thinks it will cost too much and the reconstruction could lead to mistaken identifications.'

'That's a pity. Eaves said he'd do it for free.'

Jane was surprised. 'For free?'

'Yes. The university gave him a research grant this semester. He was quite excited when I told him about the mummified nun. He wants to use the case as part of his research and development in facial reconstruction.'

'That's fantastic news, Sam! I owe you a large drink.'

'I'll hold you to that. I was going to take Eaves to the mortuary this afternoon to have a look at the body. Will that be OK?'

'Yes, it's fine by me, though it will be up to DCS Barnes whether or not we use it. How long will it take to do?'

'A full clay reconstruction can take a few weeks. He'll need to take the head back to his lab and use the skull for the reconstruction.'

'Does that mean he has to take the remaining facial tissue and adipocere off?'

'Yes.'

'I'm not sure the diocese would be happy about that.'

'It doesn't matter what they think. It's a murder investigation. I've already spoken with the coroner and he's fine about Eaves working on the skull. I've also arranged for Dr Martin, the forensic odontologist, to examine the nun's teeth and take photographs for a comparison with any dental records you might find.'

Jane was a little irritated that Sam had taken it upon herself to speak to the coroner and other experts without consulting her first, but she didn't say as much as she knew Sam was trying to be helpful.

'DCS Barnes wants the nun's cause of death kept quiet until we identify her,' Jane said.

'The only people I've told are the ones I just mentioned and Prof Martin, for obvious reasons.'

'Just let them know to keep it to themselves please,' Jane said. She then told Sam about the engraved cross they'd recovered.

'Well done, Jane. Identifying MB will be a big step forward in the investigation.'

'I've got a meeting this afternoon with the diocesan bishop. Fingers crossed I'll get a result today.'

'Let me know if you do. Speak to you later.'

* * *

Stanley and Boon were waiting in the interview room for Barry to be brought in by the custody officer.

'You take the lead, Boony.'

'Are you sure, guv?'

'Yeah, you nicked him and know more about the case than I do. I'll write the interview notes.'

'Thanks, guv,' Boon replied, looking chuffed.

Entering the room, Barry let out a big sigh. 'How long is this going to take?'

'That depends on whether or not you tell us the truth. Take a seat and listen to what my colleague has to say,' Stanley said.

Boon cautioned him again. 'You do not have to say anything unless you wish to do so, but what you say may be given in evidence. Do you understand the caution, Mr May?'

'I ain't stupid, mate.'

'Are you still happy to be interviewed without a solicitor?' Boon asked.

'Yeah.'

Boon opened his notebook. 'You said at your flat you gave the cross to your wife as a present.'

'Yeah, an early Christmas present.'

'Where and when did you buy it?' Stanley asked.

'Ages ago, from a stall in Orpington market.'

'Can you describe what's engraved on it for us?' Boon asked.

Barry hesitated before answering. 'There's a love heart on it.'

'The love heart is actually a religious emblem known as the Sacred Heart of Jesus – it's common on crosses that nuns wear,' Boon told him. 'What's written on the other side of the cross?'

'I think there's some numbers and letters . . .'

Boon removed the cross, which was in a clear exhibits bag, from his pocket and placed it on the table.

'Can you read what's written on it?'

Barry looked offended. 'I ain't illiterate . . . M, B, 20, 02, 58.'

Boon put the cross back in his pocket. 'And what do you reckon the engravings mean?'

Barry shrugged. 'I don't know.'

'Would you agree it's probably someone's initials and date of birth?' Stanley asked.

'Yeah, I suppose so.'

'Your wife's initials are KM. She also told me her date of birth is the eleventh of August 1953. Why on earth would you buy her a cross engraved with someone else's initials and birthday?' Boon asked.

'I . . . didn't notice the letters and numbers when I bought it,' Barry said hesitantly.

'We seized the crowbar from your toolbox. I'll bet when forensics do some test marks with it, they'll find a perfect match to the crowbar marks on the coffin,' Boon said.

Barry bit his lip and didn't reply. Boon and Stanley could see he was agitated and trying to concoct another plausible answer. Stanley didn't give him time to think of one.

'Forcing open a coffin and stealing from the body is a serious offence, for which you could go to prison. I can't begin to imagine what the other inmates will do to a man who stole a cross from a dead nun.'

Barry looked even more worried.

Stanley continued to twist the knife. 'I imagine the other inmates will take their own divine retribution . . .'

Barry had heard enough. 'I didn't open the coffin with the intention of stealing anything!'

Boon leaned forward. 'Then tell us exactly what happened.'

'Lee had gone off to speak with Mr Durham and Dermot went to call the police. I just wanted to see if there was a body inside. If there wasn't, we could have moved the coffin and carried on working. I used my crowbar to open it and was shocked when I saw the body.'

'Did you realise it was a nun?' Boon asked.

Barry nodded. 'She was wearing nun's clothes. Also, her hands were held together on her stomach like she was praying.'

'Show me,' Boon said.

Barry interlinked his fingers, with his thumbs up. 'She was holding a little wooden cross in her hands and some of them bead things religious people have.'

'You mean a rosary,' Stanley said.

'And where was the cross you stole from her?'

'Around her neck.'

'Why did you feel the need to steal it?'

Barry sighed. 'I don't know . . . it looked nice, and I thought I could maybe sell it for a few quid. Katie was feeling a bit down, so I gave it to her instead.'

Boon suspected he gave it to his wife as a form of apology for assaulting her.

'Did your wife know it was stolen?' Boon asked, just as a matter of procedure.

'No. I told her I found it on the building site,' Barry replied.

'Did you take anything else from the coffin?' Stanley asked.

'No.'

'Are you sure? It won't make matters any worse if you did.'

'I swear . . . it was just the cross.'

Stanley read over the interview notes. Barry agreed they were correct, then signed and dated each page.

'What's going to happen to me now?' he asked.

'You'll be charged with Theft and Outraging Public Decency. If I were you, I'd plead guilty, but don't be surprised if you get a custodial sentence,' Stanley told him.

'Prison! For stealing a poxy little cross!' Barry exclaimed.

Stanley shook his head in disgust. 'I've dealt with all sorts of criminals in my career . . . but even the worst of them would never steal from a dead nun.'

*　*　*

'How'd it go?' Jane asked seeing Boon and Stanley walk into the CID office.

Boon did a thumbs-up. 'Full confession, signed and sealed. He definitely took the cross.'

'What about the missing knife?'

'He's adamant he only stole the cross. Interestingly, he remembered that the nun's hands had been placed together like she was praying, and the wooden cross and beads were in between them. I noticed the same thing when we opened the coffin. Strange thing for someone who just murdered her to do.'

'Not if the person who did it was religious as well, I suppose,' Jane remarked.

Stanley nodded. 'That's a good point.'

'The Church must keep records of the nuns and priests who worked and lived at the convent,' Boon added.

'I'm going to the diocesan head office this afternoon with Father Floridia. We're meeting the bishop,' Jane said.

'I know. Barnes phoned me earlier after your meeting,' Stanley said.

Jane turned to Boon. 'You know Barnes wants us to keep the nun's murder quiet for now, don't you?'

Boon nodded. 'The guv told me before we interviewed Barry.'

Jane told Stanley about her conversation with Sam Pullen and Richard Eaves' offer to do the facial reconstruction for free.

'We might not need it if you get a result identifying her from the initials on the cross,' he said.

Boon put the cross on Jane's desk. 'You might want to show this to Father Floridia and the bishop.'

'Anyone know where the Bromley Council offices are?' Jane asked.

'Just down the road in the Civic Centre at Stockwell Close. It's literally a two-minute walk,' Boon told her.

'I need you to go their planning department and make some inquiries. You might want to take some notes of what we need.'

Boon removed his notebook and pen from his pocket. 'Fire away.'

'Only tell them the builders uncovered a coffin, and we've yet to open it. Ask if they have copies of the original plans and layout of the old convent. I also need copies of the plans and documents relating to the new flats and current building works. They may also know whether or not the grounds are deconsecrated.'

'Is that important, under the circumstances?'

'Barnes wants to know,' Jane said, knowing Barnes didn't really.

'Anything else?' Boon asked.

'Yes. Ask who you should speak to about records of the children who lived at the convent. If possible, get the records from the time the convent closed going back twenty years to start with.'

Boon closed his notebook. 'No problem, sarge. I'll charge Barry May and go down there.'

'Can we keep him in custody overnight? Then take him to court tomorrow morning?' Jane asked Stanley.

'Bromley Magistrates is closed on a Saturday,' Boon informed her.

'Why do you want to keep him in custody?' Stanley asked.

'He's been using his wife Katie as a punch bag,' Jane told him. 'She was covered in bruises and terrified of him. Sadly, she won't press charges at the moment.'

'He's an evil piece of shit,' Stanley said with feeling.

'I'm hoping she's left him and gone to her parents for now. Even then I'm worried he'll go round there and give her another beating,' Jane said.

'I'll tell the charging sergeant to keep May in custody for court on Monday morning. You can try and get him remanded in custody by the magistrate, but I doubt he will. Although the offence is repulsive, it's still only a theft of property that isn't worth much.'

'Well, it's worth a try,' she said. 'Maybe the magistrate will be as repelled as we are.'

'Come on, Boony,' Stanley said, walking towards the door.

'Where are we going, guv?' Boony asked.

'To charge Barry May and have a little word in his ear about what happens to scumbags who assault women.'

They were out of the room before Jane could say anything.

She did some paperwork while she waited for them to return. It was fifteen minutes before Stanley came back on his own, telling Jane that Boon had gone to the council offices.

'What did you do to him?' Jane asked.

'Let's just say he won't bother his missus again,' Stanley said.

'You didn't hit him, did you?'

Stanley shook his head. 'I just put him up against the wall and prodded his chest a few times.'

Jane thought he'd probably made matters worse. 'That's really going to help his wife.'

'I told him I know some tasty villains who detest wife beaters. He nearly shit himself when I said I'd give them his address if he ever laid one finger on his wife again.'

'Well, let's hope it works, for Katie and the children's sakes.'

The SOCO walked in and handed Jane two sets of A4 photographs. 'These are the blowups you wanted of the cross. The others are the mortuary photos which DS Johnson took. They came through in the dispatch bag from the lab this morning.'

Jane thanked him and put two photographs of the cross and some of the coffin in a folder.

She turned to Stanley. 'I spoke with Nick Durham earlier. He runs the company that's doing the new building work in the convent grounds. He was very helpful, but obviously a bit upset at the site being closed.'

Stanley shrugged. 'Tough shit. I'm sure he's not short of a few quid.'

'There's some old buildings on the site that were burnt out in the sixties. Durham wondered if they could knock them down,' Jane continued.

'Fine by me, as long as it's all surface work and no digging. Let's go over everything we've got so far in my office. We also need to write up an action plan.'

In his office, Jane sat opposite Stanley.

'Barnes was impressed with your report.'

'I was worried he'd pick holes in it. But he was actually very pleasant and listened to what I had to say – though it would be fair to point out he didn't agree with all my views. I reckon he'll form a full murder squad once we identify the nun.'

Stanley nodded. 'I asked Barnes why he wanted her murder kept quiet. He told me he was running late for a meeting and to ask you.'

Jane told Stanley about the suicide of young Stephen Phillips and what Barnes had uncovered during the investigation.

'I could see he was still quite emotional about it all,' she added.

'I'm not surprised. The death of a child is never easy to investigate, but to discover that priests and nuns could abuse kids in their care – then cover it up – is sickening. Do you want me to come with you to meet the bishop?'

'I'll be fine,' Jane said. 'Stephen's death was nearly twenty years ago now. I'd like to think the Catholic Church's attitude has changed since then. Father Floridia offered his assistance before we even knew if there was a body in the coffin . . .'

'He may be fishing for information,' Stanley said.

'I don't think so. He came across as very sincere.'

Stanley snorted. 'You've only met him once. First impressions can be misleading. Take Barnes's advice, tread carefully and don't give away too much.'

'I haven't,' Jane said quickly.

He raised his eyebrows. 'Why does it feel to me like you're trying to defend yourself?'

'I'm not. I just think you're wrong about Father Chris,' Jane said without thinking.

'On first-name terms, are you? You forget, Jane, I've known you a long time. What is it you're not telling me?'

Jane let out a big sigh. 'I've done something I may regret . . .'

'Well, it won't be the first time,' he grinned. 'Come on, spit it out!'

Jane told him about her meeting with Father Chris the previous evening and what she'd divulged about the nun's murder.

Stanley flopped back in his chair looking exasperated. 'This is more than stupid . . . it's fucking disobeying a senior officer's order. Barnes will literally crucify you if he finds out!'

'I didn't know his views at the time,' Jane said feebly.

'Common sense alone should have told you not to say anything. And you didn't even tell me you were going to see Father Floridia.'

'It was an impulse decision on the way home,' Jane explained. 'Father Floridia promised he wouldn't tell the bishop until I said it was OK.'

Stanley shook his head. 'For your sake, I hope he hasn't phoned him.'

'What do you think I should tell Father Floridia?' Jane asked.

'The truth – that you screwed up and shouldn't have said anything.'

'Are you going to tell Barnes?'

'What would you do if you were in my position?'

'I don't know . . . maybe realise I acted in good faith?'

'I won't tell Barnes,' he said.

'Thank you,' Jane said, the relief obvious in her voice.

'Don't thank me yet,' Stanley said. 'Somehow, I doubt a priest is going to oblige you by lying to his superiors the way you did. In which case, you tell Barnes you messed up – and you don't mention you told me.'

Jane knew she had no choice. 'Do you want to draw up an action plan?'

'Right now, I've nothing more to say to you, Jane. Have your meeting with the bishop, then we'll discuss what to do next.'

'I'm really sorry,' Jane said.

'So am I, Jane. I expected better of you. Just go before I change my mind,' he said, waving her away with his hand.

CHAPTER ELEVEN

Jane bought a sandwich in the canteen and ate it at her desk before phoning the mortuary. Jack, the mortuary technician, answered and she asked to speak with PC Rogers.

'PC Rogers isn't here, sergeant. I'm not sure when . . . or if he'll be back.'

'Did the coroner send him back to division?' Jane asked thinking that would be a bit harsh.

'I heard through the grapevine, the coroner told him his days as a coroner's officer were numbered. Rogers was in a right sulk when he came back here. He said another coroner's officer would be dealing with the case as from Monday and he was taking some time off. Then he left with his tail between his legs.'

'Sounds like he's learned his lesson the hard way,' Jane said.

'Well, he's only himself to blame,' Jack said. 'He's been warned about his attitude by the coroner before. Is there anything I can help you with in Rogers' absence?'

'There's a priest called Father Floridia who's helping me identify the nun. He wanted to come to the mortuary and say a prayer for her . . . if that's OK with you?'

'No problem at all, sergeant. I'll lay her out in our chapel of rest in a clean white shroud.'

'Thanks, Jack. We'll be with you in about half an hour. Oh, while I think of it, my DCS wants us to keep the nun's cause of death to ourselves for the time being.'

'I know – DI Stanley phoned earlier and told me the same thing. He's got nothing to worry about . . . my motto has always been "what goes on at work, stays at work".'

Jane thought Jack's motto rather ironic, as most people wouldn't want to hear about the dissection and examination of dead bodies anyway.

* * *

Driving to St Mary's Church, Jane felt miserable about her conversation with Stanley and anxious about her meeting with Father Chris. She was stuck in a quandary, wondering what she could do to get out of a messy situation. She knew she only had herself to blame, but hoped identifying the nun might placate Stanley and, more importantly, Barnes, if he found out she'd lied to him.

Jane knew, as a last resort, she could go to court and apply for a warrant to seize any relevant documentation from the diocesan archives, but that course of action risked creating animosity between the police and the Catholic Church, whose assistance was vital to the investigation. She sighed, knowing there was only one answer. She had to be honest with Father Chris and face the consequences, whatever they might be.

Walking up the stone path to the presbytery, Jane saw Father Chris looking out of the living-room window. He waved to her then opened the front door. He was wearing a black raincoat, black suit, and a shirt with a white clerical collar.

'Hi, Jane, thanks for coming to pick me up. How are you today?' he said, greeting her with a smile.

She couldn't bring herself to smile back. 'Before we go to the mortuary, I need to have a chat with you.'

'Is something wrong?'

'Yes, but it's nothing you've done. Can we talk inside?'

He showed Jane through to the living room, where they both sat down.

'I had my meeting with DCS Barnes this morning. He's happy for you to assist me identifying the nun. But he also instructed me not to tell anyone connected with the Church, the building site, or the press that the nun was murdered, until we discover her identity.'

He looked concerned. 'Does he know you told me she was murdered?'

Jane sighed. 'Under the circumstances I thought it best not to tell him you know.'

Father Chris looked worried. 'This puts me in an awkward position with Bishop Meade, because—'

Jane interrupted. 'I would never ask or expect you to lie to him. If you don't want to come with me to Bishop Meade's office, I totally understand. He doesn't know we've met or discussed the discovery of the coffin or the nun's death, so I'm happy to keep it that way, if you are. Then there will be no repercussions for you.'

He gave her a doubtful look. 'That's not really possible now.'

'Why not?'

Father Chris shook his head. 'I spoke with Bishop Meade last night, after you left.'

Jane was surprised. 'I thought you said you wouldn't call him.'

Father Chris looked upset. 'Don't worry, he doesn't know the nun was murdered.'

'I'm sorry, I didn't mean to offend you. This whole situation is my fault.'

'It's all right. I understand your concern. After you left last night, I realised I'd have to make an appointment to see the bishop as he's a busy man. I didn't want you to have a wasted journey, so I called him. Naturally, he asked what it was about, but I only told him I'd been informed a coffin had been uncovered at the old convent with the body of a nun inside. If Bishop Meade finds out I knew she was murdered before I called him, he's not going to be a happy man.'

'Looks like we've both dug a bit of a hole for ourselves,' Jane sighed.

He let out a nervous laugh. 'We reap what we sow. Bishop Meade also knows you are trying to ascertain the nun's identity.'

'Did he say if they had any historical records of the nuns who lived at the convent?'

'No, and I didn't ask. He said he'd do what he could to help. I told him we'd be there around half past two.'

'We best be on our way, then,' Jane said. 'Are we agreed we don't tell him she was murdered – at least for now?'

'Regrettably, yes. I'll let you do the talking when we get there,' he said solemnly.

* * *

As they got into Jane's car, she looked at her watch and told Father Chris they had time to go to the mortuary first if he wanted to say a prayer for the nun before the meeting with Bishop Meade. Jane reached over to the back seat, picked up a folder and handed it to Father Chris.

'We recovered the cross at the builder's flat this morning. He admitted forcing the coffin open and stealing it. There are some photographs of the cross and coffin in there for you to look at.'

Jane started the car and pulled away from the kerb. She noticed he was looking at a photo of the cross.

'It's exactly as you described it would be – the Sacred Heart, with a small cross and circle of thorns engraved on it. I'm assuming MB are the initials of the nun.'

'Possibly, but they could be for her given name.'

'I forgot you told me that,' Jane said.

'A common given first name for a nun is Mary. The B could also refer to a given name or even a real surname.'

'What about the engraved date? Could it be when she became a nun?'

'Possibly. It could also be when she took her final vows.'

'How old do you have to be to become a nun?' Jane asked, realising it might help narrow down the victim's age.

'These days, at least eighteen. After a woman decides she wants to be a nun, she moves into a community, like a convent, as a novitiate. They live and work with other nuns, to help them decide if they want to live a religious life.'

'Like a sort of test drive to see if you like it,' Jane smiled.

He laughed. 'That's one way of putting it.'

'Would the joining age have been younger back in the fifties and sixties?'

'Possibly, yes. I have met a nun who became a novitiate when she was fifteen, but I think that's quite rare over here.'

'How long does it take to become a fully-fledged nun?' Jane asked.

'After two years as a novice, the nun takes her first vows, then after another three years, they surrender their life to their religious order and take vows that compel them to remain unmarried, devote their work to charity, and give up most of their material goods. Then, as you put it, the novitiate is fully-fledged.'

* * *

Arriving at the mortuary, Jane asked Father Chris to wait in the coroner's officer's room while she went to speak with the mortuary technician to check if the nun's body was ready for viewing. As she entered the mortuary examination room, she saw Sam Pullen standing by the X-ray viewer with a grey-haired man in his fifties casually dressed in a white T-shirt, blue jeans, denim jacket, and white trainers.

Jack was placing a clean shroud on the nun's body, which was on a mortuary trolley. 'I'll take the nun to the chapel of rest. Give me five minutes to set things up, then the priest can do his bit,' Jack said cheerfully pushing the trolley towards the doors.

'Hi, Jane.' Sam smiled. 'This is Richard Eaves. Richard, this is Detective Sergeant Jane Tennison.'

'Thank you for letting me be involved in your investigation,' Eaves said. 'I'm looking forward to doing the facial reconstruction. As it's the weekend tomorrow, I'll pick the head up on Monday and get straight to work on it.'

'How long do you think it will take?' Jane asked.

'At least two or three weeks for a clay reconstruction.'

'I look forward to seeing it,' Jane said, but Eaves could see she looked disappointed.

'If you need something quicker, I could do a two-dimensional facial reconstruction,' he suggested.

'What does that involve?' Jane asked.

'Taking a front and side profile photograph of the skull, which I place side by side on a drawing table and cover with transparent paper. Using the shape of the bone and the tissue markers as a map, I then sketch a face back onto the skull. It will only take me a couple of days. I'll also do the clay model as part of my research.'

Jane brightened. 'Thanks, Richard, the sketch will be immensely helpful to start with. Are you able to give an estimation of the nun's age?'

'You just missed Doc Martin, the odontologist,' Sam said. 'He examined the teeth and estimated her to be between twenty and thirty years old.'

Eaves nodded. 'I've looked at the X-rays for skeletal development and anatomical growth markers in the hands, wrists and clavicles. My findings concur with Doc Martin's.'

Jane had hoped the age range might be narrower. 'The cross on her body had 20 February 1958 engraved on it. If she was sixteen when she became a nun and the date refers to the taking of her vows, which would be five years later, then her age at death could be between twenty-one and thirty.'

'That makes sense,' Sam said. 'But the date on the cross could also refer to when she became a novice nun, which means she could have been anything between sixteen and twenty-one when she died.'

'If the convent closed in the mid-sixties, that makes the possible age range sixteen to twenty-three, I think,' Jane added.

Eaves was apprehensive. 'It should always be borne in mind, whatever the case, all a forensic anthropologist or odontologist can do is give the best estimate of biological age, regardless of how far it may be from actual chronological age. Once you identify her, the age problem should be resolved.'

'Thanks for your help, Richard. I look forward to seeing the reconstruction,' Jane said.

Jack walked back in. 'The nun's ready for viewing.'

'Thanks, Jack. I'll let Father Floridia know,' Jane said.

Sam walked with Jane to the coroner's officer's room to get her coat and briefcase.

'I'm working Saturday but should be finished around five. I wondered if you fancied going out for something to eat,' Jane asked.

'I'd love to, Jane, but I'm out on a date. I could do Sunday lunch, though.'

'I'm not sure if I'll be working Sunday.'

'If you're not, give me a ring Sunday morning. I know a lovely old pub on the Thames called The Anchor. It's a short walk from London Bridge station. We could meet there first.'

'Sounds good to me. I'll let you know about work,' Jane said.

'He doesn't look like your everyday fuddy-duddy priest,' Sam remarked, having seen Father Chris from the corridor.

He stood up as the two women entered the room.

'We can through to the chapel of rest now, Father,' Jane told him.

'Aren't you going to introduce us?' Sam asked.

'Of course,' Jane said and did the introductions.

'Do you have a Christian name?' Sam asked as they shook hands.

'It's Christopher, but most people call me Father Chris,' he replied.

'Are you Italian?'

'Father Chris is Maltese,' Jane said.

'It's a lovely island. I went there once on holiday,' Sam said.

'I'm glad you liked it, Dr Pullen.'

'Please, call me Sammy.'

Jane wasn't sure if she was flirting. 'I think we best get a move on, Father, or we'll be late for the meeting with the bishop.'

'It's been a pleasure meeting you, Sammy.'

'Likewise, Father Chris.'

As he walked to the door, Sam took Jane's arm.

'It's a pity priests are celibate,' she whispered with a wink.

* * *

In the chapel of rest Father Chris took off his coat, removed a purple stole from his pocket and placed it around his neck. The nun's body was covered to the top of her neck in a white ritual blanket with a large embroidered gold cross.

'Would you like me to leave?' Jane asked.

'No, it's fine, please stay if you want.'

Jane stood with her hands behind her back and head slightly bowed so she could watch him. He remained in silent prayer for a while before speaking.

'My God, I recommend to thee the souls of my relations, my benefactors, my friends, and my enemies, and of those who are in purgatory on my account. I recommend to thee the souls of evangelical labourers, of religious and priests, and especially of those who had charge of my soul. I recommend to thee the souls of those who were most devout to the passion of Our Lord, to the Blessed Sacrament, to the Blessed Virgin Mary, the souls who are most abandoned, those who suffer most, and those who are nearest to the entrance into paradise. Eternal rest grant unto them, O Lord, and let perpetual light shine upon them. May they rest in peace. Amen.'

Jane was touched by his prayer, hearing the emotion in his voice. Thinking he had finished, she raised her head, and took a step forward. She was about to speak when Father Chris continued the prayer. She quickly stepped back and resumed a solemn position.

'In the name of the Father, and of the Son, and of the Holy Spirit. Amen,' he said, blessing the nun with the sign of the cross. He turned to Jane.

'Thank you for letting me pray for her.'

'It was a very moving.'

'An Italian saint called Alphonsus Liguori wrote it in the 1700s, when he was a bishop. Under the circumstances, I thought it appropriate.'

'I'll let the mortuary technician know we've finished, then we'll be on our way.'

*   *   *

Father Chris was quiet on the journey to Southwark. Something was clearly preying on his mind.

'I can't stop thinking about how she died . . . helpless, unable to move or shout for help,' he said after a while.

'It's bizarre . . . her body was mummified, and face contorted . . . yet I saw her as I imagined she would be . . . a beautiful young woman who devoted her life to God. Yet, as a man of faith I ask myself: where was her God when she needed him most.'

'Doesn't the bible say he moves in mysterious ways?' Jane offered.

'Actually, it doesn't,' he said. 'The words are from a poem called "Light Shining out of Darkness" by William Cowper, encouraging us to trust God's greater wisdom in the face of inexplicable tragedies.'

'As you can probably tell,' Jane admitted, 'I'm not very religious. But I do believe we will find the person responsible for her death.'

'Really, after all this time?' he asked.

'I've a good success rate investigating murders, and believe me, I don't give in easily,' Jane assured him.

'I'm sorry for being so gloomy. I have every faith in you succeeding,' he said.

'Can I ask you something about the nun?'

'Of course. I don't have a problem talking about her, although seeing her lifeless body brought back some sad memories.'

Jane thought it best not to ask about those memories. 'When a nun dies of natural causes and is placed in a coffin, would her hands be put in a praying position like you did earlier?'

'Yes, usually with a wooden cross placed in the hands.'

'What about rosary beads?'

'Sometimes they're wrapped around the hands. Why do you ask?'

'Barry May said the nun's hands were clasped together like that when he opened the coffin. A wooden cross and rosary beads were in her hands. It's possible someone religious did that after she was killed.'

Father Chris was taken aback. 'Are you suggesting someone connected to the convent killed her?'

'I can't rule it out.'

'I've never heard of a case where a priest, a nun or anyone connected with a religious order committed murder. Have you?' he asked bluntly.

'No, but that's not to say it's never happened.'

'It could have been a layperson who worked at the convent who killed her,' he suggested.

'Would a convent employ laypeople?' Jane asked.

'Of course, especially if building or electrical work needed to be done.'

'Then the diocese might have records or receipts regarding any work of that kind.'

'Let's hope they do,' he said.

CHAPTER TWELVE

Approaching the Elephant and Castle roundabout, Jane asked Father Chris for directions to the archbishop's house.

'Take the second turning off the roundabout. Go straight up and you'll see St George's Cathedral. Archbishop's House is just next to it. There's a courtyard you can park in,' he told her, sounding more relaxed than earlier.

'Do you cycle all this way?' Jane asked.

'Sometimes, but if the weather's bad, I get the train to Waterloo and walk down.'

Jane saw the cathedral tower come into view.

'It's a big cathedral. I've lived and worked in London all my life and never even knew it was here.'

'It was built in 1848 then severely damaged in a German bombing raid during World War Two. An oddly named man called Romilly Craze designed and rebuilt it as a gothic revival cathedral, which opened in 1958. Pope John Paul II will be attending a service there when he visits London next month.'

'You mentioned yesterday that Archbishop Malone was in Rome organising the Pope's visit.'

'Bishop Meade is standing in for him while he's away. The courtyard is just over there on the right,' he said, pointing.

After parking, Jane picked up the photographs and followed Father Chris to the main entrance in St George's Road, with its ancient-looking arch-shaped dark oak doors.

Father Chris lifted the heavy brass knocker and banged it down on the door three times.

'Getting a reply sometimes takes a while. I wish they'd get a doorbell or one of those fancy intercom things fitted,' he said, and knocking again.

'Just coming,' a voice called out from the inside. The door was opened by a young priest wearing a white clerical collar and black cassock with a brown tasselled rope tied around his waist.

'Good afternoon, Father Chris,' he said. 'Please come in.'

Entering the building, Jane was impressed by the vestibule with its arched ceiling, which opened onto a stone staircase. She was surprised to see a Thirties-style lift, with gold-coloured ornamental door grilles in the middle of the stairwell, looking rather rickety and out of place.

'Bishop Meade is expecting you and Detective Tennison. Would you like a coffee, tea or a cold drink?' the priest asked.

They both opted for coffee and the priest told them he would bring their drinks to the archbishop's office, which Bishop Meade was using while he was away.

'Are we using the lift?' Jane asked warily.

'We'll use the stairs. The office is on the first floor.'

'That's a relief,' she whispered to herself.

The Victorian-style room turned out to be almost as big as the Bromley CID office. The walls were covered with dark wood panelling, apart from the far end, which had floor-to-ceiling bookshelves. There were two stained-glass windows, one depicting Jesus on the cross and the other the Virgin Mary praying.

The bishop was sitting near the bookshelves at a carved oak pedestal desk. In front of the desk were two walnut armchairs with velvet-covered seats.

The bishop removed his moon-shaped glasses and stood up. He was a short, chubby-cheeked man in his late forties or early fifties, with thin black receding hair, partially covered by a rose-red skullcap. He wore an ankle-length black cassock trimmed with rose-red piping matching the buttons down the front. A large plain gold cross and chain hung from his neck down to a red cloth sash, tied around his midriff. A short, red-trimmed black cape hung from his shoulders.

The bishop raised his right hand towards Father Chris who bowed and kissed the large gold ring, set with an amethyst, that was on his third finger.

Father Chris looked at Jane. 'May I introduce you to His Most Reverend Excellency Robert Meade, Bishop of the Diocese of Southwark. Your Excellency, this is Detective Sergeant Jane Tennison of the Metropolitan Police, Bromley.'

Bishop Meade held his right hand out to Jane who gave a little bow of her head as she shook it.

'Welcome to Archbishop's House, Detective Tennison. Please take a seat.' He indicated the two chairs opposite his desk.

Jane was about to sit down when Father Chris nudged her and shook his head. They waited until the bishop was seated at his desk again and then sat down.

The young priest entered holding a tray with three coffees in bone china cups.

'Is there anything else Your Excellency requires?' the priest asked.

The bishop shook his head. 'No, thank you.' He turned to Jane.

'Thank you for coming to see me, Detective Tennison. The Church will do everything it can to help regarding the unearthed coffin. Father Floridia told me you found the body of a nun inside the coffin.'

'Yes, that's correct, sir . . . I mean, Your Excellency.'

'Under the circumstances, Bishop Meade will be fine,' he smiled. 'Father Floridia briefly told me the situation surrounding the discovery last night. I wonder, though, if you would be kind enough to go over it for me in more detail so I can take some notes and decide how I can best help you.' He opened a large leather notebook and picked up a fountain pen from his desk.

'May I take notes as well?' Jane asked.

'Of course. I was expecting you to.'

Jane recounted how the coffin had been found and how one of the builders had forced it open while on the site and stolen a cross from around the nun's neck, which they had subsequently recovered.

Bishop Meade sighed and shook his head. 'May God forgive him.'

Jane removed the photographs of the cross from the envelope. 'As you can see, the cross is engraved. We are assuming the nun lived at the convent and I was hoping the initials and date might help us identify her.'

He looked closely at the photographs as Jane continued.

'Father Floridia mentioned that you keep records of all the nuns who lived and worked in the diocese.'

'That is correct. The archives are kept in this very building. They contain a wealth of material from the establishment of the diocese in 1850 to the present day, including information on our clergy, both living and deceased. It's possible the initials MB may not be the initials relating to the nun's birth name, however.'

'Father Floridia did explain the complications concerning the initials,' Jane said. 'Would it be possible for me to visit the archives and look through the records?'

'Of course. However, it might be quicker if I spoke with our archivist, Bree Parkin. She has extensive knowledge and is experienced in searching the records for all sorts of things.'

'That would be very helpful,' Jane replied.

The bishop held up the photograph of the engraved cross. 'Could I keep this to show Mrs Parkin?'

'Certainly.' Jane recalled what Barnes had said about using the question of the land being consecrated as a cover, and explained about the sale of the Sisters of Mercy convent in the mid-sixties to a building developer.

'I remember hearing about it at the time,' the bishop said. 'It's always sad when a convent that does so much for orphaned and destitute children has to close.'

'The developer is adamant his solicitors told him there was no consecrated ground when he purchased the land. I have told them to stop all digging work until we can ascertain if this is correct.'

The bishop nodded. 'His solicitors would have liaised with the diocesan solicitors regarding the purchase of the convent and completed a "petition for faculty", which is required before any development or reconstruction work can commence on consecrated land or buildings.'

'So once that's granted, the land and buildings are officially deconsecrated?' Jane asked.

Meade smiled. 'Not quite. In basic terms, deconsecrating is the act of removing a religious blessing from something that was previously consecrated by a priest or bishop. In respect of a church, anything which has been blessed and dedicated to the use of God must be removed: the crucifix, the vestments, the stations of the cross, holy water and so on . . .'

'Would the petition cover moving the remains of any convent nuns or other bodies to another graveyard?' Jane asked.

'No. A further "faculty" would need to be granted by the bishop of the diocese for any exhumations to take place. If a body lies in consecrated ground, disinterment – without a faculty – is an offence under ecclesiastical law and the 1857 Burial Act.'

'Would the archives have a record of any consecrated ground on the old convent site?'

'I am aware the archives hold material relating to finance and property, so there may well be records regarding the sale of the old convent. I'll ask Mrs Parkin to look into that as well,' the bishop said.

'Thank you. I don't wish to appear rude, but do you know how long it might take to get a result?'

'I'll speak with Mrs Parkin this afternoon. She doesn't work weekends, but hopefully she might have an answer for you by Monday or Tuesday at the latest.'

'That would be fine. Thank you for your assistance. I really appreciate it.'

'Do you have any photographs of the nun's body?'

'Not with me, but I can arrange for one to be delivered to you.'

'Don't worry, it was merely a curiosity to know how she looked.'

'Unfortunately, her body was mummified with adipocere so she's unrecognisable.'

'How sad. Let's hope we can find out who she was. May I ask when her body will be released to us for reburial?'

'That's a decision for the coroner. He has said that he would like us to identify her first, but I think that might just be a standard formality.'

'I understand. Is there anything else I can help you with?'

'No, I think that's about it for now,' she said.

The bishop turned to Father Chris. 'You've been very quiet, Father Floridia. Is there anything you'd like to add?'

'No, Your Excellency. I've merely been an intermediary, who thought it best to let Detective Tennison explain the circumstances.'

'You've acted appropriately. When the nun's body is returned to us, I'd like you to conduct the service at her reburial.'

'Thank you, Your Excellency. I'd be honoured to do it.'

The bishop stood and proffered his right hand to Father Floridia, who stood then bowed and kissed the amethyst ring.

* * *

'I thought that went well,' Jane said as they walked back to her car.

Father Chris looked uncertain. 'Do you? I think he was suspicious of me being so quiet.'

'Then surely he'd have asked more questions,' Jane replied, trying to sound upbeat.

'That's the thing,' he said. 'Normally he asks a lot of questions and chats away for ages. Why didn't you show him the pictures of the coffin?' he asked.

'You told me a nun wouldn't normally be buried in a metal coffin. If I'd shown him the photographs, it might have made him suspicious about her death.'

He sighed. 'He's not going to be happy when he knows the truth.'

'Don't worry, that's my problem, not yours. Besides, he might realise the police were in a difficult position and be more sympathetic than you think.'

Father Chris didn't look convinced. 'Why does Barnes want the nun's murder kept quiet, anyway? Surely it would make more sense to just be open about it so as not to upset Bishop Meade.'

Jane didn't want to tell him about Barnes's painful experiences with the Catholic Church. 'I don't know. I'd never met him until this morning. It's not for me to question his decisions.'

He gave her a sideways look. 'Does he also suspect a priest or nun might be involved?'

'Like I said before, we have to consider it as a possibility . . .'

'I don't think such a thing is possible,' he said firmly.

A sad-faced Father Chris sat silently staring out of the passenger window on the journey back to the parsonage. Jane wanted to ask some more questions relating to the investigation but decided it was better to leave him to his thoughts. Eventually they pulled up outside St Mary's.

'Would you like to know the result of the archives search when I get it?' she asked, trying to engage him in conversation.

He shrugged. 'It's up to you. If I'm doing the reburial service, I'm sure Bishop Meade will give me the details. Thanks for the lift,' he said, getting out of the car.

Jane could see he was still upset. She got out of the car and followed him.

'I'm only doing my job, Father Floridia. The thought that anyone could commit such a heinous crime revolts me. All I want to do is find who is responsible . . . no matter who it is!'

He turned around sharply. 'You have no idea what it means to be a priest or nun.'

'Then enlighten me.'

'When a priest is ordained, he becomes a new man, one who can say with St Paul, "It is no longer I who live, but Christ who lives in me." He is changed not because of what he can do, but because of what he has become. He carries out his work in the power of Christ, not in his own power. It is inconceivable to me that a man or woman who has heard God's calling and accepted his Holy Orders could commit, or even contemplate, the murder of another human being.'

Jane realised it was pointless carrying on the argument, and didn't want to drive a wedge between them. 'I realise this whole situation can't be easy for you.'

He looked sad. 'You don't know the half of it, Jane. I think it would be best, for both of us, if we don't contact each other again,' he said with regret in his voice.

'If that's what you want,' she replied, taken aback.

'As I said, it's for the best.'

Father Chris walked away.

CHAPTER THIRTEEN

Driving back to Bromley, Jane regretted telling Father Chris that a priest or a nun might have been involved in the murder. She sighed, knowing she'd find it difficult to believe if someone told her a police officer had violently murdered a colleague.

But what had he meant when he said, 'You don't know the half of it'? Was he referring to something that had happened in the past or the present situation?

Returning to the station, Jane went straight to DI Stanley's office and told him about her meeting with Bishop Meade and the forthcoming archive searches.

'Sounds like you just got away with murder,' Stanley remarked.

Jane gave him a quizzical look.

'I mean, you didn't reveal to the bishop the nun was murdered. It also means DCS Barnes won't be on your back.'

'I'd prefer to describe it as a lucky escape,' Jane said.

'Whatever . . . it's still a good result and Barnes will be pleased – even more so when you identify the nun. He rang me earlier for an update. He didn't say anything about his grievances against the Catholic Church, but it sounded like he's chomping at the bit to get a result on this case.'

Jane frowned. 'I'm worried Barnes might be a bit too eager. What happened in the past might cloud his judgement. On the face of it Bishop Meade was very open and helpful.'

'Believe me,' Stanley said, 'Barnes doesn't rush anything. He's always slow and methodical. If anyone in the diocese lies or tries to cover this up, he'll give them enough rope to hang themselves . . . then come down on them like a ton of bricks.'

'Will he tell the bishop it's a murder investigation or does he want me to?'

'He didn't say, but my bet is he'll want to do it.'

She nodded. 'It looks like I won't get a result on the nun's identity until Monday or Tuesday. There's not a lot more I can do until then, so should I take the weekend off as rostered?'

'If you want. Did you ask the bishop if a priest had worked at the convent?'

'No. It might have made him suspicious. The archives will have a record.'

'Might be worth asking Father Floridia.'

Jane hesitated. 'There's a slight problem there . . .'

'Jesus Christ, don't tell me you've managed to piss off a priest as well!'

She frowned. 'He's not pissed off with me. He just doesn't want to assist me . . . for now.'

'Spit it out, Jane. What did you do to upset him?'

She told Stanley about Father Floridia's reaction when she suggested a priest or nun might have been involved in the murder.

'Sounds like Barnes is right about the clergy being in denial,' he remarked.

'I don't think he's in denial,' she said. 'I just think as a priest himself, he finds it hard to accept.'

'That's no reason to blank you. Do you think there's more to it?'

'What do you mean?'

'He could be stonewalling you because he's hiding something?'

'I don't think so. He suggested a layperson, who worked at the convent, might have been responsible, but if that was the case, you'd expect the Mother Superior or one the other nuns to have reported her missing. Unless they thought our victim had just upped and left of her own accord.'

'That's possible, but unlikely. How's it going with Missing Persons?'

'Nothing positive yet. Maybe I should check the station archives as well.'

'You'd be looking for a needle in a haystack. Old misper and crime reports are just dumped down there in no particular order.'

'I could put out an all-stations memo,' Jane suggested, 'to see if there are any serving officers who remember dealing with a missing nun from St Mary's Convent back in the sixties.'

'OK. Wait and see if the diocesan archive search gives you a name, then do it.'

'Whatever the outcome, I think Father Floridia's assistance might still be useful. The convent is a stone's throw from his church. Some of his parishioners have probably lived in the area for years and might have known some of the nuns. We might need to speak to them at some point, so Father Floridia would be a good means of introduction.'

Stanley snorted. 'He's already turned his nose up once . . . don't be surprised if he does it again.'

Jane wasn't going to be put off. 'I'll let him calm down over the weekend and contact him on Monday or Tuesday.'

'Fine. Do your report then head off home and get some rest over the weekend. I suspect you'll be pretty busy next week. Well done today. Keep up the good work.'

* * *

Jane left Stanley's office, then phoned the forensic laboratory and got put through to DS Johnson.

'Hi, Jane, what can I do for you?' Lloyd asked.

She told him about the nun's cross, the relevance of the date and initials on it and her conversation with Bishop Meade.

'How's the work on the fibres you recovered going?' Jane asked.

'I don't think the fibre expert has had a chance to start on them yet. Give me a second and I'll go and ask her.'

'It's OK, there's no rush. Could you ask her to check the fibres from the nun against the rope she was wearing around her waist?'

'You think she was strangled with her own rope.'

'No, but I saw a priest today at Archbishop's House who was wearing one that looked exactly the same.'

'Bloody hell – you think a bloody priest did it?'

'Don't you start.'

'Start what?'

'It's a long story,' she sighed. 'I've got the weekend off. Do you fancy having that drink and a catch-up on Saturday evening?'

'I'd love to, Jane, but I've already made arrangements for Saturday night.'

'Oh, right. Maybe some other time then?' she said, unable to keep the disappointment out of her voice.

'Definitely. Your choice where we go. I'm paying and no arguments. I'll speak with the fibre expert right away, then get back to you with a result – probably Monday as the lab shuts at the weekend.'

Jane thanked him, then called Sam Pullen.

'Hi, Sam, it's Jane. I'm not working Sunday, so are you still up for a lunchtime meet?'

'Of course. Do you still want to meet at London Bridge?'

'I don't mind . . . whatever's easiest for you.'

'Where do you live?'

'Chislehurst.'

'Bloody hell, we're nearly neighbours. I live in Mottingham. Tell you what, let's meet at The Bull's Head.'

'Where's that?'

Sam laughed. 'On your doorstep. Do you get out much?'

'I only moved here a few weeks ago. I don't know the area at all.'

'Give me your address and I'll pick you up at midday.'

Jane put the phone down and had started typing her report when DC Boon walked in, holding five large maps and a bulging folder.

'Looks like you've been a busy boy at the Civic Centre,' Jane remarked.

'I felt a right prat walking up the road carrying all this stuff. I could hardly see where I was going, then nearly got run over by an old boy on a mobility scooter.'

Boon dropped the maps and folder on his desk.

'So what have you got for me?' Jane asked.

'Everything you asked for . . . except the stuff on the kids,' he said, pulling his chair over to Jane's desk. Taking his notebook from his jacket pocket, he opened it and sat down. 'The council don't keep records of children who lived at the convent orphanage. However, they said many Catholic children's homes are organised by the Catholic Children's Society, who should hold records of the homes they operated. The local one is based in Westminster. If we don't have any luck with them, they suggested checking with the diocesan archives in Southwark. Talking of which, how did it go with the bishop?'

'Pretty well. Fingers crossed we should have a name by Monday or Tuesday. I see you got some plans.'

'Yes, they printed them on a big copier they had. There are drawings of the old convent, the renovations from the sixties, and the plans for the current development. The folder's full of paperwork relating to the development applications and approvals.'

'Is any of the ground consecrated?' she asked.

'They didn't know the answer to that question but did say if it were, a priest or bishop would have to deconsecrate it before any building work could start. Again, they said to check the diocesan archives. I got the impression they couldn't be bothered to look through all the documents, but they said the answer should be in there somewhere.'

'Judging by the size of the file, there's a lot to look through,' Jane said.

'I can start now if you like,' Boon suggested, getting up from his chair.

'It's OK. You've been on duty since six so why don't you head off home?'

'I'm on a bit of a high, to be honest,' he said. 'I don't feel tired. Shall I start on the plans or the paperwork?'

'Whatever suits you,' Jane said, with a smile.

'Documents it is then ... or should I do a report on the Barry May arrest and my visit to the planning office first?'

'Do the report. DCS Barnes will no doubt want to read it on Monday. I'll take the plans home with me and have a look at them over the weekend,' Jane told him.

*   *   *

By seven the office was empty apart from Jane and Boon. She'd finished her report and looked up to see how he was doing. She tried not to laugh, watching his head fall forward and jolt up again as he struggled to concentrate and stay awake whilst typing his report with two fingers.

'You nearly finished, Boony?' she asked in a loud voice.

He quickly sat upright. 'Nearly, sarge. I'm on the last paragraph.'

Jane went to the store cupboard in the corner of the room and removed a large exhibits bag. She picked up the plans from Boon's desk and put them in the bag.

'Do you want me to look at the building documents over the weekend?' Boon asked.

'Don't worry, I'll do it,' she said, picking up the folder and putting it in the exhibits bag.

'I know what to look for,' he said, sounding offended.

'I've not got anything planned for the weekend so I've plenty of time to spare. No doubt you'll be playing football for the Met.'

'That's true,' he said. 'We've got a game against Essex police tomorrow. Inter-police games are always bloodbaths.'

'Don't get yourself injured. I need you on my team, fit and healthy.'

'I'll be fine,' he grinned. 'Do you reckon Barnes will form a full murder squad?'

'I think he'll have to. So far, everything points to our victim being murdered between 1958 and 1965, when the convent was sold. That time span means whoever killed her could still be alive.'

'I hope Barnes puts me on the squad.'

'I'm sure he will. He's already let you continue working on the investigation with me. Your knowledge of the case works in your favour. It's also useful to anyone else who comes on the team. Have a good weekend and I hope you win the game. Be here at eight on Monday morning and we'll go over everything before the meeting with Barnes. Then you can head off to the magistrates' court for May's first appearance.'

* * *

Driving home, Jane felt her stomach rumbling. She stopped at the fish and chip shop in Chislehurst High Street and ordered cod and chips, then nipped to the nearby off-licence. Looking in the refrigerated section, she noticed a bottle of Blue Nun Liebfraumilch. 'Must be a sign from God,' she said to herself as she picked it up, along with a bottle of white wine for her neighbour, Gerry.

After parking on her driveway, she popped round to Gerry's to give him the wine.

'Hello, Jane, has the light bulb blown again?' he asked.

'No, it's working fine. I bought this as a thank you. I hope you like Chardonnay,' she said, handing him the bottle.

'It's mine and Vi's favourite. Thank you so much. Why don't you come in and have a glass with us?'

'I've just bought some fish and chips and I don't want them to get cold, but I'd love to another time.'

He smiled. 'I look forward to it. And don't forget I'm here if you need me.'

'Actually, as it happens, the cold water tap in my kitchen sink is dripping all the time . . .'

'I'll get my toolkit,' he said instantly.

'No. It's OK, tomorrow will be fine. I'm not working, so morning or afternoon would be great.'

'I'll pop round after I've taken Spud for his morning walk. Goodnight.'

What a lovely man, she decided as she walked to her door.

* * *

Jane thought the fish and chips were pretty good and the Blue Nun wasn't too bad, either, if a bit sweet for her liking.

She washed and changed into her pyjamas, before pouring herself another glass of wine, then fetched the exhibits bag containing the plan drawings and documents file from the hallway. She didn't feel like reading through the documents, so randomly pulled a plan out of the bag, unrolled it, and laid it out on the living-room floor. It was a copy of the original plans for the redevelopment of the convent buildings, dated August 1964. Looking at the plan, Jane remembered she'd promised Nick Durham she'd call him after her meeting with the bishop. She looked at the wall clock. It was nearly nine and she wondered if he'd be out on the town on a Friday evening, unlike herself. Removing his business card from her coat pocket, she dialled the home number.

He picked up after two rings. 'Nick Durham speaking.'

'Mr Durham, it's Detective Sergeant Tennison. Sorry it's late, but I thought I should call and update you.'

'Is it good news or bad news?'

'A bit of both,' she said. 'My DI said it's OK to knock down the burnt-out buildings but don't do any digging there.'

'Thanks, that'll keep the lads on the site busy for now. What did the bishop say?'

'He couldn't give me a definitive answer regarding any conse-crated ground on the land. But he did say the diocesan archives would keep a record. He hopes to have an answer for me by Tuesday at the latest.'

'I spoke with my dad again after you left. He's adamant his solicitor told him the land and buildings were deconsecrated before the sale of the convent. He was also told there were no grave sites on the land.'

'If he's right, the diocesan archives should confirm it and you can start work again.'

'I hope it's right, or my dad might have to move in with me,' he laughed.

'Your dad lives there?'

'Yes, in the old chapel.'

It suddenly dawned on her why she'd thought Nick Durham looked so familiar. His father had to be the man with Bella, the Golden Retriever, who went into the old chapel and returned with an umbrella.

'Hello? Sergeant Tennison? Are you still there?' Nick asked.

'Yes. Sorry, I got distracted,' she replied, wondering why Nick's father had never mentioned he was the original developer who had bought the convent and its land. 'I've got to go, Mr Durham, I have some paperwork I need to finish tonight. I'll ring you as soon as I get a definitive answer from the bishop.'

'Well, thanks for calling . . . oh, before you go, I spoke with our electrician about your wiring. He said he could have a look at it next Saturday.'

'That would be great, thank you.' She tried to sound pleased, but her head was full of unanswered questions about Thomas Durham's behaviour.

'There is one other thing . . .'

'I've really got to go, Mr Durham.'

'Will you . . . have dinner with me tomorrow night?' he asked.

Jane hesitated. She knew it wouldn't really be proper.

'Please say yes. If you don't, I'll feel totally rejected and might have to hang myself,' he pleaded.

'Go on then,' she said. 'I can't resist your charm anymore. I'll ring you in the morning for the details.'

'I'll book a table for two at the Fantail in Farnborough Village. I think you'll like it,' he said.

'I'm sure I will. Speak to you tomorrow.' She put the phone down, feeling slightly guilty.

Although she liked Nick Durham, she'd only accepted his dinner invitation to learn more about his father, who she strongly suspected was hiding something. She sat at the dining-room table, opened her notebook, and thought hard about the two occasions she had met Thomas Durham, then started to make some notes.

When Boon had said a coffin had been 'dug up', Thomas Durham had looked concerned, and yet never mentioned that he'd renovated the convent or his son's involvement in the current development. It was also odd he'd not contacted his son immediately about the coffin or told him he already knew about it when Nick had called him on Thursday evening.

Jane remembered Thomas Durham looking angry when she saw him coming out of the site office in the morning. He'd clearly had an altercation with Lee Holland, who she now knew had lied to her when he'd said he didn't know him. So what were Holland and Durham so worried about that they had to lie? Could Father Chris be right about someone outside of the Church being involved in the murder?

CHAPTER FOURTEEN

Jane was woken by the sound of someone knocking on her door. She looked at the alarm clock. It was eight o'clock.

'Hang on, I'm just coming,' she shouted as she got out of bed and put on her dressing gown, before hurrying downstairs to open the door.

'Morning, Jane,' Gerry said, holding up his toolbox in one hand and an adjustable spanner in the other. 'Oh, sorry, have I woken you up? I can come back later.'

'No, it's fine. I was already awake. Please, come in,' she said.

He looked at the tap. 'Oh dear, it's dripping quite badly.'

'I'll put the kettle on. What would you like?' Jane said.

'Cup of tea's fine. Best you fill the kettle up first as I'll have to turn the water off at the stopcock. It's usually under the sink.' Gerry squatted down while Jane filled the kettle.

'It's a bit stiff. I'll give it a squirt of WD40 to loosen it for you.'

Jane made two cups of tea, gave Gerry his and watched as he removed the tap handle and stem.

'As I thought, the washer's had it.'

'There's a hardware shop in the high street. Shall I pop down there and get a new one?' Jane asked.

'I've got plenty in my toolbox,' Gerry said, removing a plastic bag filled with different-sized washers.

It took him a couple of minutes to replace the washer and refit the tap. He turned on the mains supply, let some water run through the tap, then turned it off and stood back.

'There you go, Jane. Job done,' Gerry said looking pleased.

'You're a star, Gerry. How much do I owe you?'

'Don't worry about it. I like fixing things, and washers are two-a-penny.'

'I'll get you another bottle of wine then.'

'Oh, you don't need to do that,' he said with a smile. 'Anything nice planned for your day off?'

'I'm out for dinner this evening,' Jane told him. 'But I need to pop into work this morning to sort a couple of things out.'

'Going anywhere nice for dinner?'

'A restaurant called the Fantail in Farnborough Village. I've not been there before.'

Gerry looked impressed. 'A special occasion?'

'Not really. Someone I met through work invited me,' she replied.

'Well, he must think a lot of you if he's taking you there. I've heard it's very fancy.' Jane now felt even more uncomfortable about accepting Nick Durham's invitation. She wondered if she should cancel it, and instead speak with DCS Barnes and Stanley on Monday and ask for permission to officially interview Thomas Durham and Lee Holland.

* * *

Arriving at Bromley, Jane went straight to the custody room and spoke with the uniformed sergeant.

'There's a couple of things I need to ask Barry May. Can I have a quick word with him in his cell?'

'If it's related to the offences with which he's charged, it needs to be an official interview under caution,' he told her.

'It's not. It's an off-the-record chat about some of the people he works with.'

He handed her the cell keys. 'That's good enough for me. You might not get much out of him, though. He's not been very happy since DI Stanley and Boony had a polite word in his ear about using his wife as a punch bag. All I got when I offered him breakfast was "Fuck off and leave me alone." You want an officer with you in case he kicks off?'

'I'll be fine, thanks.'

Jane slid the cell wicket open and looked in. Barry's lip curled when he saw her.

'Barry, I need to have a word with you.'

'I've already admitted what I done, so just leave me alone.'

'It's not about anything you've done.'

'You deaf or something. I don't want to speak to you!'

'It would be in your interest to help me.'

'What do you mean?'

'If the answers you give me are helpful, I'll tell the judge dealing with your case that you made a full and frank confession and assisted my inquiries. A good word from me could mean a suspended sentence as opposed to a custodial one.'

Barry thought about it. 'All right. What do you wanna know?'

Jane opened the cell door and went in. 'Is Thomas Durham involved in the current redevelopment at the old convent?'

'He's retired, but he still pokes his nose in on the site and moans if we ain't doing things right.'

'Does that upset Lee Holland?'

'Nah. Thomas and Lee go way back. They're old mates. It's me and Dermot he moans at.'

'Lee's worked for him for a long time, then?'

'Yeah. He was a labourer first and worked his way up to site manager.'

'Did he work on the renovation of the old convent?' she asked.

'He said he did.'

'What about Dermot?'

'No. This is his first job for the Durhams.'

'Did Lee say he was going to phone Mr Durham about the coffin?'

'I can't remember exactly what he said, but he walked off towards the old convent, so I assumed he was going to speak to Mr Durham.'

'Would that be Thomas or Nick?'

'Thomas. He lives in the old chapel.' He narrowed his eyes. 'What's this all about, anyway?'

'I'm just trying to get my head around who does what in the company. Then I'll know who to talk to.'

'Nick Durham runs it all now. He's a decent guy to work for. So is Lee . . . most of the time.'

'Thanks for your help, Barry.'

'I'm really sorry for hitting Katie,' he said suddenly.

'Count yourself lucky she hasn't pressed charges against you . . . yet,' Jane said.

'It won't happen again, I swear,' he said.

'It had better not, because if it does, DI Stanley will come after you,' she said. She could see the fear in Barry's eyes. She stepped out of the cell, closed the wicket and walked back down the corridor.

* * *

Jane went to the canteen, ordered a bacon sandwich and a cup of tea then took it down to the CID office. She looked in Boon's desk tray for his report, wanting to read the part about his conversation with Dermot and what he'd said Lee Holland did after the discovery of the coffin.

It was no surprise when she read it. Dermot said that Lee told him he was going to speak to Mr Durham and walked off towards the old convent. She recalled seeing Thomas Durham come out of the site office early on Friday morning, then telling her the site manager wasn't very helpful and asking her 'what's going on'. Lee Holland had looked worried and said the man was just a nosy resident and he didn't know his name.

It was clear that Thomas Durham and Lee Holland were trying to distance themselves from each other. And whatever they were hiding, it appeared to be connected to the discovery of the coffin. She thought about Nick Durham and wondered if he was also involved in some way. She got his phone number out of her handbag and called him.

'Hi, it's Jane Tennison.'

'Please tell me you're still on for dinner tonight,' he said.

'I was just wondering where and what time I should meet you?' she said.

CHAPTER FIFTEEN

As soon as she got home Jane went upstairs to her bedroom, opened the wardrobe, and looked for something to wear for dinner at the Fantail. She selected four different dresses, held them up in front of the mirror then placed them carefully on the bed before deciding which one to wear. She picked up the red, short-sleeved boat-neck dress and tried it on. Being made of wool, she knew it would keep her warm on a cold evening. She looked in the mirror again and liked how the bust darts and banded waist accentuated her figure. She removed her hair tie, shook her head, then fluffed her hair so it hung over her shoulders. 'That'll do nicely,' she said to herself. She decided some black tights, black court shoes and a knee-length black velvet coat would go well with the dress.

As she hung it to one side in the wardrobe, Jane noticed her tracksuit and thought about her conversation with Father Chris about how he liked to run three or four times a week or go to the Walnuts Leisure Centre. *There's no time like the present*, she thought to herself and decided to go for a run.

Having changed into her tracksuit and trainers, Jane realised she didn't know Chislehurst, or the surrounding area very well, and planned out a triangular route using her *A-Z* street map book. She estimated it would be about three miles and wrote it down on a piece of paper which she put in her tracksuit pocket. She did some stretches and then set off.

As she ran along the pavement, Jane started thinking about Nick Durham. It crossed her mind he could be in cahoots with his father and Lee Holland, and the invitation to dinner was a ploy to get information out of her. They could each be playing the same game. At his office he'd seemed relaxed, though understandably concerned about his father's heart condition and the building work having to stop. And he'd readily accepted she had further inquiries to make, even offering to let her look through the company files – which suggested he had nothing to hide.

As she trudged up a steep road, Jane also realised it was irrational to think Nick could have been involved in the nun's murder since he'd have been a teenager at the time, and his father had yet to purchase the convent. It made her wonder if Thomas Durham had lied to his son when he said his solicitor told him everything had been deconsecrated before the sale of the convent. But if it was true, then why were Thomas Durham and Lee Holland so worried about the discovery of the coffin? If they'd been involved in the nun's murder, it seemed bizarre that they would bury the coffin on land they knew might be dug up in the future.

Jane was pretty sure Nick didn't know his father and Lee Holland had lied to her. But the more she thought about it, the more she worried that going to dinner with him to probe him about the case could compromise the investigation – she should cancel their dinner date under the pretext she had to work. It would be a shame, though. She realised she'd been looking forward to it.

Jane knew there were other ways she could find out what Thomas Durham and Lee Holland were up to, without using Nick or giving anything away. She made her mind up and decided to take her police hat off for the evening, just enjoy herself, and not talk about the investigation.

Jane struggled up Yester Road towards the High Street. It was a steep climb of over a mile, and she regretted not driving the route first to see what it was like. She was so hot she took off her tracksuit top and tied it round her waist.

The last mile home included another hill and halfway up she had to walk to the top. She was grateful that the final stretch was downhill. By the time she got home, she was breathing hard and soaked with sweat. She looked at her watch and was disappointed to see how long it had taken her and how unfit she'd become without regular exercise over the last few weeks.

'Been out for a run, Jane?' Gerry asked, seeing her bent over and breathing heavily.

She took a deep inhale. 'Yes, but I'm beginning to regret it. I had no idea how steep Yester Road is.'

He chuckled. 'There's a lot of steep hills in Chislehurst. In fact, the name is derived from the Saxon words *cisel*, which means gravel, and *hyrst*, which means wooded hill. There's quite a bit of woodland around here.'

'I didn't see any woods on my run.'

'There's Hawkwood and Petts Wood, which are owned by the National Trust, and Scadbury Park Nature Reserve. They're lovely for walking and running . . . you should try them out sometime.'

'I will, Gerry, thanks.'

'My pleasure. How's the tap holding out?'

'It's not dripped once since you fixed it.'

'That's what I like to hear,' he said.

Jane went inside, drank two glasses of water then collapsed on the settee and quickly fell asleep.

The room was in darkness when Jane opened her eyes. Realising the sun had gone down, she jumped up, switched on the table lamp, and looked at her watch. 'Shit.' She only had thirty minutes to get ready before Nick Durham arrived to take her to the restaurant. She ran up the stairs, peeled off her tracksuit and got into the shower, wondering if she had time to wash and dry her hair.

She had a tepid shower, not waiting for the water to heat up, put curlers in her hair and was just switching on the hairdryer when she heard a knock at the door. 'Oh my God, he's here and I look a mess!' she said, seeing herself in the mirror. She put on her dressing gown, hurried down the stairs and started apologising as she opened the door.

'I'm really sorry, Nick, I . . .' She stopped in mid-sentence as she saw a smiling Gerry holding out a booklet.

'Sorry to bother you, Jane. I forgot you were going out to dinner.'

'And I'm running late, Gerry. What can I do for you?'

'I'm a member of the Chislehurst Society. They produce this newsletter, called *The Cockpit*, two or three times a year. It gives you the latest news and goings-on in the area and I thought you might like to read it . . . or maybe even join yourself,' he said and handing it to her.

'Thanks. Sorry – I really must dash.'

'Have a nice evening . . . and don't do anything I wouldn't do,' he said with a cheeky grin as she shut the door.

She liked Gerry and knew he meant well, but Jane was beginning to regret asking for his help and wondered if his surprise visits were going to become a regular occurrence. She ran back upstairs and started blow-drying her hair.

It wasn't long before there was another knock at the door. Nick was holding a bouquet of flowers in one hand and a bottle of wine in the other.

'Sorry,' she said, 'I went for a run, then fell asleep and only woke up half an hour ago.' There was still a curler dangling from her hair. 'As you can see, I'm still not ready.'

'It's a woman's prerogative to be late.' He smiled and held out the flowers and the wine. 'These are just a token of my thanks for agreeing to have dinner with me, and not completely shutting my building site down . . . yet.'

'They might be construed as a bribe,' she teased, noticing the wine was Châteauneuf-du-Pape, which she knew was expensive. 'But thank you.'

He faked a look of shock. 'I would never bribe an officer of the law.'

Jane showed him through to the living room. She thought Nick looked quite trendy in his white shirt and navy blue suit.

'Take a seat. I'll be as quick as I can.'

'There's no rush. I booked the table for 7.30. I thought we might pop into The Olde White Lion for a drink before dinner. It's just opposite the restaurant.'

'Sounds good to me,' she said, putting the orchid on the mantelpiece.

Jane finished drying her hair, got dressed and put on some light makeup. She stood in front of the bedroom mirror, fluffed her hair and smoothed out her dress, then went downstairs to the living room.

'Right, I'm good to go,' she said.

He stood up and looked at her with wide eyes. 'Wow, you look absolutely stunning.'

Jane smiled. It had been a long time since a man had said that to her. 'You look very smart, too.'

'Thank you. It's the first time I've worn it.'

Jane locked her front door and turned to follow Nick to his car – then stopped in her tracks when she saw it.

'Is this your car?' she said, admiring the shining silver-grey convertible sports car, with its wire wheels and red leather interior.

He nodded. 'It's a 1961 Jaguar E-Type XKE and one of the first ever made. It was involved in a bad accident a few years ago and declared a write-off. I bought it for a song and made it roadworthy again.'

'You rebuilt it?' she said, amazed at the job he'd done on the car.

'Yes. It's kind of a hobby of mine. I've got a Ferrari that I'm working on just now.'

'You must have a big garage.'

'It's a double garage, which I've turned into a workshop. I find tinkering away on cars relaxes me.'

'How fast does it go?'

'It's capable of 150 miles an hour and does nought to sixty in 6.9 seconds,' he said in a matter-of-fact way, holding the car keys out. 'Would you like to drive it?'

She put her hand up. 'No thanks. It's way more powerful than my little Mini Cooper and I don't want to damage it.'

He smiled. 'You'll be fine. It's no different from driving any other car. Just relax and enjoy it.'

Jane removed her black velvet coat as Nick opened the driver's door, then handed it to him. Sitting in the soft bucket-shaped driver's seat, she savoured the rich earthy smell of the leather interior. Nick asked if she wanted to adjust the seat, but after placing her hands on the wood-trimmed steering wheel and feet on the pedals, she said it was fine.

'It's so comfortable, but strange to be sitting so low to the ground,' she said, putting her lap belt on.

'You get used to it.'

Jane turned the ignition, but nothing happened. She looked at Nick, wondering what was wrong.

'You need to push that little black button in the middle of the dashboard.'

She tried again, and the engine burst into life with a loud growl from the twin exhausts, then settled into a softer rhythmic rumble. She put it into first gear, slowly let her foot off the clutch and lightly pressed the accelerator. As the car started to pull away, she saw Gerry coming down his driveway with Spud. He stopped to admire the car, and Jane gave him a wave from the driver's seat.

Nick directed Jane to Locksbottom, which was only four miles away. She wished it had been a longer journey as driving the Jaguar was such a thrill. As she drove into the car park, Jane thought the large mock Tudor building in front of her was someone's house, until she noticed FANTAIL written above the entrance doors in large black lettering on a white background.

'Thanks for letting me drive your car. I felt like I was in a James Bond film,' she said with a beaming smile.

'You're a good driver,' he said.

'I had to pass a five-week course before I could drive a police car,' she told him.

'Well, they obviously taught you well. The pub's just over the road . . . or we can go straight to the restaurant.'

'A drink in the pub would be nice,' Jane said.

They crossed the road to the pub, The Olde White Lion.

Jane thought the interior had a warm, welcoming feel about it, with its old oak beams and a roaring log fire. There was a dancing area and stage at the back where a band was setting up its equipment.

'What can I get you, Nick?' the buxom middle-aged lady behind the bar asked him. He looked at Jane.

'G and T with ice and lemon, please.'

'Your usual, Nick?'

'Yes please, Sandra.'

'Bottle of Grolsch lager and one G and T with all the trimmings coming up,' she said. They sat down at the bar.

'I take it you've been here before?' Jane whispered to him.

'It's my local. Sandra's the landlady.'

'You should have said. I'd I have driven over here to save you picking me up.'

'You're only down the road, so it wasn't out my way. Are you OK getting a taxi home if I have a drink?'

'Of course, as long as you let me pay for it,' she replied, suspecting he would offer to.

Sandra brought them their drinks and they clinked glasses.

'You've got a nice house,' Nick said.

Jane sighed. 'It needs a lot of work doing on it, which I can't afford at the moment.'

'You don't need to spend a fortune to make a house look nice. It all depends on what you want and how you do it.'

'To be honest, I haven't a clue about what to do with it,' Jane admitted.

'I could draw up some different plans for you. Let me have a look round, give you a few ideas and see what you think. I can get materials for half the price that some traders would charge you.'

'Are you sure? I'd pay you, of course.'

'We can discuss that later. I could have a look tomorrow if you like.'

Jane remembered Sam Pullen was picking her up at midday.

'I'm out for lunch tomorrow, I'm afraid.'

'Oh, right. Well, maybe some other time then,' he said.

From the disappointed look on his face, Jane thought he assumed it was with another man. 'It's with a friend, but I'm not meeting her until midday.'

He perked up. 'I could come round at ten. It would only take me an hour to look round your house.'

'Ten it is, then,' Jane said with a smile.

'Would you like another drink?' Nick asked.

Jane looked at her watch. 'It's seven thirty. Should we go over to the restaurant?'

'It's OK if we're a bit late. They'll hold the table for me.'

'In that case, I'll have another G and T.'

'Same again, please, Sandra.'

'I'm paying for this round . . . whether you like it or not,' Jane said, opening her handbag and removing her purse.

'I don't, but I won't argue. Where did you live before Chislehurst?'

'Marylebone, in a tiny flat. I was on an investigation which led to me making inquiries in Kent. I really liked the area and wanted to live and work somewhere quieter so I could study for the inspectors' exam.'

'You could have got a bigger place for the same price if you'd moved a bit further out,' he said.

'I know. But as a Met police officer I get a housing allowance which helps towards my mortgage. But to get it, you have to live within a fifteen-mile radius of Trafalgar Square. Chislehurst is just on the edge of it.'

He nodded. 'On the plus side, a house in an area like Chislehurst is a good investment. If you do it up a bit you could easily make a five or six grand profit on it in no time.'

Nick put his half-full glass on the counter. 'Shall we head over to the restaurant?'

'Yes. I just need to pop to the ladies.'

As Jane stood in front of the mirror checking her makeup and hair, she was pleased that Nick hadn't mentioned the investigation. So far, she was just enjoying herself.

Sandra walked in.

'All right, love?'

'Yes, thanks,' Jane smiled. 'You've got a really nice pub.'

'Glad you like it. It's been hard work running it since my husband buggered off with one of the barmaids. Mind you, I'm better off without the arsehole. Is Nick taking you for dinner at the Fantail?'

'Yes. I'm looking forward to it. I've been told it's really fancy.'

'Best outside of Central London, though its prices are about the same. You and Nick been dating long?' she asked.

'We've just met, literally two days ago,' Jane replied coolly, thinking it was none of Sandra's business.

'Well, don't you go leading him up the garden path. He's one of the best is Nick. He doesn't need more heartbreak in his life.'

'Is there something I should know?' Jane asked.

Sandra sighed. 'Sorry if it seems like I'm intruding, love, but . . .'

'My name is Jane,' she interrupted.

'I've known Nick for years, Jane. You could say I've got a bit of a soft spot for him – in a maternal way, that is. He got married about a year and a half ago, then two weeks later his missus ran off with his best man. Turned out they'd being having an affair for a long time, but the bitch didn't have the guts to tell him.'

'God, that's awful,' Jane said. 'I didn't even know Nick had been married.'

'It gets worse, Jane. Six months later, his mum discovered she had cancer. She was dead within three weeks. I'd never seen Nick so depressed. His father was in a terrible state, too, but he had to be strong for his son's sake.'

Jane suddenly felt very uncomfortable about accepting Nick's invitation to dinner, worrying that she might have led him up the garden path.

'I've certainly got no intention of hurting Nick,' she said.

Sandra looked at her. 'Good. He likes you . . . a lot.'

'How do you know?'

'He was in here last night and told me about you.'

'What did he say?' Jane asked.

'Not much, but I could tell from the way he spoke and the look in his eye that he's got a soft spot for you.'

'Did he say what I do for a living?'

'No, but my guess is you're a copper.'

Jane was flummoxed. 'How can you tell?'

Sandra tapped the side of her nose with her forefinger. 'Being a landlady means I'm pretty good at guessing people's professions.'

'But we've never spoken until now.'

Sandra laughed. 'I'm only joking. Nick said he'd met a police lady who he really liked. Believe me, if your relationship does develop, you won't find a nicer or kinder man to be with.'

'Thanks for telling me about the tragedy in his life. I better get going or he'll be wondering where I've got to.'

'Take care, Jane. I've a feeling I might be seeing more of you.'

'Everything good?' Nick asked when she got back to the bar.

'Fine, thanks. I was just chatting to Sandra. She's quite a character.'

'She certainly is. Any nonsense and you're out the door with her foot up your backside.'

As they were leaving the pub, the band started playing their opening number, 'Crazy Little Thing Called Love' by Queen.

*   *   *

The maître d' of the Fantail looked stylish in a three-piece grey pinstripe suit. 'Good evening, Mr Durham. It's been a while since we've had the pleasure of your company.' He had a pronounced French accent.

'I only come here on special occasions,' Nick replied, smiling at Jane.

'Then we will do our best to make it a memorable evening for you and madame,' said the maître d'.

As they crossed the floor, Jane admired the sophisticated ambience of the 1920s Art Deco design of the room, with its bold geometric shapes and bright colours.

The maître d' led them to a table for two in the corner of the room, draped with a pristine white linen tablecloth.

He pulled out Jane's chair, picked up her napkin, wafted it open and gently placed it on her lap. He handed them each a menu and asked Nick if he would like to see the wine list or have an aperitif first. They decided just to have wine and the maître d' said the sommelier would be with them shortly.

'Are you hungry?' Nick asked.

'Absolutely starving. All I've had all day is a bowl of cereal and a bacon sandwich,' Jane said, opening the menu and looking at the starters. She gasped with surprise, realising a three-course meal in the station canteen would cost less. She fancied a steak but couldn't believe the price of that either.

The sommelier handed Nick the wine list.

'Would you like some champagne?' Nick asked.

Jane couldn't begin to imagine what a bottle would cost. 'I'd love a glass, thank you,' she replied.

'We'll have a bottle of Dom Perignon, please,' Nick told the sommelier. 'Please, Jane, have whatever you want,' he said. 'I want you to enjoy yourself.'

'What are you having?' she asked, thinking she would have the same or else something of a similar price.

'Do you like steak?'

'It's what I was thinking of having,' she admitted.

'How about the chateaubriand for two, roasted chateau potatoes and grilled asparagus?'

'That sounds good to me.'

'I'll ask for a red wine sauce on the side. Do you want a starter?'

'I don't think I'd be able to eat my main course if I had one,' Jane laughed.

Nick placed their order with a waiter. The sommelier, who was pouring the champagne, recommended Cabernet Sauvignon with the steak.

'Do you have family in London?' Nick asked.

Jane nodded. 'My parents are in Maida Vale. My sister Pam lives in Shepherd's Bush with her husband and two young sons.'

'Do you get to see your family much?'

'Not really. My mum does a Sunday lunch for us all every so often, and I keep in touch by phone. What about you ... any brothers or sisters?' she asked.

'I'm an only child. My mother died of cancer last year, so there's just me and my dad now.'

'I'm sorry, it must have been a terrible time for you both.'

'It was. Stupidly, we bottled up our grief as we felt we had to be strong for each other. Coping with her death hasn't been easy, but at least we now talk about fond memories with a smile. I do worry about my father, though, what with his dodgy heart and this coffin business. It was hard persuading him to retire after Mum's death. He said work kept him occupied, so I realised I had to find something else to keep him busy, which wasn't easy as he's pretty stubborn at times.'

'What did you find to occupy him?'

'A golden retriever puppy, which he absolutely adores. Taking her for long walks keeps him fit.' Since Nick had opened the conversation about his father, Jane took the opportunity to ask some questions about him.

'Is his dog called Bella?'

'Yes.'

'And does he live in the old convent?'

'Yes, in what used to be the chapel. How did you know?' Nick asked.

'My colleague and I couldn't find the building site the other morning. We asked a man who was walking a dog called Bella. Now I know why I thought you looked so familiar yesterday. You're the spitting image of your father.'

'Do I look that old?' he frowned.

'You know what I mean,' she grinned. 'Funnily enough, I also saw him and Bella yesterday morning. He was talking to the site foreman, Lee Holland.'

'No doubt he was badgering Lee about the coffin and what was happening with the site. I told my dad not to get involved because it's not good for his health, but he just can't help himself.'

'Does Lee know about his heart condition?'

'Yes, they're old friends. Lee worked with my dad on building sites long before he started his own company. I kind of knew Lee would speak to my father before me, even though I've asked him not to involve dad in any problems. The two of them are as thick as thieves at times. That said, Lee's been like a rock for Dad since Mum died.'

Jane wondered if she'd got it all wrong about Thomas Durham and Lee Holland. Perhaps their strange behaviour could simply be due to Thomas's ill health, and the fact that they didn't want Nick to know they'd been discussing the discovery of the coffin.

'Hopefully, it will all be sorted in the next few days and the building work can start again,' Jane said.

'That would be good,' he said. 'Anyway, enough about work. What do you like to do when you're not investigating mysterious coffins?'

Jane laughed. 'As I said, I'm studying for the inspectors' exam, so that takes up a lot of my spare time.'

'Not too much I hope,' he said.

'I'm sure I can take some time off from studying,' she said.

'Do you like cycling? I go for a cycle in the countryside and have a pub lunch now and again. I've got a spare lady's bike in my garage if you fancy an outing sometime.'

'That would be nice. I haven't been on a bike since I was a youngster,' Jane said.

The waitress served their chateaubriand and the sommelier brought over the wine and poured two glasses. He put the bottle down on the table.

'The maître d' said the wine is with compliments of the house, Mr Durham.'

Nick smiled. 'Please thank him for me. It's very much appreciated.'

Jane cut into her steak. 'It's the best I've ever tasted. It literally melts in your mouth,' she said.

'Try a bit of the red wine sauce,' Nick said.

Jane poured a small bit on the side of her plate and dipped a piece of steak in it. Her face lit up as she ate it. 'I think I've just died and gone to heaven,' she said, enjoying the dark smokiness, the sweetness, and the acidity from the wine. She poured some more on her plate and realised what she'd just said. 'I'm sorry, that was a thoughtless remark.'

He shook his head. 'Don't be silly. You're enjoying yourself and that's what matters to me. Tell me the layout of your house so I've got an idea of it before I come round tomorrow.'

'It's pretty straightforward, really. You've seen the lounge, and there's a door leading to the dining room and the kitchen. There's also a door from the kitchen into the hallway. Upstairs, there's the master bedroom at the front, small double at the back, and a bathroom at the top of the stairs.'

Nick nodded, picturing the layout in his head. 'As an off-the-cuff suggestion, I'd remove the wall between the living and dining rooms to open it up and give you a bit more space.'

'Would that be expensive?'

'Not really. You'd need to put a up a lintel to support the load above it if you take out the wall. You could use a wooden lintel which is cheaper than a steel one. Once that's done, it's just a case of making good with plaster and paint or wallpaper.'

'Sounds like a good idea,' Jane said, trying to imagine it.

'I'd need to see your kitchen before coming up with any ideas about that. But if you go open plan, you can get rid of the door to the kitchen in the hallway. Then there would be enough room to make a recess in the kitchen, into which you could fit a large fridge freezer with space for a wine rack above. It'd be really cheap and easy to do with some plasterboard.'

'That's a brilliant idea.'

'I'll draw up some rough sketches for you tomorrow and then do some proper plans. If you decide to go ahead, I can organise everything for you at cost price. I reckon the work would only take two or three weeks tops.'

'I'll have to take a loan out to pay for it . . . if the bank will give me one.'

'I'll loan you the money. You can pay me back as and when. No interest.'

'It's very kind of you to offer, Nick, but I couldn't . . .'

'I wouldn't offer if I didn't want to. And with your permission, I could use photographs of the completed job as an advertisement for my designs for smaller houses. You'd be doing me a favour.'

'Can I think about it?'

'Of course, there's no rush.'

The sommelier topped up their wine glasses and they didn't talk much as they concentrated on their food.

'Would you like a dessert?' Nick asked.

'I'm really full,' Jane said.

'What about a sorbet? It's a refreshing palate cleanser – just what you need after a big meal.'

'Can we share one?'

'Of course.' Nick got the waiter's attention and ordered one sorbet, with an extra bowl and spoon.

After the waitress had served the sorbet, Nick scooped half of it into the other bowl then picked up the champagne.

'Shame to let it go to waste,' he said, pouring it over the sorbet. 'It actually tastes really nice.'

Jane noticed the sommelier frowning as he watched Nick, barely able to disguise his disapproval. She and Nick giggled like a pair of schoolkids. Jane tried a spoonful. Nick was right: it was wonderful.

'Would you like a coffee or a liqueur?' Nick asked, finishing his sorbet.

'I'm fine, thanks.'

'I'll get the bill and ask the maître d' to call a taxi for you,' Nick said with a sigh, as if he was sad their evening had come to an end.

'I don't want to go home yet,' Jane said. 'I thought we might go back to the pub, listen to the band, and have a dance . . . if you want to.'

Nick's eyes lit up. 'I'd love to. But I have to warn you . . . I'm no John Travolta.'

'That's probably because everyone mistakes you for Robert Redford,' she said, remembering his quip when they'd first met.

'You said Woody Allen yesterday,' he retorted.

'I know, but it's also a woman's prerogative to change her mind.'

CHAPTER SIXTEEN

There was a lively energy in The Olde White Lion as the band belted out The Rolling Stones' 'Brown Sugar', and the flashing disco lights made the cigarette smoke look like a mass of swirling rainbows. The pub was packed and the dance floor full as the lead singer encouraged everyone to join in the chorus. '*Brown sugar . . . how come you taste so good?*' rang out as people sang at the tops of their voices.

'Is it always this busy on a Saturday night?' Jane asked, raising her voice above the music.

'Yes, thanks mostly to the band. If it's too noisy for you, we can go down the road to a quieter pub.'

'It's fine, I like it here,' she said.

'What would you like to drink?' Nick asked, getting his wallet out.

'Please, let me get the drinks . . . and I won't take no for an answer,' she said firmly.

'In that case, I'll have a Bacardi and Coke. I just need to nip to the gents.'

Sandra was still behind the bar. Jane ordered Nick's drink and a glass of white wine for herself.

'Did you have a nice meal?' Sandra asked.

'It was the best food I've ever tasted,' Jane said. 'And Nick is great company.'

'I hope your friendship blossoms into something more for both of you,' Sandra smiled.

'So do I,' Jane replied without thinking, realising how attracted she felt to him. She was pretty sure Nick felt the same way about her.

Jane paid for the drinks and carried them over to a small table near the dance floor. The band was playing 'London's Calling' by The Clash as Nick returned from the gents.

'Is this your sort of music?' Nick asked.

'I like all sorts really,' Jane said. 'But I do like heavy rock, like Led Zeppelin and Deep Purple. I saw Janis Joplin live at the—'

'Royal Albert Hall, twenty-first of April 1969. It was her one and only UK performance,' Nick interrupted.

'You were there as well?' Jane asked, hoping he had been.

'I certainly was,' he said. 'I remember everybody was up and dancing, which was unbelievable in a posh place like the Albert Hall. It was a night I'll never forget.'

Jane grinned. 'Same here. She put her heart and soul into every song. That raw voice she had was incredibly emotional.'

'I know just what you mean,' Nick said. 'But the highlight of the night for me was when she sang "Piece of My Heart".'

'Now that song did rip your heart out,' Jane agreed. 'It made me cry back then, and still does when I hear it now.'

'Can you remember who the support band was?' Nick asked.

'Yes,' she replied.

'Well, who was it, then?' Nick asked.

'It was Yes,' she replied, knowing she was right.

'I know you said yes, but who was it?'

'It was the band called Yes!'

Nick laughed. 'You fell for that one, didn't you?'

Jane raised her eyebrows and shook her head, '*Yes*, I did. Now it's my turn.' She walked around the dance floor and spoke to the band's bass guitarist.

'What you up to?' he asked Jane warily when she returned.

'All I can say is . . . *there is something going down and I can feel it*,' Jane replied with a grin.

Nick racked his brain to associate what she said with a song. The answer came when the lead singer made an announcement.

'Ladies and gentlemen, this next song by the Bee Gees is especially for Nick, who's also a big John Travolta fan.'

As the band started playing 'Night Fever', the audience let out a loud cheer and more couples got on the dance floor.

Jane grabbed Nick's hand. 'Come on, time to show me how you strut your stuff,' she said.

'Go on, snake hips!' Sandra shouted to Nick from behind the bar.

Nick laughed. 'I'll never be allowed back in here again after this.'

Some people formed a line and started the Brooklyn hustle dance associated with the film *Saturday Night Fever*. They moved in unison, forward and back, doing a three-step turn and clap, then moving their right hands diagonally across their bodies, pointing first to the floor and then to the ceiling.

Nick and Jane danced to one side.

'Do you want to join in?' Jane asked.

'I'll give it a go,' he said, and they moved into the line.

Jane was surprised at how good a dancer Nick was. When the song was over, Nick held Jane's hand and walked her back to their table.

'You all wanna have some more party fun?' the lead singer shouted and a loud chorus of 'yeahs' filled the air. 'OK, let's get down with a little number by The Gap Band. *Say oops upside your head, say oops upside your head . . .*'

There was another loud roar of approval and Nick took hold of Jane's hand.

'Come on, that's the rowing boat song,' he said, as people sat splay-legged on the dance floor behind each another, moving their hands and torsos backwards and forwards, as if rowing a boat, then swaying from side to side slapping the floor twice on each side.

'I don't really want to get my dress all dirty on the dance floor,' Jane said.

Nick took off his jacket. 'Sir Walter Raleigh to your rescue.'

'I can't sit on your nice jacket.'

'Yes, you can,' he said, pulling her up from her chair.

As Nick sat on the floor, his legs either side of Jane, he eased his body forward. As he pressed against her, she felt an unexpected tingle of sexual arousal. She didn't think he was doing it deliberately but wouldn't have minded if he was.

When the song was over, Nick put out his hand. Jane gripped it tightly and he pulled her up quickly from the floor, she stepped forward, put her arms around his neck and kissed him on the cheek.

'That was great fun. I can't remember the last time I enjoyed myself so much.' She hugged him.

He pulled her closer. 'You're an amazing woman, Jane. I've had a great time, too.'

His soft breath on her ear and the sweet smell of his aftershave sent another sensuous tingle through her body. She held his hand as they left the dance floor.

'Do you want to stay a bit longer.'

'I don't mind,' she said. 'It's up to you.'

'Let me know when you want to leave then, and I'll get Sandra to call a cab for you.'

'I hope you're not thinking of driving home.'

'No way. I only live over the road. I can pick up my car tomorrow.'

'I can walk with you and get a cab from yours . . . if that's OK with you.'

He looked surprised. 'Are you sure?'

'Yes. The truth is, I'd like to see your place. Is it a house you designed and built?'

'No. It was built in the 1930s. My mum and dad used to live there until they moved into the chapel and rented it out. I rented a place locally, then when I was thirty, Dad said I could move in. I've modernised the interior, though.'

'Shall we go then?'

As they left the pub the cold fresh air hit Jane making her feel light-headed. She stopped, took a deep breath and slowly exhaled.

'Are you OK?' Nick asked, looking concerned.

'Fine thanks . . . just a rush of blood to the head.'

'You had me worried there.' He smiled and held her hand.

'The houses are big around here,' she remarked as they walked to Nick's house.

'Farnborough Park is a private estate,' he told her. 'Some of the houses are new-builds and others are Victorian. Many of them were built in the Twenties and Thirties.'

'Did you design any of them?'

'A few of the newer ones. Nearly there . . . it's just round the corner.'

As they walked onto the large crazy-paved driveway, Jane was surprised at the size of the elegant red-brick house, which was three times as big as hers.

'It's lovely house,' she said. She noticed a green Range Rover parked in front of the garage to her left.

'Is your father here?' she asked, thinking it might be his car.

'No, that's my car. I use it for work. It's more suitable for muddy building sites than the Jag.'

Nick opened the front door and switched on the chandelier light, revealing a hallway with cream-coloured walls and a hard-wood floor. Nick took Jane's coat and hung it in a cupboard under the stairs.

'Come on through to the kitchen. There's a bathroom just there on the left if you need it.'

The large open-plan kitchen-diner had a terracotta tiled floor and oak cabinets. The centre island had a stainless-steel sink and a four-ring electric hob with an extractor above. The dining table, by the sliding patio doors, was made of golden oak, with a set of six matching chairs with black leather seats.

'I love your kitchen. There's so much workspace . . . and even a dishwasher!'

'I redesigned it a couple of years ago, but I didn't build it. Originally there was a wall between the dining area and the kitchen,' Nick said as he opened the fridge and removed a bottle of Chablis.

'Would you like a glass of wine or a coffee perhaps.'

'A small glass would be nice, thanks.'

Nick poured some Chablis into two crystal wine glasses and handed one to Jane.

'What's that thing above the cooker?' she asked.

'It's a microwave oven. It uses tiny, electromagnetic waves to cook food more evenly. They say it can cook a joint of meat six times faster than a conventional oven. I haven't really used it much yet.'

Jane peered through the patio doors. 'Is that a conservatory you've got in the garden?'

Nick flicked some switches next to the patio door, lighting up the conservatory and revealing a swimming pool inside it, with a gentle wave of steam fog floating above the water.

Jane was astonished. 'Blimey, this place is full of surprises. I'd have brought my swimsuit if I'd known,' she joked.

'Actually, I've got one in the utility room if you fancy a dip. My friend's wife left it behind the other week. She's about the same size as you, I reckon.'

'Go on then,' she said. 'But only if you're getting in as well.'

Nick fetched the swimsuit from the utility room and showed Jane upstairs to his bedroom, which seemed bigger than her living room, though she wondered if the floor-to-ceiling mirrored wardrobe doors made the room look bigger than it actually was. She liked the minimal décor of the geometrically shaped room, with its grey side cabinets, steel side lamps and multicoloured abstract oil painting above the king-size bed.

Nick opened the door to the en suite bathroom, grabbed his dressing gown and handed it to Jane. 'I'll get changed in the spare room, grab some towels then see you downstairs.'

Jane put the red V-neck shoulder strap swimsuit on and looked in the mirror. It was a tight fit, accentuating her breasts and hips, and she thought it looked quite sexy. She put on Nick's dressing gown and went downstairs.

Nick was sitting in his swimming trunks at the dining table looking through a black leather cassette case.

'Do you like Dire Straits?'

'Love them. Mark Knopfler is such a brilliant guitarist.'

Nick tucked the cassette into the waistband of his trunks, then topped up their wine glasses. She followed him into the utility room and through a door that led to the conservatory swimming pool. He put the glasses down on a small plastic table between two sun-loungers, then put the tape in the cassette player. The first track was 'Tunnel of Love', a song about a boy meeting a girl, liking her, but not wanting to spoil things by getting too deep. It suddenly seemed very appropriate.

As Jane removed the dressing gown and put it on the lounger, Nick looked up with a stunned expression.

'It's a bit small, isn't it?' she said awkwardly.

'Not at all. It fits you perfectly.'

As they walked along the side of the pool, Jane couldn't resist playfully nudging Nick as if she was going to knock him in the water. As he deliberately fell sideways towards the water, Nick grabbed her wrist and pulled her in with him. Jane shrieked as they fell into the warm water together. Surfacing, Jane clasped her hands around Nick's neck as he swam to the shallow end, where he could stand with his head and shoulders above the water. They gazed into each other's eyes as Nick pulled her close, enveloping her in a tight embrace. The long passionate kiss that followed was intoxicating, a magical moment of surrender that neither of them had felt before.

'Do you want to go upstairs?' Jane asked.

'It's been a long time since I've made love to a woman,' Nick said nervously.

'Then we'll have to take things slowly,' she replied.

CHAPTER SEVENTEEN

Jane woke early. Blurry-eyed and unaccustomed to the surroundings, for a moment she wondered where she was. But feeling Nick's warm breath soft on her neck, and his arm around her waist, she felt reassured, knowing she was safe and where she wanted to be. From the intensity of her emotions, Jane knew, even though she had been a bit drunk, that this was more than a casual one-night stand. From the moment they had undressed and got into bed, Nick had made her feel wanted and loved, with gentle foreplay and tender kisses, stimulating her beyond her wildest imagination. Jane had reciprocated, and drawn together like two magnets, they made passionate love, their emotions expressed without words and their eyes speaking the unsaid.

Jane slowly rolled over and gazed into Nick's eyes.

'I'm so lucky to have you next to me,' he said.

'Me too,' she replied, feeling an adrenaline rush as they kissed.

'Shall we have some breakfast, then I'll take you home and we can discuss some interior design ideas?' he said as they pulled apart.

'I'd rather just spend the day in bed with you,' she smiled.

Nick tapped her nose. 'I thought you were meeting a girlfriend for lunch?'

'I'll call her and make an excuse. I don't think she'll be too bothered.'

'Well, it's up to you.'

'Her number is at my house, so I'll have to ring her from there.'

'Do you want to use the bathroom, while I make some bacon, eggs and coffee?' Nick asked.

Jane grabbed his hand. 'Can we make love again first?'

* * *

Later, Nick picked up his car from the Fantail car park and let Jane drive it to her house. Taking a longer route this time, she felt more relaxed and better able to enjoy the experience.

'I should have the Ferrari up and running in a few weeks, and you can have a go behind the wheel,' Nick said.

'That would be great.' Jane smiled, liking the fact he wanted to see more of her, though she worried that rushing things too quickly might spoil everything. *Only time will tell*, she thought to herself, hoping that this time it would last.

As soon as she got home, Jane went upstairs to change and phone Sam Pullen, while Nick measured the wall between the dining and living rooms and made notes in a drawing book.

'Hi, Sam, it's Jane. Something has come up and I can't make lunch at The Bull's Head today,' she said, feeling bad about lying.

'No problem,' Sam said. 'To be honest, I'm feeling knackered after a late night.'

'Did you get called out to a crime scene?'

Sam laughed. 'No, I was out on a date with Lloyd and had a bit too much to drink, then one thing led to another and . . . well, I won't go into details.'

Jane was a bit taken aback by how frank Sam was being. 'You mean Lloyd Johnson, the lab sergeant?'

'Why? Have you slept with him as well?'

'*No!* Never! We're just good friends.'

'So, is there anyone in your life, Jane?' Sam asked.

'Not at the moment . . . but I'm working on it,' she said tentatively.

'It's not that handsome Father Chris, is it?' Sam asked.

'No, it isn't,' she said firmly. 'He's a priest, Sam, for goodness' sake.'

'I was only joking, Jane. No need to be so touchy.'

'Sorry, I had a late night catching up on my paperwork and didn't sleep too well.'

Sam asked if there had been any developments in the investigation. Jane told her about Bishop Meade making inquiries with the archivist and how everything had pretty much come to a standstill.

'Hopefully, we'll know who she is by Tuesday at the latest and DCS Barnes will form a squad. Then we can move forward quickly.'

'You'll solve it, Jane. Lloyd said you're one of the most dogged and lateral-thinking detectives he's come across. If you fancy going out next weekend, let me know. And get some rest, you grumpy mare,' she laughed, and Jane couldn't help joining in.

Although Sam Pullen could be a bit direct and over the top, Jane liked her and felt they shared a bond. They were both strong-willed and determined to prove themselves as good as any man at their jobs.

Jane went into the living room. The door to the dining room was open and she could see Nick looking at one of the building plans, that she'd forgotten to put away. She bit her lip, wondering how he would react.

'I've cancelled my lunch with Sam Pullen. She was fine about it,' she said.

He looked up. 'Great. We could go out for lunch and a drive in the countryside . . . if you want to?'

'I'd love to. Sorry about the mess. My DI wanted me to look through a load of plans and documents we got from the Bromley planning department,' Jane said in a casual tone.

'What for?'

'Just to see if there's anything about the land being consecrated.'

'I can help you if you want . . .'

'It's all right. I'll do it tonight. Besides, this is my day off and I'm entitled to enjoy it.'

'There is something interesting here,' he said, pointing to some markings on one of the plans.

Jane moved closer. It was the original plan of the convent dated 1851 and the markings were two parallel lines of dashes running from the convent chapel to the buildings that had been destroyed by fire.

'Is it a pathway of some sort?' Jane asked.

'I'm not sure, but I think it might be a tunnel, running from the chapel to the old outbuildings.'

'Really?' Jane replied, her curiosity piqued.

'There's a cellar in the chapel with a six-foot-long cavern off it, which my father uses for storing his wine. I think the cavern might once have been part of this tunnel but was bricked up at some point.' Nick looked at the 1965 plan for his father's original development of the convent. 'There are no similar markings on here for a tunnel.'

'Why would that be?'

'A number of reasons. The architect may not have looked at the original plans, or he might have thought the tunnel had been filled in, or decided it wasn't relevant to my dad's development.'

Jane realised the outbuildings weren't far from where the coffin had been discovered and wondered if the tunnel could have been used to secretly move the nun's body outside the convent. If it had been, common sense told her that two or more people had been involved in moving it, sometime after the murder but probably before Thomas Durham bought the land. There was a part of Jane that really wanted to tell Nick the nun had been murdered. But she knew it was best not to say anything until DCS Barnes decided to go public with the details. She just hoped Nick would be understanding when he learned the truth.

Jane's phone rang, and she picked it up.

'Hi, sarge. It's DC Lyons, early turn CID at Bromley. Sorry to bother you on your day off.'

'That's OK. What's the problem, Matt?'

'Jack, the mortuary technician at Queen Mary's, rang. He was a bit worried about an incident that occurred yesterday concerning the dead nun. I tried phoning Boony but there was no answer, so I thought I'd better phone you.'

'What's happened, Matt?' she asked, wishing he'd get to the point so she could go out with Nick.

'I don't know the full details. Jack said he was doing a suicide post-mortem with Prof Martin when a priest turned up and said he'd come to say a prayer for the nun. Jack asked him who he was, and he said the bishop had sent him.'

'Is that it?' Jane asked.

'Pretty much. Jack also said he thought the priest was behaving a bit oddly when he said his prayer for the nun. Anyway, he left his home number if you want to ring him for more details.'

'Fire away,' Jane said, picking up the pen and notepad next to the phone.

After the call, she was in two minds about phoning Jack to get more details, though she suspected it was nothing to be concerned about as Bishop Meade didn't know Father Chris had already said a prayer for the nun.

'Everything all right?' Nick asked as he entered the living room.

'Yes, just one of the detectives from the office passing on a message.'

'Do you have to go to work?' he asked with a frown.

'It's nothing that can't wait until tomorrow. Right, let's get on the road.' Jane smiled, eager to drive the Jag again.

'Do you fancy popping over to my dad's and having a look around the chapel? You might find it interesting.'

'I thought you didn't want to worry him, especially with his heart problem?' she said.

'To be honest, I'm curious about the tunnel. I don't think my dad even knows about it. He'd probably find it quite interesting.'

Jane knew she'd need to see the cellar at some point and find out if a tunnel did actually exist. 'Do you want to ring first in case he's out?

'I've got my own set of keys. He won't mind me showing you around if he's not there.'

'Can I drive again?' Jane asked with a grin.

Nick threw her the keys. 'We'll take her on the A20 first, then you can really give it some welly.'

*   *   *

As Jane drove up to the old convent, Nick said his father's car was outside so he should be in. Once inside the main entrance hall, Nick used his key to open one of the arched wooden double doors to the chapel and stuck his head in.

'Hi, Dad, you in? It's me, Nick,' he called out, but there was no answer.

Walking into the chapel, Jane was astounded by the interior. Decorative stone carved arches and pillars acted as room dividers alongside the original timber panelling, stained-glass windows and vaulted ceilings. The light and airy open-plan sitting-dining room had a stone fireplace with a wood-burning stove, and the dining area led to a luxuriously fitted kitchen.

'This is absolutely stunning. I've never seen a place like it. It's like stepping back in time yet being in the future,' Jane said.

Nick showed her round the rest of the house and the more she saw the more she fell in love with it.

'Did you design this as well?'

'I'd like to say yes, but I'd be lying. The layout was the original architect's idea, but I redesigned the interior about six years ago.'

'How do you come up with such wonderful and creative ideas?

He shrugged. 'I like to think big and bold. It's always been about a sense of scale for me. There's no particular "Nick Durham" look. Every house and interior design is different and individual to the client paying for it. Satisfying them is what it's all about, regardless of what it takes. If you care about your dream enough, you'll find a solution.'

'Well, this would certainly be my dream home,' she said. She noticed the painting of an attractive, smiling, blonde woman in her late fifties above the fireplace. 'Is that your mother?'

He nodded. 'I had a painter do it from one of the last photographs of her.'

'She's beautiful. And you have her blue eyes.'

He looked away. 'Would you like to see the cellar?'

Jane nodded. She could tell he still found it difficult to talk about the loss of his mother.

'Be careful on the spiral stairs. The stonework can get quite slippy this time of year, so use the rope rail,' he said, flicking on the light switch.

As she stepped carefully down into to the dank stone chamber, Jane was glad she'd worn her brown knee-length winter boots, as the rubber soles had a good grip on them. Nick was wearing soft leather-soled shoes and would have gone flying halfway down if he hadn't grabbed the handrail.

'It's a lot bigger down here than I imagined,' Jane said.

He nodded. 'There are some old empty stone crypts right at the back. My dad told me they used to use it as a cool storage place for nuns' bodies before their funeral.'

Jane realised it was likely empty coffins had also been stored in the cellar. She felt a cold shiver run through her body as she wondered if this could be the very place the nun had been murdered. She suddenly felt something touching her backside and let out a yelp. She saw Nick smile and was about to give him a mouthful when she saw the dog.

'Naughty girl, Bella. You mustn't jump on Jane like that,' Nick said as he bent down and stroked the dog.

'Everything all right down there?' a voice shouted from the stairwell.

'Yeah. It's just me, Dad.'

'You had me worried there, son . . . anyone'd think you'd just seen a bloody ghost,' Thomas Durham said, descending the stairs.

Nick winced as he looked at Jane and whispered, 'Sorry, sometimes he doesn't think before he speaks.'

Jane's heart was still racing, but she could see the funny side. 'That really scared the crap out of me,' she whispered back as she saw Thomas approach.

'I believe you two have already met,' Nick said.

Thomas nodded. 'Detective Sergeant Tennison, as I recall.'

'Yes, sir. Pleased to meet you . . . again.' Jane smiled and they shook hands.

'So, what brings you to my house?' he asked.

'She's not here in a formal capacity, Dad. We went for dinner last night and I offered to show Jane around the chapel.'

'It's beautiful house, Mr Durham,' Jane said.

'Please call me Thomas or Tom. Yes, it's my own bit of heaven . . . thanks to Nick's interior design talents. It was a bit drab before he got to work on it.'

Nick told his father about the 1851 plans of the convent and the markings of what he thought might be a tunnel from the cellar to the outbuildings.

Thomas looked thoughtful. 'Although we refer to it as a cellar now, most of what you see down here was in fact a crypt.' He walked towards the wine storage area. 'This end of the tunnel was already blocked off when I bought the convent.' He turned on a light switch.

Jane could see the red brick wall at the end of the six-foot-long wine cellar.

'This area was already a wine cellar,' Thomas continued. 'The racks are the original ones, and the bottles at the far end were already down here. Whether they were used for communion or the nuns' personal consumption, I don't know. I did try one once, but it tasted like vinegar. I've kept them as a reminder of the past.'

'I see you still haven't bothered to get this wall repaired,' Nick said. He looked at Jane. 'Whoever originally built this was a crap bricklayer. It's uneven and the cement mix is so poor it's crumbling away.' Nick rubbed his hand against the bricks, then tapped with his knuckle, causing some of the cement to crumble onto the floor. 'You need to get this looked at, Dad, before it falls down.'

'I know, son. I'll get one of the brickies on the site to have a look at it.'

Nick shook his head. 'You've said that before. I'll speak to Lee tomorrow and ask him to have a look; that way, I know it will get done.'

Thomas frowned. 'I'm not totally incapable. I'll speak to him myself, thank you,' he snapped.

Jane wasn't sure if he was agitated because Nick had mentioned Lee's name in front of her, or if this was the normal way they talked to each other.

'It's quite a spooky place,' Jane said. 'Nick mentioned the bodies of the dead nuns were kept down here,' she added, to see what Thomas might add.

'Apparently so,' he said. 'I was told they would hold an all-night prayer vigil down here for the departed on the evening before the funeral. I'm glad to say there were no bodies or coffins left behind when I bought the place.'

'Some of his friends think it might be haunted,' Nick grinned.

Thomas laughed. 'The only ghostly occurrence down here has been the disappearance of some of my more expensive wines, which bizarrely occurs whenever Nick visits me,' he said.

'I get the blame for everything, Jane ... even the ghosts,' Nick replied with a smile. He turned to his father. 'The tunnel on the map appeared to extend to the burnt-out buildings.' Jane was relieved he'd brought it up, so she didn't have to.

Thomas nodded. 'It did, son, but our survey at the time revealed the fire caused the collapse of the tunnel under the outbuildings.

That's why the current build is well away from the old buildings, which will be turned into a garden and a car park.'

If that was true, Jane realised, then if the nun's body had been moved using the tunnel, it must have been before the fire, so it must have been done by someone connected with the convent.

'Do you like red wine and cheese, Jane?' Thomas asked.

'Yes,' she said.

He picked a bottle from the rack and held it out. 'Would you like to try a '61 Médoc with some camembert and English cheddar?'

'Thank you, that would be lovely,' she replied, sensing he was trying to impress her.

They walked up the stairs to the kitchen, and Thomas opened the wine, sniffed it, then poured it into a glass decanter and left it to breathe. He then prepared the cheese and cut some slices of freshly baked brown bread. 'I made this myself,' he said proudly. He presented the bread and cheese on a large wooden board with a slicer, and handed out side plates, side knives and napkins. Placing three crystal wine glasses on the kitchen breakfast bar, Thomas poured the wine.

'The Médoc is arguably the most famous red wine district in the world, home to many of the greatest and most renowned names of Bordeaux. Please follow my lead, Jane.' He picked up his glass by the stem and gently swirled the wine, before sniffing it.

Nick sighed. 'I must have seen and heard this a thousand times.'

Jane whacked him on the arm. 'Don't be so rude to your father,' she said.

Thomas smiled and continued. 'With few exceptions, the region produces only red wine, and no white wine has the right to be called Médoc.' He took a sip, let it linger on his palate, then swallowed. 'Nectar of the gods,' he beamed.

Jane raised her glass. 'Cheers.'

Jane thought the cheese went well with the wine and the home-made bread was delightful. Thomas asked her about the site and when they'd be able to reopen. Jane repeated everything she'd told Nick. 'The site might be able to open again within the next few days, but the final decision is up to my DCS.'

Thomas frowned. 'I understand the decision to reopen the site is not yours to make. However, when I purchased the old convent, I had my solicitors go over everything with a fine-tooth comb. They reassured me the buildings and land had been deconsecrated.'

Jane wondered if he was telling the truth. 'Can you remember who carried out the deconsecration?'

'I don't know. I was told it took place after the nuns moved out and before the convent was put up for sale, which was nearly two years before I actually bought it.'

'Did the diocese oversee the sale?'

'Yes, a bishop and their solicitors did.'

'Can you recall who it was? I may need to speak to him.' She doubted it was Bishop Meade, as he would probably have been a lowly priest sixteen years ago.

He shrugged. 'I can't remember his name now. Their legal department consulted with my solicitors. But the original documents should be stored at our office.'

'I had a quick look but couldn't find them,' Nick said, then looked at Jane. 'Sorry, I forgot to tell you.'

'Well, I wouldn't have thrown them away,' Thomas said, testily. 'I suppose my previous secretary might have had a clear-out when we moved to our current office a few years ago.'

Jane thought he looked agitated. 'It's OK. I got a copy of the planning documents from the Bromley planning department. I've yet to read through them all but I'm sure the answers will be in there.'

When they'd finished eating, Nick cleared the table and put the dishes and cutlery in the dishwasher.

'Please excuse me, Jane, but it's time for my afternoon nap. You are welcome to stay and have a look around.'

'Nick has already given me the tour. Thank you for your hospitality.'

'We'll be off now, Dad,' Nick said. 'I know how much you need your beauty sleep.'

'See what I have to put up with, Jane? He's always been a cheeky so-and-so. If his mother were still here, she'd put him in his place.'

'Good to see you, Dad,' Nick said, giving him a hug.

'It's been a pleasure meeting you again, Thomas,' Jane said.

He shook her hand. 'You keep him in his place, Jane – and make sure he takes you to the Ivy next time.'

Thomas followed them out to Nick's car and waved them good-bye. When they were out of sight he returned to the chapel and immediately picked up the phone. It connected after three rings.

'Lee Holland speaking.'

'You're not going to believe this. Nick is dating that Tennison policewoman.'

'What, the one who's dealing with the coffin?' Lee asked.

'Yes, that one!' Thomas barked.

'Jesus Christ, what are we going to do, Tom? We could go to prison if she finds out what happened.'

'I know that! If she interviews Archbishop Malone it could open up a whole can of worms and ruin us and the company. If you'd have done what I told you years ago with that bloody coffin we wouldn't be in this mess now!'

*   *   *

On the journey back to Chislehurst, Nick invited Jane to stay the night.

'I'd love to,' she said. 'But I've got a meeting with one of my DCs at eight, then one with my DI and DCS. I've also got to look through those bloody planning documents and type up my notes for the meetings.'

'I can help you with the planning documents.'

She smiled. 'There's no way we'd get any work done sitting in the same room together.'

'I promise I'll behave,' he said.

'It's not you I'm worried about,' she said with a grin.

'OK,' he sighed, 'I give in. Can I see you tomorrow?'

'Of course. I should be finished by five.'

'I'll do some design drawings tomorrow to give you some idea of what you could do downstairs, then bring them round in the evening.'

'I'll cook a meal for us then. But I have to warn you, I'm no Delia Smith.'

'That's OK,' he said with a grin. 'I see you more as the Fanny Cradock type, anyway.'

'In that case you can be Johnnie, and I'll boss you around,' Jane quickly retorted, making Nick laugh.

'Do you like soup?' she asked, deciding she'd have a go at Father Chris's widow's soup recipe.

'What's in it?'

'If I told you, it would spoil the surprise.'

Nick followed Jane into the house to get his drawing book. They kissed briefly and he walked back to his car. Standing at the front door, Jane saw Gerry walking around Nick's Jaguar and looking inside. She watched as the two men had a brief conversation and then Gerry got in the passenger seat.

Nick waved. 'I'm going to take your neighbour for a quick spin. See you tomorrow.'

Jane waved back as they drove off. After spending time in Nick's company and then making love with him, everything felt natural and easy between them. She knew she had strong feelings for him, which he had reciprocated. 'Could he finally be Mr Right?' she asked herself.

Jane put her house keys in the bowl next to the hallway telephone, then noticed the notepad with Jack the mortuary technician's phone number on it. She was in two minds about calling

Jack but decided it might be better to do it now, as he would probably be busy on Monday morning. She dialled the number and he answered.

'Hi, Jack. It's DS Tennison here. I was told you wanted to speak to me about another priest visiting the nun.'

'Oh yes, thanks for calling me back, sergeant. It may be something and nothing, but it was quite distressing at the time, so I thought I should let you know about it. Anyway, yesterday morning I was doing a suicide post-mortem with Professor Martin. Poor chap jumped off his balcony on the tenth floor of a tower block. He was quite a mess, I can tell you—'

Jane interrupted, sensing it was going to be a long-winded account. 'DC Lyons mentioned the bishop had sent another priest down to say a prayer for the nun. In fairness, the bishop didn't know Father Floridia had already done it, so there's actually nothing to worry about.'

'I wasn't worried, sergeant. But I thought the priest's behaviour was a bit bizarre when he was alone with the nun's body in the chapel of rest. It was very different to the way Father Floridia behaved.'

'I guess they all have different ways of praying,' Jane said, losing interest.

'I've seen many priests and vicars say a prayer for the dead at the mortuary,' Jack continued, 'but this was the first time I saw one get down on his knees and cry.'

Jane was suddenly interested again, and wanted more detail. 'And you actually witnessed this?'

'He didn't know I was watching. I forgot to close the curtain on the door window. The priest had his back to me.'

Jane picked up the pen and notepad from the phone table. 'Tell me exactly what happened.'

'What, from the moment he came in . . . or just what he did in the chapel?'

'From the start would be good, but go slowly. I need to write it all down.'

Jack said that he was in the mortuary when he heard the door buzzer. He asked who it was over the intercom and a man said he was a priest, who'd been sent by the diocesan bishop to view the body of the nun found on a building site.

'I went to the door and saw a man dressed like Father Floridia, but with a purple shirt.'

'Did he say his name?'

'No. I had no reason to doubt he was a priest and didn't ask. He sat in the waiting room while I prepared the body. When I returned, he asked if I knew how she'd died. I told him I didn't, and her death was still under investigation. He also asked if he could see the coffin as he'd need to arrange for a similar one to be provided for her reburial.'

'Did you show it to him?'

'Yes. Shouldn't I have done?'

'How did he react when he saw it?'

'He didn't say anything, but he looked shocked, then I took him to the chapel of rest to pray for her.'

'Tell me exactly what he did, Jack.'

'He stood by her, laid his hand on her chest, then shook his head from side to side. Suddenly, he fell to his knees and put his head in his hands. It seemed to me he was in a very distressed state. I felt a bit awkward watching him, so I moved away and waited for him to come out, which was about three or four minutes later.'

'So, you never actually saw him crying?'

'It was pretty clear he had been from the state of his eyes. He asked me where the toilet was. I showed him and when he came out, he'd obviously washed his face and composed himself.'

'Did he say anything?'

'No. He just left the building and got in a car.'

'What sort of car was it?'

'It was a black Ford Granada. Someone else was driving and he got in the back.'

Jane could understand Bishop Meade sending someone to the mortuary, but clearly what Jack had witnessed was most odd. Then something very worrying struck her, and she knew the questions she asked Jack mustn't be leading ones.

'Did the priest wear any jewellery?' Jane asked.

'He had a large gold cross hanging from his neck.'

'Anything on his hands?'

Jack thought about it. 'Yes, he wore a gold ring with a large round purple stone.'

Jane felt her pulse quickening. 'Can you remember which hand and which finger it was on?'

'His right hand, but not which finger. Sorry.'

'Take your time and describe the man to me, please.'

'He was about five feet six, in his fifties, with a round face, black hair and slightly balding.' He paused. 'Can I ask why you need to know all these details?'

'I can't tell you at the moment, Jack. I'm really grateful for everything you've told me, and I'd ask that you keep it between us for now.'

'My lips are sealed, sergeant.'

Jane's heart was racing as she put the phone down. The man who'd been at the mortuary seemed very different from the serene and confident man she had met two days ago, but she was now certain it was Bishop Meade.

CHAPTER EIGHTEEN

Jane had a restless night thinking about Bishop Meade, Thomas Durham and Lee Holland. She woke at six and couldn't get back to sleep, so she decided to have a shower and go to work.

Sitting in a peaceful, empty office, with a sausage sandwich and cup of tea for breakfast, she started reading through the convent planning documents.

Jane came across something of interest and immediately phoned Nick. He sounded groggy.

'You not out of bed yet?' she asked.

'I was just about to get up.'

'Pull the other one.'

'What are you doing up so early?' he asked, yawning.

'Working!' she said. 'I've just found a solicitor's document which says the convent chapel and grounds were deconsecrated by the diocese in 1964, which was just after the nuns moved out and prior to the purchase of the land by your father. I'll have to run it by my DCS first, but hopefully you might be able start digging again.'

'That's great news, Jane,' he said. 'I could kiss you all over.'

'You'll have to wait until tonight for that. Got to go.' She looked up and saw Boon, who was limping badly and had a black eye.

'What happened to you?' Jane asked.

'Essex police. One of their players deliberately kicked me in the bloody shin. I had a row with him, then he head-butted me.'

'And there was me thinking rugby was a rough game,' she said, shaking her head.

He grinned. 'It was worth it, though. The twat got sent off and we won the game three-one.' He raised his leg, struggling to sit comfortably at his desk.

'Do you really think you're fit enough to work?'

He looked offended. 'I've never gone sick because of a football injury.'

'I admire your attitude, especially as some officers go sick at the first sniff of a cold.'

'Can you do me a favour, sarge?'

'Depends what it is.'

'Would you mind nipping up to the canteen and getting me a bacon sarnie and a coffee? The first flight of stairs took forever, and my legs are killing me.'

'I thought you were fit enough to work, Boony . . .'

'I'll get it myself then,' he frowned, putting his hands on the desk to support his weight as he tried to get up.

'Sit down,' Jane said. 'I'm only joking.' She picked up her purse. 'Seeing as you're so poorly, I'll even buy it for you.'

* * *

On her way back from the canteen, Jane bumped into Stanley on the stairs.

'Morning, Stanley. Nice weekend?'

'Yeah, not bad. Yourself?'

She thought it best not to tell him about her date with Nick or her visit to Thomas Durham's house. 'Pretty boring really. Spent most of it looking through the planning documents. I also had an interesting conversation with Jack the mortuary technician.'

Stanley shook his head in disbelief. 'Do you ever actually get out and have some fun on your days off?'

'Yes, of course I do,' she said defensively. 'But there's a lot to do on this investigation, and only me and Boon working on it at the moment.'

'You know what your problem is?' he said.

Jane sighed. 'Enlighten me.'

'You're becoming job-pissed,' he said, turning to walk off.

'Don't you want to hear what Jack told me?' she called after him.

He kept walking. 'Give me five minutes to get a sandwich and coffee, then we'll talk in the office.'

* * *

Back in the office Jane spoke quietly with Boon. 'There's something that doesn't sit right with me about Thomas Durham and Lee Holland. I'm convinced they're hiding something from us, but I'm not sure what it is – especially now the original development of the land seems above board.'

He nodded. 'I thought the same, but it looks like we were wrong. Are you going to tell Stanley what you think?'

Jane shook her head. 'It's just a gut feeling with no evidence to support it. I'll leave it for now. But keep digging.'

When Stanley came back from the canteen Jane told him about the planning document revealing the land had been deconsecrated and asked if he would ask DCS Barnes if the building work could resume.

'What time is the meeting with DCS Barnes?' Boon asked, looking out of the window at the station yard.

'Ten,' Jane and Stanley replied in unison.

'Looks like he got the time wrong, then,' Boon said.

Jane and Stanley leaned over and saw a grim-faced Barnes stomping across the yard.

'He doesn't look very happy,' Jane said.

Stanley stood up and addressed the office, which was now half full. 'DCS Barnes is on his way up, so stick the food under your desks and look busy.' He marched off to his own office.

Jane looked nervously towards the door. Barnes walked in holding a newspaper. Everyone stood up, acknowledging his rank.

Barnes pointed his finger at Jane and Boon. 'You two . . . Stanley's office . . . Now!'

Jane and Boon looked at each other as they got up and headed to the door. Stanley stood as they entered his office.

Barnes threw the newspaper down on the desk. 'How the fuck did this happen?'

Stanley looked stunned as he read the headline. 'I have no idea, sir.'

Barnes picked up the newspaper and threw it at Jane.

She looked at the headline and her heart sank: MURDERED NUN'S BODY FOUND ON CONVENT BUILDING SITE. She thought of Nick reading it, knowing she'd lied to him. She wanted to make an excuse to leave the room and phone him, but she knew she couldn't.

'The article even suggests the bodies of children may be buried on the grounds!' Barnes exclaimed, looking daggers at Jane and Boon. 'Have either of you been shooting your mouth off?'

'I haven't spoken to the press,' Jane said.

'Me neither,' Boon said.

'Well, someone bloody well has!' Barnes shouted. 'If I find out one of you is lying to me, your career is over!'

Boon noticed the paper wasn't a tabloid. '*The Bromley News Shopper* is a local weekly paper, sir . . .'

'Which is exactly why I think someone from this office is the leak,' Barnes said. 'I specifically said I wanted this investigation kept quiet. If someone connected with the Church was involved in the murder, you can bet your bottom dollar they'll do their best to cover it up. We had the upper hand and now we've lost it.'

Boon looked at the paper again. 'Sir . . .'

'This had better be good, Boon,' Barnes snapped.

'This article was written by Rebecca Rogers—'

'What a brilliant observation. And there was me thinking you'd tell me something I didn't know.'

Boon felt intimidated but was determined to finish. 'She might be related to PC Rogers, the coroner's officer at Queen Mary's mortuary. He had a run-in with the coroner about his handling of the nun's case.

His home address will be on file. I could check the electoral register and see if a Rebecca Rogers is shown at the same address.'

Barnes's anger abated slightly. 'Let's hope you're right. Go and do it now.'

'Yes, sir.' Boon hurried out of the room.

'I think you may be right about the Church being involved in a cover-up, sir,' Jane said, knowing this would get Barnes's attention and hopefully divert his anger.

'And why is that?' he asked, lighting one of his Sobranie cigarettes as he sat down.

Jane told Barnes about Bishop Meade's visit to the mortuary.

'I find it hard to understand why a long-standing member of the Church, who must have dealt with hundreds of deaths, would be so distressed at the death of one nun,' she said.

'How certain are you it was Meade who went to the mortuary?' he asked.

'From the detailed description the mortuary technician gave me, it had to be him. He even wore a bishop's ring and left in a chauffeur-driven car.'

Barnes took a long puff on his cigarette and sat quietly mulling things over. Jane was worried his loathing of the Church would turn into a crusade of vengeance for his thwarted investigation into the young boy's suicide. She also knew she would have to reveal her knowledge of the tunnel between the chapel and the burnt-out buildings, but somehow not give away too much detail about Nick and how she found out about it.

'There is something else of interest I have found out about the convent,' Jane began, but was interrupted by a knock on the door.

Stanley opened it. 'We're in a meeting, DC Lyons, whatever it is it will have to wait.' Stanley started to close the door.

'There's a Bishop Meade on the phone asking to speak with DS Tennison.'

Jane looked at Barnes.

'Put the call through to Stanley's phone,' he said. 'He might not be aware of the article in the paper yet. If he does start kicking off about it, hand the phone to me and I'll deal with him.'

The phone rang and Jane picked up. Barnes leaned in close so he could hear both sides of the conversation. Jane could smell the stale smoke on his breath.

'Good morning, Bishop Meade. What can I do for you?'

'Good morning, Detective Tennison. Unfortunately, I've some bad news. I spoke with Mrs Parkin, our archivist, who informed me our diocesan archives have no records pertaining to the nuns who lived and worked at the Sisters of Mercy convent,' he said in a matter-of-fact way.

'What, none at all? Are you sure?' Jane asked.

'It would seem they were all destroyed in the fire in the convent outbuildings where they were stored.'

'Even the children's records?'

'Sadly, yes.'

'What about any priests who lived or worked at the convent?'

'Only Sisters of Mercy ever lived and worked there. On a positive note, I can tell you that the convent land and buildings were deconsecrated and a "Petition for Faculty" was granted. There were about twenty nuns' graves there, all of which were officially moved to St Luke's cemetery in Bromley before the convent was sold.'

'With regard to the fire, do you know exactly when it occurred?' she asked.

'Mrs Parkin informed me it was the summer of 1962. The fire started in the bakery and destroyed all the convent's provisions, then spread to the schoolhouse. With little food to eat, no school to teach in, and the main buildings in a state of disrepair, the convent closed and it was sold to a building developer. I should add that the convent's records would have been transferred to the archives had it not been for the fire.'

'I see. Well, thank you for your assistance, Bishop Meade,' she said.

'If there's anything else you need, please feel free to call me. I won't be in my office today, though, as I'm attending a religious conference in Cambridge this afternoon.'

Jane put the phone down.

'He's hiding something,' Barnes said, his jaw set.

Stanley wasn't so sure. 'Hiding what? There was a fire, and Jane found a council planning document confirming everything was deconsecrated.'

'I'm not doubting that,' Barnes said. 'What I find odd is he never gave his name when he went to the mortuary or told you he'd been there. Also, he never asked when the nun's body would be released for burial.'

'In fairness, he did ask me when I met him on Friday,' Jane said. 'I told him it was the coroner's decision and he'd probably want us to identify her first.'

'He's just told you the records were destroyed, and he knows the land was deconsecrated . . . so why didn't he ask you to speak with the coroner? Take it from me, there's skeletons in his cupboard,' Barnes said firmly.

Jane thought for a moment. 'It's possible his emotional distress at the mortuary wasn't grief over the death of a nun. His reaction to seeing her body could be an outpouring of self-pity and regret for something he's done or was involved in. If I'm right, then it also suggests Bishop Meade knows who she is and may be lying about the diocesan records being destroyed in the fire.'

'If he's lying, then so is the lady who looks after the archives, which on the face of it would seem unlikely,' Stanley remarked.

'Then we need to have a word with Mrs Parkin . . . without Meade knowing,' Barnes said.

'I can do that, sir,' Jane said. Barnes nodded.

Boon returned, looking pleased with himself. 'The electoral register for PC Rogers' address only showed him and Mrs Rogers living there. But I phoned Jack the mortuary technician and asked him if Rogers had a daughter. He said yes and her name was Rebecca. She's twenty-two and a junior reporter for the *News Shopper*.'

'Looks like she's trying to make a name for herself,' Stanley said.

'Good work, son,' Barnes said. 'I'd like you to pay Miss Rogers a visit. I want to know exactly what information she received. Also, tell her her father could be disciplined and possibly dismissed from the force for leaking confidential information to the press.'

'Is it worth getting her to do an article about the cross and asking former nuns and orphans at the convent to contact us?' Boon asked.

Barnes shook his head. 'The *News Shopper* is just a weekly rag. We need the mainstream tabloids and TV involved. I've already spoken with our press office. They've organised a press conference for four o'clock this afternoon at Orpington where I'll make a public appeal for assistance. I'll need blown-up photos of the cross, the coffin and the victim in the coffin.'

'The anthropologist who does facial reconstruction is making a two-dimensional drawing of the nun's face. It might be worth using it in a press appeal,' Jane chipped in.

'I want to see it first,' Barnes replied.

'Are you forming a murder squad, sir?' Boon asked hopefully.

'Yes. It'll be based at Orpington. There's a conference room we can use. Stanley, I want you to set it up today, so take two more Bromley detectives with you to help. I'll call around the division and ask them to release further staff. I want everyone at the press conference and a five thirty squad meeting after it.' He looked at Jane. 'In the meantime, you speak with Mrs Parkin and Boon with Miss Rogers.'

'Are you going to arrest Bishop Meade?' Boon asked.

Barnes shook his head. 'There's not enough evidence yet. Even if Meade admits he went to the mortuary, it doesn't prove anything. Our priority is identifying the nun and finding a connection between her and Meade. Clearly it would take at least two people to move that coffin to where it was found. That said, our only suspect at present is Bishop Meade. But we need to find substantive evidence he has lied and obstructed the investigation before arresting him.'

'I have an idea where the coffin might have come from,' Jane said. 'I was about to tell you before Bishop Meade called. Can I just nip and get a plan of the convent so I can show you?'

Barnes nodded. Jane returned quickly with the 1851 plan of the convent and laid it out on Stanley's desk as the others gathered round.

'I spoke with an architect who told me these markings are for a tunnel. As you can see, it runs from the convent chapel basement to the outbuildings.'

Barnes looked thoughtful. 'It makes sense keeping a coffin in the chapel basement . . . and the tunnel would be useful cover for moving it unnoticed.'

'Between the convent and the outbuildings are gardens, surrounded by eight-foot-high walls, which give further cover once you exit the tunnel. The coffin was found just here, which is about fifty metres away.'

'At the time, no one would have thought houses or flats would be built on the land,' Boon added.

'If you're right, Tennison, using the tunnel to move the coffin implies someone living at the convent was involved.'

'I agree, sir, but there's also the possibility it could have been a layperson who worked at the convent,' she said.

'You're right,' Barnes said, 'though I doubt there'll be any records of laypeople who worked at the convent in the fifties and sixties. That said, a press appeal might help identify and locate them.'

It was becoming obvious the task ahead of them was not going to be an easy one because of the years that had passed since the murder.

'I think it might be worth us having a look at the tunnel and taking some photographs,' Barnes said.

Boon looked at Jane. 'We met the man who lives in the chapel—'

Jane was quick to interject. 'I'll ask him if I can have a look at the basement and take some photographs.'

Barnes lit another Sobranie. 'All in all, this has been a productive meeting. Is there anything else we need to discuss for now?'

Jane raised her hand. 'Can they resume work on the building site now we know the land was deconsecrated?'

Barnes shook his head. 'I would have said yes. Unfortunately, the *News Shopper* article alleging children may be buried on the land means I can't.'

Jane knew it was pointless arguing with him. She dreaded telling Nick the bad news.

'Will you be digging up the site and dredging the lake to look for other bodies?' she asked.

'I don't know yet. We'll have to see how the inquiry develops,' Barnes replied.

Stanley, who hadn't said much, looked at Jane. 'Do you know how old the children at the orphanage were?'

'No. Why do you ask?'

'We have to consider that one of the children could have committed the murder, and the nuns and Meade covered it up.'

Barnes nodded. 'I agree. The problem is, if all the children's records were destroyed, we've no way of identifying them.'

'Not necessarily, sir,' Boon piped up. 'A man at Bromley Council told me some Catholic orphanages and children's homes are run by the Catholic Children's Society, which is based in Westminster. They may keep records of the children who were sent to the convent and where they went when they left.'

'Good thinking, Boon. Give them a call and see if they can help us.' Barnes looked at each of them in turn. 'Right, you all know what you have to do. Time is of the essence, so let's get to work.'

CHAPTER NINETEEN

Jane felt anxious walking to Nick's office, not knowing if he'd read the article in the *News Shopper*.

'Mr Durham's on the phone just now,' Judy, the office secretary, said when she saw her.

Jane ignored her and went straight to Nick's office.

Nick put his palm on the speaker. 'I'll be with you in a minute.'

Jane sat on the sofa, nervously rubbing her hands, and wondering if their relationship was going to be over before it had begun.

Nick finished his call and put the phone down. 'This is a pleasant surprise,' he said as he got up.

Jane stood up. 'There's something I've got to tell you – and I don't think you're going to like it.'

'What's wrong?' Nick asked.

Jane took a deep breath – then just blurted it out. 'The nun in the coffin was murdered. We don't know who did it. I should have told you, but I couldn't. I'm really, really sorry and don't blame you if you don't want to see me anymore . . .'

Jane was talking so quickly, Nick had difficulty in understanding what she was saying.

'Whoa, slow down, Jane,' he said, putting his hands gently on her shoulders. 'I already suspected there was more to this nun thing than you were letting on.'

She took another deep breath to calm herself. 'Why didn't you say so? I've been worried sick about how you'd react. I really thought you'd be mad with me.'

He gently squeezed her shoulders. 'I'm not going to get mad simply because you're doing your job.'

'My DCS said we were to keep it to ourselves until we had identified the nun. A journalist found out and wrote the article. She also alleged there could be the bodies of other nuns and children buried in the grounds of the convent. As a result, my DCS said you can't do any work on the site until further searches are done,' Jane said, looking forlorn.

Nick smiled. 'That's not your fault. I understand your boss's reaction. I can't say I'm happy about it, but I'm not going to argue. Is he going to dig it all up?'

'Not at the moment, but he might later . . . and dredge the lake as well. I'm sorry for any distress this may cause your father, especially with his heart condition. But obviously I couldn't say anything to him either.'

'Don't worry, I'll speak with him. I'm sure he'll understand, and we will both do anything we can to assist your investigation.'

Jane looked at her watch. 'I've got to go to the diocesan archives and make some inquiries there.'

He kissed her on the cheek. 'Don't look so worried. Losing the site is only a temporary setback, I'm sure.'

* * *

Boon pressed the intercom at the *News Shopper* offices in Petts Wood, gave his details and was let in. The receptionist asked him to take a seat while she informed Miss Rogers of his arrival.

He saw the paper with Rebecca Rogers' article on a table and read it while he waited. He thought it was a bit sensationalised, but it was obvious her father had given her a detailed account of the discovery of the coffin, post-mortem and cause of death.

'Good morning, DC Boon, I'm Becky Rogers. I take it you've come about my article?'

He looked up to see a very attractive young brunette, with permed shoulder-length hair. She was dressed fashionably in a light blue jumpsuit, which had tapered legs and shoulder pads. The tight silver belt she wore showed off her slim, shapely figure.

Boon slowly stood up and shook her hand. 'Yes. Thank you for seeing me.'

'The office is quite small, and people are constantly nattering on the phone. We could pop over to Petts Wood Square for a coffee in the café and have a chat there.'

'That would be good,' Boon replied.

'I'll just nip upstairs and get my jacket, then.'

* * *

'That's a nasty limp you've got,' Becky said as they sat down at a table. 'What happened?'

'Football injury . . . nothing serious,' he said, taking a sip of his coffee. 'I'm going to be straight with you, Becky. We know who the source was for your article. I understand why you wrote it, but your father should not have released confidential information to you. He's put himself in a position where he could be disciplined and even dismissed from the force.'

She looked shocked. 'Is it that serious?'

'Yes. You were just doing your job, so you're not in any trouble. But my DCS is not happy. He didn't want to go to press until we'd identified the body.'

Becky looked concerned. 'My dad didn't actually tell me. I overheard him speaking to my mother. I assumed the police were about to release the information when I wrote the article.'

Boon suspected she was lying to protect her father, which was understandable. 'I'm not here to have a go at you,' he said. 'What I need to know is, whether or not you are willing to assist the investigation.'

'I'll do whatever I can to help,' she said.

'Thanks. Did your article result in any phone calls from the public that might help us with the identification?'

Becky leaned towards him. 'I've only had a couple of calls, both this morning, but it's early days and I'm hoping for more. One call was just someone being nosy; the other was from a woman who said she'd been an orphan at the convent.'

'What else did she say?' Boon asked.

'I can't tell you that. I have to protect my sources,' Becky said.

'I understand, it's the same for me as a police officer. Personally, I thought your article was very good,' Boon said, trying to gain her confidence.

She looked pleased. 'Thanks. I didn't want to put the bit in about children being buried at the convent. It was my editor's idea because he wanted to spice it up a bit.'

'For what it's worth, there's nothing to suggest any children were buried there.'

'Truthfully, I hope not,' Becky replied solemnly.

'I know the *News Shopper* is only a weekly paper, but you might be able to help us with a follow-up piece.'

'Really. How?' she asked, sounding eager.

'My DCS is holding a press conference at Orpington later today. He's releasing details about a crucifix we recovered which had some initials and a date on it. Hopefully, it will result in a positive identification. If it doesn't, he'll no doubt need to do a further appeal through the national and local press outlets.'

'Do you think I could go to the press conference?'

'You're a journalist, so I can't see why not. I'll make sure your name is on the press list.'

'Thank you so much, DC Boon. It'll be my first press conference.'

'Please, call me Simon.'

Becky leaned forward. 'The lady who phoned me said she still keeps in contact with one of the nuns. I'll see if I can get her name and address for you.'

'That would be really helpful, but don't get yourself in trouble on my account. Would you mind asking her if she'd be willing to speak to me?'

'Of course. I'll call her as soon as I get back to the office.'

'That would be great.' He finished his coffee. 'I was also wondering what made you want to become a journalist?'

She laughed. 'Originally, I was focused on being a fashion writer, but then I found myself drawn to investigative journalism.'

'Did that stem from your dad being a copper?'

Becky nodded. 'A bit, I suppose. Listening to the cases he was dealing with as a coroner's officer interested me . . . not in a gory way, though. I've always found it hard to understand why people commit some crimes – especially murder. Investigative journalism helps me to understand it better. And I believe journalists have a duty to write responsibly and help catch the perpetrators of any crime.'

'There are a lot of things we have in common, then.' Boon smiled, knowing they both still had a lot to learn in their chosen professions.

She smiled back. 'Yes, there are.'

Returning to the *News Shopper* office, Boon waited in the foyer while Becky went upstairs and phoned her contact. It wasn't long before she returned.

'Mrs Gorman is happy to see you,' she told him, 'but she'd like me to be there as well . . . if that's OK with you, of course?' Becky smiled.

Boon realised she was quite crafty, and not nearly as naïve as she pretended to be. He had no choice but to say yes.

*　*　*

Jane drove her car to Archbishop's House. Now that she knew there was no problem with Nick, she was able to think about the future with him. She was sure her parents would approve. Her only worry was that when she introduced him, her mother would embarrass her with too many probing questions.

She lifted the heavy brass knocker and banged it down several times. With Bishop Meade away, she had an opportunity to speak with Mrs Parkin in private. She just hoped that Mrs Parkin was unaware of the *News Shopper* article. The same priest she had met on Friday opened the door.

'Good morning, Detective Tennison. Unfortunately, Bishop Meade isn't here.'

Jane smiled. 'Yes, I know. He said he was going to a meeting in Cambridge. I've actually come to speak with Mrs Parkin, the archivist.'

'Is she expecting you?'

'Yes. Bishop Meade has asked her to assist my inquiries in identifying the nun.'

'Very good. The archives are down in the basement. Please follow me.'

They walked down the winding marble stairs which opened onto a long corridor.

'Mrs Parkin's office is just up on the right.' The priest turned and left.

Jane knocked on the door and entered.

Her eyes had to adjust to the dimly lit, musty-smelling room. She was surprised how big it was, with row after row of alphabetically arranged books, binders and boxes stretching towards the ceiling and covering every inch of the dusty shelves.

A woman was sitting behind a large desk with a table lamp. 'Mrs Parkin?'

'How can I help you?' she asked.

Mrs Parkin looked to be in her early forties, with shoulder-length blonde hair. She was short, slim, and smartly dressed in a white blouse with a bow at the neck and a black skirt.

'I'm Detective Sergeant Tennison. I wanted to thank you personally for searching your archive records on the Sisters of Mercy Convent.'

'My pleasure,' she replied.

'There were a couple of other things I was going to ask Bishop Meade about the convent so I can complete my report. Unfortunately, he's gone to Cambridge. I wondered if you might be able to help me.'

'I will if I can. I just need to pop to the ladies.'

Jane doubted Mrs Parkin would try and contact Meade but couldn't be certain. 'Actually, I need to use the toilet myself.'

Mrs Parkin smiled. 'Follow me.'

When they returned to the archives Mrs Parkin asked Jane how she could help her.

'Bishop Meade said the convent buildings and land were deconsecrated. Do you have a record of who in the diocese dealt with it?'

'It should be on the Petition for Faculty. I put it in a box with the few things I found on the convent.' She reached under her desk, pulled out the box and looked inside. 'Here it is. Signed and dated fifth of July 1964 by Bishop Malone. He's our archbishop now.' She handed it to Jane.

'Would he have performed the deconsecration alone?' she asked. She scanned the document for Meade's name, but couldn't see it.

Mrs Parkin pulled another document from the box. 'This solicitor's letter also confirms it was Bishop Malone. He's currently in Rome helping to organise the Pope's visit to the UK. I'm hoping to get an introduction when he visits London,' she beamed.

'Would he have dealt with the exhumation and removal of nuns' bodies to another grave site?'

'Yes. There's a document in here about that as well.' She showed it to Jane.

'Could I have copies of these documents for my case report, please?'

'Of course.' Mrs Parkin walked over to the copier.

Jane thought about Thomas Durham and Lee Holland and what they might be hiding. 'If other bodies had been uncovered by the builders during the original redevelopment of the convent, would they have had to notify the diocese?'

'Most certainly yes . . . and also the council. They would also have to apply for another Petition for Faculty, then the bodies could be moved and the ground deconsecrated.'

Jane thought about Father Chris's suggestion that a layperson might have been involved. 'Do you keep records of any builders or handymen who worked at the convent?'

'We don't keep their names, if that's what you mean. However, we do keep receipts regarding repair work and estimates, which would have gone through our buildings department.'

'Would you have receipts relating to the Bickley convent?'

'Possibly, but they would be stored in a separate section of the archives and might take a while to find.'

'I'd be grateful if you could have a look when you get a chance, and let me know if you find anything,' Jane said.

'Jot down your phone number on my notepad,' Mrs Parkin said, pointing to the pad on her desk. 'Is there anything else I can help you with?' She handed Jane the copies of the documents.

'About the fire, do you know how it started?'

'I'm afraid not.'

'Might there be any records?' Jane asked, recalling Meade telling her Mrs Parkin had given him the details of when and where the fire occurred.

Mrs Parkin looked in the box and removed a document. 'Just this. It's a letter from the diocesan solicitors to the developers.'

Jane read it. The only mention was a line stating that a fire had occurred in August 1962, damaging several uninsured out-buildings and the school beyond economical repair. Jane realised Meade could have the letter but wondered how he knew the fire had started in the bakery and destroyed all the convent documents.

'There's nothing else about the fire?'

'Not that I could find. You'd be better off speaking to Bishop Meade. He knows more about it than me.'

Jane didn't want to press Mrs Parkin. From what she said, it seemed Meade knew a lot more about the fire than he was letting on and was trying to distance himself from it. Jane changed tack.

'I assume when the convent closed the children were moved to another orphanage.'

'Yes, but I doubt they would all have gone to the same one.'

'Would you have a record of their names and where they were sent?'

'Unfortunately, we don't. Bishop Meade did ask me to look, but it appears the convent never passed the details on to the archives, which was most remiss of the Mother Superior in charge. Then again, with all the distress and upheaval of the convent closing, she might just have forgotten.'

Jane wasn't so sure and wondered if the records had been passed on but had then been destroyed by Meade. 'Do you know who the Mother Superior was?'

'No, it appears all the nuns' personal records were destroyed in the fire as well.'

'Did any priests live at the convent when it was open?'

Parkin frowned. 'Of course not, that would be most irregular.'

'Would a local one visit or help teach at the school?' Jane asked.

'That wouldn't be uncommon. St Mary's is the nearest Catholic church to the old convent. Father Floridia is the current priest. He's a lovely man – unlike some of the misery guts out there. You know, I've never heard anyone say a bad word about Father Floridia.'

Jane nodded. 'I've had the pleasure of meeting him. He introduced me to Bishop Meade. As a matter of interest, would you have a record of the priests who worked at St Mary's in the fifties and sixties?'

Parkin's eyes narrowed. 'Can I ask why you need all this information?'

'The coroner wants us to explore every possible avenue to try and identify the nun found in the unearthed coffin. He's a stickler for making sure we do a thorough job.'

Mrs Parkin nodded. 'Well, we wouldn't want to upset him. Give me a second while I look in the St Mary's archives.' She walked down a long row of bookshelves and out of sight.

Jane didn't hear the door open but jumped when she heard someone behind her cough to get her attention. She turned sharply and saw the young priest.

'I'll have to ask you to leave, Detective Tennison,' he said in a firm voice.

'May I ask why?' she said, suspecting the *News Shopper* article had been brought to his attention.

'I have just spoken with Bishop Meade. He is most displeased to learn that you neglected to make him aware you are investigating a murder. He feels you have deceived the Church by your actions and will be informing Archbishop Malone. Under the circumstances I think it's best you leave.'

'Fair enough. Please tell Bishop Meade my detective chief superintendent will be in touch with him to explain our position,' she said, surreptitiously folding the copied documents and tucking them in her pocket.

The priest followed her to make sure she left the building.

Mrs Parkin returned to her desk empty-handed and looked around for Jane. 'Why does everything keep disappearing round here!' she muttered to herself.

* * *

On the drive to Mrs Gorman's house in West Wickham, Becky asked a lot of questions about the investigation. Boon tried to confine his answers to things she would already have known through her father.

'Do you reckon someone connected to the Church was involved?' she asked.

'I don't know,' he said. 'We'll have to wait and see what the investigations turn up.'

'Come on, Simon, we both know it's got to be someone who lived or worked at the convent,' she insisted.

'You could be right, but then again you could be wrong. A good investigator considers all possibilities, not just the one that best fits their assumptions.'

'Very astute, officer. I shall remember that – but I'll bet you I'm right.'

'What's the bet?'

'You wine and dine me at a posh restaurant uptown, then take me dancing at the Empire nightclub in Leicester Square. If I'm wrong, it's my treat.'

Boon smiled. Win or lose, he very much fancied a night out with Becky. 'You're on.'

She shook his hand. 'And I'm going to choose the most expensive thing on the menu.'

'As long as it's only the starter, I'm happy with that,' he grinned.

Becky pressed the doorbell of the small terraced house. A plump, dark-haired woman in her mid-twenties opened the door.

'Hi, I'm Becky. Is your mother in?'

'My mother doesn't live here,' the woman replied, looking confused.

Boon wondered if Becky had been the victim of a hoax call.

'Sorry, I think we might have the wrong address. Do you know if a Mrs Gorman lives in the street?'

The woman laughed. 'I'm Annette Gorman. You spoke to me on the phone, Miss Rogers.'

Becky looked embarrassed. 'I do apologise. I was expecting someone a lot older. This is Detective Constable Boon.'

'I thought it might be,' Annette said, inviting them in.

They went to the small living room which was littered with children's toys.

'Sorry about the mess. I've got two-year-old twin girls. I just put them down for their mid-morning nap, so we shouldn't be disturbed for a while.'

Becky asked Annette if she'd mind her and Boon taking some notes.

'Not at all. I don't really know if I can help you much. I was only ten when the convent closed.'

'Can I ask why you rang Becky, Mrs Gorman?' Boon asked, wanting to get straight to the point.

'I was shocked when I read her article. I couldn't believe one of the nuns was murdered. I showed it to my husband before he went to work. He knew I'd been an orphan at the convent and said I should call you to see if I could be of any help. He also said I should call the police. But there was nothing in the article about who to call . . . other than Miss Rogers.'

Boon explained they had been keeping quiet about the murder as they had hoped to identify the nun before going public. 'When were you at the convent?' he asked.

'From about 1957 until just after the fire, which I think was in the summer of 1962. It wasn't long after that my brother and I were moved to different orphanages.'

Boon realised Annette would have been at the convent at the time the nun was believed to have been murdered. He was about to pick up on it when Becky butted in.

'Sorry, did you say your brother was there as well?'

Annette nodded sadly. 'He was my twin. I don't know where David is now . . . or if he's even alive,' she said, welling up.

'Have you spoken with the Catholic Children's Society in Westminster?' Boon asked.

'Yes, but they couldn't help. They don't keep orphanage records. Sadly, they didn't have a David Bell with the same date of birth as me on their records. I also wrote to the diocesan archives but just got a letter back saying there was no record of him.' She started to cry.

Boon felt downhearted. It seemed the Children's Society would be another dead-end inquiry, though he'd still contact them to double check.

'I'd like to try and help you find your brother, Annette,' Becky said.

'How? I've exhausted every avenue there is.' She wiped her eyes with a tissue.

'I'll ask my editor if I can do an article on the orphanage, the loss of your parents and the struggle to find your brother. It might help to locate him.'

'That's very kind of you. Not all the children were orphans in the true sense of the word. Some had been abandoned or were from broken homes. When I was sixteen, I ran away from the children's home I was in to look for my brother. Then I met my future husband, who was eighteen at the time. His family took me in and helped me look for mine.

'We managed to trace a close friend of my parents. Through her, I discovered David and I had lived in a big house in Sussex. When we were three, our father was seriously assaulted during a break-in and died of his injuries some months later. As a result, our mother had a breakdown and started drinking heavily. She confided in the local priest about her depression and drinking.' Annette's brow furrowed. 'He rewarded her plea for help by informing the authorities and having us taken away,' she said with bitterness in her voice.

'My God, that's awful,' Becky exclaimed. 'I thought the Church was supposed to help people in need!'

'Were you reunited with your mother?' Boon asked, moved by her painful story.

She shook her head. 'No. Thanks to the priest, she ended up in Graylingwell asylum. She committed suicide when David and I were nine. My mother's friend found out we were at the convent and wrote a letter to the Mother Superior, but we were never told about it.'

'What possible reason could she have for not telling you?' Becky asked.

'In the eyes of the Catholic Church, suicide is a mortal sin, and she was an evil cow.'

'Do you mind if I ask you some questions about your time at the Sisters of Mercy orphanage?' Boon asked.

Annette let out a cynical laugh. 'We used to call some of them the Sisters Without Mercy.'

'Why was that?'

She looked sombre. 'Because the Mother Superior and her minions were heartless and brutal in the way they treated us. Although I was only five, I'll never forget my first day there.'

'What happened?' Becky asked, apprehensively.

Annette sat motionless, her lips trembling as she recalled the event. 'We were in the dining room having breakfast when we were made to stand in a line. Mother Superior said she was going to show us what happens to girls and boys who misbehave. The door opened and four girls, not much older than me, were marched in by Sister Margaret who whacked them across the back of the legs with a bamboo cane if they walked too slow. At first, I thought it strange as they were all wearing white headscarves and carrying silver bowls. They were then made to stand in front of us and remove their headscarves. All their hair had been shaved off and it was in the silver bowls they held in front of them. Mother Superior produced a big wooden ladle from up her sleeve then proceeded to walk behind the girls and whack each of them hard on the head. I could see they were terrified, but they didn't dare cry in case they got hit again.'

Becky gasped, putting her hand over her mouth. 'What did she do to the boys?' she asked.

Annette licked her dry lips and clasped her hands together. 'Sister Margaret marched the boys in and paraded them round the room. All of them were wrapped in bedsheets.' She paused and took a deep breath.

'Why on earth where they made to wear bedsheets?' Boon asked.

'Because they had wet themselves during the night. It wasn't until they were made to pull the sheets from their heads that I saw David was one of the boys. He started to cry when he saw me. I took a step forward, then one of the elder girls tugged me back. She whispered I'd make it worse for him if I did anything.' Annette's sadness was turning to anger. 'Mother Superior then gave them a whack with the ladle as well.'

Boon shook his head in disgust. 'In my few years as a police officer, I've seen some terrible things but the thought that anyone, especially nuns, could do that to children . . .'

'Having all your hair cut off or being made to wear a wet sheet was nothing compared with being made to sit in the chapel crypt in the dark, on your own. Mother Superior would say it was so we could "reflect on our sins in the presence of the Lord".'

'Were there dead bodies down there?' Becky asked, wide-eyed.

'Just the man who founded the convent. He was in a stone sarcophagus. Occasionally a nun who died would be in a coffin awaiting burial, but that was rare. It was terrifying and so cold down there you'd sit on the floor with your knees under your chin, pulling your dress down and your jumper sleeves over your hands to try and keep warm. Thankfully, I only ever got sent down there once. I never wanted it to happen to me again, so I made sure I always did as I was told.'

The thought of being alone in the crypt sent a shiver through Becky. 'Do you think there might be the bodies of abused children buried in the grounds of the convent?'

Annette shrugged. 'I don't remember anyone suddenly disappearing while I was there, but that's not to say a child hasn't been killed since the convent opened.'

Boon knew it was a possibility but doubted it. 'I'm really sorry for making you recall such traumatic events, Annette. Yours, David's, and every child's life in the convent must have been a living nightmare,' he said.

'I was never so happy as when I left that place, but it's stayed with me ever since and robbed me of growing up with my brother. There was a constant atmosphere of fear, but it wasn't all bad. Some nuns were kind and even lied to protect us. Although they didn't argue with Mother Superior about her strict rules, they didn't enforce them with an iron rod like some of her cronies.'

'They should all be ashamed for doing nothing about it,' Becky said fiercely.

'Believe me, I know they were. Those that did challenge Mother Superior quickly found themselves transferred to another convent, usually in some godforsaken country, or so I was told.'

'How many children lived at the convent?' Becky asked.

'About thirty . . . there were slightly more girls than boys.'

'Have you kept in contact with any of them?'

'No. A couple of girls were moved to the same new orphanage as me. But I lost contact with them when I left.'

'How many nuns were there?' Boon asked.

'It varied, but generally I'd say about twelve, including Mother Superior.'

'Can you remember the Mother Superior or any of the nuns' names?'

'I haven't a clue what her name was,' she said. 'Everyone just called her Mother Superior. Sister Margaret was her deputy, and she was even more sadistic. She always took great delight in beating and humiliating us.'

'Do you know her surname?'

Annette shook her head. 'All the nuns were just called Sister and we used their Christian names for those that let us.' She paused for thought. 'There was Sister Suzanne, Sister Julie, Sister Jane and Sister Melissa. I remember them mostly because they were the nicer ones. It's hard to recall the others.'

'Can you remember the Christian names of any other nuns beginning with an "M"?' Boon asked.

Annette thought with her eyes closed, then opened them. 'There was Sister Maria, at least two Sister Marys, and I think a Sister Madeline. I'm sorry, but that's all I can remember just now. Do you think the nun who was murdered might be one of them?'

'It's possible. We believe our victim was between eighteen and thirty and had the initials MB. If I read the names out, could you give me a rough age of each of them?'

'Sorry, I was ten years old . . . I couldn't even begin to guess how old they were back then. Mother Superior and Sister Margaret looked the oldest. Sister Maria and Sister Suzanne were definitely younger.'

'I know this is a long shot, but do you know if any of them still live or work in the area?'

Annette sighed. 'Sister Julie does, though she's no longer a nun. We speak on the phone and meet up quite regularly, actually. I didn't want to give you her details until I spoke to her personally and made sure it was OK.'

'I understand . . . and thank you for your honesty. Obviously, Julie might be able to provide some useful information. Would you mind calling her just now and asking if she'd be willing to talk to us?'

'I'll try but she might be at work. She's a nursing sister at Farnborough Hospital.'

While Annette went to the kitchen to make the call, Boon checked his notes to see if there was anything else he needed to ask.

Becky let out a sad sigh. 'It's made me realise how lucky I was to be raised by loving parents who always made me feel wanted and safe. Although we've had a few big rows over the years, I can't ever recall a time when my parents raised a hand to me.'

'Same here,' Boon replied.

'Could you prosecute the nuns for assault after so many years?'

'It would need Annette and other victims to give evidence in court. I'll certainly be telling my superiors what she told us. Are you going to write an article about what happened to her?'

'I feel the public has a right to know. Those responsible should be named and shamed, but I won't write it without Annette's approval. And I will still try and help her find her brother.'

Boon smiled. 'You're a good person, Becky Rogers.'

She smiled back. 'As are you, Simon Boon.'

Annette came back and told them Julie must be at work as she wasn't answering. She turned to Boon. 'I'll call her later and give her your office number. I'm pretty sure she'll do her best to help with the investigation.'

'Thank you,' Boon said.

'How did you meet up with Julie again?' Becky asked.

'It was about two years ago while I was shopping at Allders department store in Bromley. I noticed this woman staring at me and shaking as if she'd seen a ghost. I asked if she was all right, but she didn't answer. I was about to walk away when she asked me how I got the mark on my face.' Annette pointed to a three-inch scar on her left cheek. 'I told her a nun hit me with a bamboo cane and she looked close to tears. I'd never seen Sister Julie in casual clothes, so at first it didn't register who she was. When she asked me if I was Annette Bell, it came to me in a flash. We hugged each other and cried our eyes out. In many ways, finding each other has been a blessing for both of us. Our long talks and lots of tears have helped us come to terms with what happened in our lives.'

Boon was about to ask Annette a question when he heard one of the babies crying.

Becky stood up. 'We'd best be going and let you see to your children.'

'There's just a couple of other questions I'd like to ask before we go,' Boon said.

'If she carries on crying, she'll wake the other one up. I'll be back in a second.' Annette dashed up the stairs and returned cradling one of the babies.

Becky's eyes lit up. 'Ah, she's beautiful. What's her name?'

'Davina, after my brother. Her sister is called Julie.'

'Can I hold her?' Becky asked.

Annette handed Davina to her and then sat down opposite Boon.

'Were there any non-religious people who worked at the convent?' he asked.

'Not that I recall. Most things in the convent were done by the nuns. You'd be surprised how skilled they were at fixing and making things. We had to do chores every day, keeping the place clean, helping with the laundry, tending the gardens and vegetable patches. Mucking out the pig pens was the worst punishment – you had to grab the shit with your bare hands and put it into a bucket.'

'That's gross,' Becky said.

'Were there any priests who worked there?' Boon asked.

'There was one who'd come in and read us Aesop's Fables in class. Sometimes the bishop would visit ... we'd be given clean clothes and inspected by Mother Superior before he arrived.'

'Can you remember the priest's or bishop's names?'

'We were only allowed to call the bishop "Your Excellency", if he deigned to speak to us. We called the priest Father Bob. He was a nice man, everyone liked him. He used to give us all a boiled sweet in class, hold his finger to his mouth and say we must not tell Mother Superior, or he'd get in trouble.'

Boon closed his notebook. 'Thank you, Mrs Gorman. I know it must be hard, talking about your life at the convent, but it's been really helpful to our investigation.'

Boon couldn't wait now to get back to the station. Father Bob, he wondered . . . could he be Bishop Meade?

CHAPTER TWENTY

Driving Becky to Petts Wood, Boon asked if she'd mind keeping the conversation with Annette Gorman to herself, at least until DCS Barnes had held the press conference.

'I don't have a problem with that,' she said, 'as long as you buy me a drink.'

'Are you blackmailing me?' Boon grinned.

'If it weren't for me, you wouldn't have met Annette. So, I figure you owe me.'

'All right then, where do you want to go?'

'Do you know The Chequers in Southborough Lane?'

'Yes. It's a quiet, cosy little pub . . .'

'That's why I chose it,' she smiled, with a twinkle in her eye.

'The Chequers it is, then,' Boon replied.

'If Sister Julie is willing to talk to you, can I tag along?' she asked.

'I doubt it will be me who speaks to her. Julie could be the key to a lot of unanswered questions. As a significant witness my DS or DI will want to speak to her.'

'Will you tell me what she says?'

He sighed. 'I can't do that, Becky. But if Julie wants to speak to you, that's a different matter.'

'Do you think this Father Bob is involved?'

His forehead creased. 'No, but obviously he needs to be traced and interviewed.'

She laughed. 'I can tell you're fibbing by the way you reacted when Annette told you his name. And the way you just looked at me was another giveaway.'

Boon sighed. 'I can't tell you, Becky . . .'

'Come on! You wouldn't have found Annette or Julie if it hadn't been for me. I won't tell anyone else.'

'You promise this is between us?'

'Of course. It's not in my interest to piss you off, is it?'

Boon told her about Bishop Meade and why he suspected he may have been involved in the nun's murder.

Becky's eyes widened. 'Bloody hell. If your timeline is right and Meade was the priest who visited the convent, then he must have known the murdered nun.'

Boon nodded. 'If he killed her, the big question is why – and who else was involved. We found out there's a tunnel from the convent chapel that leads to near where her body was found.'

'Have you checked it out?' Becky asked.

'Not yet.'

'Do you think the nun's murder had anything to do with the sale of the convent?' Becky asked.

'How do you know about the sale?'

'I'm a journalist. I do my homework before writing an article,' she said indignantly.

Boon suspected who her source was. 'You mean your father told you about the coffin being found on the building site.'

'Yes, but I made my own enquiries to find out about the history of the convent, the fire and then the sale to the building developer, Thomas Durham. If the nun found out there was something hooky going on between Meade and Durham, then maybe they thought she might tell the police.'

Boon laughed. 'Now you *are* in fantasy land. Durham bought the land well after the nuns left. Even if he was remotely involved, why bury the coffin somewhere you know it would be dug up?'

'That's a good point . . . but I still think it's a possibility worth exploring.'

'Please, Becky, leave the detective work to us,' he said. 'Or you could find yourself in trouble.'

* * *

Jane returned to Bromley to do her report on the meeting with Mrs Parkin. She phoned Nick first to see if he was in.

'Hi. It's me. I'm due a lunchbreak. If you're not busy, I could pop to the café and get a couple of sandwiches.'

'I'd love to, but I've got to go to my dad's,' he said.

Jane thought he sounded stressed. 'Is he all right?'

He sighed. 'Not really. One of the other residents at the convent showed him the *News Shopper* article. He's got himself in a right state about the site being closed down. He's convinced no one will buy any property there if they think bodies of murdered children and nuns are buried in the grounds. His breathing sounded heavy and a bit erratic, so I'm quite worried about him, to be honest.'

Jane wondered if there was more behind Thomas Durham's distress. 'I'm really sorry, Nick. Obviously, we have to reassure the public we are investigating the allegation, but personally I think it's just sensationalism by a young journalist. I found a document in the diocesan archives confirming the land was deconsecrated prior to the sale, so that should help put your father's mind at rest.'

'Thanks. That should cheer him up a bit. Hopefully I'll see you tonight if he's feeling better.'

'No problem. Give him my best,' she said, and ended the call, realising Nick was in a hurry.

Jane had started typing her report when Boon walked in.

'How's your leg?'

'Bloody sore.' He sat down, rubbed his shin, then looked at Jane with a sly grin. 'I've just spoken to a woman who was a child at the convent from 1957 to 1962. She told me about a priest who used to visit and read them stories. The children called him Father Bob.' He paused for Jane to answer.

Her eyes lit up. 'Robert Meade! The bishop!'

He nodded. 'She didn't know his surname, but I'd bet my life it was Meade.'

'That's brilliant work, Boony. I was at the diocesan archives earlier. I think Meade knows more about the convent fire than he's letting on. I'm beginning to wonder if it was arson.'

'Pity no one examined it at the time,' Boon remarked.

Jane held her right finger and thumb close. 'I was this close to getting my hands on a list of former St Mary's priests. With Meade's name on it and Annette's recollection of "Father Bob", we'd have undeniable evidence to link him to the convent and the nuns.'

'You might not need the list,' he suggested. 'Mrs Gorman is in regular contact with a lady called Julie. She used to be a nun at the convent. I'm waiting to see if she'll speak to us. If she says Meade was a regular visitor to the convent, he's screwed.'

'You've had a productive day, Boony. Barnes will be pleased. How on earth did you find Annette Gorman?'

'Believe it or not, PC Rogers' daughter, Becky. She is really nice – unlike her old man. As a thanks for her help, I said she could attend the press conference.'

'Be careful, Boony. I know from personal experience that journalists can be very underhand. They turn on the charm to get what they can out of you.'

'She's just a junior reporter,' he said, 'and her heart's in the right place.'

Jane raised her eyebrows. 'Sounds as if you like her.'

'I'm not so stupid I'd mix business with pleasure,' Boon said quickly.

Jane didn't comment further. She knew many of her colleagues would disapprove of her dating Nick if they found out. It was early days, but she'd tell them when the time was right and duly suffer the raised eyebrows and cynical remarks.

'What else did Mrs Gorman tell you?' Jane asked.

Boon opened his notebook and went through his conversation with Annette.

Jane felt physically sick hearing how the children had been treated by some of the nuns. 'Those poor kids. An orphanage is supposed to be a safe place, not a bloody prison camp.'

'I just can't understand why the nuns Annette said were nice, like Sister Julie, didn't do something about it,' Boon remarked.

Jane thought for a moment. 'Maybe our victim tried to . . . and that's why she was murdered.'

Boon nodded. 'If you're right, it points to nuns being involved more than Meade. Mrs Gorman said all the children liked him.'

'I don't doubt that, Boony. But what Annette told you raises a stronger possibility for me. Men who abuse children need to win their trust. Father Bob's stories and boiled sweets may have been a means to an end.'

'You think he was sexually abusing young girls?' Boon asked in a shocked tone.

'It could be boys as well as girls,' she said. 'When he handed out sweets, he said not to tell Mother Superior, or he'd get in trouble. Children who are abused don't understand right from wrong or what is happening to them. They trust the abuser. They will do whatever they say. If our victim knew Meade was abusing children and threatened to expose him, his life would be over. He'd be defrocked and go to prison.'

'His only way out would be to silence her,' Boon concluded.

Jane's desk phone rang. She picked it up, giving her rank and name.

'It's Father Floridia. Are you free to talk?'

She sensed an uneasiness in his voice. 'Yes. Go ahead.'

'Bishop Meade just phoned me in an absolute rage. He's been made aware of an article in the *Bromley News Shopper* about the nun's murder and the bodies of children—'

Jane interrupted him. 'I know. I was at the diocesan archives earlier. I got asked to leave by a priest who'd just spoken with Bishop Meade.'

Father Chris's tone changed. 'Did you know about the newspaper article as well?'

'Not until it was published this morning.'

'You could at least have had the decency to warn me as soon as you knew about it,' he said.

'I'm sorry. It was thoughtless of me. It hit us out of the blue as well. What did Bishop Meade say?'

'He accused me of being in cahoots with you, a liar and a disgrace to the Church. He said we have been deceitful, and the police were underhand by not being honest from the start.'

'I'll speak with Meade and tell him you didn't know about the murder,' Jane assured him.

'I've already told him that, but I don't think he believes me. He said I was not to talk to you again without his authority or a representative of the Church being present.'

'Then why are you talking to me now?' she asked.

'There's something you need to know, but I'd rather not say it over the phone. Can you come over to the presbytery?'

'I'm quite busy at the moment . . .'

'It's about Bishop Meade. He's lied to us.'

'I'm on my way.' Jane got up and grabbed her coat.

'Where are you going?' Boon asked.

'I'll tell you later. Write up your report on the Annette Gorman information,' she said, hurrying out.

*   *   *

Father Floridia was dressed casually in his tracksuit when Jane arrived. He took her through to the living room. She could see the anxiety on his face as he took a deep breath.

'Since we parted on Friday, the thought that someone connected to the convent might be involved in the nun's death has eaten away at me. On Sunday, after mass, I spoke with one of my older parishioners about the convent. She didn't know much about the nuns so I asked if she could remember who the priest at St Mary's was in the late fifties and early sixties.'

'And she told you it was Bishop Meade.'

Father Chris raised his eyebrows. 'How did you know?'

Jane told him about her visit to the archives and Annette Gorman's account of her time at the convent.

'I don't want this to sound insensitive,' he said, 'but ... do you believe her?'

'My colleague who interviewed her has no doubt she's telling the truth. Her distress while recounting such painful memories was not an act.'

Father Chris shook his head in disgust. 'Those poor children will have been scarred for life. Do you think Bishop Meade knew what was going on?'

'If Meade had nothing to hide, why didn't he just tell us he was the local priest and visited the convent on a regular basis? It's clear he'd know who the Mother Superior was, and at least the names of some of the nuns, including possibly our victim. He's deliberately obstructed police inquiries and distanced himself from the convent. The question is, why?'

'Are you going to arrest him?'

'That's not for me to decide ... but I think it's inevitable.'

Father Chris sighed. 'This just gets worse and worse. But I can't believe Bishop Meade would be capable of murder. It seems more likely he's concealing the wrongdoing of others.'

Jane decided to be open with him. 'It's possible he was sexually abusing children at the convent and our victim found out.'

Father Chris was stunned. 'You think he's a paedophile?'

'Bishop Meade is clearly hiding *something*. Under the circumstances we have to consider it a possibility,' Jane said. She told him about Meade reading stories to the children and giving them sweets.

'Has anyone said they were actually abused by him?' Father Chris asked.

'No, but his acts of kindness may have had an ulterior motive,' Jane suggested.

'That's ridiculous!' he said. 'Hundreds of priests, vicars and nuns read bible stories to children and give them sweets at Easter, Christmas, or other special occasions. Are you saying they are all paedophiles as well?'

'No, but Meade also told the children not to tell Mother Superior. And now he's not telling us the truth.'

'I really can't get my head around all this. It flies in the face of everything I've been taught and hold dear as a Catholic priest.'

'Does Meade have a chauffeur-driven black Ford Granada?' she asked.

'The archbishop does, but Bishop Meade's been using it in his absence. Why do you ask?'

Jane told him about a man matching Meade's description going to the mortuary on Saturday morning to say a prayer for the nun.

'He didn't know I'd prayed for her soul. It could have been a priest he sent to the mortuary,' Father Chris said defensively.

'The mortuary technician said he was dressed in a purple shirt and wore a gold ring, with a large round purple stone in it. When he saw the nun's body, he had what can only be described as an emotional breakdown. I think Meade knows who she is and was full of self-pity and regret for something he'd done.'

Father Chris tilted his head back and sighed. 'No, no, no, this can't be right.'

'I know the truth can be hard to accept,' she said gently, 'but the evidence speaks for itself. It's also clear one person alone couldn't have moved the coffin. There are others out there who were involved or know what happened. And they've covered up the truth for at least twenty years.'

Father Chris looked miserable. 'I know. That's why I will do what I can to help you. Archbishop Malone is flying back from Rome tomorrow morning. Meade said he'll probably want to speak with me on Wednesday. I can't lie to him as well, Jane. I have to tell him everything I know.'

'You don't need to get involved,' she said. 'There's a record of the parish priests in the archives which will prove Bishop Meade worked here. The last thing I want is for you to get in trouble or lose your job. As far as I'm concerned, this conversation never took place and you never knew about the nun's murder.'

Father Chris shook his head. 'There are no priests' records in the archives . . . apart from mine.'

'How do you know that?'

'I spoke with Mrs Parkin on the phone just after you left. I told her I was writing an historical article on the church and needed some details about the previous parish priests. I wanted to confirm what my parishioner told me.' He sighed. 'The strange thing is, I wasn't really surprised when I was told they were missing.'

Jane shook her head in disbelief. 'Bishop Meade must have removed them. He must be a complete fool to think we wouldn't find out he was the parish priest. My DCS is holding a press conference this evening. He's confident a public appeal will identify other nuns and children who were at the convent. We can also make discreet inquiries with local residents. I'm sure there will be plenty of people out there who remember "Father Bob ".'

'Thank you,' he said. 'You've been very understanding.'

'I hope everything works out for you, Chris.'

'So do I, Jane. But right now, I don't know what my future holds,' he said darkly.

Jane wondered what he meant. 'Do you mind if I ask you a personal question?'

He forced a smile. 'That depends on what it is.'

'What made you want to become a priest?' She hoped he wouldn't be offended by the query.

Father Chris sighed. 'That's a question I've repeatedly asked myself these last few days.' He paused and looked at Jane with a sadness in his eyes. 'I've never told anyone the real reason before.'

'You don't have to tell me if you don't want to,' she said, sensing his discomfort.

'I was seeking God's forgiveness, by giving my life to Him.'

'Forgiveness for what?' Jane asked.

'The death of my parents,' he said softly as his eyes glazed over. 'If it wasn't for me, they'd still be alive.'

'What happened?' Jane asked in a quiet voice.

'We had a small restaurant in Valetta, and my parents and I lived above it. My father Aaron looked after the guests and my mother Tamyra was the cook. My brother Michael and I took turns working in the kitchen and serving the guests. We closed early one Friday night as it wasn't very busy. Michael went home to his wife and baby son and I went to a nearby nightclub with a girlfriend.' He paused and took a deep breath.

'I can still remember hearing the explosion above the sound of the music. Everyone ran into the street to see what had happened. The sky was red with flames and filled with smoke. Somehow, I knew it was our restaurant. I ran down the road to find the front of the building blown out and the inside on fire. The upper floor we lived on was in a state of collapse . . . then I saw my mother at the smoke-filled bedroom window trying to open it . . . but she couldn't. I tried to go in, but I was driven back by the flames. I tried again, but a friend grabbed me and said it was too dangerous. Eventually the fire brigade came . . . but it was too late. After they put the fire out, I found my father in the kitchen. He had died from severe blast injuries. My mother was in the bedroom . . . there wasn't a mark on her body. I cradled her in my arms, but she was dead from smoke inhalation.' He put his hands over his face and wept.

Jane wanted to comfort Father Chris by putting her arms round him, but knew it wouldn't be appropriate.

'Oh, Chris, I'm so sorry for your loss. It must have been terrible for you and your brother. What caused the explosion?'

He looked up at Jane slowly. 'I did. And I can't forgive myself for what I've done . . . only God can.' His voice trembled.

Jane felt numb. 'But how . . .?'

'Through my negligence and stupidity. I was so hasty to go out and enjoy myself that I forgot to turn off the propane gas bottle in the kitchen. My father switched the light on, then the spark of electricity ignited the gas,' he said, his voice full of guilt and self-loathing.

'Is that what the fire brigade said or what you believe happened?' Jane asked.

'They said it was a gas leak, so it had to be the propane bottle. I was last out of the kitchen that night. It was my responsibility to check the bottles were turned off . . . and I obviously didn't.'

Jane remembered the burn marks on his mother's cherished recipe book. Now she knew why it was so precious to him.

'You can't blame yourself and let it eat away at you, Chris. I dealt with a case where a faulty gas bottle accidently exploded in a garage.'

'This bottle wasn't faulty, Jane. If it were, we would have smelt the gas before that fateful night.'

'No one smelt gas in my case, either. The truth is, you don't know whether or not you turned the gas off or if the bottle was faulty. Sometimes we carry so much guilt and doubt, we blame ourselves for what happens to others, but you have to learn to move on.'

'My brother blamed me. We haven't spoken since it happened, which was ten years ago.'

'Does he know you became a priest?' she asked.

Father Chris shook his head. 'I couldn't face him or my demons, which is why I left Malta. At first, I was suicidal and confessed to a priest. He said suicide would be a mortal sin in the eyes of God, a sin that defies the love I owed Him. His words had a positive influence on me. I believed if I placed myself in the hands of God, He would forgive me and see me safely through life.'

'Believe me, Chris, the world is a better place with honest, caring priests like you in it.'

'That's kind of you to say. Anyway, that's the end of my story. Now, would you like some *kwarezimal* and a coffee?'

'You're tempting me,' she said with a smile. 'But sadly, I have to get back to work.'

'I'll walk you to your car.'

* * *

After calming his father down, Nick left him asleep in bed. Driving his Range Rover up St Mary's Lane, Nick thought he saw Jane's Mini Cooper. He pulled over, deciding to play a joke on her. He looked in the glovebox and found an old parking ticket to place under her windscreen wiper. As he was about to get out of his car, he saw Jane emerging from an alleyway beside the church, talking to a man in a grey tracksuit. Nick closed the car door and watched in his wing mirror.

Chris spoke as they walked. 'With all that's happened concerning the nun's murder, I find my faith in the priesthood and Catholic Church being tested to its limits. It's like a dark shroud has descended on me . . . and I can no longer see the light.'

'There's rotten apples in every profession,' Jane said. She placed her hand on his arm. 'Whatever happens, you have to do what is right for you, Chris.'

'God bless you, Jane. It's been a pleasure knowing you. I wish you well in your investigation.' He leaned forward, hugged her and gently kissed her on the cheek before walking off towards the presbytery.

Jane was lost for words. It was like a final, sad goodbye, yet she had also felt a surge of arousal when he held and kissed her.

As she drove off, Nick ducked down until she had turned the corner. Sitting upright and close to tears, he punched the steering wheel.

'You're all the fucking same!' he said through gritted teeth.

CHAPTER TWENTY-ONE

Entering the Orpington incident room, Jane was surprised at how organised and well-equipped it was, given how quickly it had been set up. The conference-room table was pushed up against one wall and twelve chairs were set out for the press to sit at. A4 photographs of the nun's coffin, body and the cross were stuck on one wall. Large Bromley planning department maps and plans of the convent – from 1851, 1964 and 1981 – were on another wall. A large whiteboard had 'Victim – MB?' written on it, her estimated age range, height, and hair colour. Under it was written 'Pathologist – Dr Samantha Pullen', with details of her post-mortem findings and cause of death. DS Johnson's name had 'Lab liaison sergeant' written next to it with plenty of space for the forensic results when they came in. A tall filing shelf was filled with statement forms, action and information sheets, message pads, writing paper, pens, and as-yet-empty filing trays.

'You've done a good job here, guv,' Jane told Stanley.

'Looks all right, doesn't it? I spoke with your man Eaves this morning. He worked from photographs and X-rays of the head over the weekend and produced these for the press conference.' He opened a folder and showed Jane two A4-sized artist's impressions of the murdered nun, one wearing a veil and the other without.

Jane thought they portrayed her as an attractive, serene-looking young woman.

Stanley stuck them on the wall. 'They look quite lifelike. If we identify our victim, it'll be interesting to see how closely Eaves' impression resembles an old photograph of her.'

'Is Barnes happy to use them in his appeal?' Jane asked.

'He was in two minds at first, but having seen them he said it was worth a shot. I've got desks, typewriters, phones, and an index

LYNDA LA PLANTE | 239

carousel to put in after the press conference. I'll add details about our suspect Bishop Meade and the information Annette Gorman gave us once the press people have gone.'

'How many other officers have you got joining us?' Jane asked.

'Ten detectives and two civilian indexers, which will make a total of sixteen, including Barnes.'

'I thought we might have had more officers,' she said.

'Barnes said he wants to see where the press appeal leads us, then review things after a couple of days. I get the impression he wants to crack this case within a week or two.'

'Somehow I don't think it will be that easy,' Jane remarked. She saw Boon walk in. 'Any news on Sister Julie?'

He gave her a thumbs-up. 'Her name's Julie Dorton and she's willing to speak to us. I've got her address. She lives in Hurst Road, Sidcup with her husband.'

'Well done, Boony,' Jane said.

'Would someone like to explain who this Julie is?' Stanley said.

Boon told him about his meeting with Annette Gorman.

'Did Julie Dorton confirm what Annette Gorman said about the nuns and Father Bob?'

'I didn't ask, though Mrs Gorman had obviously told her why we wanted to interview her.'

'Why not?' Stanley asked, frowning.

'Because I didn't want to scare her off over the phone. An interview in the comfort of her home is more likely to produce the best results, like it did with Mrs Gorman,' Boon said.

'Well, let's hope you're right,' Stanley replied.

'He knows you're right, Boony. He just hates to admit it,' Jane teased, giving Stanley a grin.

'You've done well, Boony. Barnes will be pleased.' Stanley looked at his watch. It was half past three. 'I've told the duty sergeant to keep the press in the foyer until we're ready for them. I'll go down just before four, hand out the press passes and bring them up to the incident room.'

'I'll do that for you, guv. I'm sure DCS Barnes will want you by his side as he enters the room,' Boon said, wanting to keep his promise to Becky.

'Good point. I'll go and get the passes and leave them on the desk over there,' Stanley said, walking off.

Jane guessed why Boon was being so helpful. 'You'd best tell Becky Rogers to just listen and learn.'

'I already have,' Boon replied with a grin.

Jane looked at the photograph of the cross. 'Do you know if Barry May got remanded in custody this morning?' she asked Boon.

'The bastard got bail. DC Lyons took the case for me. He detailed our objections, but the magistrate didn't think they warranted a custodial remand. It was also in May's favour that he had no previous convictions.'

Jane wasn't surprised about the bail. She just hoped Katie had gone to her parents' house.

*　*　*

There were eight members of the press and two cameramen waiting in the foyer. Boon was disappointed not to see Becky amongst them as he handed out the press passes.

'Please follow me,' he said, opening the door.

'Sorry I'm late,' Becky said loudly as she rushed into the foyer.

Everyone stopped in their tracks and looked at her.

'I didn't know *Newsround* covered murders,' a journalist said sarcastically, and a few of the others laughed. Boon handed Becky a pass.

'Well, that was a good start,' he whispered.

'Sorry, it took me ages to find somewhere to park. My editor's well chuffed I'm attending this. I've got a list of questions to ask,' she said waving a sheet of paper at him.

'Please, Becky, just let the seasoned journalists ask the questions,' he cautioned.

'Shall we make our own way upstairs officer?' an impatient journalist asked.

Boon was beginning to regret inviting Becky.

Barnes welcomed everyone and waited for the cameramen to set up before starting. The detectives on the squad stood at the side of the room. Jane noticed Lloyd Johnson walk in and waved to him. He waved back, then went and stood at the back of the room.

Barnes opened by introducing himself and Stanley, then addressed the journalists. 'I'm sure most of you are aware of the article in the *Bromley News Shopper*.'

Members of the press nodded, while Becky looked at Boon with a satisfied grin.

Barnes continued. 'I've called this conference today because we need the help of the mainstream media, press and the public to solve the murder of our unknown victim. Whilst the *News Shopper* is correct about some aspects of the nun's death, there are also many inaccuracies. Most notably about the bodies of children being buried on the grounds of the former Sisters of Mercy convent. Sensationalist journalism doesn't help our investigation. At present there is no evidence to support the claim that any children were murdered. Our primary focus is to identify the nun, which I'm confident will lead us to whoever killed her.'

Boon noticed Becky's grin change to an indignant frown.

'At this point, I'd like to hand over to Detective Sergeant Jane Tennison, who initiated the investigation. She will take you through the circumstances surrounding the discovery of the body and the post-mortem. Jane, if you please.' Barnes beckoned her over.

Jane was taken aback at being put on the spot. Barnes hadn't given her any warning she was going to address the press.

'Knock 'em dead, sarge,' Boon whispered.

Jane walked over to the maps on the wall, then used the most recent one to show where the coffin had been found and described how it had been uncovered by the workmen. She then moved over to the wall with the photographs on it. She touched the photograph of the nun in the coffin with her index finger.

'It was fortunate the body was mummified. This helped to preserve evidence of injuries on the body that might not have been found if advanced decomposition had occurred. Dr Samantha Pullen, the forensic pathologist, concluded the victim had been initially strangled to unconsciousness then put in the coffin. Scratch marks and broken fingernails on the inside indicate she regained consciousness and tried to get out. At or about this time, she was then stabbed in the back of the neck. The knife severed her spinal cord, which would have caused total paralysis. She may have died instantly or lost the ability to breathe properly and suffered a slow death by asphyxiation.'

The room fell silent as everyone took in the disturbing details of the murder.

'How old do you think she was?' a journalist asked.

'Expert opinion from a forensic dentist and anthropologist suggests between eighteen and thirty.' Jane pointed to Richard Eaves' drawings. 'These artist's impressions of her face were done by the anthropologist. We can't say they are an exact likeness of our victim but we're hoping they may help to identify her. We have copies for you to take with you.'

Jane pointed to the photographs of the cross. 'We recovered this cross she was wearing around her neck. As you can see from the enlarged photograph, it's engraved with the initials MB and the date 20.02.58. Clearly this date is significant as the convent closed in 1963. It could relate to the date she became a novice or took her final vows, which would generally be five years later. We believe the nun—'

'Could it be her date of birth?' Becky interrupted without thinking, eliciting some mocking laughter around the room.

Jane was polite in her reply. 'We excluded that possibility as it would mean the nun would only have been five when the convent closed.'

Becky blushed and looked at Boon apologetically.

Jane continued. 'We believe the nun lived and worked at the convent. It's reasonable to surmise she was murdered between 1958 and 1963.'

'Do you think someone else at the convent was involved?' a journalist asked.

Jane knew his question required a guarded answer. Before she could reply, Barnes stepped forward.

'On the evidence so far, yes, I do. But that's not to say it is the only line of inquiry we are looking at.'

'Do you have any suspects?' the same journalist asked.

'Yes, but for obvious reasons I can't disclose who they are at this stage.'

'Is the diocese helping you with your inquiries?' a female journalist asked.

'We have spoken with Bishop Robert Meade. He informed us all documentation relating to the nuns and children was destroyed by a fire at the convent in 1962, shortly before it closed.'

'What . . . everything?' she asked, looking surprised.

'So it would seem. As you can imagine, it has made our task of tracing the nuns and children who lived at the convent a difficult one. I would appeal to anyone who lived or worked at the convent to call the incident room at Orpington police station. With your assistance, I am confident we can put a name to our victim and solve this monstrous crime,' Barnes concluded.

Becky raised her hand. Boon looked at her and shook his head, but she ignored him.

'Just a couple of questions if I may, sir.'

'Yes, go ahead, young lady,' Barnes said.

'Do you think the nun's death could be linked to the convent land being developed into flats?'

'Are you asking if I think the developers were in some way involved?' he said.

Becky nodded. 'Yes.'

'We have considered that possibility,' he said, 'but we have excluded it for a couple of reasons. Firstly, we now know all the buildings and land were deconsecrated before purchase. Secondly, it would make no sense to bury a body on land that you are going to dig up.'

There was another ripple of laughter at Becky's expense.

A couple of journalists raised their hands. Barnes pointed to one of them, but Becky hadn't finished.

'DS Tennison mentioned a forensic dentist examined the victim's teeth. Does that infer she'd had some dental work done?'

Barnes shook his head in disbelief and looked at Jane to answer.

'That's correct,' she said. 'We're checking missing persons with dental records on their files against the victim's teeth. Obviously, we haven't had a match yet.'

'If the nun was never reported missing, you won't get a match, will you?' Becky said.

'It would be negligent of us not to check missing persons' dental records,' Barnes said tersely. He pointed to another journalist, but Becky still wasn't done.

'Did the nuns at the convent drive cars?'

'I don't know!' Barnes said, unable to disguise his exasperation.

'Nuns don't generally drive cars,' a seasoned-looking journalist in a grey pinstripe suit remarked. 'They take a vow of poverty. You might occasionally see one on a bike though,' he said wittily.

'Next question, please?' Barnes said, pointing to a journalist.

Becky interjected yet again with a confident smile. 'Have you checked local dentists near to the convent? If nuns don't drive cars, they'd probably walk to the nearest one if they needed a filling.'

The room fell silent waiting for an answer from a flustered-looking Barnes. It was a simple line of inquiry that had so far been overlooked. Boon nodded at Becky, pleased she had silenced the mockers.

Barnes cleared his throat. 'Thank you for that astute observation, Miss . . .?

'Rogers, Becky Rogers . . . investigative reporter for the *Bromley News Shopper*.'

Barnes pointed to the journalist who had his hand raised.

'I spoke with someone at the diocesan offices this morning. I was reliably informed they were not aware the nun was murdered until after the *News Shopper* article. Why weren't they or the press informed immediately after the post-mortem last Thursday?'

'Because I wanted to try and identify the victim first,' Barnes replied, with an edge in his voice.

'If you'd informed the diocese immediately or done a press appeal, you might have identified her by now,' the same journalist said.

'As I already said, the convent records were destroyed in a fire and the diocese was unable to help us,' Barnes said.

'Unable or unwilling?' the journalist in the pinstripe suit interjected.

'We will continue to seek their assistance. It's up to them whether or not they want to help or hinder us,' Barnes replied, clearly losing his cool.

The same journalist picked up on Barnes's comment. 'As an investigative journalist for *The Times*, I know of many allegations of child abuse made against Catholic priests and nuns. In my experience, the hierarchy of the Church withholds information from investigators and the press. They turn a blind eye and protect their own using medieval canon law. They allow the abuser to confess their sins without fear of a public prosecution. Do you think the nun's murder is being covered up by members of the Catholic Church?' he asked pointedly.

There was an air of expectation in the room after such a direct question. Everyone looked at Barnes, keenly awaiting his reply. Jane knew this was Barnes's opportunity to air his feelings of injustice over Stephen Phillips' death. She watched as all the journalists hold their pens to their notepads, ready to write down his reply.

Barnes took a sip of water. 'I had a similar experience investigating the suicide of a twelve-year-old convent orphan. At his post-mortem we discovered he'd been beaten so badly you could see the outline of a belt and buckle on his skin. Old bruises and scars revealed this was a regular occurrence. I wanted to interview other children at the orphanage, but my request was refused by senior members of the diocese who said they would carry out an internal investigation.'

'And did they?' the journalist asked.

'I was told by a bishop that the priest who "chastised" Stephen had been moved to "pastures new",' Barnes said in a sarcastic tone. 'Personally, I'm in no doubt Stephen took his own life as a direct result of the pain he suffered. Those responsible for his injuries should have been charged with assault and held accountable in the Crown Court. The diocesan investigation was nothing more than a cover-up. I will not let that happen again. My team of officers will not rest until this case is solved . . . with or without the help of the diocese.'

'Bloody hell, that was some revelation,' Boon whispered to Jane.

She didn't reply. Jane feared the Met's senior officers would view his remarks as an unnecessary attack on the Catholic Church, and unbecoming to an officer of his rank. She wondered if Barnes was unburdening himself and didn't care he was putting his career on the line.

'Do you think children at the Sisters of Mercy convent were abused?' the journalist asked.

Becky looked at Boon, who whispered to Jane.

'I hope Stanley told him about Mrs Gorman . . .'

'We have no direct evidence of that at this time,' Barnes said. 'But it is something we are looking into as part of our investigation.'

'Obviously not,' Boon sighed as Barnes continued.

'I would encourage anyone who was abused in any way whilst at the convent to contact us. We will treat your information as confidential and support you. Unless there are any further questions, I think we can conclude this press conference.'

As members of the press left the room, the journalist in the pinstripe suit approached Barnes.

'Thanks for answering my question about the cover-up. I intend to write an exposé about child abuse by priests and nuns. It has gone on for too long now and something needs to be done about the archaic laws the Catholic Church uses to deal with those who abuse children.' He handed Barnes his business card. 'You can rest assured I never reveal my sources.'

Barnes put the card in his breast pocket. 'Thanks. I'll keep you informed of any developments,' he said, and they shook hands.

Becky had a quick chat with Boon and thanked him for letting her attend.

'I was wondering if you still fancied going out for a drink?' she asked.

'I think I'm going to be busy with work for a while,' he replied, remembering what he'd said to Jane about mixing business with pleasure.

Becky pulled a sad face. 'Pretty please. I promise, I won't ask a single question about the investigation.'

'Go on, then. Tomorrow night will probably be best for me work-wise. I'll give you a ring. What's your home number?' he asked, handing Becky his notebook.

* * *

Once the press had left, Barnes spoke to the detectives and civilian staff. He told them the office meeting would start in half an hour, but first he wanted to speak with Stanley, Jane, Boon and Lloyd Johnson in his office.

As Barnes opened the bottom drawer of his office filing cabinet, they heard the chink of glasses. He removed a bottle of Glenmorangie malt whisky and five glasses, which he lined up on his desk.

'I keep this for special occasions,' he said as he pulled the cork stopper out. 'I thought the press conference went well, didn't you?' He poured some whisky into the glasses.

They looked at each other, wondering who was going to reply first. Lloyd elbowed Stanley, forcing him to respond.

'Yes, sir. You spoke very well. Stephen Phillips' death and the Church's cover-up certainly got the press's attention. It will no doubt cause a bit of a stir in the diocesan offices.'

'Good. It was my intention to put the cat amongst the pigeons. Help yourselves.'

Once everyone had picked up a glass, he said, 'Cheers. Here's to putting Bishop Meade and his co-conspirators behind bars.'

Everyone raised their glasses and said 'Cheers'. Barnes downed his whisky in one, poured another and lit one of his Black Russian cigarettes, then looked at Boon.

'Good work with Annette Gorman today, son. I thought it best not to mention her in the conference. Her statement will be another nail in Meade's coffin. Stanley also told me you've traced a Sister Julie who lived at the convent.'

'Julie Dorton. She's no longer a nun. She lives in Sidcup,' Boon replied.

'I'd be interested to know why she left,' Barnes said.

'Annette Gorman gave me the impression she'd had enough of the way the Mother Superior and some of the other nuns treated the children,' Boon told him.

'Abusing kids seems to be a way of life in the Catholic Church,' Stanley remarked.

'There may be other reasons she left. I want Boon and Tennison to interview her this evening after the office meeting,' Barnes said.

'Yes, sir,' they replied in unison.

'Thanks for coming in, DS Jackson. I know you're busy dealing with the forensics on a number of murder investigations, so I won't keep you long. Can you bring us up to speed with what you have so far?' Barnes asked.

Lloyd looked at Jane. 'Your hunch about the nun's cincture matching the fibres around her neck was spot on.'

'What's a cincture?' Boon asked.

'It's the brown, rope-like cord the dead nun was wearing round her waist,' Lloyd told him.

Boon looked at Jane with a bemused expression. 'You think she was strangled with her own rope, then someone took the time and effort to tie it neatly around her waist?'

'Of course not,' she said, 'though I suppose it's not an impossibility. Nuns of the same order have the same cinctures.'

Boon twigged. 'Ah, I get it. A nun using her own rope to strangle our victim, thus the matching fibres.'

'Hemp fibres to be precise,' Lloyd said.

'What, as in cannabis?' Boon asked.

'Hemp is a variety of the same plant, used to make rope,' Lloyd replied.

'Would you two shut up and let Tennison finish?' Barnes said.

Jane continued. 'I saw a priest at the diocesan offices wearing a cincture like our victim's.'

Barnes sat up. 'Which means the fibres on the nun's neck could be from Meade's cincture.'

Lloyd shook his head. 'The problem is that forensics can never match an individual rope to the hemp fibres on the nun's neck. All they can tell you is that there's a high probability a hemp rope was used to strangle her.'

'That's not much bloody use to us. Have you got any good news, Lloyd?' Barnes said curtly.

'We examined the broken knife tip under a high-powered microscope. There was a minuscule sliver of wood on it. Two further slivers were found on the hole in her clothing where she was stabbed in the neck. A forestry expert concluded from the cellular structure they were all birch tree fragments. This suggests the knife had recently been used for cutting wood.'

Barnes sighed. 'The chances of us finding the knife now are virtually nil. Is that it, Lloyd?'

'We're still examining the stomach contents. It's amazing how the food inside her has dried and solidified. Looks like her last meal was a vegetable stew with broccoli, cauliflower and seeded bread.'

Barnes was losing interest. 'Are you likely to find anything forensically we can use as direct evidence against Meade?'

'From what the scientists tell me, it's unlikely,' Lloyd admitted.

'I'll take that as a no,' Barnes said. 'How'd you get on at the diocesan archives, Tennison?'

'Parkin, the archivist, confirmed there were no documents relating to the nuns or children at the convent. Meade lied; she didn't tell him about the fire because it was the other way round. I've got a copy of a letter from the diocesan solicitors to the developers. All it says is the fire occurred in August 1962 and the buildings were damaged beyond repair. It raises the question of how Meade knew the fire started in the bakery and destroyed all the convent documents.'

'Are you thinking Meade committed arson to destroy the records?' Stanley asked.

Jane nodded. 'I know it's a long shot, but it might be worth getting a fire investigator from the lab to have a look at what's left of the buildings.'

'It's worth a try,' Barnes said.

'I'll get it sorted for tomorrow morning,' Lloyd said.

'Anything else of interest, Tennison?' Barnes asked.

'The list of priests who worked at St Mary's has also mysteriously gone missing.' Jane was glad she didn't have to reveal she got the information from a priest.

'That's another coincidence with Meade's name written all over it,' Boon remarked.

'The man is digging his own grave,' Stanley added.

Barnes lit another cigarette. 'I agree . . . but it's not deep enough yet. I've no doubt he's involved in the nun's murder, but without a confession we don't have enough to charge him. If he murdered the nun, he must have got someone to help him move and bury the coffin. If we can find that person and get them to roll over, we've got a good chance of convicting Meade.' He turned to Jane. 'Any other revelations from the archives?'

'I obtained a couple of documents confirming the buildings and land were deconsecrated in 1964.'

'Good, that's put that issue to bed and should please the developers.'

Jane wondered if she should tell him Thomas Durham and Lee Holland had been acting strangely and might be hiding something that could be connected to the murder, but she decided to hold back until she had some hard evidence.

'Anything else?' Barnes asked.

'Unfortunately, no, as I was escorted off the premises.'

They all looked at Jane, wondering what she'd done.

'By Meade?' Barnes asked, taking a sip of his whisky.

'No, he was in Cambridge. But he'd heard about the *News Shopper* article and phoned the priest who's his personal assistant. He must have told him I was in the archives. The priest told me Meade said I had deceived the Church and Archbishop Malone was returning from Rome, so—'

Barnes nearly choked on his whisky. 'Did you say Malone?'

'Yes. Andrew Malone is the archbishop of Southwark.'

Barnes wiped the whisky from his chin. 'Andrew Malone was the name of the priest who took pleasure in beating Stephen black and blue. If it's him, he will do everything he can to protect Meade and the Church. When's he due back in London?'

'I think he's flying back tomorrow sometime,' Jane informed him.

Barnes shook his head. 'We need to act quickly. I want Meade arrested before Malone can get to him.'

Stanley worried Barnes was being impetuous. 'I don't want to appear rude, sir, but I suspect Malone has already spoken to Meade. No doubt he will have told him to say nothing until he gets back from Rome. It might be to our advantage to interview Dorton and evaluate the calls we get from the public after the six o'clock news first.'

Barnes frowned. 'Why?'

'Like you just said, we haven't got enough to charge Meade. Arresting him now could be futile. If he made a no-comment interview, we'd have to release him. Julie Dorton may be able to identify Meade as the local priest and confirm he knew our victim. There's also a chance someone watching the news might call us with more damning evidence. Waiting until the morning to arrest him might be a better option. I can also check what time the first flight from Rome arrives.'

Barnes rubbed his chin and thought about it. 'Tennison, you and Boon skip the office meeting. Go and see Julie Dorton. Show her Eaves' drawings. Then come straight back here. This could be a long night,' he said. He downed his whisky, then poured another. 'And get someone to check out the local dentists for nuns who had a fucking toothache!'

CHAPTER TWENTY-TWO

While Boon phoned Julie Dorton from Barnes's office, Jane went to the incident room to get her bag and coat. A few detectives were setting up their desks and others were looking at the photographs and maps on the walls. She overheard one on the phone to his wife, telling her he probably wouldn't be home until late. She picked up the phone on an empty desk in the corner of the room and rang Nick's office.

'Hi, it's me. How did it go with your dad?'

'He'll survive,' he said.

'Look, I don't think I'll be able to see you tonight. I've got to interview someone and I don't know how long it's going to take. My DCI wants me to report back to the incident room afterwards. I've a suspicion he'll want us all in early morning as well. I don't want to disturb you, so I'll stay the night at mine tonight if that's—'

'Yeah, fine. Do what's best for you,' Nick replied.

'Are you OK?' Jane asked, bemused by his off-hand tone.

'Yeah, shouldn't I be?'

Jane couldn't understand why he was talking to her like this. 'Have I done something to upset you?'

There was a brief pause. 'No, it's not you. My dad can be pretty exhausting at times.'

'I understand. Look, it might be late, but I'll come round to your house when I finish. We can cheer each other up,' she said.

'If it's all the same, I'd like to stay at my dad's tonight and keep an eye on him.'

Jane was taken aback. 'Right, fine . . . I understand.' She didn't see Boon approaching.

'Mrs Dorton's happy to speak with us. You good to go, sarge?' he asked.

She put her hand over the mouthpiece. 'Can't you see I'm on the phone?' she said tersely. 'I've got to go. I'll speak to you tomorrow.' She waited for a reply then realised Nick had already put the phone down.

Driving to Julie Dorton's, Jane couldn't help but feel concerned about her brief conversation with Nick. She knew he was close to his father, but his curt replies were out of character. She racked her brain but couldn't think of anything she'd done that could have upset him. She wondered if the whole business of the nun's murder, the site being closed and his father's illness was getting to him more than he was letting on.

'You all right, sarge?' Boon asked, but she didn't answer. 'Hello, Boon to DS Tennison, are you receiving . . . over?' he joked.

She bit back a sharp reply. 'Sorry, I was thinking about what we need to ask Julie Dorton.'

'I was surprised Barnes never had a pop at me about Becky Rogers being at the press conference,' Boon remarked.

'I think his mind was on more important things. Personally, I was quite impressed with her. She's dogged and she certainly speaks her mind.'

'Not dissimilar to you then, sarge,' Boon grinned.

'Don't be cheeky,' Jane said.

'Dorton's house should be just up here on the left,' Boon said as they drove along Hurst Road.

* * *

Julie Dorton was an attractive, fresh-faced woman in her late forties, with dark curly auburn hair and bright eyes. She was wearing a dark blue hospital dress and a nurse's belt around her slim waist. Jane noticed she also wore wedding and engagement rings.

'I've not long been back from work. Please come through to the living room,' she said nervously.

'Are you all right, Mrs Dorton?' Jane asked.

'I just watched the evening news. I think I know who the nun is, but . . . it just doesn't seem possible she was murdered.' Her voice trembled. 'The artist's impression they showed looked familiar, but I wasn't sure it was her. Then when they showed a picture of the cross with the initials on it . . .' Julie started to cry.

Jane and Boon looked at each other, realising this was a significant development. Boon got out his notebook and pen, having agreed that Jane would interview Julie and he would take notes to be made into a full statement later. Jane sat next to Julie on the settee.

'Who do you think MB is, Julie?' Jane asked, handing her a tissue.

'Sister Melissa . . . but we all called her Missy.'

'Do you know her surname?'

'It was Bailey.'

'And you were at the convent together?' Jane asked.

Julie blew her nose and nodded. 'She was my best friend.'

'I know this must be difficult for you, Julie, but I need to ask you some questions about Missy . . . is that OK?'

'Yes. I want to help . . . but I can't believe she was murdered . . . I thought Missy left the convent because she'd had enough of the way it was run. Do you really think it's her body you found?'

'We don't know for certain yet. But with what you've just told us, it's an even stronger possibility. When did you first meet Missy? If you can recall any dates, it would be very helpful.'

'We joined the convent as novices in February 1953 and shared a room together. I was nineteen and Missy was eighteen. We felt segregated from some of the older sisters, who stuck to a strict religious routine and rarely spoke to us younger novices. Missy and I got on well and quickly became close friends.' Julie undid the top button of her dress and withdrew a cross on a chain. She took it off and handed it to Jane.

'We were given these when we took our final vows. Mine is the same as Missy's, apart from the initials, of course.'

'Can you recall if there was anyone else at the convent with the initials MB?' Jane asked.

'There were a couple of sisters called Mary. I think one's surname was Brown; the other one I can't remember. Mind you, they were both a lot older and probably took their vows in the 1940s.'

'Do you know what part of the country Missy was from?'

'She told me her parents emigrated to Canada just after the war. She came back to the UK to become a nun when she turned eighteen.'

'Do you know where they lived in Canada?

'Whenever we said how cold it was in winter, Missy would laugh and say, "Try living in Kingston, Ontario. It's so cold you poop snowflakes."' Julie smiled at the memory.

'Did she talk about her parents by name? What they did for a living or anything like that?' Jane asked, knowing she would need to trace them.

'I'm sorry. I don't know their names. I recall her saying something about her dad being a university teacher.'

'Do you know when Missy's birthday was?' Jane asked.

'The fifth of August. I remember making a cake for her twenty-seventh birthday . . . just before she left.'

'Can you give me a bit more detail on why you think Missy left the convent?'

'She couldn't stand how the children were treated by Mother Superior and Sister Margaret. At the time I thought it had been eating away at her so much she just decided to walk out the door one night and never return.'

'Annette Gorman told us about some of Mother Superior's horrendous punishments and assaults on the kids,' Boon said.

'I know. I spoke with her earlier. Everything Annette told you is the truth.'

'I don't for one second doubt her, or you, Julie,' Jane assured her.

'Annette also told me about the article in the *News Shopper*. I read it myself. The bit about the bodies of murdered children being buried at the convent is utter nonsense.'

'I know,' Jane said, 'but as investigators we can't totally ignore it as a possibility.'

'In fairness, Mother Superior wasn't abusive when Missy and I first joined the convent,' Julie said. 'Although she used her wooden ladle to smack the children, it was in a gentle good-natured way – a light tap on the head or back of the hand, nothing vicious. She even reigned in Sister Margaret when she saw her being overzealous in her punishments.'

'So what happened to change everything?' Jane asked.

'The convent was getting rundown and in constant need of repair, which was costly for the diocese. Mother Superior heard a rumour they were thinking of selling it to raise funds. The convent was her life. She became depressed then started drinking heavily.'

'How did you know Mother Superior was drinking?' Jane asked.

'She'd always liked a tipple, but her drinking got worse and she was often drunk, particularly of an evening. She stank of alcohol, slurred her words and staggered about. We suspected her booze was hidden in the chapel crypt as she spent so much time down there. The more she drank, the more bad-tempered and aggressive she became, often lashing out at the children and us for really trivial transgressions of the rules. Sister Margaret used it to her advantage and became Mother Superior's self-appointed deputy. Together they started to run the convent with a rod of iron.'

'I take it that upset Missy.'

'It upset many of us. Missy was quite strong-willed and often spoke her mind. She told Mother Superior and Sister Margaret their physical abuse of the children made them live in constant fear and misery.'

'What did they say to that?'

'Missy told me they laughed at her. Mother Superior started to bully Missy and constantly punish her for trivial things that didn't really matter.'

'How did she punish her?'

'She gave her the worst chores, stopped her writing home and generally made her life a misery, day in and day out.'

'How did Missy react?'

'She sort of took it on the chin and accepted her punishments. I know it must have upset her, but Missy was tough; she wasn't going to let them break her down. Sometimes I could see she was fighting back the tears. I'd ask her if she was all right. She'd smile and say, "Don't worry about me . . . I'm fine."'

'Can you tell me anything else about what made Missy so angry?'

'When Sister Margaret cut Annette's face with her cane, Missy was incensed. She told me she was going to report Sister Margaret and Mother Superior to the bishop. I'm ashamed to say I tried to dissuade her. I was afraid they would make Missy's life even more of a misery . . . and take their anger out on the children as well,' Julie added, welling up.

'You mustn't blame yourself for anything that happened at the convent,' Jane said. 'I understand why you were scared. Did Missy tell the bishop?'

'I don't think so, because Mother Superior and Sister Margaret didn't change their ways. I think Missy also thought in the end it would be a waste of time.'

'Why?' Jane asked.

'Because Mother Superior was good at putting on an act. She was ambitious. She often said she would become the next Superior General and have a private audience with the pope—'

'Sorry to interrupt, but what's a Superior General?' Jane asked.

'It's also known as Mother General. Basically, they oversee all the Sisters of Mercy convents. Mother Superior was determined to achieve her goal and make sure the bishop and other visitors were properly impressed when they came to the convent.'

'How did she do that?' Boon asked. 'Considering how badly the children were treated.'

'There was a room in the convent that was always kept locked by Mother Superior. Inside was everything a child could wish for: a lovely playroom full of toys, books and dolls, all donated by a local Catholic charity. She only opened the playroom on days that dignitaries like the bishop or other officials visited the convent. They would see a room full of happy, smiling children and walk away with a false impression all was well and she was wonderful. As soon as they were gone, the children were marched out and the door was locked. Any child who resisted was given a whack on the head by Mother Superior with her wooden ladle or caned on the backside by Sister Margaret.'

'Can you remember anything about Missy's behaviour just before she left?' Jane asked.

'She hadn't been her normal easy-going self. She was quiet and subdued. We always confided in each other when something was bothering us, but Missy was becoming more and more distant and keeping her feelings to herself. The last night I ever saw her we were in our room. It was after lights-out and I heard her crying. I asked what was upsetting her. Missy said she was really unhappy at the convent and didn't know if she could continue to devote her life to the sisterhood and uphold the vows she had taken. I realised she was thinking of leaving. I told her not to do anything rash and suggested she should ask for a move to another convent. She said she would think about it, though it seemed to me she'd made up her mind. It wasn't unusual for sisters to give up their faith, though generally they were novices. A few left while I was at the convent.'

'Excuse my ignorance, but what exactly are the vows you take as a nun?' Boon asked.

Julie smiled. 'We were not nuns in the strict sense of the word. Although nuns and sisters are addressed as "Sister", there is a difference. Nuns take solemn vows and live a cloistered life. They live, pray and work within the confines of a convent or nunnery. As "Sisters" we take simple perpetual vows of chastity, poverty and obedience. We can live in a convent or amongst the community, serving in healthcare or educational institutions. Nuns under solemn vows can only be released by the Pope, while sisters under simple vows can be released from them by the bishop.'

'You learn something new every day,' Boon smiled.

'Do you think there was anything else, besides convent life, that was making Missy unhappy?' Jane said.

Julie nodded. 'I did wonder that, but I figured if Missy wanted to tell me she would, in her own time. I woke up in the early hours of the morning, Missy wasn't in her bed . . .' Julie started to cry. 'I . . . looked on top of the wardrobe for the little case she'd brought with her when we first joined the convent. But it wasn't there. She'd also taken her underwear and toiletries. At the time I thought she must have slipped out in the middle of the night. I was heartbroken she hadn't said goodbye, but I understood why.'

'How did Mother Superior find out?'

'She asked me why Missy wasn't at breakfast. I said I didn't know and thought she'd got up before me. I was trying to give Missy as much time as possible to get far away from the convent. Mother Superior was furious when she realised Missy had run away. She accused me of helping her and Sister Margaret waved her cane in my face demanding to know where Missy had gone. I kept saying I didn't know and Sister Margaret flew into a rage and beat me with her cane. Mother Superior said if anyone asked about Missy, I was to say she had decided to leave the sisterhood and left during the night. Back then there was an unspoken rule: when a sister left the community, we were not to mention her name again.'

'That's awful, Julie. I understand now why you believed she had run away. If I were in your shoes, I'd have thought the same thing,' Jane said.

'Me, too,' Boon added.

'Did they send anyone out to look for Missy?' Jane asked.

'Mother Superior said she was going to inform the police.'

'Do you know if she did?'

'No, but I very much doubt it, as a nun running away would be an embarrassment and could have caused them problems, especially if their abusive behaviour was ever revealed. However, she did tell Bishop Malone.'

Jane wasn't surprised to hear his name come up again. 'Isn't he the archbishop of Southwark now?'

'Yes, I heard he is.'

'How did you know she told Malone?'

'The next day I was called to Mother Superior's office. Bishop Malone was there. He was angry and demanded to know if I knew Missy was going to run away, and if so, where she had gone. Initially I stuck to my story but was so incensed about the beating Sister Margaret had given me I told him Missy said she was going to write a letter to him about how abusive they were to the children.'

'How did they all react?' Jane asked.

'He pointed his finger at me and accused me of lying. He said Missy had broken her vows and betrayed God and the Church by running away. Bishop Malone was only interested in protecting the good name of Mother Superior and the convent. He said Mother Superior would inform everyone that Missy had sought dispensation from her vows, which he had granted.'

Jane sighed. 'Archbishop Malone seems to have a history of covering things up that look bad for the Church. He was also suspected of being abusive to children when he was a priest. Do you know if he was abusive to any of the children at your convent?'

'I don't think so. He rarely visited and was usually with other people when he did.'

'Did no one think it strange that Missy didn't say goodbye?' Boon asked.

Julie shook her head. 'There's a "shroud of secrecy" when a Sister chooses to leave. They are under strict orders not to tell anyone or say goodbye and usually leave during the night. You have to understand that obedience was paramount in everything we did.'

'What happened to you after the meeting?'

'Mother Superior removed me from teaching the children and I ended up doing all the worst jobs around the convent for months. But I didn't regret what I'd said to Bishop Malone about the abuse because I knew Missy would have been proud of me.'

'I don't wish to sound insensitive, but did you ever wonder why Missy didn't try and make contact with you?' Jane asked.

'I like to think she wrote to me, but Missy knew all our incoming and outgoing mail was checked and censored by Mother Superior and Sister Margaret in case it contained something offensive to our vocation. They would have destroyed any letters Missy sent me. Some of my own letters from home were so inked out by them there was hardly anything left to read. I used to cry, worrying over what my mother had been trying to tell me, but there was no way I could ever know. It never occurred to me Missy might be dead. To now know she was murdered is beyond belief. Are you really sure it's her?'

'I hate to say it, Julie, but even more so now.'

'But why? It just doesn't make any sense. Who on earth would want to kill Missy?'

'Right now, I can't answer that, but I promise you we will find out who and why,' Jane said reassuringly.

'Could it have been an accident?'

'I'm afraid the injuries she received rule that possibility out. Can you remember the date when you thought Missy ran away?' Jane asked.

Julie closed her eyes and thought about it. 'I think it was in August 1962. Shortly after her birthday.'

'Was that before or after the fire?'

Julie closed her eyes again. 'I'm not sure now . . . but I think it was before the fire.'

'What do you remember about the fire?'

'I was asleep in bed when I was woken by Sister Maria shouting that the outbuildings were on fire. I could see the flames as I ran through the gardens. When I got there, the bakery and schoolhouse next to it were ablaze and the flames were spreading rapidly to the other buildings. Mother Superior and some of the nuns were throwing water from the well on it. The heat got so intense they couldn't get close enough with the water and had to stop trying to put it out. By the time the fire brigade got there, all the outbuildings were on fire.'

'I was told the fire started in the bakery. Do you know if that's correct?' Jane asked.

Julie nodded. 'That's what Mother Superior thought. She was convinced one of us had failed to make sure the baking oven fire was extinguished at the end of the day. She thought a cinder must have started it. After the fire Mother Superior became an emotional wreck and started drinking even more. I think she knew in her heart the buildings wouldn't be rebuilt and the convent would close . . . which of course it did.'

'Do you know the Mother Superior's full name and Sister Margaret's surname?'

'Adele Delaney was Mother Superior.'

'Do you know where she is now?'

'She died some years ago.'

'How do you know?'

'Sister Suzanne Lincoln told me. We were at the convent together and still keep in touch. She works at St Joseph's Hospice in Mare Street, Hackney. She went there after the convent closed.'

'Do you know where she lives?' Boon asked.

'The convent is situated in the midst of the hospice buildings. Mother Superior was in palliative care there, suffering with
hepatocellular carcinoma.'

'What's that?' Boon asked.

'A form of liver cancer that occurs in people with alcoholic
cirrhosis.'

'The demon drink got the better of her in the end,' Boon
remarked.

Jane thought his remark inappropriate and glared at him before
Julie continued.

'Sister Margaret's surname was Wilde. Which we all thought
rather apt due to her fierce temper.'

'Do you know where she is now?' Jane asked.

'I haven't a clue. Suzanne might know.'

'Does the name Father Bob mean anything to you?'

Julie smiled. 'Yes. He was the priest at St Mary's. He used to
come to the convent and read stories to the children. He was a
lovely man. I shouldn't say it, but some of us younger sisters fancied him . . . but not in a carnal way, of course,' she said with a grin.

'Did Missy like him?' Jane asked.

Julie laughed. 'Yes, she used to refer to him as the "forbidden
fruit".'

Jane suddenly found herself thinking of Father Chris and the
moment he'd kissed her.

'Why did you ask about Father Bob?' Julie asked.

'Annette Gorman mentioned him, but wasn't sure about his
surname.'

'It's Meade.'

Jane didn't want to press Julie about Meade possibly abusing the
children, as it was clear she liked and trusted him, so she changed
the subject.

'There's a tunnel from the crypt to the outbuildings. Was it in
use while you were there?' Jane asked.

'Yes. We used it to take food from the bakery and gardens to the main building in bad weather. During the fire, part of it collapsed. Mother Superior had a builder look at it. He said it was dangerous, so we were all banned from using it. As I recall, the tunnel door in the crypt was removed and bricked up.'

'Do you know who the builder was?'

'No, I'm afraid not.'

'Did any builders ever carry out repair work at the convent while you were there?' Jane asked.

'Sometimes, but I didn't really take any notice. I recall a leaky roof in the chapel being repaired by a couple of men.'

'Can you describe them?'

Julie shook her head. 'Like I said, I didn't really take any notice.'

Boon took a picture of the coffin from a folder and handed it to Julie. 'Did you ever see this coffin when you were at the convent?'

'I recall some metal ones like that in the crypt. And there were also a few wooden coffins down there.'

'Would a nun be buried in a metal coffin?' Boon asked.

'No, the wooden ones were for us.'

Jane stood up. 'That's all we need to ask you for now, Julie. I'm sorry our conversation has been so upsetting for you. What you've told us has been incredibly useful to our investigation. DC Boon will compile an official statement at the station from his notes. Would you be happy to sign it and give evidence in court if required?'

'Of course. I'll do whatever you need if it helps catch whoever killed Missy.'

Boon tentatively raised his hand. 'Can I ask you a personal question, Mrs Dorton?'

'Of course.'

Jane gave him a sideways glance as a warning he'd better not upset her.

'What made you leave the sisterhood?'

Julie smiled. 'I found my own piece of forbidden fruit, fell in love and married him. My surname is Davidson now. Carl, my husband, is an ambulance driver,' she said proudly.

As they walked to the front door, Jane remembered something.

'Do you have any photographs of Missy from when you were at the convent?'

'I'm sorry. Our vow of poverty meant we couldn't have things like cameras.'

'I guess the artist's impression will have to suffice then,' Jane said.

'Actually, come to think of it, I've got a group photograph of us all with the children in a cupboard upstairs. Give me a second while I look for it,' Julie said.

After a few minutes she came downstairs holding a large, framed black-and-white photograph. She handed it to Jane.

Boon leaned forward to look at the photograph, which had clearly been taken outside the schoolhouse. Three older sisters were sitting on a garden bench, with the rest of the sisters, a priest, and some children in a semi-circle behind them. The youngsters sat on the ground, cross-legged. Everyone was smiling as if they didn't have a care in the world. Jane visualised Eaves' artist's impression but didn't see anyone she could positively identify as Sister Missy. The fact that they were all dressed the same and wearing white wimples made it even more difficult.

Julie looked glum. 'They say every picture tells a story . . . the truth is, this one lies. Although it brings back some happy memories, we all smiled because Mother Superior said anyone who didn't would be for the high jump. That's Missy,' Julie said, pointing, 'and that's me on her left. Annette's sat on the ground in front of Mother Superior who is in the centre on the bench, with Sister Margaret on her right. That's Father Bob in the back row.'

'Would you mind writing down the names of everyone in the photograph you can remember?' Jane asked.

'Of course.' Julie went and got a notepad and set to work.

'Do you have any more photos like this?' Boon asked.

Julie shook her head. 'We had a convent group photograph taken every summer. Mother Superior hung them in the "off limits" play-room. When we knew we had to leave the convent, I got the job of packing up the stuff that was in there. I took this as a memento of me and Missy and the year we took our final vows.'

Jane realised Meade looked a lot different now and doubted she'd have recognised him without Julie pointing him out. She saw the photograph had 'Sisters of Mercy Convent 1958' printed on the bottom and turned it over. She found what she was looking for. On the back was a sticky label with 'Scott Davies Photography' and an address in Market Square, Bromley.

'Would you mind if I took this photograph with me?' Jane asked.

* * *

The incident room was a hive of organised activity and urgent voices. Every phone was manned by detectives, trying not to talk over each other as they spoke with members of the public who had seen the six o'clock news. The caller's details and information were recorded on the appropriate forms, which on completion were taken to Barnes's office, where he and Stanley assessed and prioritised them for any immediate action.

'You got anything that mentions Mead or Malone yet?' Barnes asked Stanley.

'Nope, nothing. I've got a few with possible names for nuns at the convent, but they're all Sister this and Sister that – not a surname on any of them.

'Same here. I thought we might at least get a call from a nun who'd lived there,' Barnes sighed.

'If they lead a sheltered life, they might not watch TV or read newspapers,' Stanley remarked.

'That's true. At least we are getting people calling in, so fingers crossed.'

Stanley held up a few information forms. 'There've been a few calls from people who said they were kids at the orphanage. They all mention the strict regime handed out by the Mother Superior and some of the nuns.'

'I've got a few here too, but no mention of Meade being an abuser. We need to prioritise the calls we've received, then I'll get some of the team to interview the former pupils.' There was a knock on the door. 'I've already told you there's no need to knock,' Barnes shouted, thinking it was a detective with more information forms.

Jane walked in, with Boon behind her carrying the convent photograph.

'You two took your time.'

'Less haste, more speed, sir,' Jane beamed.

'I'm not in the mood for flippancy, Tennison.'

'We think we've identified our victim,' Jane said.

'And we've got proof Meade knew her,' Boon added, holding up the photograph.

Barnes's face lit up.

'Who is she?' an energised Barnes asked.

'Her name's Melissa Bailey, also known as Sister Missy, born fifth of August 1940. Her parents live in Kingston, Ontario. She became a novice at the Sisters of Mercy convent in February 1953 and took her final vows on the twentieth of February 1958.'

'The date on the cross. That's bloody brilliant. Well done, you two.' Barnes beamed.

Boon put the photo down on Barnes's desk and pointed out Melissa and Julie.

'The priest in the back row is—'

'The illustrious Father Bob,' Barnes said, picking up the photograph to have a closer look.

'Julie Dorton confirmed it's Robert Meade,' Boon added.

'Meade was clearly well-liked, so I didn't press her about him abusing the children. I figured it would be better coming from an actual victim if we trace one.'

Barnes nodded. 'Tell me everything that Dorton said, chapter and verse.'

Jane recounted the interview from memory and Boon added other salient details from his notebook.

'Well done, the pair of you. Dorton's information is another step in the right direction. It yet again proves Meade is lying.'

'I can't say I was sorry to hear Mother Superior was dead after the way she treated those poor children,' Boon remarked.

'Julie's account suggests Missy didn't even get out of the front door of the convent before she was murdered,' Jane said.

'Dorton might have lied about her relationship with Missy because she was involved in the murder?' Stanley suggested.

Jane shook her head. 'I've no reason to doubt her whatsoever. I certainly don't think Julie was putting on the tears for effect. She also got a severe beating from Sister Margaret.'

'OK, fair enough, but it's a question that needed to be raised,' Stanley said defensively.

'If Missy was murdered inside the convent when she was attempting to leave, it was probably in the early hours of the morning, which rules Meade out as he lived a mile—'

Barnes interrupted. 'Come on, Jane, it's bloody obvious Meade is lying through his teeth and involved in some way. Who's to say Sister Missy didn't go there to confront him if he was abusing the children?'

'I'm not doubting he's involved. I'm just saying it makes him less likely to be the killer if he was tucked up in bed. It's also a bloody long way to drag a coffin from the presbytery to the convent,' Jane replied.

'Not if there's two people carrying it. I'd bet a pound to a penny Malone is involved in some way,' Barnes insisted.

Jane told Barnes about Julie's meeting with the then Bishop Malone: how he wanted to protect the good name of the convent and grant Sister Missy a dispensation so it appeared she'd left the sisterhood of her own free will.

He nodded. 'That just confirms my suspicions about Malone.'

Boon raised his hand. 'Can I say something?'

'I know Julie's account suggests Mother Superior and Sister Margaret thought Sister Missy ran away, but it's clear they both had violent tempers.'

'It's a valid point, son, but Missy's post-mortem revealed her death was extremely violent and has all the hallmarks of a male assailant,' Barnes said.

Jane thought there was more merit to Boon's idea. 'They could have been involved in a cover-up . . . or forced into one by Meade or Malone.'

'I agree, that's possible,' Barnes conceded.

'Well, Mother Superior can't help us as she's dead,' Stanley remarked.

Barnes rubbed his chin. 'We still need to confirm it, and trace Sister Margaret.' He looked at his watch. 'Boon, go and phone the hospice and see if you can get hold of Sister Suzanne. Tell her you spoke with Julie Dorton. Confirm Mother Superior's death and see if she knows where Sister Margaret is. Also, ask if someone from the team can interview her tomorrow.'

'Yes, sir,' Boon said. He quickly left the office.

'This case is a real can of worms,' Barnes said. 'The diocese will close ranks. They'll speak to us, but they will lie through their teeth to protect their own and the reputation of the Church.'

After the meeting, Jane spoke privately with Stanley in the squad room. She asked him what was happening about searching the convent grounds and development site for other bodies. He told her that Barnes had spoken with Richard Eaves, the anthropologist, and sought his advice about looking for buried bodies.

'What did Eaves say?' Jane asked.

'He's going to speak with the university archaeology department. Apparently, they've got some new-fangled machine called a ground penetrating radar that looks for underground anomalies.'

'Can it find human bodies?'

Stanley shrugged. 'They've never used it for that, but they're willing to give it a try. To be honest, I just think he's going through the motions to cover his back, since we've not a shred of evidence any children or other nuns were murdered.'

'Did they say how long it will take?' Jane asked, thinking of Nick's predicament.

'A week or two. If they find nothing, then I guess the building work can recommence.'

When Stanley was out of earshot, Jane picked up a phone and dialled Nick's office. There was no answer, so she tried his home phone.

'Hi, it's me. I've got a bit of good news for you. You might be able to reopen the site in a week or two.'

'I'll believe that when it happens,' he replied dismissively. 'My father just called. He's not feeling well, so I need to go.'

'Have I done something to upset you?' Jane asked anxiously.

'I don't know, have you?'

'What's that supposed to mean?'

'Nothing. I'm really stressed at the moment. I'll speak to you tomorrow.' Nick put the phone down.

Jane wondered what on earth was bothering Nick. If he was having second thoughts about their relationship, she'd rather he be honest and say so. She racked her brain thinking of what she might have said or done to upset him, but nothing came to mind. She couldn't go on like this, however: she had to talk to him face to face to find out what was going on.

Barnes walked into the squad room with a wad of information forms, which he handed to the civilian indexers.

'I've marked up the ones that need further action and NFA'd the others. Some of the information received from former convent pupils is high priority. Allocate them to members of the squad to carry out interviews ASAP.'

Barnes saw Boon putting the phone down. 'Any luck with Sister Suzanne?'

'She's happy to be interviewed and confirmed Adele Delaney is dead. She'd also heard through the grapevine that Sister Margaret Wilde is at a convent on Canvey Island. I rang the local Essex Old Bill. They said there's a Sisters of Mercy convent on the island, which also has a large Catholic school on the site.'

'Another home for abusers and the abused, no doubt,' Barnes said, shaking his head.

'According to the officer I spoke with, there's no orphanage. But the school has a couple of hundred local kids. I've got the address and phone number. Shall I give them a ring and make an appointment to speak with Sister Margaret tomorrow?'

'No, I don't want her to know we're coming,' Barnes said. He called Stanley and Jane over. 'Tomorrow morning, me and Stanley will pay Bishop Meade a visit. Boon's got a possible location for Sister Margaret. Tennison, I want you to go with Boon to the convent on Canvey Island. If Sister Margaret is there, interview her – and don't go easy on her.'

'Yes, sir,' Jane replied.

'As things stand, are you going to arrest Meade tomorrow?' Stanley asked.

'You were right to question my decision earlier,' Barnes replied. 'The press conference and talking about Stephen's death got me worked up. I think we need to turn the heat up slowly with Meade. Make him squirm a bit in a preliminary interview.'

Stanley nodded in agreement. 'I gave Special Branch at Heathrow a call. Malone is booked on the seven o'clock BA flight which lands at ten. It will take him at least forty-five minutes to travel back to Archbishop's House.'

'We'll leave here about half nine to interview Meade,' Barnes replied.

'Don't you think we should aim to be there for nine, in case the archbishop returns?' Stanley said.

'On the contrary. I hope the son of a bitch does turn up!' Barnes said.

'What happens if they don't let us into the diocesan offices?' Stanley asked.

'Then I'll kick the bloody door in,' Barnes said.

'Are you going to interview Malone as well?' Stanley asked.

'Not yet. I want to make him squirm a bit first, too,' he grinned.

CHAPTER TWENTY-THREE

Jane established the time in Ontario was three in the afternoon. She phoned the Kingston police department and spoke with a Detective Inspector Tremblay. Jane told him she was investigating the murder of a woman they believed to be Melissa Bailey, who'd been a Kingston resident until 1953, when she came to the UK to become a novice at a convent in Bickley. The inspector seemed shocked when Jane told him how Melissa had been murdered.

'I'll do whatever I can to help,' Tremblay said.

'We're almost certain our victim is Melissa Bailey, but we don't have a confirmed identification due to the state of her body. I don't have Christian names for her parents, but I'm led to believe her father is a university lecturer,' Jane told him.

'There's a university here called Queen's,' he said.

'I'd imagine Mr Bailey must be in his fifties or sixties by now, so he may be retired,' Jane replied.

'Leave it with me. I'll get on to Queen's University right away. If I trace the Baileys, would you like me to inform them their daughter might be dead or ask them to call you?' Tremblay asked.

'I'd be grateful if you could tell them in person,' Jane said. 'I think it would be better if they know what happened to Melissa before speaking to me hundreds of miles away over the phone. I'll fax you over a copy of the dental chart our forensic odontologist made. Hopefully, if you trace Melissa's parents, their family dentist might still have her old records and could do a comparison to give us a positive ID.'

'If I do get your victim's dental record, I'll get our forensic dentist to check it as well. I wish you well in your investigation, Detective Tennison. As soon as I locate the Baileys, I'll call you.'

After a meal in the canteen, Jane typed up her reports, and it was nearly nine before she got home. She was so tired she went straight to bed but tossed and turned, unable to get to sleep. She couldn't stop thinking about the last two phone conversations she'd had with Nick, and his coldness towards her. She knew she'd done nothing to upset him, so why did it feel as if he wanted to end their relationship?

Jane thought about Thomas Durham and wondered if he was one of the builders Julie had seen fixing the convent roof. If it was him, and maybe Lee Holland, too, it meant they had deliberately not mentioned their connection to the convent before Missy had been murdered. Thomas Durham suggested he'd had nothing to do with the convent until long after the fire, but Jane also wondered if he was the builder who'd deemed the tunnel unsafe and bricked up the crypt door. Then something else worrying struck her: was it possible Thomas had revealed something to Nick about the convent, and that was what was forcing him to end their relationship?

* * *

Jane woke early, still tired from a restless night. She had a quick shower and got dressed.

'Morning, Jane,' Gerry said as she was about to get in the car. Spud relieved himself on the grass verge.

'Morning, Gerry. How are you and Spud today?' she replied, walking over and stroking the dog.

'We're both well, thank you. Another early start?'

'Yes, I've got a really busy day ahead of me.'

'That's a nice Range Rover your boyfriend Nick has, though I prefer the Jag.'

'He uses the Range Rover for work. It's more reliable on muddy building sites than the Jag,' Jane told him.

'I thought about getting a Range Rover myself. But I realised it wouldn't be very practical for a small dog like Spud trying to get in and out of it.'

Jane tried not to laugh. She doubted very much he could afford a Range Rover. But she also wondered how he knew Nick had one.

'Did Nick take you for a spin in it?'

'No. I saw him parked up when I was walking Spud last night.'

Jane raised her eyebrows. 'Outside my house?'

He pointed. 'No. Just up the road. I went over and said hello.'

'What did he say?' a curious Jane asked.

'Not much. He said he had to go and see his father. Then he drove off.'

'What time was that?'

'About nine.'

Jane wondered if she'd just missed Nick before getting home, or perhaps, feeling guilty for his earlier behaviour, he hadn't had the courage to knock on her door. Either way, she wished she'd been able to talk to him and sort things out between them. As she drove to work to pick up DC Boon, she tried to focus on the day ahead.

*   *   *

Knowing the Dartford Tunnel into Essex would be busy during rush hour, Jane and Boon decided to go to the photography shop in Bromley before travelling to Canvey Island.

It was just before nine and the small shop in Market Square wasn't open yet, but the sound of a man singing loudly inside could be heard on the street.

'He's got a good voice,' Boon remarked.

'The song sounds familiar,' Jane said.

'It's the Toreador song from *Carmen*.'

Jane smiled. 'Since when were you into opera?'

'I'm not but my dad is.'

Jane knocked on the door and the singing stopped.

A man in his mid-fifties with shiny grey hair opened the door. He was dressed in a tweed suit, white shirt, and tartan bow tie.

'Come away in. I was just about to open. Are you delivering for development or collecting photographs?' he asked cheerily. He had a pleasant Scottish accent.

'Neither. I assume you are Scott Davies, the owner?' Jane asked, holding up her warrant card.

'I am indeed, and have been for nearly thirty years. How can I help you, officer?'

Jane told him she and Boon were investigating the murder of a nun from the convent.

'I couldn't believe it when I read the *News Shopper*. I used to go to the convent every summer and take a photograph of them all. It was such a shame it had to close after that dreadful fire. The sisters were lovely lassies, and the wee 'uns were so well-behaved. It was a lot easier to get them organised for a group photo than it was a bloody wedding party, I can tell you.'

'We were wondering if you kept copies of the photos you took at the convent,' Jane asked.

'Aye, I do, but it's the negatives I keep as they're easier to store. Funnily enough, I was looking at them just now.'

'Why was that?' Boon asked.

'To see if any of the sisters looked like the drawing in today's newspaper.' Davies picked up the *Daily Mail* to show them Richard Eaves' artist's impression on the front page.

'Did you spot a likeness?' Jane asked.

'Ach, it's hard to say, as the pictures are no' very big in the viewer. You can have a wee look yourself if you like, or I can set the projector up so you can see them on a screen.'

'The screen would be helpful, thanks,' Jane replied.

'Give me a wee minute and I'll set it up in the darkroom,' Scott said, turning the sign hanging on the door back to CLOSED. 'Please come on through.'

There was a strong odour of rotten eggs in the darkroom, and Davies could see Boon was feeling nauseous.

'Sorry about the smells. It's the chemicals I use for processing.' He turned on the ventilator fan. 'I've arranged these in the order I took them. The first being in 1953,' he said, pressing the slide control. The first one was a bit blurry, so he adjusted the focus.

Having seen Julie Dorton's photograph, Jane and Boon were able to spot Sister Missy right away in the middle of the back row. They also recognised Julie standing next to her. Seeing the large projected image of a smiling Missy when she was eighteen and had just entered the convent as a novice brought a lump to Jane's throat. She was a picture of innocence and beauty, blissfully unaware of the abusive world she had entered and the fate that would so cruelly befall her.

As Scott flicked through the photographs, Missy was always in the back row next to Julie and Meade was on the far left of the picture – until they came to the 1962 slide.

'This was the last one I took before the convent closed. The lady on the left of Father Bob looks most like the drawing in the newspaper, compared with the other photos,' Davies remarked.

'I agree with you, Mr Davies, there is a similarity,' Jane said, not wanting to give too much away, though she wondered why it was the only photo where Meade was standing next to Missy.

'Did you know Father Bob?' Boon asked.

'Only through visiting the convent to take the annual photograph. He came to my shop once as well.'

'Why did he come here?' Jane asked.

'He wanted a small copy of the 1962 photo as it was the last picture I took before the convent closed.'

Davies's comment made Jane look more closely at the projected image. She noticed that Meade and Missy were standing so close together their shoulders and upper arms were touching. She moved nearer and peered at the photo following the position of their arms and hands. It was hard to tell, but it looked as if their hands might have been touching.

'Seen something of interest, sarge?' Boon asked.

'No. I was just trying to see if I could identify Annette Gorman,' she said casually.

'Did you know any of the sisters by name, Mr Davies?' Jane asked.

'I knew the Mother Superior, but not by name. I only ever really spoke with her or Sister Margaret when I went to the convent.'

'Do you have any photos of the sisters in casual clothes?' Boon asked.

'No. They were always dressed in their habits when I went there.'

'What about at work or play?' Jane asked, wondering if there might be an individual close-up of Missy.

'I did ask if I could take some photographs of their daily life, but the Mother Superior said no. I've got some colour ones of the convent gardens, though. I suggested the flower gardens would look nice in a calendar I wanted to make to promote my business. She took me on a guided tour, explaining what all the different flowers and shrubs were. I remember she referred to them as part of her own Garden of Eden.'

'Sounds like she was a keen gardener,' Boon remarked.

'Oh, yes. The gardens were the Mother Superior's pride and joy. She was a very knowledgeable horticulturalist. Would you like to see the slides?' Davies asked.

'We have an appointment on Canvey Island, I'm afraid. Do you have a copy of the calendar I could take with me?' Jane asked, not wanting to appear dismissive.

Davies looked in a filing cabinet, pulled out the calendar and handed it to Jane.

'Could I also borrow the 1962 slide? I'd like to get it enlarged by our photographic department.'

'I can do that for you,' Davies said.

'We might need it for evidential purposes in court, so I have to get it done in-house,' Jane told him.

'I understand.' He removed the slide and put it in an envelope.

'Thanks for your help, Mr Scott,' she said.

As they walked to the car, Boon could tell something in the last photograph had piqued Jane's interest.

'Spill the beans, sarge. What got you excited about that 1962 photo?'

Jane told him what she'd noticed. 'I want to get their hands enlarged to be sure.'

'Bloody hell, you've got eyes like a hawk!' he said.

'Every picture tells a story, Boony,' Jane smiled.

CHAPTER TWENTY-FOUR

Barnes knocked on the door of Archbishop's House and waited impatiently for someone to answer. Eventually, the young priest, Bishop Meade's assistant, opened the door.

'Can I help you?' he asked with a pleasant smile.

Barnes held his warrant card up. 'I'm Detective Chief Superintendent Barnes. This is Detective Inspector Stanley. We would like to speak with Bishop Meade.'

The priest's smile turned to a frown. 'I'm sorry, but he's not available right now.'

'Then we'll wait outside his office until he is,' Barnes replied.

'I'm sorry, but you can't come in,' the priest said, starting to close the door.

Barnes kept it open with his hand. 'Please, don't make me have to arrest you for obstructing police. Be sensible and show us to Meade's office.'

'This is most improper,' the priest replied, shaking his head.

They walked in and the priest hurried up the stairs. Barnes and Stanley followed close behind.

The priest knocked once on the door of the archbishop's office and entered quickly. Meade was sitting behind his desk doing some paperwork.

'I'm really sorry, Your Excellency. I told these police officers you weren't available, but they forced their way in . . .'

'It's all right,' Meade said calmly.

Barnes and Stanley showed him their warrant cards and introduced themselves.

'Please sit down. Would you like a coffee or tea?' Meade asked.

Barnes and Stanley declined his offer and Meade said the priest could go.

'How can I help you?' Meade asked.

'I think you know why we're here,' Barnes said.

'I assume it's about the nun's death.'

'Murder, to be more exact,' Barnes said.

'I've read the article in the *News Shopper* and seen your appeal for information on television. I find it rather deceitful that Detective Sergeant Tennison didn't tell me all the facts when she came here last week. It would seem she even lied to Father Floridia.'

'She was acting under my instructions,' Barnes said. 'I told her not to reveal how the victim died until we had identified her ... which I'm pleased to say we have.' Barnes noticed Meade's eyes widen slightly.

'May I ask who she was?' he said.

'Sister Melissa Bailey. But I think you already knew that,' Barnes said.

Meade shook his head. 'I can assure you I am not familiar with the name.'

'That's surprising, especially as you were the priest at St Mary's and regularly visited the convent while Sister Melissa was a nun there.'

'I went to the convent once or twice a month to read stories to the children. My interaction was mainly with the Mother Superior. She was quite strict and made it clear I was not to fraternise with the sisters, apart from Sister Margaret who was her deputy. My only communication with the others was a pleasant nod, hello or good morning.'

'Why didn't you tell DS Tennison any of this?' Stanley asked.

'She never asked, and I didn't think it relevant. Her failure to inform me it was a murder investigation made me believe there was nothing untoward. As far as I was concerned, the body could have been there since the 1850s. I made inquiries with our archivist, Mrs Parkin, then promptly informed DS Tennison of the results.'

'I know, I was there when you called.' Barnes looked in his notebook. 'DS Tennison asked you if any priests had worked at the convent. You replied, "Only sisters ever lived and worked there," so by your own admission that statement is clearly a lie.'

Meade sighed. 'I didn't work there in the true sense of the word. As I just said I merely visited the convent now and again.'

Barnes looked at his notes. 'You also said Mrs Parkin told you the fire started in the bakery then destroyed all the convent records and the schoolhouse.'

'Yes, that's correct.'

Barnes closed his notebook and tucked it back in his jacket pocket. 'When Mrs Parkin was asked about the fire by DS Tennison, she referred to an archive document which stated it occurred in August 1962, damaging the outbuildings and school beyond economical repair.'

'DS Tennison used subterfuge to gain entry to the archives. She lied to Mrs Parkin as to why she was there.'

'Again, she was acting under my instructions. My question is, how did you know where the fire started and that it destroyed all the convent documents?'

'Regrettably, I appear to have inadvertently caused some confusion. It was in fact the Mother Superior who told me the fire started in the bakery. When Mrs Parkin said there were no records relating to the convent in the archives, I assumed the fire must have destroyed them all.'

Barnes gave him a hard look, realising his answer was plausible.

'When did the Mother Superior tell you about the fire?' Stanley asked.

'I can't remember exactly when. I went to the convent to offer my assistance as soon as I heard about it.'

'I take it you know Mother Superior Adele Delaney is dead?' Barnes asked, knowing he couldn't refute Meade's answers if the information had supposedly come from her.

Meade nodded. 'I heard she died from cancer a few years ago.'

'Did she or Sister Margaret say anything to you about a Sister Melissa Bailey leaving the convent?' Barnes asked.

'No. They'd have no reason to either. If a sister chose to leave, it would be a matter for them and the bishop.'

'Which at that time would have been Andrew Malone, I believe?'

'That's correct. He's now the archbishop and currently on his way back from Rome. He will no doubt want to meet you personally, DCS Barnes. He's as eager to solve this horrendous crime as you are.'

'I'm looking forward to meeting him again,' Barnes smiled.

Meade looked surprised. 'He didn't mention you knew each other.'

'I'm not surprised. When he was a priest in North London, I investigated a serious assault on a twelve-year-old boy who had committed suicide. My inquiries revealed Malone repeatedly beat children black and blue. He believed it was God's will that those who were unruly be severely chastised. I was never in any doubt his actions led directly to Stephen Phillips' suicide.'

Meade looked aghast. 'I've known Archbishop Malone for many years. He would never condone violence in any way, shape or form. If your allegations were true, the Church would have investigated it and dealt with him appropriately, I'm sure.'

'They weren't interested in why Stephen killed himself. Their investigation was a sham to protect Malone and the reputation of the Church. Everything was swept under the carpet.'

'I find that hard to believe, officer,' Meade replied.

Barnes shrugged. 'Unlike some, I have no reason to lie. And let me assure you, I will not allow the same thing to happen again. I will find out who killed Sister Melissa and ensure they stand trial – as well as anyone attempting to pervert the course of justice in a cover-up.' He glared at Meade before continuing. 'It's also come to our notice that the Mother Superior and Sister Margaret were violent towards children at the convent. Were you aware of that?'

'No, I was not. If I had seen either of them treating a child improperly, I would have done something about it.'

'Did you give the children sweets?' Barnes asked.

'Yes. What's that got to do—'

Barnes interrupted. 'Why did you ask them not to tell the Mother Superior?'

'Because I knew she wouldn't approve. I really don't see what that has to do with Sister Melissa's death.'

'Sometimes an act of kindness towards a child may have an ulterior motive,' Barnes said.

Meade scowled at Barnes as he interrupted. 'I resent your insinuation. I certainly did not give the children sweets to gain their affection or trust for any immoral purpose.'

Barnes could tell he'd touched a nerve. 'I never said you did . . . but thanks for answering my next question.'

'Don't insult my intelligence, officer. It's clear you think I was involved in Sister Melissa's death.'

'Were you?' Barnes retorted.

Meade's eyes narrowed as he stood up. 'No. I was not! I didn't even know who she was until now. I've had enough of your unfounded and outrageous allegations. I'd like you both to leave.'

'Why did you go to the mortuary on Saturday morning?' Barnes pressed him.

Meade licked his lips. 'I wanted to pray for her.'

Barnes eyes narrowed. 'Even though you thought there was nothing untoward and the body could have been in the convent grounds since the 1850s?'

'Yes. I felt it was my duty under the circumstances.'

'According to the mortuary technician, you got very emotional and fell to your knees in tears.'

'That's ridiculous. I knelt to pray for her departed soul. And I had some grit in my eye.'

Barnes shook his head. 'You got emotional because you knew it was Sister Melissa Bailey in that coffin. You know what happened to her and who's responsible. You shed tears of remorse for what you'd done.'

'How many times do I have to tell you? I never knew Missy Bailey!' Meade banged his hand on the desk.

Barnes was about to push further when he heard a voice behind him.

'What is going on here, Bishop Meade?'

Barnes turned round and saw a tall man wearing a purple skull cap, a black cassock with a purple sash and an ankle-length black silk cape standing by the door. It was like a flashback in time for Barnes as he recognised the unblinking eyes, pale skin and pock-marked face of Malone.

Meade instantly composed himself, then bowed. 'Your Grace, these police officers forced their way into the building. They have been most underhand in their questioning and are accusing us of trying to cover up the death of the sister who they say was murdered. I've asked them to leave twice now.'

Malone frowned, looking at the two police officers. 'In future, if you want to speak to Bishop Meade or anyone connected to the Church, please make a formal request to my office. That way I can arrange for them to be represented by one of our solicitors. Tell your senior officer I will be in contact with him.' He smiled condescendingly.

'This is Detective Chief Superintendent Barnes. He's in charge of the investigation, Your Grace,' Meade cut in.

Barnes stood up and looked Malone in the eye. 'You don't remember me, do you?'

'Should I?' Malone replied dismissively.

'You might remember the name Stephen Phillips,' Barnes said.

Malone shrugged and shook his head. 'Can't say I do.'

'Let me refresh your memory, then. He was the twelve-year-old you beat with a belt so frequently he lost the will to live and then hanged himself.'

Malone's eyes narrowed as he stared at Barnes. 'I will be contacting the commissioner about your aggressive and underhand behaviour.'

'I'm sure you will, Archbishop Malone. But let me tell you this, murder is a crime the police investigate, not the Church.' Barnes turned to Meade. 'Your halo is slipping, bishop. If you wish to confess your sins, I suggest you do it to me . . . not Malone.'

'Get out, now!' Malone said through gritted teeth.

As he walked out, Barnes stopped by Malone and whispered, 'You may not have murdered Sister Melissa, but I know you were involved in her murder. Believe me, this time I won't let you cover up the truth!'

Malone waited until Barnes and Stanley had left the room, closed the door, then turned sharply to face Meade.

'What did you tell them?' he asked tersely.

'Nothing, Your Grace. I did as you told me and denied knowing Sister Melissa.'

'Well, they clearly didn't believe you. Mark my words, they'll be back, and Barnes will be out to destroy me as well. If you hadn't had carnal desires for her, we wouldn't be in this unfortunate mess.'

'I'm truly sorry, Your Grace . . .'

'I protected you from the start and promoted you because you had repented. I've been told I will be made a cardinal after the Pope's visit. I'm not going to let you jeopardise my future. It might be best for you move to an overseas mission in Africa as soon as possible.'

'But I don't want to leave here.'

'If it wasn't for me you wouldn't be here at all! Did you find the letter of dispensation in the archives?'

'Not yet, Your Grace.'

'Why not?' he scowled.

'I thought it best not to speak with Mrs Parkin personally. I didn't want to make her suspicious . . .'

'It's a bit late for that now!'

'I'll tell the police the truth and say you knew nothing about my relationship with Melissa.'

'You'll tell them nothing. You've done enough damage as it is. We'll discuss the matter further after I've spoken with the police commissioner. You had better hope I can persuade him to call his hounds off! Now get out of my sight.'

* * *

Out in the street, Barnes inhaled deeply, then lit a cigarette. 'I feel a lot better after that.'

'I don't think we'll be on their Christmas card list anymore, let's put it that way,' Stanley joked. 'The look on Malone's face when he heard Stephen Phillips' name and realised who you were was priceless,' Stanley remarked.

Barnes grinned. 'Did you notice Meade's little screw-up just before Malone walked in?'

'No. It's clear he's lying but he seemed to have a plausible answer for everything you put to him.'

'In his fit of anger, he blurted out that he never knew Missy Bailey. If he didn't know her, how on earth did he know her nickname?' Barnes said, taking a long drag on his cigarette.

* * *

Before leaving for Canvey Island, Jane popped into Bromley and spoke with the SOCO. She asked him to take the negative Scott Davies had given her to the Met's photographic department and have an A3 enlargement done of the group, as well as an individual photo of Meade and Missy and a close-up of their hands.

As Jane drove, Boon flicked through the 1963 flower calendar Davies had given them.

'There's a flower in here called *Camellia japonica*, commonly known as Sweet Jane. There's also *Digitalis purpurea*, which is foxglove and—'

'I didn't know you were into plants?' Jane remarked.

Boon held up the calendar with a grin. 'I'm not. I'm just reading out the photo captions.'

Jane shook her head, smiling. 'Right. We're in Canvey Way. Can you grab the map and give me the directions to the convent?'

He put the calendar away and picked up the AA route map. It wasn't long before they got to their destination.

'Blimey, it looks just like a big modern house. I'd never have guessed it was a religious building if it didn't have that cross on top,' Boon remarked as they pulled up outside the convent.

They were let in by a young sister, who took them to the Mother Superior, Mother Lynne's office. Jane told her why they were there.

Mother Lynne nodded sadly. 'I heard the appeal for information on the radio. It beggars belief that someone could do that to a child of God.' She made the sign of the cross. 'What brings you to our convent?'

'One of our priorities is to trace and interview anyone who used to live or work at the Bickley convent during the relevant time period.'

'I never worked there myself, so I don't think I can help you,' Mother Lynne said.

'We believe a Sister Margaret Wilde did, and were told she now lives here,' Jane said.

'Yes, she does. Sister Margaret's been with us for about three years.'

'If it's convenient we'd like to speak with her, please.'

Mother Lynne looked concerned. 'Sister Margaret is in our care wing. She's seventy-seven now and has dementia.'

'Then she'll have no memory of her time at the Sisters of Mercy, I expect,' Jane said. It looked as if they'd made a wasted journey.

'She has good days and bad days with her memory,' Mother Lynne said. 'She can also be quite cantankerous at times. I'm more concerned about the effect discussing a murder might have on her peace of mind.'

'Is she aware of our press appeal?' Jane asked.

'Not as far as I know. She doesn't have a television and has no interest in the newspapers. Most of the time she listens to music on her old record player and reads books . . . though it takes her weeks to get through them as she often forgets what's happened and has to start all over again.'

Jane nodded. 'I understand your concerns, Mother Superior. We were told Sister Margaret knew our victim. It's also possible she reported her to Bromley police as a missing person. I'm happy not to mention that our victim was murdered, but anything Sister Margaret can remember might help us to find who was responsible for her death.'

Mother Lynne paused for thought before answering. 'To engage with Sister Margaret, you will need to speak slowly and clearly, using simple words and short sentences.'

Jane nodded. 'We won't cause her any undue stress.'

As they walked along the care wing corridor Jane could hear the sound of loud music coming from one of the rooms.

'Someone likes their music,' Jane remarked.

Mother Lynne sighed. 'It's coming from Sister Margaret's room. We're constantly having to tell her to turn it down. It upsets the other residents on the wing.'

Boon whispered to Jane, 'It's "And the Glory of the Lord" from Handel's *Messiah*.'

'Another opera?' Jane said, wondering if he was pulling her leg again.

'Actually, technically it's an oratorio,' he added.

Sister Margaret's room was modestly furnished with a reclining hospital bed, a comfortable armchair, a wardrobe, and a chest of drawers with six small wood carvings of animals on it.

Sister Margaret was sitting in the armchair next to the bed, staring out of the window. She was a plump woman with long grey hair and a lined face. Jane thought she looked a lot older than Mother Lynne had said.

'Hello, Sister Margaret. How are you today?' Mother Lynne said.

Sister Margaret continued staring out of the window and said nothing. Mother Lynne turned the record player on the bedside cabinet off.

Sister Margaret glared at her. 'Why did you do that?'

Mother Lynne knelt down beside her and touched her hand. 'There are some police officers here who'd like to speak to you,' she said.

Sister Margaret looked at Jane and Boon with a stern eye. 'If they're real police why aren't they wearing uniforms?'

Jane showed Sister Margaret her warrant card. 'We're detectives, Sister Margaret. We don't wear uniforms,' she said.

'Would you like me to stay while they talk to you, Sister Margaret?' Mother Lynne asked.

'Do what you want. I don't care, now you've turned my music off,' she replied tersely.

'I think she might be having an off day,' Mother Lynne whispered to Jane. 'I need to have a word with one of the nursing sisters. I'll be back shortly.'

Jane realised it would be a difficult, as well as pointless, interview. 'I'm Jane and this is Simon . . .'

Boon showed her his warrant card. 'I'm a detective as well.'

Sister Margaret laughed. '*Simple Simon met a pieman, going to the fair.*' She laughed again and Boon smiled.

Jane knelt next to her. 'Do you remember when you lived at the Sisters of Mercy convent in Bickley?'

'Where's that?' Sister Margaret asked with a puzzled look.

'Bickley, in Bromley, London. The Mother Superior was called Adele Delaney.'

'Was she?'

'Yes. You were both there together and used to run the orphanage.'

'What orphanage?'

Jane turned to Boon who was looking at the carved ornaments on the dressing table.

'Can I have the folder a minute?'

He handed it to her and Jane took out a copy of Julie Dorton's 1958 convent photo.

'Do you recognise anyone in this picture?'

Sister Margaret peered at it, then smiled. 'Is that me, sitting on the bench?'

Jane smiled. 'Yes, it is. Do you know who this is next to you?' she asked, pointing to Adele Delaney.

'It's the Mother Superior?'

'Yes! Can you remember her name?'

'No.'

Jane was baffled. 'Then how did you know it was the Mother Superior?'

Sister Margaret looked at Jane as if she was stupid. 'Because a Mother Superior is in charge and always sits in the middle.'

Jane sighed, put the photo back in the folder and looked at Boon.

'I think this is a pointless exercise. We may as well head back to the office.'

'Can I have a chat with her?' he asked.

'Is there any point?'

'Hi, Margaret. I'm Simon.'

She smiled. 'The pieman's friend!'

'That's right, you remembered me,' he replied with an over-exaggerated smile, then picked up the record sleeve. 'What's your favourite piece in Handel's *Messiah*?'

'"The Hallelujah Chorus",' Sister Margaret replied.

He smiled. 'That's my favourite as well. It's at the end of part two, isn't it?' Sister Margaret nodded. 'Were the words taken from the bible?' Boon asked.

'They're from the Book of Revelation. "Alleluia: for the Lord God omnipotent reigneth . . . And He hath on His vesture and on His thigh a name written, King of Kings, and Lord of Lords . . . And He shall reign for ever and ever . . ."'

'Hallelujah!' Boon said. He turned on the turntable, gently placed the needle on the LP and turned the volume up a little. As the violins came in and the chorus of 'hallelujahs' began, Margaret smiled, closed her eyes and started to move her hands as if she was conducting.

Jane whispered to Boon, 'We haven't got time to sit and listen to music with her.'

'Be patient, sarge,' he replied as Sister Margaret started to sing along softly to herself.

To Jane's surprise Boon suddenly joined in:
'*King of Kings . . . forever and ever. Hallelujah! Hallelujah!*'

Sister Margaret opened her eyes, then she joined in the chorus singing, '*Forever and ever. Hallelujah! Hallelujah!*' in a cracked but still impressive voice.

Jane began to understand what Boon was trying to do. He turned the music down.

'May I say, Sister Margaret, you have the most beautiful voice. It's as if I were listening to an angel singing!'

Sister Margaret smiled. 'And you are a very good baritone, Simon.'

'I see you have other skills as well,' Boon said, picking up a large hand-carved wooden ladle from the chest of drawers. 'This is lovely. Did you make it?'

'No. My friend made it. She gave it to me as a present.'

'What was your friend's name?' he asked.

'Mother Adele.'

'Did she make all these lovely little animals, too?' Boon asked, pointing to the miniature figures, amongst which were a mouse, a rabbit and an owl.

'Yes. She's very good at carving wood,' Sister Margaret replied.

'Could I borrow the little owl to show my friend the pieman?' Boon asked.

'As long as you bring him back,' Sister Margaret replied, wagging her finger.

'I will, and thank you.' Boon slipped the owl into his pocket, then removed the calendar from the folder and handed it to her.

'This is for you. There are some pretty flowers in it.'

Margaret looked at the cover picture, then the next. By the fifth one a tear was trickling from her eye. 'These are the gardens where I used to live.'

'Did you plant the flowers and look after them?' he asked.

'Yes. We all did.'

'Mother Adele as well?'

'Yes. She taught me a lot about plants and how to make tea and herbal remedies from them.'

Boon removed the copy of Dorton's photograph. 'Is your friend Mother Adele in this picture?'

Margaret scrutinised it, as if she'd never seen it before. 'That's her there, on the bench next to me.' She pointed to Adele Delaney.

'You never cease to amaze me, Boony,' Jane said with a smile.

He didn't acknowledge her, maintaining eye contact with Sister Margaret. 'Is there anyone else you remember in the picture?'

Sister Margaret scanned it again. Her eyes started to widen, and her nostrils flared. She pursed her lips and her head started to shake angrily.

'Who is it you recognise, Sister Margaret?' Jane asked.

'He's a bad man. God will punish him for his sins!' she exclaimed.

Jane and Boon knew she was talking about Meade as he was the only man in the photograph.

'What was his sin?' Jane asked, watching Margaret's face turning red with rage.

There was fury in her eyes. 'He broke his vow of chastity to Almighty God! He is a fornicator, a sinner who will suffer in purgatory,' she shouted.

'Who did he break his vow with, Sister Margaret?' Jane asked.

She prodded the picture with her finger. 'With her, with her. May God forgive us our sins.' Sister Margaret threw the photograph to the floor and broke down in tears.

'What on earth is going on!' Mother Lynne exclaimed as she entered the room. She embraced Margaret to calm her.

'She became upset when we showed her an old group photograph taken at the convent, I'm afraid,' Jane said.

Mother Lynne glared at Jane and Boon. 'I'd like you both to leave.'

'I'm really sorry, Mother Superior. We didn't intend for this to happen,' Jane said.

'Please, just leave.'

*   *   *

Jane and Boon walked in silence to the car, trying to make sense of what had just happened.

Boon spoke first. 'She was obviously talking about Meade and Missy Bailey.'

Jane nodded. 'This is a step forward for us, but as evidence in court it's worthless, due to her state of mind. Did you hear the last thing she said?' Jane asked.

'I was distracted by Mother Lynne walking in. I heard something about forgiving sins,' he replied.

'She said, "May God forgive *us* our sins." It could be she was referring to herself and others.'

Boon removed the owl from his pocket. 'I wonder if this is made from birch wood like the slivers found on the knife tip and Missy's habit.'

'If it is, that makes things even more interesting. Mother Adele clearly knew how to handle a whittling knife. Phone Julie Dorton when we get back. Ask her if she knew anything about Mother Adele being a whittler. At least she's a reliable witness.'

'You think Adele Delaney might have killed Missy?' he asked.

Jane sighed. 'I don't know, it's all so bloody confusing now. You could argue Mother Adele and Meade both had a motive. However, if Meade and Missy were intimate enough to be touching hands in the photo, it begs the question, why would he want to kill her?'

'Maybe Meade just turned on the charm because he wanted to have sex with her,' Boon suggested.

Jane found herself thinking about Nick and wondering if he had used her in the same way. Could it be that his surly, offhand attitude was a deliberate ploy to get her to end the relationship now that he'd got what he wanted?

'If they were in a sexual relationship, it would have to have been away from the convent. Maybe at the presbytery,' Jane said. 'Then again, if Missy realised Meade had an ulterior motive, or thought she was being used, she might have threatened to report him to the bishop, which could be a motive for killing her.'

'I'd say it would be a pretty strong motive,' Boon agreed. 'He'd lose everything if the Church threw him out.'

Jane couldn't stop thinking about Nick and changed the subject. 'That was good work, getting Margaret to connect with her past. At first I thought you were pulling my leg about the music being from Handel's *Messiah*.'

'My father was a professional musician, so I grew up listening to that kind of music. I'm sorry the conversation with Sister Margaret went a bit pear-shaped at the end.'

'Don't be hard on yourself. You've got a good way with people. I was getting nowhere with her.'

'My grandad suffers from dementia. Thankfully, he's not in a home as my grandmother looks after him. She taught me how to communicate with him. I visit when I can. We do jigsaw puzzles, word games, listen to classical music and look at old photographs to try and stimulate his mind. Sometimes he knows who I am, but more often than not he doesn't,' he said sadly.

'I'm sure he's very fond of you, Simon, and your company means a lot to him.'

'I've got a confession to make,' he said with a grin.

'Spit it out,' she said.

'What I said yesterday about mixing business with pleasure was wrong.'

'What made you say that?' Jane asked, wondering if he'd over-heard her on the phone to Nick.

'I'm meeting Becky Rogers for a drink after work later. I've told her it's strictly social and I won't discuss the case with her.'

'That's fine by me, but I wouldn't tell anyone else for now.'

'We're also going on a proper night out on Saturday.'

Jane forced a smile. 'She's a nice girl . . . I really hope it works out for the pair of you.'

CHAPTER TWENTY-FIVE

'How did it go with Meade?' Jane asked Stanley as she and Boon walked into the incident room.

He waited until she was up close before replying. 'It's best we discuss it in Barnes's office.'

'I'll give Julie Dorton a call about whittling, then join you,' Boon said.

'What's whistling got to do with anything?' Stanley asked with a bemused look.

Jane laughed. 'Whitt-ling, as in carving wooden animals. It might be integral to the investigation.'

'You've totally lost me,' Stanley said.

'I'll explain why after you've told me about Meade.'

'Do you want a coffee?' Stanley asked.

'That would be nice,' Boon replied.

'Then get us a coffee when you've finished your phone call,' Stanley said, handing him a pound note.

'Where's Barnes?' Jane asked, seeing he was not in his office.

'The commissioner wanted to speak with him,' Stanley said, sitting at Barnes's desk.

'Has the shit hit the fan?' Jane asked.

'We won't know for sure until Barnes gets back. Sit down and I'll tell you all about it.'

'Do you want to wait for Boony?'

'You can fill him in later.' Stanley proceeded to tell Jane about the meeting with Meade.

Jane listened carefully, taking notes so she could compare what Meade had said with everything they knew so far about him.

'Meade totally distanced himself from knowing Sister Melissa. But he lost his composure when Barnes suggested he offered sweets to the kids for "ulterior motives".'

'Does Barnes really think that? We've had a lot of calls from people who were at the orphanage. Not one of them has alleged sexual abuse.'

'Barnes was just trying to goad him. You could see Meade was getting hot under the collar . . . excuse the pun.'

'I've got a feeling Meade and Missy were in a relationship. It may even have been sexual,' Jane said.

'You're kidding me!' Stanley exclaimed.

'Why shouldn't priests and nuns have sexual desires like the rest of us?'

'Is that a come on?' he grinned.

'Piss off,' Jane retorted. She then told him about the photograph in which she thought Meade and Missy were touching hands.

'Maybe he led her on just to get in her knickers, she got upset, then . . .'

'What is it with you men and sex?' Jane said testily. 'Or are you speaking from experience?'

Stanley held his hands up. 'Blimey, it was only a suggestion.'

'What did Meade say when Barnes asked how he knew Melissa's nickname?' Jane asked.

'He didn't ask.'

'Why not? Evidentially, that would be enough to arrest him and interview him under caution.'

'Archbishop Malone walked in at that point. He didn't recognise Barnes until he told him he was the officer who investigated Stephen's suicide . . . then said he suspected Malone was involved and there'd be no cover-up this time.'

Jane winced. 'I bet that didn't go down well.'

'It was like a red rag to a bull. Malone asked us to leave and said he'd speak with the commissioner. Which, by the looks of things, he has.'

'I worry Barnes's loathing of Malone and the Catholic Church over Stephen Phillips' suicide is clouding his judgement.'

'We all have our demons, Jane. The death of a child is one of the hardest things to deal with as a police officer.'

'I know, but pissing off the archbishop won't help our investigation.'

He shrugged. 'Barnes is in charge and we have to do as he says, like it or not.'

Boon walked in. 'I got a positive result with Julie Dorton about the whittling.'

Stanley sighed. 'For Christ's sake, would somebody explain this whistling thing – I mean, whittling.'

'Shall we just call it wood carving if it's easier for you?' Jane teased.

'Call it what you bloody well like. Just tell me what happened at Canvey Island,' Stanley said.

Jane told him about Sister Margaret's condition and the conversation they had with her.

'I've got to say Boony was brilliant with her. If it wasn't for him . . .'

'If she's as nutty as a fruit cake we can't rely on anything she said,' Stanley remarked.

Boon frowned. 'That's a bit harsh.'

'I don't have any sympathy for sadists who take pleasure in beating young children,' Stanley said bluntly.

'Neither do I. But calling someone with dementia a fruit cake is offensive,' Boon replied in the same tone of voice.

Stanley huffed. 'She'd forget it in two seconds if I did.'

Boon shook his head. 'It's nothing to joke about.'

'Who's rattled your cage?' Stanley asked.

'You have, sir.'

Stanley leaned forward. 'Who do you think you are talking to, son?'

Jane was afraid Boon was about to say something he'd regret. She kicked his foot.

'Please, stop this bickering,' she said quickly. 'We're all under a lot of pressure. Arguing amongst ourselves will get us nowhere.'

'Sorry, sarge,' Boon said. 'Sorry, guv.'

Stanley sat back. 'OK, tell me about this whittling thing you uncovered.'

Barnes's desk phone started to ring. Stanley picked it up.

'How did it go with the commissioner, guv?'

Stanley didn't say anything as he listened to Barnes. A minute later he put the phone down.

'What did Barnes have to say?' Jane asked.

'Not much. He sounded really pissed off. Malone made an official complaint to the commissioner about Barnes's behaviour. He also said he signed a dispensation order for Sister Melissa, which—'

Jane interrupted. 'I'll bet no one's actually seen it.'

'Malone said he can show us the document. The commissioner has an official meeting with him tomorrow.'

'It could be forged and backdated,' Boon suggested.

'Possibly,' Stanley said. 'But it could also be genuine. Malone told Julie Dorton in 1962 that he was going to sign a dispensation. If he was trying to cover up Melissa's murder it makes sense the dispensation was issued back then.'

'Is Barnes coming back here?' Jane asked.

Stanley shook his head. 'He's going home. He wants everyone in the incident room for a nine o'clock meeting when he'll brief us all on what the commissioner said and where the investigation is going from here.'

'That doesn't sound good,' Boon remarked.

'I have an awful feeling history might be repeating itself for Barnes,' Jane said.

Stanley shrugged. 'We won't know until he's briefed us, Jane. For now, we crack on as normal.'

Boon removed the little owl from his pocket and put it on Stanley's desk. 'Mother Adele made this. As well as lots of other animals, she also made a ladle for Sister Margaret, like the one she used to hit the kids with. Obviously, she had to use a knife of some sort.'

Stanley raised his hand. 'I get where you're going with this. The problem is, we can't rely on anything Sister Margaret said.'

'That why I spoke with Julie Dorton. She confirmed Sister Margaret was a keen whittler. She said she kept little animals she made on her study desk and had a small box in which she kept an array of different whittling knives.'

'All very interesting but circumstantial,' Stanley said.

'We can't just rule out Mother Adele as a suspect,' Jane said. 'Julie also told us Mother Adele was ambitious. She saw herself as the next Mother General and fantasised about having a private audience with the pope. If Missy threatened to expose her cruelty and drinking, her ambitions would have been destroyed.'

'True,' Stanley agreed. 'But I don't think Barnes will buy it. He's convinced Meade is responsible.'

'We have to tell him what we know about Mother Adele so he sees there are other possibilities,' Jane said.

'I'll leave that to you two, then,' Stanley said.

'Thanks a lot,' Jane replied.

'Look,' he said. 'You both know this case better than any of us. I suggest you sit down and compile a report detailing all the evidence you have against Mother Adele and Meade. Stick to the facts and don't forget to consider a joint enterprise.' Stanley handed Boon the owl.

Jane found herself remembering Barnes's Sherlock Holmes quote: 'Once you eliminate the impossible, whatever remains, no matter how improbable, must be the truth.'

Returning to the incident room, Jane thought about phoning Nick, but knew if he was surly again it would really upset her and she wouldn't be able to focus on compiling the evidential report. Boon went to the canteen to get a sandwich and a drink for both of them.

'The Bromley SOCO dropped off some photos for you, sarge,' the female civilian indexer said, holding up a large envelope. 'DS Johnson, the lab sergeant, asked if you'd call him regarding the seeds in the victim's stomach.'

Jane thanked her and took the envelope to her desk. The only photo she was really interested in was the close-up of Meade and Missy's hands. When she looked at it closely, her suspicion was confirmed. Their hands were touching, with their little fingers entwined together.

'I got two cheese toasties with tomatoes and a bowl of chips. Is that OK?' Boon said, carrying in a tray of food and two coffees.

'It's fine, thanks. Have a look at this,' she said, showing him the photograph.

'Bloody hell, you were right. That's a strong bit of evidence for the report,' Boon said.

'It's enough to arrest Meade,' she said, 'since he's denied knowing her. And what you said about him using Missy could be right. If she threatened to expose their relationship, he'd know he'd be defrocked.'

'It also makes it more likely she went to the presbytery the night she left the convent,' Boon suggested.

'Only Meade knows the answers. I think Barnes will arrest him when he sees this photo. It proves beyond a doubt he's lying through his teeth. What time are you meeting Becky Rogers?'

'It's supposed to be seven o'clock at The Chequers in Bickley. I'll phone her and cancel,' he said.

'No, you won't,' Jane said. 'We've got a couple of hours yet. If we haven't finished by half six, I'll complete the report.'

'Thanks, sarge,' Boon beamed. 'I gave the owl carving to the SOCO. He said he'll take it up to the lab in the morning to see what kind of wood it's made from.'

Jane phoned Lloyd Johnson at the lab.

'I got a message to call you about the seeds in Melissa's stomach.'

'Right. We got a botanist to look at them. Turns out they are *Digitalis purpurea* seeds, which are poisonous and commonly known as—'

'Foxglove,' Jane interjected

'How did you know that?' Lloyd asked.

Jane explained about the Scott Davies calendar.

'Bloody hell, that was a good find,' Lloyd said.

'So how does it work as a poison?' Jane asked.

'The botanist said foxglove contains digoxin, which is commonly used as a drug to treat cardiac arrhythmia because it slows the heart rate down. Large doses can cause symptoms like vomiting, giddiness and unconsciousness. In excess, it slows the heart rate so much the brain becomes starved of oxygen; the body's reflex response is to try and increase the heart rate, which can result in a heart attack and death.'

'So you'd have to have a good knowledge of plants to know how to use it?' Jane asked, thinking of Mother Adele.

'I'd say so. The botanist said there have been many cases of accidental poisoning due to foxglove penetrating the skin when handled without gloves. People have even unwittingly made tea from the leaves and poisoned themselves. It has also been used to murder people. The botanist told me of a case where a German doctor killed his girlfriend with it. Under the guise of conducting a physical examination, he placed digoxin on his glove and administered the poison rectally . . .'

Jane winced at the thought. 'Yes, thank you, Lloyd, I get your drift. I'll need to get Sam Pullen's opinion on the poisoning angle.'

'I already have. She said it's most likely the seeds were put in Sister Melissa's food or a hot drink at the last meal she had before she was killed.'

'Julie Dorton said Sister Melissa was very emotional and incoherent the last night she saw her.'

'That makes sense. Pullen said the poison could have a delayed reaction of up to eight hours. She also suggested it was possible, when Sister Melissa was first strangled, that the fear factor caused her heart rate to accelerate so much she became unconscious.'

'So whoever strangled Sister Melissa might have thought she was dead and put her in the coffin,' Jane suggested.

'That's exactly what Pullen suggested. She's going to get a specialist to examine the heart for any signs of damage due to sudden cardiac failure. I've got to say, whoever had it in for Sister Melissa was determined to kill her one way or the other.'

'Now you've told me this, it seems likely the Mother Superior was involved. We also found out she made herbal remedies from garden plants, so she must have known what was and wasn't poisonous.'

'Have you been able to trace her?' Lloyd asked.

'Yes, to a grave in Hackney. She died a few years ago.'

'So if others were involved, they could put the blame on her.'

Jane sighed. 'I know. This investigation gets more and more complicated by the minute. Thanks for calling.'

'I'll say a prayer and hope for some divine intervention,' he joked.

'Worth a try,' she said, putting the phone down.

* * *

After Boon had left for his date, it took Jane another hour to finish the report. Having read it twice, she was satisfied everything of evidential value was in it. She was leaning towards Barnes's view that Meade had killed Sister Melissa, but it was clear others had to be involved in the cover-up or at least knew the truth of what had happened. She was still suspicious of Thomas Durham and Lee Holland because they'd lied to her, but she was no closer to finding out why.

She was just about to leave when the indexer's phone started ringing.

'Orpington incident room, how can I help you?'

'I'd like to speak with Detective Sergeant Tennison, please.'

She recognised the Canadian voice. 'Hi, Inspector Tremblay, it's Jane speaking.'

'I'm with Melissa's parents, Lawrence and Fiona Bailey. They showed me her birth certificate and letters she wrote home when she was at the convent. I've told them about your investigation and the likelihood the victim is Melissa. Mr Bailey would like to speak to you,' Tremblay said.

'Of course,' she replied.

These were the conversations Jane dreaded. It was never easy talking to a parent who had lost a child, and even harder when they had been murdered. Jane knew the Baileys must have suffered years of torment wondering what had happened to Melissa. Their last physical contact would have been the day they lovingly embraced her, aged eighteen, as she left home to devote her life to God. Then, nine years later, she would go silent and they would never hear from their daughter again. Not knowing where Melissa was, or how she was being treated, must have driven them to the depths of despair. All they would have wanted was to know Melissa was alive, safe and well, but now their worst fears had become a reality.

'Thank you for finding us, detective. My wife and I have always dreaded this day would come. I have to ask, but are you sure it's Melissa?' Lawrence asked.

'I'm sorry, but all the evidence points towards Melissa being our victim. We recovered a cross engraved with her initials and the date she took her vows. Sister Julie Dorton, a good friend of Melissa's who was also at the convent, has identified it as being hers.'

'Melissa often spoke about her in her letters. She said Julie always cheered her up when she felt homesick.'

'How often did Melissa write to you?' Jane asked.

'Once a month, which was what she was allowed under the convent rules. There were a couple of times we didn't hear from her for two or three months, but it didn't worry us at the time.'

'May I ask why not?'

'She did say in a letter that one punishment for breaking the rules was the withdrawal of writing privileges, so we assumed that was why there were sometimes gaps between her letters. Melissa could be a bit hot-headed and impulsive. She often got in trouble at junior high school for speaking her mind. In fact, I think she spent more time in detention than she did in the classroom. Then when she was seventeen and decided she wanted to be a nun she calmed down.'

Jane recalled Julie Dorton mentioning the sister's letters were checked and edited by the Mother Superior, thus making it impossible to write anything negative about the convent or life there to family or friends. Although Jane thought she knew what Lawrence's answer was going to be, she still had to ask her next question.

'Did Melissa ever write about wanting to leave the Sisterhood or anything that was troubling her?'

'No. She'd tell us about the work she did in the convent, the orphaned children and how much she loved them. She often said she missed us and hoped if ever we were visiting the UK we could come to the convent and see her. Regrettably we never got the opportunity,' he added, his voice tinged with sadness.

'Can you recall when Melissa last wrote to you?'

He took a deep breath before continuing. 'The fifth of August 1962. The day of her twenty-seventh birthday. She said Julie was baking a cake for her.' His voice started to tremble. 'We became concerned when we hadn't heard from Melissa for nearly six months. I asked the advice of a Canadian detective I knew here in Kingston. He contacted Bromley police on our behalf about our concerns.'

'Do you know the name of the officer he spoke to?'

'Detective Jim Harris. I spoke with him a couple of times myself.'

'Did he carry out an investigation?'

'He told me he visited the convent and spoke with the Mother Superior who informed him Melissa had left in August as she no longer wished to be a sister. He also said the bishop had granted her a dispensation, allowing her to leave.'

'Do you know if Detective Harris recorded Melissa as a missing person?' Jane asked.

'He said he would, and he'd also make some local inquiries, but beyond that there wasn't a lot more he could do. At the time I thought Melissa might have been embarrassed about telling us she'd left the sisterhood. I thought she would eventually make contact with us . . . but now I know why she didn't.'

'Did you have any further contact with Detective Harris?'

'I called him a couple of times, but he told us there were no further developments. A year later I travelled to London and went to Bromley police station. I spoke with a sergeant who told me Detective Harris had retired. He checked the station missing persons records and told me Melissa's file was still there, but there was no update on her whereabouts.'

It was clear to Jane that DC Harris had accepted Mother Adele and Bishop Malone's word as gospel and let her missing person file gather dust in a filing cabinet. Worse still, he hadn't even bothered to notify the Missing Persons Bureau at Scotland Yard.

'Did you make any other inquiries while you were in London, Mr Bailey?' Jane asked.

'I went to the convent, but it was closed down. I spoke with a priest at the local Catholic church. He told me there had been a fire at the convent and it was going to be sold.'

'Can you remember the priest's name?' Jane asked.

'I'm sorry. It escapes me now.'

'Do you remember exactly where the church was?'

'Yes, it was just down the road from the convent.'

Jane knew it was St Mary's. 'Did you ask the priest if he knew Melissa?'

'He said he didn't but he offered to make some inquiries at the diocesan offices for me. I spoke with him again a couple of days later. He said he'd spoken with the bishop who showed him the letter of dispensation he'd signed for Melissa to leave the sisterhood. He told me the bishop said all the convent sisters' details had been destroyed in the fire, and there wasn't a lot the Church could do to help me find Melissa because she had renounced her faith and left the convent. But he was very understanding. I gave him my address and phone number in Canada. He said he'd contact me if he heard anything about Melissa's whereabouts. But I didn't hear from him again.'

'Did he mention the bishop's name?' Jane asked.

'Probably, but again, I can't remember now. I didn't know what else to do, so I returned to Canada. I hoped and prayed that one day Melissa would contact us, but as the years went by Fiona and I knew something bad must have happened.' Jane thought she could hear him choking back a sob.

'I'm deeply sorry for your loss, Mr Bailey. Our investigation is progressing quickly and I believe we are getting close to discovering who killed your daughter.'

'Do you have any suspects?' he asked.

'Yes, but legally I can't tell you who they are at present. We hope to make some arrests in the next few days. I will phone you to update you. If you want to speak to me, or there's anything else you remember that might be important, just call me in the office. If I'm not here leave a message and I'll get back to you as soon as I can.'

'Do you think someone at the convent killed her?' he asked, sounding bitter.

'We are looking at a number of possibilities. I can tell you Melissa had packed her suitcase and was going to leave the convent. We think she may have been killed on the night she tried to do so. It would be wrong of me to speculate any further . . . but rest assured we will find whoever was responsible for her death.'

'I hope you do. Inspector Tremblay asked about Melissa's dental records. I have them. The Kingston officer who advised us said it would be worthwhile getting them from our dentist in case our fears became a reality, which they now have. I was thinking of flying over to view Melissa's body and arrange for her to be flown back to Canada for burial.'

'That's understandable, Mr Bailey. I will speak with the coroner and ask if Melissa's body can be released. He will probably ask for a second post-mortem to be done first. I will call you as soon as I've spoken to him.'

Lawrence started to cry and must have handed the phone to Tremblay, because his was the next voice Jane heard.

'I've had the dental records and your faxed copy taken to our forensic odontologist. I'm expecting a result in the next hour or so. I'll get straight back to you when it comes in,' Tremblay said.

Jane thanked him and said she would be on her home number in half an hour.

*　*　*

When she got home, Jane poured herself a glass of wine and waited for the phone to ring. It wasn't long before Tremblay called.

'Melissa had a filling, a chipped tooth and two wisdom teeth removed when she was sixteen so braces could be fitted. Your odontologist noted the same in his report regarding the chip and missing teeth. It would seem Melissa Bailey is your victim. I've faxed a copy of our odontologist's confirmed identification and Melissa's dental record to double check your end. I also phoned Mr Bailey to let him know the result. As you can imagine, he and Fiona were even more devastated having their fears finally confirmed. Lawrence wanted to fly to the UK tomorrow, but I persuaded him it was best to wait until you'd spoken with the coroner.'

'Thanks for all your help, inspector . . . especially for informing the Baileys. I know it can't have been easy.'

Tremblay sighed. 'They say knowing what happened to a loved one is supposed to give some kind of closure, but the truth is, it never does. I wish you well in your investigation. Please let me know the outcome.'

'I will,' Jane said, and put the phone down.

She found herself thinking of Nick again and started to dial his home number but stopped halfway through. She was tired, it had been a stressful day and she didn't think she could deal with an emotional argument.

Jane finished her glass of wine then went upstairs to change into her pyjamas. As she closed the bedroom curtains, she noticed a green Range Rover go past her house and stop about forty yards up the road. The streetlights were too dim to be able to read the number plate, but Jane suspected it was Nick's car. She switched the bedroom light off, then peered through the curtains and watched as the driver did a U-turn and parked up. If it was Nick, she wondered why he didn't park outside her house. She waited to see if the driver got out of the car, but there was no movement. Then, as a small car drove past the Range Rover, its headlights lit up the driver.

'What the hell are you playing at?' Jane said to herself, watching Nick sink down in the driver's seat.

Jane put her slippers on, hurried downstairs and opened the front door. She heard the Range Rover's engine start and watched as it slowly pulled away from the kerb with no lights on. She walked into the middle of the road and stood with her hands on her hips blocking the way. The car stopped in front of her, and she marched up to the driver's side window.

'Are you bloody well spying on me?' she demanded.

Nick slowly wound down the window, shame-faced. 'No. I was trying to build up the courage to knock on your door and talk to you.'

'Did you come here last night as well?' she asked brusquely. Nick nodded.

'We definitely need to talk, then,' she said, spotting Gerry watching from his living-room window.

'Are you seeing—' Nick began.

'Not out here!' She stomped indoors.

Nick parked his car and followed her inside.

'What the hell is going on, Nick?' she asked as he entered the living room.

'I saw you kissing another man,' he said. 'If there's someone else, I'd rather you just told me and ended our relationship.'

She raised her eyebrows. 'There's nobody else. It certainly wasn't me you saw kissing someone.'

'I know what I saw, Jane,' he replied.

'Where and when was this supposed to have happened?'

'Yesterday afternoon. I'd just left my father's place and saw you outside the house next to St Mary's. You were with a tall, dark-haired man in a grey tracksuit. You were touching his arm . . . then you hugged and kissed him.'

Jane was dumbstruck as she realised Nick had seen her with Father Chris.

'It was you, wasn't it?' Nick asked, accusingly.

Jane let out a big sigh. 'Yes, it was, but you've misread the whole situation. The man you saw is Father Floridia. He's the priest at

St Mary's. I didn't kiss him . . . he hugged and kissed me. It was one small parting peck on the cheek – but believe me, I was as shocked as you were.'

'Then why were you touching his arm?'

'He'd been helping me with the investigation. He was upset about Sister Melissa's murder – so much so that he was questioning his role as a priest. I was just trying to comfort him, that's all.'

'Why did he kiss you then?'

'It was a final goodbye. He'd been told by his superior not to speak to me again. We both thought it best we didn't have any further contact. He wished me well with the investigation and kissed me on the cheek. I was surprised because I didn't think it was the sort of thing a priest would do.'

'Exactly! You must have encouraged him.'

'This is ridiculous! I did nothing to encourage him.'

'I don't believe you.'

'Well, it's the bloody truth! If you don't believe me there's nothing more to be said and we may as well end our relationship here and now!' Jane snapped.

Nick was taken aback. 'I'm sorry. I didn't mean to upset you.'

'Well, you have. If you want this relationship to work, we need to trust each other.'

'I know. I've been a complete and utter idiot.'

'Yes, you have, by jumping to the wrong conclusions. If I'd told you about Father Floridia, then I suppose none of this would have happened. I wondered why you were being so off with me on the phone.'

'My head was all over the place. To be honest, seeing you with another man was like a flashback to some really bad memories which made me panic and overreact.'

'What were they?' Jane asked, knowing it was to do with his wife.

'I'm divorced. I was married for two weeks then my wife ran off with my best man. I'd never suspected for one minute she'd been having an affair with him. At the time I felt so humiliated, I became depressed and didn't go out socially for a long time.'

'That's awful. Why on earth did she go through with the wedding?'

'She said she was confused and didn't know what to do. She thought she still loved me but realised, after the wedding, she didn't. The truth is, Brenda didn't give a toss about me before or after the wedding. What also hurt was a friend of mine suspected the affair but didn't have the guts to tell me. I know if I'd been in his position, I would have said something.'

'I'm so sorry, Nick . . . you didn't deserve to be treated like that.'

'I shouldn't have doubted you, Jane. Stupidly, I thought the priest must be your boyfriend. I even wondered if you were using me to find out more about the building site and convent. Can we put this behind us and move on . . . or would you rather I just left?'

Jane knew she ought to be honest, but couldn't bring herself to tell Nick she had initially considered going out with him to learn more about his father. 'I understand now why you reacted like you did. If I'd been in your shoes, I'd probably have felt the same.' She reached out, took hold of his hand, and drew him closer. 'I want to move on in our relationship, Nick Durham. So you can leave . . . but not until the morning.'

CHAPTER TWENTY-SIX

When Jane woke, Nick wasn't there. She was anxious, until she saw the note he'd left on the pillow.

You truly are a sleeping beauty. Didn't want to wake you as I know you must be tired after the long hours you've been working. Have to be at a site survey for 8 a.m., so need to pop home and get changed. Thank you for being so understanding. I will never let my past come between us again. I think I'm falling in love with you, Jane Tennison . . . Love, Nick xxxx

Jane smiled, and as she got ready for work, a warm glow stayed with her. She arrived at the incident room just after eight. It was already full, as officers on the inquiry completed their reports for the meeting with DCS Barnes. She checked the fax in-tray for the Canadian odontologist's report and quickly scanned it. He was in no doubt that Melissa Bailey was the victim. Although it wasn't in itself a big step forward, it would allow the coroner to release the body to her parents and they could take her home. It was a sad thought, but in some ways comforting that after years of heartache they could finally lay her to rest and know she was at peace.

Jane sat at the desk opposite Boon who was reading over their report.

'Morning, Boony. Anything you want to add to the report?'

'No, it looks fine to me,' he replied with a hang-dog look.

'You all right?' she asked.

'I got stood up by Becky. I sat in the effin' pub for an hour waiting for her.'

'Oh, I'm sorry. Maybe something important came up and she couldn't get hold of you?' Jane suggested.

'I tried calling her, but there was no answer. I thought she might have gone out with her flatmate instead . . . or another bloke,' he said glumly.

'Have you tried ringing her at work?'

'Yes, but she's not in yet. I knew it was all too bloody good to be true. I feel like she's just used me to get information about the investigation.'

'I doubt that's the case. Becky did take you to meet Annette Gorman, which led us to Julie Dorton and Sister Margaret, after all.'

He perked up a bit. 'I guess so. I'll try calling her again after the meeting.'

Jane told him about the foxglove seeds.

'Bloody hell. As if strangling and stabbing Melissa wasn't enough. The foxglove stinks of Mother Adele's handiwork.'

'Not necessarily. She might have warned others about the danger of handling or digesting the plants, thus innocently passing on her knowledge – possibly even to Meade, who was a regular visitor to the convent.'

'Fair point,' Boon said.

'I spoke with Melissa's father in Canada last night,' Jane said. She told Boon about her conversation with Lawrence Bailey.

'So, Meade also lied to him about knowing Melissa. The evidence against him is definitely mounting.'

* * *

'Interestingly Malone's name came up again last night,' Jane said. 'Meade told Mr Bailey that Bishop Malone signed a dispensation and the Church couldn't help him find Melissa because she'd renounced her faith. If Malone was involved in a cover-up about her disappearance it has to be because he knew what happened or was directly involved – plus it would take at least two people to move the coffin.'

'The pieces of the jigsaw are falling into place,' Boon smiled.

'Hopefully. I got a confirmed ID the body is Melissa.' Jane showed Boon the dental match report.

'That's good news, sarge. I'm glad you found the Baileys. You'll have brought them some closure.'

'*We* found them, Boony. *We* brought them that closure. This is a team effort. You've played a big part in this investigation and raised some interesting points others didn't think of. You are going to make a good detective. I'm looking forward to doing your annual report.'

Boon looked scared. 'Now I'm worried,' he said.

'Is Stanley or Barnes in yet?' Jane asked.

'Barnes isn't. Stanley's in his office reading a copy of our report. He said he doesn't want to be disturbed. I think Stanley's worried Barnes might be taken off the case.'

'Between you and me, he's only got himself to blame if he is. He let his emotions get the better of him when he interviewed Meade. Then the way he spoke to Archbishop Malone was naïve for a man of his experience.'

It was nine on the dot when a dour-faced Barnes walked into the incident room, followed by Stanley, also looking downcast.

'This doesn't look good,' Boon whispered to Jane.

Barnes cleared his throat. 'Good morning, everyone. I'll keep this brief and to the point. I am to be relieved of my command later this morning and moved to a desk job at the Yard. DCS Salmon, a devout Catholic, will be taking over. In the meantime, complete your reports for a two o'clock meeting with my replacement. I'd like to thank you all for your hard work and support during my brief time on this investigation . . . especially Stanley, Tennison and Boon.'

His announcement was greeted by a stunned silence. Then one of the detectives said, 'Why have you been replaced, guv?'

'It would seem my remarks to the press on Monday about the Catholic Church and cover-ups did not go down well with the commissioner, or the current archbishop of the diocese, Andrew Malone. That said, I am certain, if you carry on with the same determination and enthusiasm, you will as a team solve the murder of Sister Melissa Bailey.'

Barnes left the room. While the rest of the officers started talking animatedly amongst themselves, Stanley told Jane and Boon that Barnes wanted to speak with them in his office.

'Can I make a quick phone call, guv?' Boon asked Stanley.

'Is it important?'

'Yes, very. It's connected to the investigation.'

'Go on then, but don't be long. Barnes is in a bad enough mood as it is.'

Boon waited until Stanley had left the room, then phoned the *News Shopper* office, asking to speak to Becky Rogers.

Stanley told Barnes that Boon would be a couple of minutes, and Jane went to get some coffees while they waited for him.

When Boon finally walked in, she thought he looked anxious.

'You all right?' she whispered, handing him a coffee.

'Becky still isn't at work. I'm a bit worried about her. I'll tell you why later.'

They were interrupted by Barnes. 'Is there something you two would like to share with me and Stanley?'

'No, sir,' they replied in unison.

'Just so you both know, the commissioner told me not to go near Meade or Malone without his approval. He's meeting Malone at the Yard at ten. He said he'd assess the situation and decide what was to happen after their meeting.'

'So you might still be running the investigation, sir?' Boon asked hopefully.

'Afraid not, son. I'm history.' He shrugged. 'I'm not particularly bothered. I've done my thirty years, so I can retire if I want on a full pension. Did you contact the Kingston police, Tennison?'

Jane nodded, then told Barnes about locating the Baileys, her conversation with Lawrence Bailey and the dental records matching Melissa.

'Fucking Malone is involved up to his neck. He knows Meade murdered Melissa and now we can't speak to either of them!'

'Things might change once the commissioner is aware of all the evidence,' Stanley said.

'And pigs might fly,' Barnes retorted. 'Stanley updated me about your visit to Sister Margaret. Although I despise the woman for what she did to those poor children, it's bad news she has dementia. That said, her reaction to seeing the photo of Meade and pointing out Melissa can be used against him as evidence.'

'She wouldn't be a credible witness,' Jane said.

'You two would be. You witnessed her reaction; you saw her point at Sister Melissa.'

'We couldn't actually see who she was pointing to,' Boon said.

'Come on, it's bloody obvious, so what's the harm in saying it was her?' Barnes shot back.

Jane knew what Barnes was suggesting, but she wasn't going to lie in court. She handed him the close-ups of Meade and Sister Melissa touching hands. 'This is stronger evidence they were in a relationship, which proves he's lied to us and implicates him in her murder.'

Barnes looked at the photos as Jane continued.

'There's something else that's come up which suggests Mother Adele may have been involved.' Jane then explained about the foxglove seeds in Melissa's stomach.

'All very interesting, but as Mother Adele is dead, not much use.'

'It's also possible Meade knew foxglove plants contained a poison,' Jane suggested.

'Would the amount of foxglove in her stomach have killed her?' Barnes asked.

Jane shrugged. 'I don't know, but it's clear it didn't, since she was stabbed to death.'

Stanley picked up on Jane's remark. 'Then it is possible Mother Adele was angry with Melissa and slipped some foxglove in her food to kill her but for some reason it didn't work. Then later that night, Melissa met secretly with Meade in the crypt where he killed her because she posed a threat to his career.'

'It still leaves the question of who moved the coffin outside and when,' Boon said.

'It could have been Meade and Malone,' Stanley suggested.

'God, how I'd love to arrest that bastard Meade! I know I could force the truth out of him and get the evidence we need against Malone as well,' Barnes said.

Although Jane knew Barnes was fixated on Meade and Malone, she decided it was time to raise her concerns about Thomas Durham and Lee Holland.

'There's something else that's come up in the course of the investigation that I need to ask you about. Thomas Durham and Lee Holland are hiding something, but I don't know what it is or why.' She was interrupted by a knock on the door.

'I'm busy,' Barnes shouted.

The door opened and PC Roger Rogers, the coroner's officer, walked in. He glared at Boon.

'Where's my daughter?' he asked aggressively.

Everyone looked at Boon, waiting for a reply.

'I don't know,' he replied.

'Her flatmate said she was meeting you last night and she never came home. She hasn't turned up for work this morning either. So, where is she?' Rogers demanded to know.

'We were supposed to meet at The Chequers in Bickley last night, but she never turned up,' Boon said.

'What were you meeting her for, Boon?' Barnes asked with a frown, clearly wondering if he was passing on information about the investigation.

Boon started to look uneasy. 'We were just going to go for a social drink, nothing more, sir. I phoned her work a few minutes ago because I was worried about her. I'm even more worried now.'

'Why?' Barnes asked.

'I asked when they had last seen Becky. Her editor told me she had arranged to meet someone from the diocese yesterday afternoon and left the office at about two.'

'Who was she meeting?' Rogers asked.

'I don't know . . . and neither did her editor,' Boon said.

'Did you tell her about our interest in Bishop Meade?' Barnes asked.

Boon hung his head. 'Not at first. After we spoke with Annette Gorman, Becky kept pressing me about who Father Bob was. I said I didn't know, but she knew I was lying. In the end I told her about Bishop Meade and said we suspected he may have been involved in the murder.'

'I'll swing for you, Boon, if any harm has come to my daughter!' Rogers shouted.

'Excuse me, but you were the one who told Becky about the post-mortem results. You know your job stipulates not to pass on information about a deceased person or an ongoing investigation,' Stanley said.

Rogers pointed at Jane. 'She never told me it was to be kept quiet!'

Barnes slammed his hand on the desk. 'All right, everyone, calm down. Sitting here blaming each other is getting us nowhere. My concern right now is for Becky. Stanley, I want you to go with Rogers and search her flat; see if there's anything there that might indicate where she's gone. Boon, you go to her work with a couple of detectives and speak to all the staff. Tennison, you're coming with me.'

'Where to, sir?' she asked.

'Meade's office, to arrest him and find out what he was doing yesterday afternoon. Arrange for a uniform car to take us there on blues and twos,' Barnes said.

'Is that advisable after what the commissioner said?' Stanley asked.

'Right now, I couldn't give a flying fuck about the commissioner. Finding Becky is all I care about,' Barnes said, putting on his jacket.

CHAPTER TWENTY-SEVEN

Barnes said nothing during the high-speed journey to Archbishop's House. Jane knew there would an uproar after Meade was arrested and Barnes might well find himself suspended from duty. He also risked being sacked for disobeying the commissioner's orders and even losing his pension. Jane sighed to herself. She knew nothing and nobody was going to stop Barnes in his quest to bring down Meade and Archbishop Malone.

Arriving at their destination, Barnes asked the two uniformed officers to accompany him. He knocked on the door and the young priest answered.

'Where's Meade?' Barnes grunted.

'The archbishop said you are not allowed on these premises. I'll have you know he's presently with your commissioner.'

Barnes's eyes widened. 'I couldn't care if he's with God himself.' He grabbed the priest by the front of his cassock. 'Is he in Malone's office?'

The priest looked terrified and frantically nodded.

Barnes raced up the stairs followed by Jane and the uniformed officers. He tried to open the door, but it was locked from the inside.

'Open the bloody door now, Meade, or I'll kick it in!' Barnes shouted.

There was no reply from within. Barnes nodded at the burly uniformed officer, who knew what to do. It took him two running shoulder charges to force the door open with a crash.

'Robert Meade, I am arresting you—' Barnes stopped, aghast at what he saw.

A motionless Meade, eyes bulging and tongue protruding, was hanging from the tall bookshelf, his red cloth cincture tied round his neck as a noose.

'No!' Barnes exclaimed, grabbing a pair of scissors off the desk. He quickly climbed up the library ladder. The uniformed officers supported Meade to ease the tension on the cincture as Barnes hurriedly cut through it.

Jane noticed a six-by-four-inch photograph on the desk. Looking closer she could see it was a copy of the 1962 Sisters of Mercy group photograph, where Meade was standing next to Sister Melissa with their little fingers entwined. She turned it over and was shocked to see 'May God forgive me my sins' written on the back. Jane put the photograph in her coat pocket.

As Meade was laid on the floor, Barnes jumped down from the ladder.

'Don't you dare die on me!' Barnes said, kneeling beside Meade. He started mouth-to-mouth resuscitation and chest compressions.

Jane knew Meade was dead. She placed two fingers on his wrist to feel for a pulse, then looked at Barnes.

'He's gone,' she said softly.

'No, he's not getting away with it like this!' Barnes said, continuing the resuscitation attempt.

Jane gently put her hand on Barnes's arm. 'Sir, I can assure you he's dead . . . you can't save him.'

Barnes clenched his fist and slammed it down on Meade's chest in anger. 'That bastard was our best hope of finding Becky Rogers.'

He stood up and walked over to the young priest who was in a state of shock. 'Did Meade leave this building yesterday afternoon?'

The priest nodded.

'He left here just after two. He didn't say where he was going.'

Jane recalled Boon saying Becky had left her office at about the same time to meet someone from the diocese.

'I want you to remember his exact words,' Barnes said.

'He asked me to hail him a cab, then said, "I'm going out to see someone. I'll be back in a few hours."'

'Did you hear him say to the cab driver where he wanted to go?'

'No.'

'Did you see him when he got back?'

'Yes, it was between seven thirty and eight.'

'Can you be more exact with the time?'

'I went to his apartment just before seven thirty to see if he wanted some supper, but he wasn't there. I called on him again at eight and he was there. He said he didn't feel hungry, so I left and didn't see him again until this morning in his office.'

'What sort of mood was he in last night?'

'He was fairly quiet and looked tired.'

'And this morning?'

'He seemed all right. He had a meeting with Archbishop Malone before he went to see your commissioner. He remained in the archbishop's office on his own and said he didn't want to be disturbed. That was the last time I saw him . . . until now.'

'What was he wearing when he left here yesterday afternoon?' Jane asked.

'His clerical suit, purple shirt and white collar.'

She knew Meade would stand out dressed like that, particularly if he had met Becky in a public place.

'Does the name Becky Rogers mean anything to you?' Barnes asked the priest.

He nodded. 'She called yesterday and asked to speak with Bishop Meade.'

'What did she say?'

'Just that she wanted to speak personally with him about a delicate matter.'

'Did Meade speak to her?'

'I put the call through to him. A minute or so later he came to my office. He seemed annoyed.'

'Why?'

'She never told me she was a newspaper reporter. I thought it was a personal call when I put her through. Bishop Meade told me who she was. He said if she ever called again, I was to put the phone down on her.'

'Did she call again?'

'Not to my knowledge.'

Something didn't add up for Jane. She very much doubted Meade would agree to meet Becky in the first place, much less harm her, as she posed no direct threat to him. Although Melissa's death had been brutal, there was no direct evidence that Meade was ever violent or abusive. Malone, on the other hand, regularly beat children.

Barnes looked at the uniformed officers. 'I want this room treated as a crime scene. Get on your radio and ask for DS Johnson from the lab to attend. Also ask for four detectives from the incident room. I want Meade's office and apartment searched top to bottom. I need one of you to drive me back to Orpington, and one to guard the scene until DS Johnson and my detectives arrive.' He turned to Jane. 'Let's go, Tennison.'

'Can you give me a couple of minutes please, sir? I just want to nip down to the archives and speak with Mrs Parkin.'

'What for?'

'She might know something about the letter of dispensation Malone purportedly signed. If she says there wasn't one in the archives, then the letter he's taken to the commissioner must be a fake.'

'Good thinking . . . I'll come with you.'

'She might be a bit tetchy after our first meeting – even more so if there's two of us. It might be best I go on my own.'

'I'll wait for you in the car then.'

As Jane entered the archives, she knew Mrs Parkin would not yet be aware of Meade's death.

'What do you want?' Mrs Parkin asked with a stern expression.

'I need your help, Mrs Parkin.'

'You tricked me into helping you last time. Archbishop Malone said I was not to speak to the police. So please just go away and leave me alone.'

'I'm sorry I was underhand. I regret not being upfront with you. At the time I believed Bishop Meade was lying to me and wouldn't let me speak with you personally,' Jane explained.

'Bishop Meade is as honest as the day is long,' she said primly. 'He wouldn't—'

'Bishop Meade is dead. We just found his body in the archbishop's office.'

Mrs Parkin looked mortified. 'Dead! How?'

'It looks like he may have taken his own life.'

'Why . . . why would he do that?' she asked, clearly distraught. 'Bishop Meade is a kind and gentle man.'

'Other people have said that as well. I understand how distressed you must be, and I'm sure you want to go home right now, Mrs Parkin. But my job is to get to the truth of what happened and why. There's something very important that's come up in our investigation and we need to resolve it as soon as possible.'

Mrs Parkin wiped her eyes with a tissue, then took a deep breath before replying. 'What is it?'

'We now know the murdered woman was a sister at St Mary's Covent. Her name was Melissa Bailey. We have reason to believe Archbishop Malone signed a dispensation letter allowing her to renounce her faith and leave the convent. Do you know if that document exists?'

'No, but it might. Archbishop Malone came down here yesterday morning and said he needed to look through some old documents.'

'What time was that?'

'About eleven or eleven-thirty. I offered to get the documents for him, but he said he'd get them himself.'

'Did he appear angry?'

'He did, actually. Anyway, he went into the archives and came out a few minutes later holding a document, then left the room without saying anything. It might have been the dispensation letter.'

'How do you find Archbishop Malone?'

'To be perfectly honest, he's an arrogant pig of a man with a terrible temper. He talks down to everyone and shouts when you make a mistake or are too slow in doing something for him. The truth is no one here likes him, but you don't dare talk back, or he'll have you sacked. He's been known to move priests who have upset him to churches in all sorts of godforsaken places.'

Jane remembered Boon telling her Becky had been making inquiries at the council planning offices about the sale of the convent.

'Remember last time I was here I asked you about quotes or invoices for building work at the convent? I wondered if you found any.'

'I haven't really looked, but I can do it now if you want.'

'Are you sure?' Jane asked.

'God rest his soul,' she said. 'But a woman was murdered. Whoever did it needs to be found and punished.'

'Thank you, Mrs Parkin. 'I've got to go back to the station. If you find anything could you fax a copy over to the incident room for me?' Jane said, handing her the station fax number.

'That's fine. But please don't tell Archbishop Malone I've helped you or I'll lose my job.'

* * *

Jane told Barnes about her conversation with Mrs Parkin, but decided not to mention her request for any documents about building work at the convent until she knew if there were any. Barnes said nothing on the journey back to Orpington, clearly in deep thought. As they walked across the station yard he finally spoke.

'I have to say I wasn't expecting Meade to top himself.'

'I found this on the desk,' Jane said, handing him the photograph.

Barnes looked at it briefly, read what was written on the back and returned it to Jane. 'A veiled confession, I suppose. Suicide is considered a mortal sin in the Catholic faith. He won't get God's forgiveness, a funeral mass or burial in a Catholic cemetery.'

'I didn't know that,' Jane replied.

'That's because you're not a Catholic. And before you ask, I was until I dealt with Stephen Phillips' death and then renounced my faith. Mark my words, there's going to be an uproar at the Yard over Meade's suicide. My career is over, Jane, but I don't want you, Stanley, or anyone else getting dragged down with me. When the top brass start asking questions, I want you all to say you acted under my orders.'

'I think you'll find the officers on the squad are all on your side,' she said.

'Thank you. But now Meade is dead, the investigation into Sister Melissa's murder is all but over. I suspect the commissioner and Malone will agree to sweep everything under the carpet. But I'm not going to let that happen.' Barnes looked at his watch. 'DCS Salmon will be here in a couple of hours to take over. Let the team know I want an office meeting in an hour. See if Stanley and Boon are back from their inquiries. Tell them to come to my office so we can discuss Becky's disappearance. We need to find her.'

* * *

Stanley had not yet returned from searching Becky's flat. A dejected-looking Boon was sitting at his desk with his head in his hands.

'You, all right, Simon?' Jane asked.

'This is all my fault. I should never have told Becky about Bishop Meade being a suspect. Does he know anything?' he asked.

Jane sat next to him and put her hand on his shoulder. 'Meade's dead. He hanged himself in the archbishop's office this morning before we got to him.'

Boon looked stunned. 'Did he have a meeting with Becky yesterday?'

'It's possible, but we don't know for certain,' Jane replied.

He shook his head. 'If he's killed Becky, we may never find her.' He was close to tears.

Jane saw Stanley walk in. 'Barnes wants a meeting with us in his office.'

'I know. I just saw him in the corridor. Looks like Meade took the coward's way out once he knew we were on to him,' Stanley said.

'I'm not so sure you are right about Meade. There may be other reasons he took his own life that we've yet to discover,' Jane said.

Boon glared at her. 'Why are you defending him? He clearly killed Sister Melissa, and he's probably killed Becky. I hope Meade rots in hell.'

'It's possible Melissa was going to the presbytery to see him the night she was killed, but never got there,' Jane suggested.

'You've changed your tune,' Stanley remarked.

'Meade could have gone to the convent to kill Sister Melissa, then packed her bag to make it look like she'd run away,' Boon said.

'It's possible that's what happened, but he'd have been taking a big risk of getting caught in the convent or waking Julie Dorton.'

Boon stood up. 'People commit suicide for a reason. Meade couldn't live with what he'd done. Stanley's right, he took the coward's way out.'

'We'd better go see Barnes,' Jane said. She had never seen Boon so worked up. She knew he wasn't thinking clearly and trying to reason with him, or Stanley, would be pointless.

'Did you find anything of interest at Becky's flat?' Barnes asked Stanley.

He handed Barnes a notebook. 'This was beside her bed. Meade's name is in it, along with some others. I think it's her thoughts about the investigation.'

'Strange she didn't take it with her to work,' Barnes remarked, flicking through it.

'She's got a small pocketbook for work,' Boon said. 'Becky told me she kept a notebook beside her bed. She'd often wake in the night and think of something important. She said if she didn't write it down, she'd have forgotten about it by the morning.'

'I know that feeling well,' Barnes replied. He put the notebook down on his desk. 'There's tons of stuff in there, but it's all in shorthand.'

'I can read shorthand,' Jane said.

Barnes handed her the notebook. 'Transcribe and type it up for me, please.' He turned to Stanley. 'Did you speak to Becky's flatmate?'

'Yes, at her workplace. Her name's Jayne Burman. She was at school with Becky and has been her flatmate for two years. She said Becky had become obsessed with the murder, thinking it could be her breakthrough to working for a mainstream paper.'

'Did she mention Meade?' Barnes asked.

'Not by name. Burman said Becky was very perky yesterday morning. When Jayne asked why, Becky said she had a lead on someone connected to the Church to follow up on, which might prove interesting.'

'That's got to be Meade,' Boon said.

Barnes nodded. 'It certainly looks that way. Even more so now we know Meade left his office at around the same time. What did Becky's editor have to say?'

'He and two others confirmed Becky left just after two,' Boon said. 'She said she was following up on a lead and would be out for a couple of hours.'

'I take it she has a car?' Barnes asked.

'Yes,' Stanley replied. 'A red 1972 Citroën 2CV, with a black canvas roll-back sunroof. I've already circulated the registration Met-wide and to the surrounding county forces. I also contacted Becky's bank. She's made no withdrawals or card purchases. They'll notify us if she does. I've got a recent photograph of her from her flat.'

'Contact our press office at the Yard,' Barnes said. 'Give them a full description; what she was wearing when last seen and details of her car. Get a patrol car to drop her photo off as well. I want it on the six o'clock news, TV and radio, and in all tomorrow's papers. Can anyone think of anything else we can do to locate her?'

Jane made a suggestion. 'This is a long shot. We could contact the Public Carriage Office to get the word out to the black cab community. Tell them we are looking for any cabbie who picked up a man outside Archbishop's House yesterday afternoon who fits Meade's description.'

'That's worth a try,' Barnes said.

'I've got her address book from the flat. We could ring round all her contacts. See if they know anything,' Stanley said.

'Share it out amongst the team to make it quicker,' Barnes replied. 'How's PC Rogers?' he asked Stanley.

'Frantic with worry and wishing he'd never told his daughter about the post-mortem. As a cop, he knows the prospects of finding her alive are not looking good. He's at home comforting his wife. I promised we'd contact him as soon as we have any news – good or bad.'

'I'll phone him in a minute and tell him about Meade's suicide, as well as what we've just discussed.'

Barnes's phone rang. He picked it up and had a brief conversation before ending the call.

'That was Lloyd Johnson. Dr Pullen just attended the scene. She did a cursory examination of Meade's body and found no marks indicating he had been in a struggle. She also thought the bruising and cincture marks on his neck were consistent with Meade hanging himself.

'Now, this may sound odd coming from me, but we need to keep an open mind about Becky's disappearance. Although there's evidence that points to Meade being involved, she could have been abducted by a stranger. She may be alive and being held against her will. Time is of the essence. We need to think laterally and do everything we can to find her.'

* * *

Most of the team were gathered in the office for the meeting with Barnes, apart from the officers who were searching Meade's apartment and office, who so far had found nothing of interest.

Jane phoned the Public Carriage Office who said they would do what they could to trace the cab driver who picked Meade up outside Archbishop's House. She then phoned British Telecom and requested details of all outgoing calls from Archbishop's House the previous day, and the names and addresses of who the calls were made to. She said it was urgent and the person she spoke to said they would fax the details through to her within the hour.

Barnes addressed the team. 'I'm sure you've all heard about Bishop Meade's suicide. As tragic as it is, depending on which way you look at it, he is no longer my main concern. We now need to concentrate on finding Becky Rogers. To that end, I've asked for an urgent press appeal to be made. I want you to treat every call or piece of information we receive as a possible lead. Follow it up until you are completely satisfied it is a dead end. If you have something positive, inform DI Stanley immediately.' Barnes noticed DCS Salmon and the deputy commissioner entering the room.

Everyone stood to attention.

'I thought the commissioner himself might have been here,' Barnes remarked drily.

'He's busy trying to appease Archbishop Malone . . . thanks to you,' the deputy commissioner scowled.

'The floor is yours, Salmon,' Barnes said with an ill-disguised sneer.

'I'd like to speak to you in your office, DCS Barnes,' the deputy commissioner said.

'If you want to talk to me, sir, I'd rather you did it in front of my team.'

'I won't ask again,' he said.

'Then don't, because I'm not budging.'

'DCS Barnes, you are relieved of your command and suspended from duty until further notice,' the deputy commissioner said.

Barnes laughed and shook his head. 'May I ask on what grounds, sir?'

'Disobeying the commissioner's orders and misconduct in a public office.'

'Did the child abuser – sorry, Archbishop Malone – influence your decision?' Barnes asked.

The deputy commissioner was losing his patience. 'No, he did not. But he has made a formal complaint about your conduct and your hounding of Bishop Meade.'

'And so the cover-up begins. You're all as bad as each other.'

'That's enough, Barnes. Leave these premises now or I will have you forcibly removed!' the deputy commissioner snapped.

Barnes took his warrant card out of his jacket pocket and held it up as he addressed his colleagues. 'Like you all, I took an oath of office the day I joined the police force. We swore to serve the Queen, without favour or affection, malice or ill-will. We learned our primary objective was the prevention of crime and the detection and punishment of offenders. As you progress in your service, never forget the oath you took and what you stand for. It has been a pleasure working with you all. You should be proud of what you've achieved in a short time on this investigation. Keep up the good work and I wish you a successful outcome. The last thing I ask of you is to find Becky Rogers . . . not for me, but for her family.'

As Barnes walked out, he stopped by the deputy commissioner. 'We both know you can't punish or discipline me if I retire.' He handed him his warrant card. 'Tell the commissioner to stuff this up his arse.'

Boon started to clap slowly. He was joined by another officer, then another, until the whole room was filled with applause for Barnes. Jane could see he was deeply moved by their show of respect and admiration. He raised his hand in acknowledgement and left the room.

Salmon shook his head in disbelief. 'Just so you all know, I am Detective Chief Superintendent Rufus Salmon. I am now in charge of this investigation and need to be brought up to speed with everything. To that end, I will hold a full office meeting in twenty minutes. I want to hear what each and every one of you has been doing and what evidence you have accumulated.'

Stanley whispered to Jane, 'What a load of bullshit. Now Meade's dead, he knows full well the investigation is all but over. This is all about damage limitation with the diocese.'

'I agree, but he needs to get his priorities right. Excuse me, sir,' Jane said, trying to get Salmon's attention.

'And you are?' Salmon asked.

'DS Tennison. Are you aware we are also investigating the disappearance of a young journalist called Becky Rogers?'

'No, I was not, though I did hear DCS Barnes mention her name just now.'

'She hasn't been seen or heard from since yesterday afternoon. We have evidence that—'

Salmon raised his hand. 'You can tell me all about it during the office meeting.'

Jane was astonished by his lack of interest. 'It's possible Becky has come to some harm.'

'Did you not hear me, Tennison?'

'Becky is a serving police officer's daughter,' she continued undaunted. 'He and his wife are worried sick about her.'

'We have evidence that suggests Bishop Meade arranged to meet her,' Stanley chipped in, 'and a witness who saw him leave his office at the same time Becky left hers. The press has been informed of her disappearance and will shortly be making an appeal for assistance to find her. Needless to say, we can expect a deluge of phone calls. I doubt Becky's parents, or the press, would be impressed if we didn't answer the calls because of an office meeting.'

Boon decided to add his voice to their pleas. 'I'm DC Boon. I know I can speak on behalf of us all. Investigating Becky Rogers' disappearance must be a priority. Every second is precious if we want to find her alive and well.'

Salmon looked embarrassed. 'OK, the office meeting can wait. Carry on as you were. I'll read through the reports and we can have a meeting tomorrow if need be. I've a few things to do back at the Yard. Keep me informed of any developments, DI Stanley.'

'I will, sir.'

Stanley waited a few minutes in case Salmon returned, then spoke to the team.

'I think we all know what's going on here. As far as I'm concerned, Sister Melissa Bailey's death is still under investigation, since it could be connected to Becky Rogers' disappearance. Meade may or may not be responsible, but either way we need to find out what's happened. If you get any calls or information that you feel needs an immediate response, tell me, not Salmon.'

CHAPTER TWENTY-EIGHT

Jane sat at her desk to read through the shorthand in Becky's notebook. She felt sad thinking of the aspiring young journalist writing notes on her first major investigation, full of enthusiasm and keen to impress her editor. It reminded Jane of herself as a young detective, going over the evidence in her mind and writing down her thoughts.

'This fax just came through for you from BT,' the civilian indexer said, handing over four sheets of paper.

Jane put the notebook to one side and looked through the calls. She found nothing of relevance until she spotted a number she recognised. Stanley was reading through some reports in Barnes's office when Jane walked in holding up a fax sheet.

'There's a two-minute call on here made from Meade's office yesterday afternoon.'

'What's interesting about a bishop phoning a presbytery?' Stanley asked.

'The call was made at a quarter to two, just before Meade left in a cab. He phoned St Mary's Church presbytery. Father Floridia lives there. He's the resident priest.'

'So, Meade phoned a priest . . . what's the big deal?'

'You are hard work at times, Stanley,' she said.

'Then get to the point.'

'I've two thoughts here. One, Meade simply phoned Father Floridia and asked if he could speak with him at the presbytery. Two, Meade asked if he could use the presbytery to meet Becky Rogers in private.'

Stanley nodded. 'Now you're making sense. Do you think Father Floridia could be involved in Becky's disappearance?'

Jane sighed. 'I very much doubt it. Father Chris has helped me from the start of this investigation. Meade told him not to talk to me and he put his job on the line by doing so. Maybe Meade went there to discuss our investigation and see if I'd been in contact with him.'

'Why would Meade go all the way to the presbytery when he could just as easily ask over the phone?'

'I agree, that's odd. However, there are a lot of prying eyes and ears in Archbishop's House,' Jane suggested. 'But if Becky did go to the presbytery, I don't believe she would have come to any harm there.'

'You can't be certain of that,' Stanley said, opening the phone book and picking up the phone.

'Who are you calling?'

He started to dial a number. 'The presbytery. I want you to speak with Father Floridia, ask him if he's spoken with Bishop Meade recently and gauge his reaction.'

Jane put her finger on the disconnect button. 'I'll do it, but face to face.'

'Take Boon with you,' Stanley said.

'No. I need to go alone. I'll know if he's lying.'

'Just because someone is nice, it doesn't mean they are not dishonest. Meade being a prime example.'

'I know that, but Father Chris isn't like him or Malone.'

'Sounds like you've got to know him well in a short space of time,' Stanley remarked.

'I consider him a friend,' Jane said.

Stanley raised his eyebrows. 'Just a friend?'

'Yes,' she said, frowning. 'And I resent your insinuation.'

* * *

Jane knocked on the door of the presbytery. Father Chris opened it, looking pleased to see her.

'Hello, Jane. What brings you to my door?'

'I'm here in an official capacity. I need to ask you some questions about Bishop Meade.'

His smile faded. 'You'd better come in. Is Bishop Meade not willing to talk to you?'

They walked through to the living room.

'I've some bad news about Bishop Meade.'

Father Chris looked concerned. 'Has he been arrested?'

'Bishop Meade is dead, Chris. He hanged himself in Archbishop Malone's office this morning.'

Chris slumped onto the sofa, a stunned expression on his face.

'I was one of the officers who found him.'

Chris looked upwards. 'Where were you, my God, when he needed you most?' Then he bowed his head. 'Eternal life grant unto him, O Lord, may perpetual light shine upon him and may he rest in peace. Amen.' He made the sign of the cross, then looked up at Jane. 'What is it you need to know?'

'Did Bishop Meade phone you yesterday?'

'Yes, he said he needed to speak with me and asked if he could come to the presbytery.'

'Can you remember what time he called?'

Father Chris thought for a second. 'About quarter to two, I think. Then he came here just after two.'

'Do you know how he got here?'

'I assume it was in a taxi cab. He asked me to call one when he was leaving.'

'And what time was that?'

'Just after seven. What's this all about, Jane?'

She told Chris about Becky Rogers and her unexplained disappearance.

'I have to ask you this, and please don't take it the wrong way. But did Becky come here to speak with Bishop Meade?'

'No. He never even mentioned her name while he was here. I can assure you Bishop Meade had nothing to do with her disappearance.'

'What did Bishop Meade want to speak to you about?'

Father Chris sighed. 'I'm sorry, but I can't tell you, Jane.'

'Why not?'

There was sadness in his eyes as he looked at her. 'Roman Catholic law forbids me disclosing what was said during a confession.'

'Meade confessed to you?'

'If I break the sacred seal of confession, I will be excommunicated from the Church.'

'But this is a murder investigation. And a young woman has gone missing.'

'That makes no difference. I can't tell anyone what Bishop Meade said, not even the police, no matter how serious the crime is. I shouldn't even disclose the identity of a penitent who has confessed.'

'We know Bishop Meade lied to us. I have evidence that suggests he had been in a relationship with our victim. If he didn't kill her, I suspect he knew who did.'

'You have to believe me, Jane. Bishop Meade did not kill Sister Melissa.'

Jane knew only Meade could have told Father Chris her name.

'Can you tell me who did?'

He looked forlorn as he shook his head. 'There's no point in continuing this conversation. My answer will always be no.'

'Now Bishop Meade has killed himself, he will be seen as a murderer who could no longer bear his guilt. Surely you want to clear his name.'

'I don't want to argue with you, Jane, but I beg you to keep this conversation between the two of us.'

Jane sighed. 'I understand your position in the eyes of the Church, but if you know who killed Sister Melissa and don't tell me, you're letting whoever is responsible get away with murder.'

'I don't know who murdered her, but I pray you will find the answers you seek.'

* * *

Returning to Orpington, Jane went straight to Stanley.

'How'd it go with the priest?' he asked.

'Meade was with him during the time frame Becky went missing. Bottom line is, we were wrong about Meade being involved in Becky's disappearance. If she was following up on a lead, it was with someone else.'

'Was there anything in her notebook that might help us?' Stanley asked.

'I haven't had a chance to go through it yet. I'd just started when I got the fax through from BT. I'll go and do it now.'

Jane opened the notebook and decided it was best to work backwards from the last shorthand entry Becky had made.

Thomas Durham — developer — bought convent — was land and chapel deconsecrated? — did Durham bribe Meade to say it was to council planners? — did dead nun know? — tunnel under chapel — coffin found near it — maybe used to move coffin unnoticed?

After transcribing the last entry, Jane checked the rest of the notebook for anything that might help trace Becky's last movements. But there was nothing beyond the mention of Thomas Durham and the tunnel. Jane looked over to Boon who was sitting opposite typing a report.

'Did you tell Becky Rogers about the tunnel at the convent?'

'Not . . . that I recall,' he replied hesitantly.

'Read this and explain to me how you think she knew about it,' Jane said, handing him the transcript.

He licked his lips as he read it, then handed it back to Jane.

'I don't know,' he said, unable to look her in the eye.

'Please, Boony, don't dig a big hole for yourself by lying to me,' she said.

Boon sighed. 'We were talking about Meade being a suspect. I let slip there was a tunnel, and the coffin was found near it. She asked if I'd checked out the tunnel, and I said no.'

'What about her interest in Thomas Durham? Did you tell her about him?'

Boon looked offended. 'No. Becky said she'd made her own inquiries about the history of the convent, the fire and the sale to Thomas Durham.'

'Did she say where?'

'No, but it was probably at the Bromley planning department. Becky reckoned something dodgy might have gone on between Meade and Durham over the sale of the convent. She thought Sister Melissa might have been killed because she found out about it. I told her Durham bought the land after the nuns had left, so it would be stupid of him to bury the coffin on land he was going to build on.'

'Did she agree with you?'

'Sort of. But she still thought it was a possibility worth exploring. I told her to leave the detective work to us or she could find herself in trouble. Becky was right about Meade, though, and now he's probably silenced her as well.'

'Meade had nothing to do with Becky's disappearance,' Jane said firmly. 'We have a credible witness who spent yesterday afternoon and evening with him. I need to speak with Stanley about this,' she said, holding up Becky's notebook.

'Are you going to tell him what I told Becky?' Boon asked, looking worried.

Jane felt Boon was already suffering enough emotional stress over Becky. 'Not if I can help it,' she said.

'Thanks, sarge. Sorry I messed up.'

'Don't worry. We all make mistakes. The important thing is that we learn from them,' she said.

* * *

Having read the transcript, Stanley handed it back to Jane.

'How did Becky know about the tunnel and Thomas Durham being the developer?' he asked.

'It looks like she did some investigating of her own at the council planning department,' Jane said. 'She probably looked at the same documents and maps as we did.'

'Her notes don't really help us much,' Stanley remarked.

'I'm not so sure. I'm wondering if there's something in her idea that Thomas Durham committed bribery to get the chapel and land deconsecrated.'

'Well, it can't have connected to Meade as he had nothing to do with it,' Stanley said.

'I know, but Archbishop Malone did.'

Stanley looked bemused. 'You seriously think he's involved in Becky's disappearance?'

'Thomas Durham and Lee Holland lied to me from day one. I didn't know why, but having read Becky's notes, I think she may have inadvertently given us the answer.'

Stanley leaned forward. 'Why is this the first time you've mentioned speaking to Thomas Durham?'

'I thought I had . . .' she started to reply.

'You only ever mentioned you'd spoken to Nick Durham. As I recall, you said he was very helpful, just upset at the site being closed.'

Jane realised she had unintentionally put herself in a difficult situation and wondered how best to tell Stanley about Thomas Durham and Lee Holland.

Stanley folded his arms. 'I'm waiting for an answer, Jane.'

She recalled her words of advice to Boon.

'I was about to raise it at the meeting with Barnes when PC Rogers walked in. I should have said something earlier, but I had no evidence to support my suspicions.'

'I want to hear everything, chapter and verse. And don't try and wheedle your way out!' Stanley said angrily.

Jane told him about the first time she and Boon met Thomas Durham and Lee Holland, their strange behaviour, their lies about knowing each other and the argument she believed they had the morning she and Boon went to the site to arrest Barry May.

'If Nick Durham and Barry May told you Thomas Durham and Lee Holland were long-standing friends, it must have been blatantly obvious they were hiding something from you. Why didn't you interview them?' Stanley demanded.

'At first I thought they were concerned about the discovery of the coffin. I even wondered if they were involved in moving it.'

'Then why didn't you bloody well say something?'

'It seemed absurd to me that they would bury a coffin on land they intended to develop. And even if they had, surely they would have moved it before the digging work began,' Jane said defensively.

'Which also suggests Becky Rogers might have been right, and she's not even a bloody detective!'

'I was also made aware that Thomas Durham suffers from a heart condition and wasn't supposed to get involved in any of the new development work. I thought he and Holland might be acting strangely because they didn't want Nick Durham to know his father was distressed about the discovery of the coffin.'

'What fucking planet are you on, Jane? If Durham was upset about the coffin, he must have been apoplectic when he read Becky's article in the *News Shopper*.'

'When I met Thomas Durham, he didn't seem that perturbed about it. He accepted we had a job to do, and the site would have to remain closed.'

'Be honest, he didn't have much choice, did he!'

'I know, but . . .'

Stanley raised his hand. 'Hang on a minute . . . when did you meet Thomas Durham?'

'I went to his house at the weekend. He lives in the convent chapel.'

'Were you there on official business or pleasure?'

'A bit of both, I suppose,' she said uncomfortably. 'Nick Durham showed me round the old chapel and crypt. Thomas came in while I was there. He said there were no coffins in the crypt when he moved in. I didn't have any reason to doubt him after confirming the chapel and land had been deconsecrated.'

Stanley looked squarely at Jane. 'What is it with you and Nick Durham?'

Jane looked him in the eye. 'I'm seeing him . . . we've been out to dinner. It's nothing serious yet, but—'

'Jesus Christ, this just gets better and better. And there was me thinking it was the priest who was shagging you!'

'That's uncalled for!' she snapped back.

'If Barnes was still here, you would be out the door with his boot up your backside.'

'Why? I haven't revealed anything about our investigation to Nick or Thomas Durham,' Jane argued.

'You can't see the wood for the trees, can you? You seem to forget Becky Rogers is obsessed with Melissa Bailey's murder. She told her colleagues she was going out to follow up on a lead and has vanished off the face of the Earth. Her notes clearly show an interest in Bishop Meade and Thomas Durham. We know Meade refused to speak to Becky, so where in that detective's head of yours do you think she might have gone?' Stanley asked scornfully.

Jane closed her eyes and sighed as the realisation hit her. 'To speak to Thomas Durham.'

'Exactly! The Durhams stand to lose everything because of Becky's article. No one in their right mind would want to buy a property where they thought murdered children might be buried. How would you feel if a young journalist who just lost you millions of pounds turned up on your doorstep asking questions?'

'I'd be upset, but it doesn't mean I'd kill them,' Jane replied.

'We both know it doesn't take a lot to send people over the edge and lash out. One punch, one stab and a life can be over.'

Jane knew she'd messed up and it was pointless arguing. 'Are you going to interview Thomas Durham?'

'You've met him on three occasions and been to his house. You're best placed to search his premises, arrest and interview him . . . with Boon.'

Jane was stunned. 'I don't think that would be appropriate under the circumstances.'

'If you don't like it, then go back to the Bromley office and deal with the simple everyday crimes.'

'Do you not think there's a conflict of interest if I arrest Durham?'

'No. Not now you've told me what you know. Unless, of course, you think your boyfriend Nick might be involved in Becky's disappearance?' Stanley said.

'As far as I'm aware he was in his office all afternoon, then he spent the night at mine. I didn't get the impression he'd just murdered or kidnapped anyone,' Jane retorted.

'We need to confirm his exact movements for the afternoon Becky went missing,' Stanley said. 'So I'll interview him. Due to your unfortunate relationship with Nick Durham we need to do things by the book when we search his father's place. I want you to type up a search warrant for Thomas Durham's house. Get it signed by the on-call magistrate, then come straight back here. While you're doing that I'll get as many uniformed officers as I can to help you search the grounds. I also want inquiries made at every flat to see if anyone else saw Becky or her car.'

'Should I get DS Johnson involved as well? He could look for any traces of blood or hairs matching Becky's.'

Stanley nodded. 'For what it's worth, I hope we're wrong – not just for Becky's sake, but yours as well.'

There was a knock on the door and Boon entered holding some papers. He looked at Jane.

'These were just faxed over from the diocesan archivist.'

She looked through them. 'There's a document headed "Durham Building Company Ltd", giving a quote for repair work to the chapel roof. There's also an invoice for the work done, both signed by Thomas Durham and dated a year before Melissa went missing. There are other quotes and invoices from the same company for repair work over a two-year period . . . again before Melissa went missing. There's also a report on the fire damage and an estimated cost of repair to the buildings.'

'Jesus Christ! If he did all this work on the convent back then and kept quiet about it, he's also a potential suspect for Melissa's murder!' Stanley exclaimed.

CHAPTER TWENTY-NINE

The magistrate asked a few questions about the investigation, signed the warrant and Jane returned to the incident room shortly after the six o'clock news broadcast about Becky Rogers' disappearance.

Once again the detectives were busy on the phones, gathering information from members of the public who had called in. Jane noticed Lloyd Johnson putting up some photographs of the foxglove seeds and silver birch slivers on the wall.

'How's it going?' she asked him.

'I was at the convent earlier with the fire investigator,' he said. 'You were right about it being arson. It's bloody amazing what they can tell from burnt-out buildings, even years later. He could tell from the burn damage where it started and how it tracked from one building to the next.'

'So where and how did it start?' Jane asked.

'In the bakery. The fire investigator examined a rusty old paraffin heater which was still in there. The screwcap on the oil container was missing and there were three separate seats of fire in the bakery. He reckons whoever committed the arson poured the oil out in three locations then set light to each one individually.'

'Thanks, Lloyd. It's good to know I got something right.'

'You seem a bit down . . . something up?'

'Stanley's pissed off with me.'

'What have you done now?' Lloyd asked.

Jane sighed. 'It's a long story. I'll tell you later.'

* * *

Jane knocked on Stanley's door and went in.

'Any sightings of Becky?' she asked apprehensively and showed him the search warrant.

Stanley nodded. 'It looks like she went to the convent on Tuesday afternoon. An elderly couple who live in one of the flats phoned in. They were on their way out at a quarter past two when they saw a young woman getting out of a red Citroën 2CV near the main entrance. The description matches Becky and the clothing fits with what her colleagues say she wore to work on Tuesday.'

'Did they see her again?'

'No, but her car was still there when they returned home at six o'clock. They said it wasn't there the following morning. This is not looking good. I've called in the Special Patrol Group and dog section to help with the search. I'm going to speak with PC Rogers, let him know what's happening. I understand that you're in an awkward position. If you don't want to be part of the search and arrest team then—'

'No, I want to do it,' she said firmly. 'You were right. I should have interviewed Thomas Durham as soon as I suspected he was lying. If I had, then maybe right now Becky Rogers would be sitting in the comfort of her home writing her investigative journal.'

'You can't change what's happened, Jane, but you can make a difference to how it ends.'

'I'll do my best,' Jane said.

'We've all made mistakes on this investigation,' Stanley said, 'me and Tony Barnes included. The reality is, it's you and Boon who have uncovered the vital evidence. You should both be proud of that.'

'Is Boon coming on the search?'

Stanley nodded. 'I spoke with him while you were out. I told him we think Becky went to Thomas Durham's house and you were getting a search warrant. He was pretty cut up, but he's still hoping we might find her alive and being held against her will.'

'If we find her body there it might be too much for him,' Jane said.

'If Boony wants to go I'm not going to stand in his way. Finding out what's happened to Becky might even be cathartic for him.'

Stanley opened his briefcase and took out a clear plastic property bag. He removed a rag doll and handed it to Jane. The doll had button eyes, smiling red felt lips and yellow yarn hair. It was dressed in a pink floral dress, red apron and red shoes.

'This was on Becky's bed. Her flatmate said her mother made it for her fifth birthday. I took it in case we needed a scent for the police dogs during a search,' he said with a grim look.

Jane recalled the rag doll her parents had bought her when she was a toddler. She felt close to tears thinking of Becky hugging the doll and talking to it when she felt downhearted. Jane held the doll close to her chest and whispered, 'I'm sorry, Becky.'

* * *

By seven there were thirty uniformed officers, two dog handlers, twelve detectives and a van full of search equipment on their way to the old convent in a convoy of vehicles, with Jane and Boon in the lead. Prior to leaving the station, Stanley and Jane briefed everyone regarding the exterior search parameters and inquiries to be made with all the residents. Stanley decided that if Becky's body was discovered in the old chapel, the search of the woods, land and lake could stop, and be continued in daylight if necessary.

Arriving at the convent, Jane was relieved that neither of Nick's cars was there. She sent two officers round to the rear of the chapel, even though she doubted Thomas Durham would try and escape out of the back. Boon pressed the intercom for Flat 10, the residence of the couple who had seen the red Citroën 2CV and a young woman matching Becky's description.

The woman pressed the door release to let them in. Jane, Boon, Stanley, two detectives and a dog handler went into the chapel.

Jane knocked on Thomas Durham's door while the others stood to the side.

'Hello, Jane. Come in. Is Nick with you?' Durham asked when he saw her.

'This is not a social visit, Mr Durham,' Jane said.

He noticed the other officers. 'I can see that. What on earth is going on?'

'We are investigating the disappearance of Becky Rogers,' she said.

'Who is Becky Rogers?' Durham asked.

'If you'd like to let us in, I'll explain further,' Jane said.

Durham frowned. 'No. You can speak on my doorstep.'

'I have a warrant to search your property. If needs be, I can force entry,' Jane said firmly.

He opened the door, and they all went through to the living room. Boon switched the TV off and Durham picked up a cup of coffee from the table.

'So, what's this all about?' he asked, taking a sip.

Jane handed Durham a copy of the warrant. 'Becky Rogers is a reporter for the *Bromley News Shopper*. She wrote the article about the discovery of the coffin and the murdered nun—'

He interrupted gruffly. 'I read the article, but I never looked at who wrote it.'

'We have reason to believe Becky came here to interview you yesterday,' Jane continued.

'Your information is wrong,' Durham said huffily. 'I have never met or spoken to the woman . . . nor would I ever want to.'

His dismissive manner was getting to Boon. 'A woman matching her description and driving the same make and colour of car was seen outside these premises . . .' he began.

'Then she must have come here to interview someone else!' Durham interrupted. 'This is bloody ridiculous. I'm phoning my solicitor.'

'I can't allow you to make any calls until we have finished our search,' Jane told him.

Durham gave an exasperated sigh. 'Then bloody well get on with it!'

Jane asked Boon and the two detectives to search the upstairs bedrooms, while she, Lloyd and the dog handler dealt with the downstairs and crypt.

'Where's Bella?' Jane asked.

'In her bed in the kitchen. The door is closed, so you don't need to worry about her disturbing you,' Durham replied indignantly.

The dog handler opened the bag containing Becky's rag doll, removed it, and let his German Shepherd have a good sniff.

'Track, Rumpole, track,' the handler said, letting the dog off the lead.

'Rumpole?' Lloyd remarked.

'You know, *Rumpole of the Bailey,*' the handler said.

Durham snorted. 'You're wasting your time and mine.'

Rumpole scurried round the living room sniffing around the furniture with his tail wagging. He suddenly stopped and sniffed in one area, then with his head down and nose to the ground walked towards the entrance door.

'He's on to something. Good boy, Rumpole, good boy,' the handler said.

Rumpole sniffed by the door, spun around, and moved his head from side to side as he padded towards the stairwell to the crypt.

The handler looked pleased. 'He's picked up her scent.'

'How can you tell?' Lloyd asked.

'By the way he moves and keeps his nose to the ground.'

Rumpole stopped at the top of the stairwell, took a few sniffs, and started going down the stairs, sniffing each one as he went.

'Be careful on your way down, the stonework is slippery,' Jane told the dog handler. She turned to Lloyd. 'Can you stay with Mr Durham, please?'

'Don't worry yourself, I assure you I won't try and escape,' Thomas said scornfully.

At the bottom of the stairs Rumpole stopped, had another good sniff, then started to sneeze and whine.

The handler pulled Rumpole away. 'That's how he reacts to cleaning agents like bleach.'

Jane took a few sniffs but couldn't smell anything. The handler got down on his knees and sniffed the floor.

'There's a very faint smell of bleach if you get close enough,' he said.

'Could you please come downstairs, Mr Durham,' Jane shouted up.

'She was drinking my best '61 Médoc a few days ago. Now look how she repays me,' he muttered.

'DS Tennison is just doing her job,' Lloyd said.

'She did a good job on my son, that's for sure,' Thomas retorted, starting down the stairs.

'Rumpole's not reacted anywhere else down here. The trail ends at the bottom of the stairs,' the handler said, putting him on the lead.

'How sure can you be it was Becky he was following?' Jane asked.

'Obviously I can't say one hundred per cent it's her. But I know my dog and he's never let me down. Something happened down here that necessitated the use of bleach. I'm going to see how he tracks from the hallway to the outside. I'll also check the bin areas.'

Boon followed Lloyd and Thomas down to the crypt.

'Nothing upstairs so far, sarge,' he said.

'Well, there's a surprise,' Durham scoffed.

'The dog has tracked Becky Rogers' scent down into the crypt. It ends at the bottom of the stairs,' Jane told Durham.

'Did Rumpole tell you that?' he mocked.

'He also reacted in a manner that suggests a cleaning agent was used just there.' Jane pointed to the spot.

'This is bloody ridiculous. I have a cleaner who comes here twice a week. She uses bleach to clean the stone floors.'

'What, even in the crypt?' Boon asked.

'She's very fastidious. Speak to her if you don't believe me,' Durham replied.

While Lloyd examined the stairs and hand rope, Jane went to look in the wine cellar area. She immediately noticed the wall blocking the tunnel had been repaired with some new bricks in the middle. Jane recalled Nick telling his father the wall needed fixing.

'I see you've had the wall repaired,' Jane remarked.

Thomas laughed out loud. 'Please don't tell me you think a body might be behind the wall.'

'Boony, nip out to the equipment van and see if they have any sledgehammers and pickaxes,' Jane said.

Thomas's eyes bulged and his face turned red with anger. 'That's it! I've had enough of this nonsense! I'm not having you destroying my house! I'm calling my solicitor now!' He stomped off towards the stairs.

'Come back here now, please, Mr Durham,' Boon shouted.

He went after Durham and grabbed him by the shoulder. Durham spun round and punched Boon hard in the face, knocking him to the ground. Boon winced in pain as he landed hard on his coccyx.

Durham realised what he'd done. 'I'm sorry, I'm sorry. I didn't mean to do that. I wasn't thinking straight.' He put his hand out to help Boon up.

'You fuckin' arsehole!' Boon exclaimed, knocking Durham's hand away.

Durham stood upright, his face turning blue as he struggled to breathe.

'Oh God, please help me,' he pleaded, clutching his chest as his face contorted with pain.

Boon was struggling to get up. He could only watch as Durham staggered backwards, fighting to breathe. As Thomas fell, Lloyd managed to catch him and lay him gently on the floor.

'He's having a heart attack. Keep an eye on him, Jane, and I'll call an ambulance,' Lloyd said.

She shook her head. 'That'll take too long. Get some of the uniformed officers to take him to the hospital in the police van.'

As Lloyd ran up the stairs, Durham's breathing was getting shallower, and his eyes began to close.

Boon knelt beside him. 'Where's Becky?'

'He's unconscious. We need to try and resuscitate him,' Jane said, pinching Durham's nose and putting her mouth over his.

It wasn't long before some uniformed officers arrived with a large riot shield which they used as a makeshift stretcher to take Durham to the hospital. Jane instructed one of them to remain at the hospital with Durham as he was a suspect for abduction and murder. She gave another officer Nick Durham's home phone number and asked him to get the duty sergeant to tell him about his father's heart attack.

Jane used Durham's phone to call Stanley and told him what had happened.

'Bloody hell. How bad is he?' Stanley asked.

'Not good. But Boon and I resuscitated him. And he was breathing with a slow pulse when the uniformed officers took him away. I've asked that the duty sergeant contact Nick Durham.'

'So it looks like Becky was in Durham's house, then,' Stanley said.

'It looks like he killed her in the crypt,' Jane said. 'Her body might be in the old tunnel, so I'm going to knock the wall down.'

'Do it,' Stanley said.

'And if she isn't, I'm going to keep searching,' Jane replied.

'Don't exhaust yourself. Take a rest if you need one. Salmon wants a briefing with the team tomorrow morning at nine.'

'Did you tell him about the search warrant?' Jane asked.

'Yes, he was pissed off that I didn't ask him first. I reminded him that he buggered off to the Yard and left me in charge.'

'Are you going to update him?'

'No. He's spent most of his career behind a desk in planning and development. He scurries off when you confront him with a difficult situation because he doesn't know what to do.'

'Let's hope he stays that way,' Jane remarked.

'I'd best let you get on. I'm not going anywhere, so keep me updated.'

As Jane put the phone down, Lloyd approached her.

'I examined the stairwell rope. There are traces of blood going up it on the underside. Someone with a bloody hand used it to support themselves as they climbed the stairs. It's possible Durham carried Becky's body upstairs and put it in a car to bury her elsewhere.'

'I'm still going to knock that wall down. You any good with a sledgehammer?'

'I always hit the high striker bell at the funfair,' Lloyd grinned.

It didn't take long to knock a hole in the wall and search the tunnel, but there was no sign of Becky.

'DS Tennison . . . I've found something of interest in one of the wheelie bins,' the dog handler shouted from the top of the stairs.

Jane and Lloyd followed him to a dimly lit wooden hut at the far end of the parking area. Inside were four large metal wheelie bins, one of which was on its side with the contents strewn across the floor. To one side, placed neatly on police exhibits bags was a bleach bottle.

'I found that bleach bottle in the bin. It looks like it might have a blood smear on it. One of the residents told me the bins are emptied every Tuesday morning at around ten.'

'Which means the bottle could only have been put in the bin on Tuesday after ten or today,' Lloyd remarked as he put on protective gloves and placed the bottle in an exhibits bag.

'The uniformed lads helped me search the other bins. There were no blood-stained items in them,' the dog handler said.

'He probably burned any towels or cloths he used to clean up . . . or dumped them with Becky's body,' Lloyd said.

'How quickly can you test that bleach bottle for fingerprints?' Jane asked Lloyd.

'Is there any rush with Durham being in hospital?' Lloyd asked.

'If a doctor says he's fit to be interviewed, I'll do it by his bedside. I want as much evidence against him as possible.'

'I'll take the bottle back to the lab and get to work on it first thing in the morning. Has Thomas Durham ever been arrested?'

'Not as far as I know – unfortunately,' Jane replied.

'No problem. I can use the coffee mug he drank out of earlier for comparison to any marks on the bleach bottle. I'll also take lifts off other items likely to have his prints on them.'

'If Becky was murdered here, Durham must have disposed of her car as well. It's possible he put her body in the boot and used the car to transport it. If that was the case, he'd need to hide the car, which isn't easy,' Jane said.

'He could have set light to it with her body inside,' Lloyd suggested.

'Possibly, but I'd have thought someone would have seen the fire or found it burnt out by now. It's also a big risk to drive a car a long distance with a body in the boot. Do you know if the underwater search unit work at night?' she asked.

'They come out at any time if it's an emergency. Why do you ask?'

'There is a small lake down by the woods. He might have weighted Becky down and dumped her body in it, then hidden the car elsewhere,' Jane said.

Jane rang Stanley while Lloyd took some fingerprint lifts from the coffee cup and other items in Thomas Durham's house. Jane asked Stanley for permission to call out the underwater search unit. He said he would call them and come down to the scene.

As they waited for the underwater search unit, Jane and other officers went down to the lake with seek-and-search torches. One of the officers found some narrow tyre marks leading from the building-site track to the edge of the lake and down into the water. Jane was certain the marks were from Becky's car and her body would be in it.

When the underwater search unit arrived they set up four big arc lamps powered by a petrol generator, which lit up the surrounding area, creating an eerie glow on the surface of the still water. Two divers went into the lake with submersible torches. A few minutes later, one of them surfaced and did a thumbs-up. The underwater unit had a cable winch attached to their large truck, which one of the divers attached to the submerged vehicle.

Everyone watched in silence as the red Citroën 2CV was slowly pulled out of the lake and water cascaded out of the vehicle. As Jane moved forward, an officer turned one of the arc lamps towards the boot, casting an ominous shadow of Jane's body over the car. Jane's hand trembled as she placed it on the boot lever. She knew she was about to find Becky's body but dreaded the moment. As Jane lifted the boot lid, she saw a black canvas suitcase wedged inside. She asked the search officers to remove it. It took two of them to lift it out, then place it on the ground. Jane unzipped it. Becky's body was curled up in a foetal position with a blood-stained towel tucked into one corner of the case. Fighting back the tears, Jane stepped to one side to allow Lloyd to take some photographs. She walked over to Stanley and Boon.

'Durham must have put her body in the suitcase to get her out to the car,' Jane said.

'DS Johnson can bag the body and arrange for it to be taken to the mortuary,' Stanley said. 'We'll do the post-mortem first thing tomorrow morning. You two go home and get some rest. I'll go and tell PC Rogers and his wife we found Becky,' he added in a sombre tone.

Walking to the car, Jane could see Boon was struggling to hold himself together. She had dealt with grieving parents, friends, and relatives too many times to remember, but at this moment she couldn't think what to say to him.

CHAPTER THIRTY

As Jane drove back to Orpington Boon sat quietly staring out of the passenger window. She parked the car in the station yard and switched the engine off.

'I know how you're feeling, Simon . . .'

'I don't think you do, sarge,' he said, shaking his head. 'In fact, I'm beginning to wonder if I'm cut out to be a police officer anymore.'

'I lost two colleagues during a bank robbery explosion when I was a probationer at Hackney,' Jane said. There was a catch in her voice.

Boon turned and looked at her with an expression of surprise.

'WPC Kath Morgan was my best friend. I was in a relationship with the other officer at the time. His name was Len Bradfield.'

'I'm sorry,' Boon said. 'It must have been a terrible time for you.'

'It was. And I still miss them both. But I came to realise you can't change what's happened and have to move on.'

'But how did you do that?' Boon asked.

'Through my work, and helping to bring those who caused their death to justice. You're a good detective, Simon, and have the potential to go a long way in the CID. I think Becky would have wanted you to carry on.'

He let out a deep breath. 'Thanks for the advice, sarge, I appreciate it.'

'If you want to take a few days leave, I'm sure Stanley won't mind,' Jane said.

He shook his head. 'I'd rather carry on working the investigation for now.'

'OK, but don't bottle things up. If you're feeling down or want someone to talk to, I'm always here for you.'

'OK,' he said, smiling. 'I appreciate it.'

* * *

Inside the station, Jane spoke with the duty sergeant and asked what hospital Thomas Durham had been taken to.

'Queen Mary's in Sidcup,' the sergeant replied.

'Has Nick Durham been informed about his father's heart attack?' she asked.

'I've just spoken with the officer who's guarding Thomas Durham. He's in the intensive care ward and his son is with him.'

'Is he expected to live?' she asked.

'The doctors don't know at present. He's in a coma.'

'A coma?' Jane gasped.

'He took a turn for the worse on the way to the hospital. The doctor said the coma was due to a lack of oxygen to his brain after the heart attack.'

'Does Nick Durham know it happened during our search?'

'Yes, but I didn't give him details of who you were looking for or why. The PC at the hospital said he's very distressed and has been asking a lot of questions.'

'What did the PC tell him?'

'Nothing, other than what I told him to say.'

'Which was?' Jane asked.

'That he didn't know anything about the search as it was a CID matter, and DI Stanley was in charge. I hope that didn't give away too much for you,' the sergeant replied brusquely.

Jane could see her questions were irritating him. 'I only ask because I may have to interview Nick Durham.'

'I'd leave that for a while as you suits ain't his favourite people at the moment,' the sergeant said, before walking off.

Jane wanted to go to the hospital and speak with Nick but knew a heated confrontation with him wouldn't do anybody any good.

It was nearly two in the morning by the time an exhausted Jane got home. After a large glass of wine and a sandwich, she went to bed and fell into a deep sleep.

* * *

Jane woke to the sound of her bedside phone ringing. Worried it might be an angry Nick, she was relieved to hear Lloyd's voice.

'Morning, Jane. Sorry to bother you so early.'

'It's six o'clock, Lloyd. What do you want?' she yawned.

'You should moan. I've been up all night working on the bleach bottle. Thomas Durham's prints weren't on it.'

'He must have wiped them off, then,' she said. 'Anyway, it doesn't matter. Durham's in a coma so I can't question him. I'll call you back when I get to work.'

'God, you are crabby in the morning. Hear me out, will you?'

'All right, I'm listening,' she yawned.

'I found two prints on the bottle, which didn't match any of the ones I took from Durham's house.'

'They're probably the cleaner's then.'

'For Christ's sake, let me finish! I asked the fingerprint bureau to check them against criminal records. They just rang me with a result.'

'Whose were they?'

'Lee Holland's. I thought I best let you know ASAP in case Holland tries to do a runner.'

Jane swung her feet out of bed and perched on the edge. 'My God, the two of them were involved in Becky's murder.'

'It looks that way. Durham might have committed the murder and got Holland to help him clear up the mess.'

'What's Holland's previous?' Jane asked.

'He's got a conviction for Actual Bodily Harm in 1972. He broke a bloke's nose after he drove into the back of Holland's car.'

'Can you ring Stanley while I get dressed. Tell him I'll be in the incident room in half an hour.'

* * *

Stanley, Jane and Boon parked up a street away from Lee Holland's house, along with four uniformed officers in a marked police van. Stanley told two of the officers to cover the back of the premises and two to join him.

'Boony, you can have the pleasure of nicking Holland,' Stanley told him.

'Thanks, guv,' Boon said.

'How is your leg this morning?' Jane asked.

'Still sore, but it hasn't affected my ability to kick a door in if I have to,' Boon said.

'Good, because I don't intend to announce our arrival,' Stanley said.

Once the uniformed officers radioed that they were around the back, Boon ran at the door, jumped in the air and kicked it open. Lee Holland was in the hallway tying a luggage label to a large suitcase. He casually slipped the tag into his jacket pocket.

'Going anywhere nice, Lee?' Stanley asked him.

'No. I'm taking a load of old clothes to the charity shop,' Lee said nervously.

'Bit early for that, isn't it?' Stanley remarked. He nodded to Boon.

'Lee Holland, I am arresting you on suspicion of the murder of Rebecca Rogers. You do not have to say anything unless you wish to do so, but what you say may be given in evidence,' Boon said as he handcuffed Lee.

'I swear I didn't kill her. It was an accident,' Lee said.

'Is your wife upstairs?' Stanley asked.

'I'm single,' he said.

They took him through to the living room and made him sit in an armchair. Stanley said he wanted a word with Jane and Boon and they all went into the hallway.

'It's better you interview him here, Jane, if he's willing to talk, which it appears he is. If we take him back to the station and he requests a solicitor, we could end up with a no-comment interview. Boony, make sure you write every question and answer in your pocketbook. Get him to sign every page if he confesses. I'll tell the uniformed officers they can go. I'll search the house.'

Jane and Boon returned to the living room.

'Would you like a drink, Lee?' Jane asked him.

'Could I have a glass of water, please?' he sniffed.

Boon went to the kitchen and got Lee a glass of water.

'We need to keep you here while we search the house. Are you willing to answer some questions without a solicitor?'

'OK. Can I have a tissue, please. There's some in a box over there.'

Boon handed him the box and Jane said it was OK to undo the handcuffs as she wanted him to be more at ease. She doubted he'd try and escape as he'd be no match for Boon. Lee blew his nose and wiped the tears from his eyes.

'I'd like you to tell me what happened to Becky and who else was involved in her death,' Jane said.

'It was only me. Tom had nothing to do with it.'

'I take it Tom is Thomas Durham?'

'That's right.'

'Were you at Tom's house on Tuesday afternoon?'

'Yes. I was fixing the wall in his wine cellar.'

'Where was Tom?'

'He got fed up with the banging as I knocked some of the bricks out. He said he was going to Nick's house for some peace and quiet and took Bella with him.'

'Is that the truth or are you just trying to protect Tom?'

'I swear it's the truth.'

'Tell me about Becky Rogers.'

'I was in the kitchen making a coffee when I heard a knock at the door. I opened it and this young girl was there. I said, "Can I help you?" and she just walked in. I didn't have clue who she was. At first, I thought she might be the daughter of one of the residents and wanted to speak with Tom. I asked her who she was. She said she was a reporter, her name was Becky and she'd like to speak to me about the sale of the convent and the coffin that was found on the building site.'

'Did you know she was the reporter who wrote the article in the *News Shopper* about the discovery of the coffin?'

'No. Tom told me about it, but I never read it. I told her I wasn't Mr Durham, and he was out for the afternoon, but she didn't believe me. She wagged her finger at me, then said, "Good try, Mr Durham, but I don't give in that easily." I told her again I wasn't him, just a friend of his.'

'What happened next?' she asked.

'She said she'd like to see the crypt because she thought that might be how the coffin was moved to the building site. I asked her to leave, or I'd call the police. She looked around the room and saw the stairwell, then just started towards it. I got annoyed and shouted at her to leave. She just ignored me. I shouted at her again, but she just wouldn't listen. She was a couple of steps down when, when I . . . Oh God, please forgive me . . .' Lee started to tremble, his breathing became erratic and he put his face in his hands.

Boon looked at Jane, worried that Lee was about to go the same way as Thomas Durham.

'I know it's hard for you, Lee, but I need you to tell us what happened,' she said.

He blew his nose and looked at Jane. 'I grabbed her coat ... I was only going to escort her out of the house. She spun round and knocked my hand away ... then she lost her balance. She started to fall backwards ... it was like everything was in slow motion ... there was a look of panic in her eyes ... she was waving her arms around to try and stay up. I tried to grab her coat to stop her falling but I didn't get a proper hold. She slipped away from me ... the next thing I knew she was rolling over and over down the stairs. I froze in panic, then heard the thud as she landed at the bottom. I went down. She was just lying there ... then I saw the blood trickling across the floor by her head. I knelt down and spoke to her, but she didn't move or say anything. I knew then she was dead.'

Jane got him another glass of water and gave him time to compose himself before continuing. Lee's account of what had happened was plausible but he could just as easily have lost his temper and pushed Becky down the stairs.

'You said a minute ago you knew Becky was dead. How did you know that?' Jane asked.

'She wasn't moving.'

'Did you check if she had a pulse?'

'No. I couldn't bring myself to touch her at that point.'

'What did you do when you thought Becky was dead?' Jane asked.

'I panicked. I thought I'd be blamed for what had happened. I was worried about Tom coming home and his heart condition if he saw a dead body in his house.'

'What did you do with Becky's body?'

'Tom uses part of the crypt as a storeroom. I got an old suitcase from there and put her in it, then I put the suitcase in the boot of her car.'

'How did you know which car was hers?' Jane asked.

'I took the key out of her coat pocket; it was on a key ring with a miniature 2CV on it.'

'What did you do with her body and the car?'

'I waited until it was dark and drove it down to the lake by the woods. I took the handbrake off and pushed the car down the slope into the water.'

'I thought you were worried about Tom coming home.'

'I was, but I phoned him at Nick's. I said I'd nearly finished the wall and asked what time he'd be home. He said he was going to have some supper with Nick so he wouldn't be back until late.'

'We found a bleach bottle in one of the outside bins. Did you use it to clean up?'

'I used a towel first to clean up the blood on the floor, then put it in the case and took it out to the car. When I came back, I used the bleach and some toilet roll to make sure there was no blood left. I flushed it down the toilet and put the bleach bottle in the outside bin.'

'OK, I need to ask you a few questions about your relationship with Tom.'

Lee nodded.

'When we first met, I asked you who the man with the dog was. You said you didn't know him, and then Thomas Durham never mentioned he owned the convent and land. Was there something you were hiding from us?'

'Tom was mad at me about the discovery of the coffin.'

'Why was that?'

'When Tom first bought the property, the chapel and the land it had been deconsecrated so he was OK to start the renovation work. He was exploring the crypt and found the coffin hidden under a tarpaulin with some other old rubbish right at the back. I helped him drag it out to the stairwell area. We suspected there was a body in it but we didn't open it. Tom said his wife would be upset if she knew there was a dead body in the house and told me to bury it well away from the convent.'

'Did Tom know he should have informed the diocese?'

'We both did. Tom was worried the renovation work would have to stop and he'd need to get solicitors involved to apply for some petition thing . . . all of which would cost him more money.'

'Why on earth did you bury the coffin on land you knew you were going to dig up?' Boon asked.

'I told a couple of labourers we'd been given permission by the bishop to bury the coffin down by the lake. I paid them to move it. The lazy beggars must have thought it was too far to carry and buried it near the burnt-out buildings.'

'What were their names?'

'I can't remember now. I think one was called Jordan.'

'Why didn't you rebury it when you dug it up last week?' Jane asked.

'Because Dermot phoned the police while I went to tell Tom about it.'

'Why the big pretence you didn't know each other?'

'Because we didn't want anyone to find out what we'd done with the coffin. We were also worried it might affect the current building work and we'd lose thousands.'

'You're a pair of idiots. If you'd just told us the truth about the coffin none of this would have happened,' Jane said.

Lee sighed. 'I know.'

Jane decided it was time to ask Lee some crucial questions about Becky's death.

'You said earlier you were angry with Becky because she wouldn't leave when asked.'

'I was more annoyed than angry,' he replied.

'Did you lose your temper and push her down the stairs?' Jane asked.

Lee looked distraught. 'No. It was all a terrible accident. If she hadn't tried to go down to the cellar, none of it would have happened.'

'Why didn't you just call the police and say there'd been an accident?' Boon asked.

'Because I thought no one would believe me and I'd be arrested for something I didn't do.'

'Why have you packed a suitcase?' Boon asked.

'Nick phoned me late last night. He told me about Tom's heart attack while you were searching his house. I was scared. I didn't want to go to prison for something that wasn't my fault. I was going to stay with a friend in Spain.'

Boon glared at him. 'Which conveniently happens to be a country we have no extradition treaty with.'

'I swear on my life, I didn't push her.'

Boon shook his head. 'I don't believe you and I doubt a jury will either.'

A terrified Lee looked at Jane. 'Am I going to be charged with murder?'

'That's not for me to decide. A post-mortem is being carried out later this morning. We will interview you again after the pathologist has completed her examination of Becky's body. There are a couple of other things I need to ask you about the convent. Did you or Thomas Durham ever do any work there prior to the purchase?'

'No.'

'How long have you been working with Thomas Durham?'

'Since he started the company, which was about twenty-five years ago.'

'What was the name of the company when he first started it?'

'Thomas Durham Builders. He changed it to Thomas Durham and Son when Nick started working for him.'

'I'll ask you again, did you or Thomas Durham ever do any work at the convent prior to the purchase of the buildings and land?'

'No, I told you.'

'Then can you explain why we have found quotes and invoices for repair work at the convent with the letterhead Thomas Durham Builders, some of which are dated 1960, 1961 and 1962?'

He started to look nervous. 'I don't know anything about them . . . honest.'

'All of them are signed by Thomas Durham . . . who you worked for.'

Lee licked his lips. 'I suppose we might have done some work back then. Actually, come to think of it we did repair the chapel roof at one time.'

'There is a quote and invoice for that job,' Jane told him. 'By we, do you mean yourself and Thomas Durham?'

'Yes.'

'And did you do other repair work back then?'

'Probably, but it was so long ago it's hard to remember now.'

'Does the name Melissa Bailey mean anything to you?'

'No, should it?'

'She was a sister at the convent. It was her body we found in the coffin. She was murdered during the time you and Thomas worked at the convent.'

Lee looked shocked. 'We didn't know any of the nuns. We never even spoke to them other than to say good morning.'

'Did you or Thomas Durham murder Melissa Bailey?'

'No! Why on earth would you think we'd do a thing like that?'

'Because you both lied about knowing each other, never mentioned you'd worked at the convent and now Becky Rogers is dead.'

Lee started shaking his head from side to side. 'I swear I've told you everything.'

'There's something you're hiding from me, Lee, and I think it's to do with Melissa Bailey's murder. If you're trying to protect Thomas Durham, I can assure you you'll only make matters worse for yourself.'

'Thomas is a good man . . . he's not a murderer,' Lee said, putting his head in his hands.

It suddenly dawned on Jane what he might be hiding.

'Amongst the documents we recovered was a quote to repair the fire-damaged buildings. Obviously, a survey must have been done first. Did you do that survey?'

'No, Thomas did it. But the diocese couldn't afford to repair the buildings.'

Jane could see he was getting agitated. 'And as we all know they then sold the convent to Mr Durham.'

'Yes, that's right.'

'Do you know how the fire started?' Jane asked.

'No,' he said, nervously shaking his head.

'Do you know where it started?'

'Thomas said it was in the bakery.'

'When did he tell you that?'

'Just after he did the survey.'

'The thing is, Lee, we had the bakery examined by a fire investigator. Even after all these years he was able to tell it was a case of arson. In his expert opinion, someone poured oil from a paraffin heater in three separate areas and set light to it.' Jane noticed Lee's eyes widen. 'The Mother Superior and the sisters at the convent had nothing to gain by setting fire to the outbuildings – whereas you and Thomas Durham had everything to gain. So, my question is, did you set light to the bakery?'

Lee's lips began to tremble, and he put his head in his hands.

'You wouldn't be in this situation if it wasn't for Thomas Durham. Everything dishonest he's asked you to do has now ruined your life.'

Lee looked up at Jane. 'Yes, I started the fire.'

'Tell me Thomas Durham's part in it all.'

'The Mother Superior told Tom the diocese was concerned about the cost of the constant repair bills and she was worried they might close the convent. Thomas went behind her back and spoke with the bishop. He said if the Church ever put the convent on the market, he'd be interested in buying it. The bishop said the Church didn't want to sell just yet, but if and when they did, he'd give Thomas first refusal.'

'Was that Bishop Malone?'

'Yes. We figured if the outbuildings were destroyed by fire, the Church wouldn't repair them and it'd be forced to sell. I snuck into the bakery late at night and set light to it. Thomas then overinflated the quote to repair the buildings.'

'DC Boon will read over the questions we asked and your answers,' Jane said. 'If there's anything you want to add or change, then tell him before you sign his notes.'

Jane went to see how Stanley was getting on with the search and found him in the hallway.

'He's saying Becky fell down the stairs. He's either telling the truth or he's a bloody good liar.'

'I was listening by the door. That was a good interview, Jane. Connecting Lee and Thomas Durham to the arson was brilliant. I really thought it was Meade.'

'So did I at first. It doesn't look like they murdered Melissa Bailey. If they had, I can't see them putting her in a coffin, then having it buried in the convent grounds. It also looks like Thomas Durham wasn't at the house when Becky died,' Jane added.

'Holland could be covering for him. We need to speak to Nick Durham about his father's alibi.'

'I'll do it after the post-mortem,' Jane said.

'Are you sure? I don't mind speaking with him,' Stanley said.

'I've got to face Nick at some point – though I suspect he won't want anything more to do with me,' Jane said sadly.

CHAPTER THIRTY-ONE

Jane and Boon took Lee Holland to the charge room and booked him in, whilst Stanley informed DCS Salmon of his arrest and interview.

'How are PC Rogers and his wife?' Salmon asked.

'Absolutely devastated. They were heartbroken. When I told them where we had found Becky's body, Mrs Rogers had a total breakdown. It was that bad I asked the police doctor to attend. He gave her some sedatives. I'm dreading telling them that Lee Holland said it was an accident.'

'It's going to be hard to prove murder in court,' Salmon remarked.

'If the post-mortem reveals injuries that are inconsistent with a fall, Holland's screwed.'

'Let's hope it does, then. When is the post-mortem?'

'Half past ten at Queen Mary's. Will you be attending?'

'Unfortunately, I've got a meeting at the Yard. I'll leave it in your capable hands, DI Stanley.'

Stanley suspected Salmon was just squeamish.

'Is everyone ready for the meeting?'

'Yes, sir.'

'Good, then let's go. I don't expect the commissioner's decision will go down well.'

'That's an understatement,' Stanley mumbled.

'Sorry, what did you say?' Salmon asked.

'That I'm sure the team will respect the commissioner's decision,' Stanley said.

Salmon walked into a silent room of dour-looking detectives. The discovery of Becky's body had saddened them all, and they suspected the investigation into Melissa Bailey's murder would now be shelved after Bishop Meade's suicide.

'I'm sure you are all aware of the discovery of Becky Rogers' body. Her death is a tragic loss to her family and everyone who knew her. Lee Holland was arrested for her murder this morning. Although he claims her death was an accident, I'm sure we all hope justice will prevail and a jury will come to the right decision. The commissioner has asked me to thank you all for your dedication and hard work investigating the death of Sister Mary.'

There were snorts of derision and a shaking of heads round the room.

'It's Sister Melissa . . . sir,' Boon said, unable to keep the disgust out of his voice.

Salmon looked flustered. 'Yes, sorry, slip of the tongue. Where was I?'

'You were about to tell us the commissioner is shutting the investigation down,' Stanley said.

'Unfortunately, yes. The commissioner had our solicitors look at the evidence. They concluded that there is at present no reasonable prospect of convicting anyone for the murder of Sister Melissa. However, the investigation will be classified as a cold case and remain open, pending the discovery of any new evidence.'

'There's a stack of evidence against Bishop Meade. Not to mention the cover-up by Archbishop Malone . . . for which the commissioner is also culpable,' Boon said.

Salmon looked sternly at him. 'I think solicitors have a better understanding of legal intricacies than you or me, officer. Let me assure you, this is not a cover-up. The commissioner agrees with the views of our solicitors. As from now, you can all return to your respective stations. DI Stanley, DS Tennison and DC Boon will complete the necessary reports and deal with Lee Holland.' Salmon walked quickly out the room before anyone else could challenge him.

'Looks like our hands are tied,' Jane said to Stanley.

'We may not be able to do anything about it, but I know someone who can, now he's handed in his warrant card,' Stanley said.

'Are you going tell Barnes what's happened?' Jane asked.

'Too right I am. He can tell the press what he likes without fear of repercussions.'

* * *

Jane found it hard to watch as Sam Pullen examined Becky's body. She'd been to many post-mortems, but this was the first one where she'd known the victim. She thought about PC Rogers. As a coroner's officer he would have attended hundreds of post-mortems, but the thought of his daughter lying on a cold slab being dissected would be a nightmare he had never imagined.

Only a few days had passed since Jane had watched Becky stand her ground amongst seasoned journalists at the press conference. She'd been laughed at and ridiculed but didn't let it bother her. Jane fondly remembered Becky irritating Barnes with her naïve questions. He did his best to ignore her, but she would not give in. And in the end she'd shown him up.

No one spoke during the three-hour post-mortem. When it was over, Sam Pullen, Jane and Stanley went to the mortuary office to discuss her findings.

Pullen referred to her notes and drawings. 'There are multiple bruises and cuts to Becky's body which are consistent with a fall down a stone staircase. I can't say if she was pushed. There is also a fracture on the back of her head. This probably occurred when she landed at the bottom of the stairs and her head impacted with the floor. The impact caused an acute subdural hematoma.'

'Remind me what that is,' Stanley said.

'A subdural hematoma occurs when a blood vessel in the space between the skull and the brain is damaged. Blood escapes from the vessels, leading to the formation of a blood clot that places pressure on the brain and damages it. Head injuries that cause a subdural hematoma are often severe, such as those from a fall or violent assault. An acute subdural hematoma is among the deadliest of all head injuries. Blood fills the brain area rapidly and compresses the brain tissue, which can result in unconsciousness, a coma and subsequently death.'

'So, Becky died because of the fall,' Stanley concluded.

'No. The head injury may well have rendered her unconscious or in a coma, but the cause of death was drowning.'

Jane was stunned. 'She was still alive when Holland put her car in the lake?'

'Yes. I found white froth in her nose and airways, as well as water in her stomach, which is consistent with death by drowning.'

'Would Holland have known she was alive after she fell down the stairs?' Jane asked.

Sam shrugged. 'It's possible she was in a coma and he thought she was dead. If he'd checked for a pulse, she'd still have had one.'

'He said he didn't,' Jane said.

'The sad thing is, if he had – or had even bothered to call an ambulance – Becky might have survived, though she might have suffered brain damage.'

'Then technically he's guilty of gross negligence manslaughter by failing to render any form of first aid or call an ambulance,' Jane suggested.

* * *

Before they left the mortuary, Stanley made a quick call to the office then spoke with Jane.

'I just spoke to the duty sergeant. Thomas Durham is still unconscious. The doctor said he's in a vegetative state and may have permanent brain damage. It's too early to tell if he'll recover or not. Nick is with him.'

'I'd better go and see him. I'll ask where his father was on Tuesday afternoon.'

'I had Boon speak to him while we were at Becky's post-mortem. I thought it would make things easier for you.'

'Thanks. Was Thomas with Nick on Tuesday?'

'Yes. He was in his office most of the afternoon. The receptionist confirmed it as well. Thomas left Nick's house at about nine o'clock. He's in the clear over Becky's murder.'

'What about the arson?'

'Lee Holland will obviously be charged. If Thomas Durham makes a recovery he'll be interviewed and charged as well,' Stanley replied.

'What about Malone?'

'He told the commissioner he was shocked to discover she had been murdered.'

'But he falsely signed a letter of dispensation when Melissa supposedly ran away.'

'It's not a criminal offence. Even if we told the Pope, nothing would happen to him. Besides, we won't be allowed anywhere near Malone without the commissioner's approval and that's never going to happen. Are you going to tell Nick about Holland's confessions?'

'Not just now. He's got enough to worry about as it is.'

'Do you want me to wait for you?' Stanley asked.

'No, it's OK. I'll get a cab back to the office or see if a patrol car is free.'

'Sorry it's all ended up in such a mess for you,' Stanley said.

'So am I . . . but life goes on.'

'That's the Jane I know best,' Stanley smiled.

* * *

Thomas Durham was still in intensive care. Jane didn't want to go onto the ward in case there was a scene with Nick. She showed one of the nurses her warrant card and asked her just to tell Nick there was a detective outside who'd like to speak to him.

As soon as he saw her, Nick's expression changed. He looked at her as if she was a piece of dirt.

'What do you want?'

'Can we go outside and talk in private, please?' Jane asked, noticing a couple of nurses watching.

'I don't think we've got anything to talk about.'

Jane didn't want to get into an argument. 'Fine, I'll go then.' She started to walk away.

'How could you think my father was involved in that girl's disappearance?' he asked angrily.

'We had evidence she went to the convent and wanted to speak to your father. I couldn't just ignore it.'

'If you had bothered to speak to me, I could have told you where he was. But oh no, you were so hellbent on arresting him, it didn't even cross your mind. You don't care about me ... you just used me because you wanted to know more about my father.'

'That's not true, Nick. I do care about you.'

'Well, I don't give a fuck about you! You are a devious bitch who can't be trusted ... just like my ex-wife. I never want to see you again,' he said, raising his voice.

'I'm genuinely sorry about your father, Nick.'

'Sorry! You are responsible for the state he's in. I'll never forgive you for as long as I live!' He turned and walked away.

* * *

As she stared out of the cab window, Jane knew there was no way back with Nick. In some ways she wondered if it was for the best, as he'd clearly not got over what his wife had done to him. She recalled his reaction to seeing Father Chris kiss her and suspected Nick had in fact been spying on her a few nights ago. It seemed that underneath his charming façade there lurked a jealous, possessive man who would question where she'd been every time she had to work late.

The cab dropped Jane off at the police station. As she walked through the reception-desk door, the duty sergeant handed her a small envelope with her name on it.

'A member of the public dropped this off for you earlier. He said it was important and asked that I made sure you got it.'

'Did he say who he was?'

'His name was Chris. He said he was a friend of yours.'

Jane thanked the sergeant and tucked the letter in her pocket.

'Is it OK if I have a quick word with Lee Holland? I just need to tell him we will be interviewing him later.'

'No problem,' the sergeant said. He unclipped the cell key from his belt and handed it to her. 'I just gave him a copy of the *Sun*. There's an article in it about Becky Rogers' disappearance and a photo of her. I thought the evil bastard might like to read it.'

*   *   *

Holland was sitting in his cell looking sorry for himself. The newspaper had been screwed up and thrown on the floor.

'Becky Rogers' post-mortem has been completed. Are you still happy to be interviewed without a solicitor?'

'I asked to speak to one earlier. He said I wasn't to speak to you.'

'That's fine by me. Just so you know, Becky drowned. She was still alive when you put her in the lake.'

Lee looked stunned. 'No . . . no . . . you're lying. She was dead . . . she wasn't moving.'

'She was in a coma. There's part of me that thinks you knew that, and having pushed her down the stairs you needed to finish her off by dumping her in the lake.'

Lee shook his head. 'I honestly thought she was dead.'

'If you'd bothered to check for a pulse, you'd have found one. Becky had a chance of surviving if you'd bothered to call an ambulance, but you didn't. Your actions ultimately led to her death.' Jane slammed the door shut as she left the cell. As she passed an empty interview room, she went in, sat at the desk, and opened Father Chris's letter.

My dearest Jane,

I know you will keep what you are about to read to yourself. However, for reasons that will become obvious, please destroy this letter once you have read it.

As you know, Bishop Robert Meade asked me to take his confession on Tuesday afternoon. I want you to know, as God is my witness, I believe everything he told me to be the truth.

Robert and Sister Melissa fell in love and had a brief sexual relationship. He knew what they were doing was against their vows and feared, if caught, they would be excommunicated. He also thought the Mother Superior had become suspicious of them. For both their sakes, he decided to end the relationship and arranged to meet Melissa at midnight by the outbuildings tunnel to tell her.

As Robert waited, he heard the voices of women arguing in the crypt and wondered if Melissa had been caught trying to sneak out to meet him. As he walked towards the crypt, he heard a muffled voice shouting to be let out. He thought it sounded like Melissa and looked through the keyhole of the crypt door. He saw the Mother Superior and Sister Margaret, who was holding her cincture in her hand, leaning over a metal coffin trying to hold the lid down. Then a muffled voice shouted, 'I am going to tell the bishop what you've done!' The Mother Superior pushed Sister Margaret to one side and opened the coffin lid. Robert saw Melissa sit up as Mother Adele shouted, 'No, you won't!' and stabbed her in the back of the neck with a small knife. Melissa screamed, her eyes closed, and she fell back in the coffin. Then Mother Adele closed the lid.

Robert was ashamed to tell me he panicked and ran back to the presbytery. He assumed Melissa was dead and blamed himself for what had happened. At first, he didn't know what to do, then decided he had to tell Bishop Malone. To his surprise, Malone turned up at the presbytery later that morning.

It transpired Mother Adele had called Bishop Malone and informed him that Sister Melissa had left the convent, but prior to doing so she had confessed she was in a sexual relationship with Robert. Robert knew Mother Adele and Sister Margaret were unaware he'd witnessed Melissa's murder and were attempting to use him as a scapegoat to cover their sins.

Robert admitted the relationship but told Bishop Malone what had really happened to Melissa. Malone was incensed but wanted to avoid a scandal that would bring the Church into disrepute. To that end he told Robert to say nothing and in turn he would protect him and resolve the situation. Malone said he wouldn't tell Mother Adele he knew Melissa had been murdered, but would play along with their story and sign a dispensation so it appeared Melissa had renounced her vows and left the sisterhood of her own accord.

When Robert made his confession to me, he was a broken man and full of remorse. I had not expected him to take his own life. I can only assume he wanted to unburden himself of his sins and could no longer live with his guilt over Melissa's death.

My other reason for writing this letter is to tell you I have decided to leave the priesthood. It was not an easy decision but after all that has happened, I no longer feel I have chosen the right path in life.

I called my brother in Malta. He was overjoyed to hear my voice after so many years. He had had no idea where I was or what had happened to me. We both felt guilty about the way we had treated each other and agreed to resolve our differences. He wants us to open a restaurant together in memory of our parents. Everything on the menu will be from my mother's recipe book.

I will never forget you, Jane. You are a wonderful woman, and I will always cherish meeting you and our friendship. If ever you are in Malta, please come to our restaurant where I will make you the best soppa tal-armla, and kwarezimal for dessert.
With love.
Christopher x

Jane felt deeply sad, knowing Chris was returning to Malta, but pleased that he valued their short time together. She wished she could have got to know him better but knew she would see him again one day. She read the letter one more time before tearing it into tiny pieces and putting it in the bin.

Jane could only surmise what had happened to Melissa before Meade had witnessed her brutal death. It seemed Mother Adele and Sister Margaret suspected Melissa had feelings for Meade and caught her going to meet him. Whether Sister Margaret had attempted to strangle Melissa with her cincture would remain unknown. She thought Bishop Meade's confession was credible and Malone was guilty of a cover-up, not just for the sake of the Church, but his own career as well.

Jane sighed, knowing she could never reveal the contents of Father Chris's letter and Archbishop Malone would yet again escape prosecution.

CHAPTER THIRTY-TWO

Jane, Stanley and Boon spent the next few days in Stanley's office, compiling a report of the investigation for the commissioner. They had been instructed by DCS Salmon to 'stick to the facts', detail the interviews they had carried out and evidence they had uncovered. They were not to express any personal views as to who they thought might have been responsible for Sister Melissa Bailey's death. When the report was completed, Salmon took it straight to the commissioner who had arranged a live press conference for nine o'clock, six hours prior to Pope John Paul II landing at Gatwick airport.

Stanley brought a portable colour television to work so they could sit in his office and watch the press conference.

The commissioner introduced Archbishop Malone, who was standing to one side dressed in his formal attire.

'That smug smile on Malone's face is a giveaway,' Stanley remarked as he turned the volume up.

The commissioner smiled. 'This is an auspicious and historic day, with the first ever visit of a reigning Pope to the United Kingdom. With that in mind, I won't keep you long as I know you will be wanting to get to Gatwick for Pope John Paul II's arrival in a few hours. As you know, a coffin containing the body of a woman was unearthed at a building site in Bickley nearly two weeks ago. She has been positively identified as Sister Melissa Bailey, who lived and worked at the former Sisters of Mercy convent. It is believed she died in August 1962. Following a post-mortem, the Bromley coroner asked for a criminal investigation to be carried out. This was overseen in a meticulous manner by Detective Chief Superintendent Salmon, who compiled a report for the coroner and our solicitor's department.'

'I hope Barnes isn't watching this!' Stanley exclaimed as the commissioner continued.

'Although Sister Melissa's death has been deemed an unlawful killing by the coroner and a thorough investigation has taken place, I'm sad to say there is insufficient evidence to identify those responsible. However, Sister Melissa's death will remain on file, and should any new evidence come to light the investigation will be reopened. I'll now hand over to Archbishop Malone to say a few words.'

Malone stepped forward. 'I would like to thank the commissioner, DCS Salmon and his detectives for their hard work and dedication in investigating Sister Melissa Bailey's death. When I was the diocesan bishop, I often visited the Sisters of Mercy convent up until the day it sadly had to close. To the credit of the now departed Mother Superior Adele Delaney and all the sisters who lived and worked there, I found it to be a happy and peaceful place where orphaned children were lovingly cared for. I'm relieved to say there is no evidence that anyone in the convent was involved in Sister Melissa's death. However, I hope that one day the person, or persons, responsible will be caught and brought to justice.'

'Why did Bishop Meade commit suicide?' a journalist asked.

'Since his death, I have been made aware Bishop Meade was suffering from severe depression. I can't go into the details as his suicide is currently being investigated by the diocese and there will be a coroner's inquest. However, I can tell you it is not connected to the death of Sister Melissa Bailey. Thank you for your time and may God be with you.' He made the sign of the cross.

Jane felt sickened by Malone's lies, but knew she could never betray Father Chris by revealing the truth.

The commissioner stepped forward. 'I would like to add that the tragic death of the *Bromley News Shopper* journalist, Rebecca Rogers, is not connected to the Melissa Bailey investigation and a man has been arrested and charged with her murder. Now,

unless there are any further questions, we need to make our way
to Gatwick airport.'

The journalists, cameramen and photographers quickly packed
their belongings away and hurried out of the room to make their
way to Gatwick.

'What a load of shite. They water it down by saying "her death",
when they know full well Missy was murdered!' Boon exclaimed.

Stanley shook his head in disgust and turned the television off.
'It's just as Barnes predicted – a fucking cover-up!'

Boon frowned. 'As I see it, the commissioner is perverting the
course of justice. We should do something about it.'

'There's nothing we can do, Boony,' Jane said.

'The coroner said it was an unlawful killing – that can't just be
ignored!' Boon argued.

Jane understood why Boon was upset but thought his remarks
naïve. 'The commissioner knew he couldn't suppress Dr Pullen's
post-mortem statement or the coroner's verdict of unlawful killing, especially after Becky's article in the *News Shopper* revealed
our investigation to the public.'

Stanley nodded. 'The Met solicitors would have told the commissioner any criminal proceedings were futile, especially as Mother
Adele and Bishop Meade are dead, and Sister Margaret is immune
from prosecution due to her state of mind.'

Jane put her hand on Boon's shoulder. 'You win some, you lose
some . . . you move on.'

'Bloody hell, that's a bit rich coming from you,' Stanley remarked.

Jane shrugged. 'Maybe, but as much I respect him, I don't want
to become like DCS Barnes. He's made me realise bitterness will
eat away at you and end up clouding your judgement. We need to
put this investigation behind us, not let it tear us apart.'

'Sorry to interrupt,' the duty sergeant said as he entered the
room. 'I thought you might like to know that Barry May has
been arrested for assaulting his wife. She's in Queen Mary's

Hospital with two black eyes and broken ribs. She said to tell DS Tennison she wants to make a statement and press charges against him.'

* * *

Returning from the supermarket, Tony Barnes walked into his living room carrying two bags of shopping. His wife was sitting on the sofa watching the television as Pope John Paul II descended the steps of a plane at Gatwick. He was dressed in a white skull cap, cassock and pellegrina, girded with a fringed white fascia. A large pectoral cross hung from a gold cord around his neck. On reaching the concrete, he fell to his knees and kissed the ground.

Barnes felt repulsed as he watched Archbishop Malone help the Pope up and then kissed his hand. He dropped the shopping then turned off the television.

'Sorry, but I can't bear watching that crap,' he snorted.

She frowned. 'Well, I want to watch it, like thousands of others. History is being made today and you should appreciate it.'

'That's Malone with the Pope and I can't bear the sight of him! Yet again, he's made a fool of me!'

'For Christ's sake, Tony, let it go. You've allowed him to eat away at your soul for nearly thirty years now. You're retired. You need to put the police service behind you and move on . . . for both our sakes.' She turned the television back on.

The commentator expressed his thoughts. 'There is nothing sentimental about this pope. He comes to proclaim the truth as he wrote in a poem twenty years ago. "*If I have the truth in me it will break out one day – I cannot repent.*"'

Barnes opened his wallet and removed the business card *The Times* investigative journalist had given him, then left the room.

'Where are you going?' his wife shouted after him.

'To proclaim the truth!'

* * *

After interviewing Barry May, Jane went to speak with Stanley. He was watching the Pope's visit on the television and drinking a glass of whisky.

'The Pope's just arrived at Victoria station on the Gatwick train. Malone is with him. The smug son of a bitch is waving, and smiling to everyone,' Stanley said.

'He'll probably be made a cardinal after arranging the visit,' Jane remarked.

'Fancy a quick snifter?' Stanley asked, holding up his glass.

'Go on then,' she replied.

Stanley opened his bottom desk drawer, removed a bottle of Glenmorangie, poured some into a glass and handed it to Jane.

'That's the same whisky Barnes likes on special occasions.'

'I know, he left it in his filing cabinet. Be a shame to let it go to waste,' Stanley grinned.

'You thieving git,' Jane laughed as she raised her glass. 'Cheers.'

Stanley raised his glass in turn. 'Cheers. I wonder if the Pope and Malone will discuss Bishop Meade's suicide?'

'Probably, then sweep it under the carpet,' Jane replied.

'They're all lying bastards. I reckon Bishop Meade would have confessed if we'd had the chance to interview him.'

'For what it's worth, I don't think he was involved in Melissa's death,' Jane said.

'Are you being serious?' Stanley asked.

'Yes, it's just a gut feeling,' Jane replied. 'We all have our own views about what happened to Melissa and who killed her, but only she, and the person who killed her, know the truth. We worked hard and did our job to the best of our ability. One day the abuse and cover-ups carried out by the Catholic Church will come out. When it does, we can hold our heads high and say, "I told you, but you didn't listen."'

'You and I might be long retired before that day comes,' Stanley replied. 'How'd it go with Barry May?'

'Boon's charging him with grievous bodily harm.'

'Boony's turning into a good detective.'

'Well, he's learning from the best, isn't he?' Jane grinned.

Stanley laughed. 'Don't flatter yourself ... it's me he models himself on.'

Jane raised her eyes. 'God help us, then. Do you mind if I head off home? My house is in desperate need of some TLC, so I'm going to multitask with a paint brush in one hand and a large glass of wine in the other.'

'One for the road?' Stanley asked, lifting the bottle.

'Just a wee dram,' Jane replied.

Stanley poured some whisky into both glasses. 'How's things between you and Nick Durham?'

'He made it quite clear that he never wants to see me again. I haven't heard a word from him since and I don't expect to.'

'Sorry about that, but it's probably for the best. And there's plenty more fish in the sea.'

'Like I said before – you win some ... you lose some.'

'And then you move on,' Stanley said, and they both raised their glasses.

ACKNOWLEDGEMENTS

I would like to thank Nigel Stoneman and Tory Macdonald, the team I work with at La Plante Global.

All the forensic scientists and members of the Met Police who help with my research. I could not write without their valuable input.

Cass Sutherland for his valuable advice on police procedures and forensics.

The entire team at my publisher, Bonnier Books UK, who work together to have my books edited, marketed, publicised and sold. A special thank you to Kate Parkin and Bill Massey for their great editorial advice and guidance.

Francesca Russell and Blake Brooks, who have introduced me to the world of social media – my Facebook Live sessions have been so much fun.

The audio team, Jon Watt and Laura Makela, for bringing my entire backlist to a new audience in audiobooks. Thanks also for giving me my first podcast series, *Listening to the Dead*, which can be downloaded globally.

Allen and Unwin in Australia and Jonathan Ball in South Africa – thank you for doing such fantastic work with my books.

All the reviewers, journalists, bloggers and broadcasters who interview me, write reviews and promote my books. Thank you for your time and work.

Dear Reader,

Thank you very much for picking up *Unholy Murder*, the seventh book in the Tennison series. I hope you enjoyed reading the book as much as I enjoyed writing it.

Throughout the series, Jane Tennison has solved many kinds of mysteries, but in *Unholy Murder* I wanted to present her with a different kind of challenge – solving a murder which was committed almost two decades ago. Faced with a situation where those involved in the crime may be untraceable, unwell, or no longer alive, not to mention the challenges of investigating a crime under the watchful eye of a powerful institution, Jane finds herself having to think outside of the box. I enjoyed exploring the different forensic technologies that would have been available to her in the 1980s, and how she would use the information they provided along with her detective's instincts to follow the trail to the truth.

If you enjoyed *Unholy Murder*, then please do keep an eye out for news about the next book in the series, which will be coming soon. And in the meantime, early next year sees the publication of the next book in my new series featuring DC Jack Warr, in which Jack finds himself embroiled in an international drugs operation, art theft – and a murder investigation . . .

The first two books in the Jack Warr series, *Buried* and *Judas Horse*, are available now. And if you want to catch up with the Tennison series, the first six novels – *Tennison*, *Hidden Killers*, *Good Friday*, *Murder Mile*, *The Dirty Dozen* and *Blunt Force* – are all available to buy in paperback, ebook and audio. I've been so pleased by the response I've had from the many readers who have been curious about the beginnings of Jane's police career. It's been great fun for me to explore how she became the woman we know in middle and later life from the *Prime Suspect* series.

If you would like more information on what I'm working on, about the Jane Tennison thriller series or the new series featuring

Jack Warr, you can visit **www.bit.ly/LyndaLaPlanteClub** where you can join my Readers' Club. It only takes a few moments to sign up, there are no catches or costs and new members will automatically receive an exclusive message from me. Zaffre will keep your data private and confidential, and it will never be passed on to a third party. We won't spam you with loads of emails, just get in touch now and again with news about my books, and you can unsubscribe any time you want. And if you would like to get involved in a wider conversation about my books, please do review *Unholy Murder* on Amazon, on GoodReads, on any other e-store, on your own blog and social media accounts, or talk about it with friends, family or reader groups! Sharing your thoughts helps other readers, and I always enjoy hearing about what people experience from my writing.

With many thanks again for reading *Unholy Murder*, and I hope you'll return for the next in the series.

With my very best wishes,

Lynda

TENNISON
from the very beginning

TENNISON

HIDDEN KILLERS

GOOD FRIDAY

MURDER MILE

THE DIRTY DOZEN

BLUNT FORCE

and

UNHOLY MURDER